The Dragon Revenant

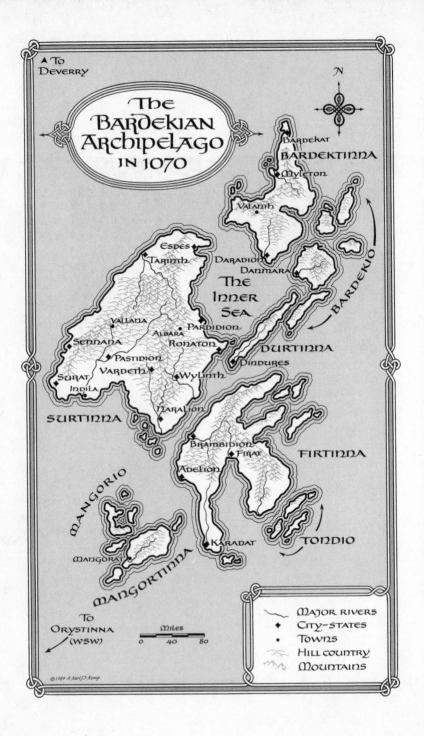

The Dragon Revenant

KATHARINE KERR

A FOUNDATION BOOK

DOUBLEDAY

NEW YORK • LONDON • TORONTO • SYDNEY • AUCKLAND

Sci.Fic.

ALSO BY KATHARINE KERR

Daggerspell
Darkspell
The Bristling Wood
Polar City Blues

A FOUNDATION BOOK

PUBLISHED BY DOUBLEDAY

A DIVISION OF BANTAM DOUBLEDAY DELL

PUBLISHING GROUP, INC.

666 FIFTH AVENUE, NEW YORK, NEW YORK 10103

FOUNDATION, DOUBLEDAY, AND THE PORTRAYAL OF THE LETTER F ARE TRADEMARKS OF DOUBLEDAY, A DIVISION OF BANTAM DOUBLEDAY DELL PUBLISHING GROUP, INC.

LIBRARY OF CONGRESS
CATALOGING-IN-PUBLICATION DATA

KERR, KATHARINE.
  THE DRAGON REVENANT / KATHARINE KERR.—1ST ED.
    P.   CM.
  "A FOUNDATION BOOK."
  I. TITLE.
PS3561.E642D7   1990
813'.54—DC20   89-23602
                                         CIP

ISBN 0-385-26140-3
ISBN 0-385-41098-0 (PBK)

PRINTED IN THE UNITED STATES OF AMERICA
MAY 1990

FIRST EDITION

RRD

IN MEMORY OF
HOWARD "JAKE" JACOBSEN
1934–1988
HE IS AND WILL BE SORELY MISSED.

ACKNOWLEDGMENTS

For my translations from the Llywarch Hen corpus I used Patrick Ford's edition of the text in his *The Poetry of Llywarch Hen*, University of California Press, 1974. Since I was also swayed by his arguments in the introduction to that edition, I have translated *hen* in this context as "the ancestor." Any errors in these translations are of course mine alone, as are such minor acts of magic as my turning winter into summer for the epilogue's epigraph.

My special thanks go to:

John Boothe of Grafton Books for his support of and enthusiasm for this entire project,

Judith Tarr for sage advice and encouragement at the line of battle,

Eva, Jean, Linda, and Elaine of Future Fantasy Books in Palo Alto, California, for backing my books early on and for running a splendid bookshop,

and, as always, my husband, Howard Kerr, for everything.

A Note on the Pronunciation of Deverry Words

The language spoken in Deverry is a member of the P-Celtic family. Although closely related to Welsh, Cornish, and Breton, it is by no means identical to any of these actual languages and should never be taken as such.

Vowels are divided by Deverry scribes into two classes: noble and common. Nobles have two pronunciations; commons, one.

A as in *father* when long; a shorter version of the same sound, as in *far*, when short.

O as in *bone* when long; as in *pot* when short.

W as the *oo* in *spook* when long; as in *roof* when short.

Y as the *i* in *machine* when long; as the *e* in *butter* when short.

E as in *pen*.

I as in *pin*.

U as in *pun*.

Vowels are generally long in stressed syllables; short in unstressed. *Y* is the primary exception to this rule. When it appears as the last letter of a word, it is always long whether that syllable is stressed or not.

Diphthongs generally have one consistent pronunciation.

AE as the *a* in *mane*.

AI as in *aisle*.

AU as the *ow* in *how*.

EO as a combination of *eh* and *oh*.

EW as in Welsh, a combination of *eh* and *oo*.

IE as in *pier*.

OE as the *oy* in *boy*.

UI as the North Welsh *wy*, a combination of *oo* and *ee*.

Note that **OI** is never a diphthong, but is two distinct sounds, as in *carnoic* (KAR-noh-ik).

Consonants are mostly the same as in English, with these exceptions:

C is always hard as in *cat*.

G is always hard as in *get*.

DD is the voiced *th* as in *thin* or *breathe*, but the voicing is more pronounced than in English. It is opposed to **TH**, the unvoiced sound as in *th* or *breath*. (This is the sound that the Greeks called the Celtic tau.)

R is heavily rolled.

RH is a voiceless R, approximately pronounced as if it were spelled *hr* in Deverry proper. In Eldidd, the sound is fast becoming indistinguishable from R.

DW, **GW**, and **TW** are single sounds, as in *Gwendolen* or *twit*.

Y is never a consonant.

I before a vowel at the beginning of a word is consonantal, as it is in the plural ending *-ion*, pronounced *yawn*.

Doubled consonants are both sounded clearly, unlike in English. Note, however, that **DD** is a *single letter*, not a doubled consonant.

Accent is generally on the penultimate syllable, but compound words and place names are often an exception to this rule.

Accent is generally on the penultimate syllable, but compound words and place names are often an exception to this rule.

I have used this system of transcription for the Bardekian and Elvish alphabets as well as the Deverrian, which is, of course, based on the Greek rather than the Roman model. On the whole, it works quite well for the Bardekian, at least. As for Elvish, in a work of this sort it would be ridiculous to resort to the elaborate apparatus by which scholars attempt to transcribe that most subtle and nuanced of tongues. Since the human ear cannot even distinguish between such sound-pairings as B> and <B, I see no reason to confuse the human eye with them. I do owe many thanks to the various elven native speakers who have suggested which consonant to choose in confusing cases and who have labored, alas often in vain, to refine my ear to the elven vowel system.

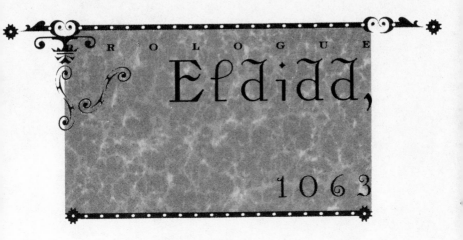

Eidid,

1063

ALAF YN AIL; MAIL AM LAD;

LLITHREDAWR LLYRY; LLON CAWAD,

A DWFN RHYD; BERWYD BRYD BRAD.

COWS IN THE BYRE, BEER IN THE BOWL.

RAIN FLOODS THE FIERCE-FLOWING FORD

AND SLICK PATHS. A SOUL STEWS OVER TREASON.

Llywarch the Ancestor

Even though dark clouds hung close to earth all day in what might have been either a heavy fog or an outright drizzle, out in the sacred grove beyond the city walls of Aberwyn the ancient oaks glowed with a light of their own, the autumnal splendor of their scarlet and gold leaves. A few sparks of that flame had fluttered down to lie in the muddy grave like golden offerings to match the grave goods already in place, jars and ewers of mead and oil, loaves of bread, a fine sword in a gilded scabbard, pottery statues of the gwerbret's favorite horses, all set around the wickerwork chariot. Although Deverry men had stopped fighting from chariots some thousand years earlier, their memory persisted as a thing belonging to heroes, and great men were buried in them, but lying down, unlike their ancestors, who were sometimes propped up in a parody of action that seemed indecent to Deverrian minds.

Lovyan, Tieryn Dun Gwerbyn, regent to the gwerbretrhyn of Aberwyn, stood at the edge of the grave and watched the shaven-headed priests of Bel clambering around in the mud as they laid the body of Rhys Maelwaedd, her eldest son, down for his last rest. By then the rituals were long over, and most of the huge crowd of mourners gone, but she lingered, unable to cry or keen, weary to the very heart, as they arranged his fine plaid, the silver, blue, and green of Aberwyn, around him. Once they began to fill in the grave, she would leave, she decided. She had watched wet earth fall on the faces of other men she had loved, her husband, her second son Aedry, the third son dead in childbirth that they'd never even named; she had no need to watch it again.

Beside her Nevyn laid a comforting hand on her shoulder. A tall man, with a shock of white hair and piercing blue eyes, he had skin as wrinkled as one of the fallen leaves and hands spotted all over from age, but he stood as straight and walked as vigorously as a young warrior. Although everyone who knew him considered his energy a marvel, Lovyan was one of the few who knew the truth, that he owed it to the dweomer of light, because he was one of the greatest sorcerers who had ever lived in Deverry. Just lately he had come into her service as a councillor, but in truth, she assumed, she was the one who was serving his particular ends. It mattered not to her, because not only did she trust him, but their particular goals were, at the moment at least, the same.

"It's cold out here, Your Grace," he said, his voice soft with sympathy.

"I'm well aware of that, my thanks. We'll be leaving soon."

The priests were fastening the enormous golden ring brooch to the plaid and clasping it closed around the dead gwerbret's neck. She looked away and saw two men pushing a slab of stone, balanced on a handcart, toward the grave. The epitaph was already carved, an englyn of praise for the ruler of Aberwyn, lost to a hunting accident, but of course it never mentioned the true cause of his death: evil dweomer. She shuddered, remembering the day when they'd ridden out together to fly their hawks. They'd been calmly trotting down the river road when Rhys's horse had gone mad, bucking and rearing, finally falling to crush its rider. Even at the time the accident had seemed inexplicable; late she had learned that dark dweomermen had caused the horse's madness and thus had murdered Rhys as surely as if they'd used a sword. Why? That, no one knew.

The priests climbed out of the grave and signaled to the diggers, leaning on their shovels nearby. Lovyan blew a kiss at her dead son.

"Sleep well, little one," she whispered, then turned away. "Come along, all of you. We'd best get back to the dun."

Nevyn took her arm, and the small crowd of pages and serving women fell in behind her as they made their silent way to the edge of the grove, where her escort was waiting. Twenty-five men of Rhys's warband and fifteen of her own stood at respectful attention beside their horses. As she approached, her captain, Cullyn of Cerrmor, led over her horse, a beautiful golden mare with a silvery mane and tail, and held it for her as she mounted and adjusted her long dresses and cloak over the sidesaddle.

"My thanks, captain." She took the reins from him, then turned in the saddle to make sure that the rest of her retinue were ready to ride. "Well and good, then. Let's get back home."

At the captain's signal the men mounted, and the procession set off, Lovyan and Nevyn at the head, her women and pages just behind, and bringing up the rear, the warbands. As they rode up to the high city walls, the men on duty at the gates snapped to smart attention, but Lovyan barely saw them, so wrapped in numb grief was she. It's all been too much, she thought to herself, simply too much to bear. Yet in her heart she knew that she could indeed bear it, that she would somehow find from somewhere the strength to see her through the difficult months ahead. Many noblewomen, it seemed, lived lives that allowed them the luxury of hysterics; they could wallow in fits of weeping, or shut themselves up dramatically in their chambers and get sympathy from half the kingdom with no one being the worse for it; she, however, had always had to stifle her griefs and rise above her weaknesses. At times, such as that moment in the chilly drizzle, she resented it, but even in her resentment she knew that she'd been given the better bargain by the gods.

As the procession wound through the rain-slick cobbled streets of Aberwyn, the townsfolk came out of house and shop to pay their respects quite spontaneously to the tieryn, who had been well-liked here when she'd been the wife of the then-gwerbret, Tingyr, before their sons Rhys inherited the rhan. Their heads bared to the drizzle, the men bowed and the women curtsied, and here and there someone called out, "Our hearts ache for you, Your Grace," or "Our sorrows go with you." Lovyan's heart ached more for them. Soon, unless she and Nevyn were successful in averting it, war would ravage Aberwyn's prosperous streets, and these people would have more to sorrow over than her mourning.

The rank of gwerbret was an odd one in the Deverry scheme of things. Although by Lovyan's time the office passed down from father to son, originally, back in the Dawntime, gwerbrets had been elected magistrates, called "vergobretes" in the old tongue. A remnant of this custom still survived in the Council of Electors, who met to choose a new gwerbret whenever one died without an heir. Since the rank brought with it many an honor as well as a fortune in taxes and property, every great clan and a few optimistic lesser ones as well vied among themselves to be chosen whenever the line of secession broke, and more often than not, the contest turned from a thing of bribes and politicking into open war. Once the Council got to fighting among themselves, the bloodshed could go on for years, because not even the King could intervene to stop it. Any king who marched in defiance of the laws would find himself with long years of resentment and rebellion on his hands. The most His Highness could do was use his honorary seat on the Council to urge peace if he were so minded or to politick along with everyone else for the candidate he favored. The latter was the more usual occurrence.

Since Rhys had died childless, the members of the Council were already jockeying for position at the starting line of this possible horse race. Lovyan knew full well that they were beginning to form half-secret alliances and to accept gifts and flatteries that were very nearly bribes. She was furious, in a weary sort of way, for, though Rhys had no sons, he did leave a legal heir, one marked with the approval of the King himself, Rhodry, Rhys's younger brother and her last-born son. If only Rhodry were home safe in Aberwyn, there would be no need for Council meetings disguised as social visits, but he had been sent into exile some years before by a fit of his brother's jealousy and not better cause. Now, with the King's own decree of recall published and all Aberwyn waiting for him as heir, he had disappeared, as well and thoroughly gone as a morning mist by a hot noontide. When the King had made his proclamation of recall, some days before, His Highness had set the term as a year and a day—just a year and a day for them to find the heir and bring him home. Less than that now, she thought; an eightnight's almost gone.

Although she was certain that Nevyn knew his whereabouts, the old man was refusing to tell her. Every time she asked, he put her off, saying that someone was on their way to bring Rhodry back home and no more. She knew perfectly well that her son was in some grave danger. By trying to spare her feelings, Nevyn was making her anxiety worse, or so she assumed, thinking that her troubled mind would no doubt make up worse dangers than her lad was actually in. She suspected that some of those who coveted Aberwyn had kidnapped him, and she lived in terror that they would kill him before Nevyn's mysterious aid could rescue him. If, however, she had known the truth, she would have seen the wisdom in Nevyn's silence.

That night the drizzle turned into a full-fledged winter storm, a long howl and slash of rain pounding out of the south. It was only the first of many, Nevyn knew; the winter promised to be a bad one and the Southern Sea impassable for many a long month. In his chamber, high up in the main broch of Aberwyn's dun, the shutters strained and banged in their latches, and the candle-lanterns guttered in the drafts. Although the charcoal brazier was glowing a cherry-red, he put on a heavy wool cloak and arranged the peaked hood around his neck to ward off the creeping chill. His guest was even more uncomfortable. A Bardekian, close to seven feet tall and massively built, Elaeno had skin so dark that it was as blue-black as ink, a color indicating that he was at home in hot climates, not this damp draftiness. That particular night he was muffled up in two cloaks over a pair of linen shirts and some wool brigga that had been specially sewn to fit him. Even so, he shivered at each gust of wind.

"How do you barbarians manage to survive in this godforsaken climate?" Elaeno inched his chair a bit closer to the brazier.

"With great difficulty, actually. You should be glad we're here on the coast, not way up north, say in Cerrgonney. At least it rarely snows in Eldidd. Up to the north they'll be over their heads in the stuff in another month."

"You know, I've never seen snow. I can't say I'm pining away from the lack."

"It wouldn't ache my heart if I never saw the nasty stuff again, either. I'm cursed grateful you'd winter here."

"You don't need to keep saying that."

"My thanks, but ye gods, I feel so weary these days. There's so blasted much riding on our Rhodry, and there he is, off in Bardek where we can't reach him till spring, and the gods only know how he's faring. When I think of the worst possibilities—"

"Don't think of them. Just don't. There's naught we can do now, so don't dwell on what might be. Easier said than done, I'll admit."

With a sigh Nevyn took a scoopful of charcoal out of the bucket and scattered it into the brazier, where the Wildfolk of Fire were dancing and sporting on the pinkish-red coals. Although he wasn't sure who had hired them, Nevyn knew that Rhodry had been kidnapped by one of the Bardekian blood guilds, who permanently removed little problems like rivals for an inheritance for those that had the coin to hire them. He could only hope that the lad was still alive, and that if he were, he hadn't been put to the—resolutely he turned his mind away. The blood guilds were known to amuse themselves with their prisoners in ways that did not bear thinking about. When he heard distant thunder crack, he jumped like a startled cat.

"I've never seen you this worried," Elaeno remarked.

"Naught's come along to worry me this badly in close to a hundred years."

"I keep forgetting just how long you've lived."

"It's a hard thing to remember, no doubt. I tend to forget it myself. Along with a great many other things about the past, let me tell you. It all blurs together after a while."

"I see." Elaeno hesitated for a long while on the edge of a question. "You know, I've often wondered what's given you your—I mean, why—well, I suppose it's none of my affair."

"Hum? Haven't you heard the tale? You see what I mean about my ancient mind? I'd been thinking I'd told you already, and here I'd forgotten I hadn't. All those long years ago, when I was young—and truly, I was indeed young once no matter what I look like now—I loved a woman named Brangwen, and I got myself betrothed to her. But I thought I loved my dweomer studies more." Nevyn heaved himself out of his chair and began to pace by the brazier. "There are a great many ins and outs to this story, most of which I've forgotten, but in the end, I betrayed her. Because of me, Brangwen died, and her brother, and an innocent man who loved her, too. That part I'll never forget. And it fell to me to dig her grave and bury her. I was beside myself with guilt and grief that day, well and truly shrieking mad with shame. So I swore a vow, that never would I rest until I'd put things right. And from that day to this, I've done my best to put them right, over and over, as Brangwen and the others were reborn and crossed my path, but I've failed every time, and so I've never gone to my rest."

"Are you telling me that the Great Ones accepted a vow like that?"

"They did. Well, I'd broken one vow, hadn't I? I suppose they wanted to see if I could keep the new one." He laughed, but there was no mirth in it. "Does it seem wonderful to you, living over four hundred years?"

"It doesn't, and especially not when I hear the weariness in your voice."

"Good. You'll go far in the dweomer, Elaeno." Nevyn sat down again and sighed with a heavy exhaustion. "But keep that vow, I will. Brangwen belongs to the dweomer, and by every god in the sky, I'll make her see it this time or die trying—oh by the hells, what a stupid excuse for a jest!"

"This time? She's been reborn, then, has she?"

"She has. Jill, Cullyn of Cerrmor's daughter."

Elaeno gaped.

"The same lass that's off with that lackwit Salamander," Nevyn said. "On her way to Bardek after Rhodry. The very same one indeed."

The storm blew itself out finally after two long days of rain. Everyone was glad to get free of the enforced leisure of drowsy hours spent huddled near the hearths in the great hall, and the ward was a-bustle that morning when Cullyn went out just to be going out, walking in the fresh and rain-washed air. He was strolling across the ward, aiming for the main gates merely to have a goal, but about halfway there he paused, struck by some odd observation that for a moment he couldn't identify. Someone he'd passed, back by the washhouse, was somehow out of place. He turned back and saw a young man he vaguely recognized, Bryc by name, one of the undergrooms, but he was carrying a load of firewood, and his walk was wrong, not the shuffle or scramble of a servant, but the confident stride of a warrior. Cullyn hesitated only a moment before following him. Sure enough, Bryc carried the anomalous firewood right past first the washhouse, then the cookhouse as well. There was no other building where that firewood might belong between him and the outer walls.

Cullyn stayed with him until the lad passed the armory, then ducked into it, ran down to the door at the far end, and opened it a crack to look out. His hunch paid off. Bryc was indeed looking back to see if anyone was following him, but he never noticed that the armory door was ever so slightly open. When he angled round a shed toward the broch complex, Cullyn slipped out and followed at a good distance, keeping close to the shadows of the various buildings. The lad never glanced back again until he reached the low brick wall that separated the gwerbret's formal garden from the workaday rest of the ward. Cullyn hid in a doorway as Bryc unceremoniously dumped his load of firewood, looked cautiously around him, then leapt over the wall. As Cullyn went after, Bryc hurried across the lawn, where, some distance away, little Rhodda, Rhodry's illegitimate daughter and only heir, played with a leather ball, while her nursemaid, Tevylla, sat and sewed on a small stone bench. There was absolutely no reason for Bryc to be in the garden at all.

With an oath, Cullyn drew his sword and broke into a run. He leapt the wall just as the fellow made a grab at the child. Screaming, Tevylla jumped up and hurled her sewing scissors at his head—a miss, but he had to duck and lost a precious moment. As he charged across the lawn, Cullyn saw that Bryc had a dagger and that he was swinging down.

"Run, lass!"

Rhodda twisted away and dodged as Bryc spun around, saw Cullyn coming, and turned to flee. Tevylla grabbed the leather ball and threw it under his feet. Down he went just as the captain reached them. He grabbed Bryc by the shirt, hauled him up, and broke his wrist with the flat of his sword. The dagger spun down to the grass. He kicked it far out of his prisoner's reach.

"Thanks be to the gods!" Tevylla snatched it up. "Cullyn, I'm so glad you were right there."

"Oh, I don't know. You seemed to be handling things pretty well on your own."

Tevylla shot him a weary sort of smile, then tucked the dagger into her kirtle and scooped Rhodda up. The child herself was oddly calm, only a bit pale as she stared at her rescuer for a moment, then turned in her nurse's arms to look at the whimpering Bryc.

"Get him," she said to no one in particular. "He's nasty."

The lad screamed, twisted in the captain's grasp, then threw himself this way and that in sincere pain while he screamed over and over again. When Cullyn, utterly startled, let him go, he fell to the ground full-length and writhed and screamed the more.

"Stop it!" It was Nevyn, racing across the lawn. "Stop it right now, all of you! Rhodda, you wretched little beast!"

Sobbing and gasping for breath, Bryc flopped onto his stomach and hid his face in folded arms. Cullyn realized that the lad's arms and face were nicked and bleeding, as if a hundred cats had been clawing at him. While Tevylla stepped back in horror, Rhodda giggled and snickered until Nevyn glared her into silence.

"Never ever do that again," the old man said.

"But he had a knife. He was nasty, Gran."

"I know. I saw it all from the window. You waited until he was helpless, and that's dishonorable. Well, didn't you?"

The child hung her head in shame.

"What a sweet little poppet you have in your charge, Mistress Tevylla," Nevyn said. "She's Rhodry's daughter, sure enough."

"She's a handful at times, truly, but here, good sir, you can't be saying that she did all that." Tevylla pointed with one clog at the bleeding man on the ground.

"You'll have to take it on faith that she did, and you too, captain. Come here, Rhodda. I'm going to talk to you, and then we're all going to go see your grandmother. Cullyn, drag that young dog along to the great hall."

When Nevyn left, Tevylla started after, but the old man irritably waved her away. Trembling a little, as if the shock had finally just caught up to her, she lingered to watch while Cullyn knelt down, grabbing Bryc by the shoulders and flopping him over like a caught fish. In his pain the lad cried out and stared up at the captain in bewilderment. Something was wrong with Bryc's eyes, or so Cullyn thought of it. He'd never seen any man look so bewildered, so utterly lost and confused, as if his very eyes themselves had clouded over until he stared without truly seeing a thing.

"Here, lad, have you gone blind?"

"Not at all, but, captain, where am I? My wrist!" Whimpering from the effort, he held up his broken hand and stared at the blood running. "Did I fall? Did the dogs do this to me? What is this?" His voice rose to an utterly sincere hysterical wail. "Tell me, for the love of the gods! What am I doing here like this?"

Cullyn grabbed him again, but this time to steady him.

"Hold your tongue, lad. I'll explain in a bit. Can you stand? We've got to go see old Nevyn about this."

"The herbman? Oh truly." His voice was a bare whisper. "It was like being asleep, then waking."

"Indeed? Well, come along. You're safe now."

Even though he'd spoken without thinking, Cullyn suddenly went cold, knowing that he'd told the truth, that Bryc had been in as much danger as the child. Tevylla caught her breath in a gasp.

"How do you fare, lass?" Cullyn said.

"Well enough, captain. I just remembered somewhat."

"And it was?"

"I won't tell anyone but Nevyn, but I think me I'd best tell him straightway."

Since as regent it was one of Lovyan's duties to administer the laws of the gwerbretrhyn, Nevyn had her convene their private hearing in the chamber of justice, yet they were a scruffy little crew among the splendors. On the wall hung the dragon banners of Aberwyn and the golden sword of justice; the massive oak table and the high-backed gwerbretal chair stood on a floor made of slate tiles, inlaid in a key pattern, but Lovyan perched on the edge of the chair with Rhodda in her lap, while Nevyn had Bryc sit on the table itself so that he could bind the lad's wrist as everyone gave their testimony. To Lovyan's right Tevylla sat on a low bench with Cullyn hovering behind her. Once the testimony was over, the tieryn gave her granddaughter a little squeeze.

"Oh ye gods," Lovyan said. "It seems obvious this lad tried to kill our Rhodda, and yet somewhat makes me doubt his guilt."

"Quite so, Your Grace," Nevyn said. "To be precise, his body was being used for the attempt, but his soul and mind are blameless. Now, Tevva, what's this urgent story you have to tell?"

"This morning when I woke, my lord, I had what I thought was a strange dream. Have you ever had one of those dreams where you think you're wide awake? Our chamber, Rhodda's cot, the hearth—it all looked exactly right, and dawn was coming in the window, but when I tried to move, I couldn't, and I realized that I was still asleep."

"Dreams of that sort do happen." Nevyn finished binding the lad's wrist and turned to look at her. "What came after?"

"I dreamt there was a witch in the chamber with me. My Mam used to say that a witch could draw out your soul and put it into a little jar. I laughed, then, but this morning I felt just that, like someone was trying to steal my soul."

Nevyn felt that weary sort of annoyance that comes from seeing your worst fear confirmed.

"How did you fight this witch off?"

"I don't know." She looked profoundly embarrassed. "I couldn't move to give the sign of warding, and I couldn't even really see where the witch was. I just knew that she was there with me. So, I . . . well, I just sort of pushed back. I called on the Goddess to protect me, and pushed the witch away. Does that make any sense, my lord?"

"It does to me, Mistress Tevva. Just one thing, though. That witch was more likely to be a man than a woman. You see, our enemies were trying to do to you what they eventually did to Bryc. They can take over a person's body for a little while, if he's weak enough, and use it like their own."

Bryc moaned, tears starting in his eyes.

"Your Grace," he said to the tieryn. "I never would have. Never would I have hurt the lass. Please believe me."

Lovyan flicked Nevyn a questioning glance.

"I believe him, Your Grace. Now that I know what they're doing, I can put a stop to it, too. If I may make suggestions, Your Grace?"

"Of course."

"Two things. Bryc needs to be sent away—not out of blame, mind, but for his sake." He turned to the heartsick boy. "They've made a link with you now, lad, and they might try to use it again. If they're successful, this time they'll kill you. Do you understand? They'll use you, then toss you aside."

His face pale, Bryc nodded a slow agreement.

"The other thing is, the captain should be the child's bodyguard from now on. Whenever you go outside, Mistress Tevva, you take him along with you. I can't imagine anyone taking over Cullyn's mind."

"No more can I," Cullyn said. "I agree with Nevyn, Your Grace. Since they can't work their stinking trickery anymore, they might send someone in here with a sword."

"Done, then." Lovyan gave them each a firm nod. "And as for you, Rhodda, you obey the captain's orders from now on."

"I will, Granna."

Everyone smiled, doting on the pretty little lass because she was such a welcome relief from the dark things around them. Only Nevyn knew that the child was touched by strange magicks, that thanks to the elven blood she'd inherited from her father, not only could she see the Wildfolk, she also could command them. Poor Bryc's scratched and bruised face made it clear that she had a good streak of elven vengefulness, too. Even with all his other worries and burdens weighing him down, Nevyn knew that he'd have to scrape out a little time for her.

That night, his worries pressed heavily upon him. Just after sunset he went up to his high chamber and threw open the shutters to let in the brisk autumn air. The evening was so brilliantly clear that he could see far beyond the town down to the harbor, where the ghostly white wave-foam mirrored the stars just coming out in the velvet dark sky. Distantly he heard the booming of the bronze bell at Manannan's temple, announcing that the gwerbret's men were raising the iron chain to close the harbor for the night. In town, a few dogs barked in answer, and the dark was pricked or slashed here and there by a lantern bobbing down a street or a crack of light from a window. At the sight of the stars and the rising moon some of his weariness ebbed away, and he stood there for some minutes, leaning on the sill and thinking of very little, until a soft knock at his chamber door roused him. With a muttered apology, Elaeno slipped in, shutting the door softly behind him. It always amazed Nevyn that the enormous Bardekian moved as gracefully and quietly as a cat.

"I was just taking a look at our prisoner," Elaeno said. "He seems much better today. It looks like he's mending cursed fast. That fever he had should have killed an ordinary man . . . well, not that I'm any sort of a chirurgeion."

"Oh, I agree with your diagnosis well enough. Did you look at his aura?"

"I did, and it seems a good bit stronger. I can't get over that peculiar color, a mucky sort of green it is, with those odd purplish stripes and specks."

"I've never seen one like it before, truly. Well, let's go down and have a look at him. If he's well enough, we'll try a working. Let me just put together the herbs and things I need."

The prisoner in question was housed in a small chamber in one of the half-towers that clustered round the main broch. Outside his door stood an armed guard, because Lord Perryn of Alobry had been until his recent capture one of the worst horse thieves in the kingdom, an offense punishable by a public hanging after a public flogging. He had committed another, more serious crime as well, but Nevyn was keeping that a secret for several good reasons. The summer before Perryn had abducted and raped Cullyn of Cerrmor's only daughter, Jill, but he'd done it by a muddled dweomer in circumstances so unusual that Nevyn had no idea of whether or not he were a criminal or a victim of some peculiar spell. Although the matter would require more study before he reached his conclusions, if Cullyn found out, Perryn wouldn't live long enough to be studied. As it was, he'd nearly died already from a consumption of the lungs brought on by his misuse of his instinctive magical powers.

That evening, though, he did seem much recovered, a peculiarity in itself. As Elaeno had said, that consumption was severe enough to have killed an ordinary human being. Nevyn was beginning to suspect that Perryn was far from ordinary, and, in fact, perhaps not truly human at all. On the tall side, Perryn was a skinny, nondescript sort of young man, with dull red hair and blue eyes, a flattish nose, and an overly generous mouth. At the moment he was also deathly pale, his eyes still rheumy as he sat up in bed and coughed into an old rag. When the two dweomermen came in, he looked up, whimpered under his breath, and shrank back against the heap of pillows behind him.

"Still coughing up blood?" Nevyn said.

"None, my lord. Er, ah, well, is that all right?"

"It's a very good sign, actually. Will you stop cowering and sniveling like a wretched field mouse? I'm not going to hurt you."

"But when are they going to come to . . . er, you know . . . hang me?"

"Not until I tell them to, and if you do exactly as I say, they may not hang you at all."

Perryn arranged a totally unconvinced smile.

"I see you ate a good dinner. Do you feel like getting up and getting dressed?"

"Whatever you say, my lord."

"I want to know how you feel."

"Well enough, then." Perryn threw back the covers and swung himself up to sit on the edge of the bed. In his long white nightshirt he looked like some impossibly awkward stork. "Er, ah, I'm a bit light-headed."

"That's to be expected. Elaeno, hand him his clothes, will you?"

Once Perryn was dressed Nevyn sat him down in a chair right by the charcoal brazier, which was heaped with glowing coals. He'd brought with him a small cloth sack filled with chips of cedar, juniper, and a strange Bardek wood with a sweet but clean scent called sandalwood. Casually he strewed the chips over the coals, where they began to smoke in a concatenation of scent.

"Just somewhat to cleanse the stale humors from the air," Nevyn said, lying cheerfully. "Ah, we've got some good coals. I always like to look into a fire. It always seems that you can see pictures in the coals, doesn't it?"

"So it does." Automatically Perryn looked at the lambent flames and the gold-and-ruby palaces among the heaped-up sticks and knobs. "When I was a lad I used to see dragons crawling in the fire. My Mam had lots of tales about dragons and elves and suchlike. I used to wish they were real."

"It would be pretty, truly."

Nodding a little, Perryn stared into the brazier while the sweet smoke drifted lazily into the room. When Nevyn opened up the second sight, he noted with a certain professional pleasure that the lad's aura had expanded to normal from the shrunken size it had been during his illness. The Seven Stars were glowing brightly, but they were all oddly colored and slightly displaced from their proper positions. Nevyn sent a line of light from his own aura to the Star that drifted over Perryn's forehead and made it swirl, slapping it like a child lashes a top with a whip.

"You see pictures in the coals now, don't you, lad?" Nevyn whispered. "Tell me what you see. Tell me everything you see."

"Just a fire. A leaping fire." Perryn sounded as if he were drunk. "Big logs. It must be winter."

"Who's nearby? Who's sitting at the hearth?"

"Mam and Da. Mam looks so pale. She's not going to die, is she?"

"How old are you?"

"Four. She *is* going to die. I heard Uncle Benoic yelling at the herbman last night. I don't want to go live with him."

"Then go back, go back to the fall of the year. Do you see your Mam? Is she better?"

"She is."

"Then go back, go back further, to the spring."

"I see the meadow, and the deer. The hunters are coming. I've got to help them, warn them."

"The hunters?"

"The stag. He's my friend."

In his trance Perryn twitched, his mouth working, as he went running into that meadow of memory and chased the deer away before the hunters came. Nevyn supposed that his childish mercy had cost the little lad a good beating, too. He took him back farther, to the winter before, and back again until Perryn saw the face of his wet nurse as she held him to her breast for the first time. And back further, to the pain of his birth, and back yet more, as his soul was swept into the unborn body that grew into the one he now wore, and back and back, until all at once he cried out, twisting in pain, speaking, half-choked, in some language that Nevyn had never heard before.

"By every god!" Elaeno hissed. "What is that tongue?"

Nevyn held up his hand for silence. Perryn talked on, his voice gasping as he relived his last death. Even though his facial features had changed not a jot, he no longer looked like the weasely lad he had moments before—stronger, somehow, his eyes blazing in an ancient hatred as he spat out angry words. At the end his body jerked, half-rising from the chair, then falling back as his voice broke off. Nevyn caught him by the shoulders and shook him, but gently, calling out his name until he awakened.

"My apologies," Perryn stammered. "I must have fallen asleep or suchlike, looking at the fire. Ye gods, that was a miserable dream."

"Indeed? Tell me about it."

"I was skewered. A spear, you see, right through me, pinning me to the ground, and there were enemies, mocking me. Horrible horrible enemies, like goblins or suchlike." He let his voice fade to a whisper. "They had these big noses and bushy eyebrows, all black and bristly." Suddenly he shook himself. "I must have been remembering one of those tales my Mam used to tell me."

"Most like, most like. Here, lad, I must have pushed you too hard. You go back to bed now and rest. We'll try sitting up again tomorrow."

Once they had Perryn settled and the guard back at the door, Nevyn and Elaeno returned to the old man's chamber in the main broch. They sat down with a tankard of mulled ale each to discuss what they'd witnessed.

"I suppose his killers looked ugly to him now because he's grown used to human beings," Elaeno said.

"Oho! You're assuming that those beings were his own kind of people."

"Aren't you?"

"I'm tempted, truly, but I also think that it's very unwise to make any assumptions about Perryn at all."

"Now there I'd most certainly agree with you. Huh. Big noses and bristling black eyebrows. I suppose they could be the goblins or ogres of many an old tale, either from the islands or your kingdom. Odd, how our folk stories do seem to be pretty much alike, with sorcerers, dragons, and some sort of evil ugly being."

"Except this isn't a tale, but a memory."

"True." Elaeno had a thoughtful sip of his ale from the tankard cradled in his enormous hands. "Well, if they weren't his people, then he's from some race or other that lives near our big-nosed friends."

"What is clear is that he died violently and in anger and hatred. It might be enough to make his spirit flee at the death moment and stray far enough away to get caught up in the wrong sort of birth vortex."

"So it seems. And it was his ill luck that the womb that caught him was kin to Tieryn Benoic."

"Who by all accounts was the last man in the kingdom to understand what a strange fish his wife's sister had netted." Nevyn shook his head in bafflement. "Well, when he's stronger we'll try the fire-vision again, but I think me we'd better wait some days."

"He couldn't take the strain right now, truly. How goes the other hunt?"

"For our murdering troublemaker? Very badly indeed. For a while there I thought I was on his trail, but he's disappeared. The stinking gall of him, trying to attack the child! If I get my claws into him, I'll tear him limb from limb, I swear it."

"He doubtless knows it, too. Once he realized that you were looking for him, he probably ran off somewhere to hide." Elaeno considered the problem for a moment. "Well, maybe if he's properly scared, he'll leave us alone."

"Always full of hope and raw optimism, aren't you? No doubt he'll lie quiet for a while, but he'll come back. His kind always does, like a witch's curse."

After being in attendance on the King for two long months, both pleading his cousin Rhodry's cause and tending to business of his own, Blaen, Gwerbret Cwm Pecl, was profoundly relieved to ride home to his own city of Dun Hiraedd. With the fall harvest his taxes were coming in, and he spent a pleasurable pair of days playing the role of the rough country lord, standing round his ward with the chamberlain and bailiffs and counting up the pigs and chickens, cheeses and barrels of apples, sacks of flour (both white and barley), tuns of mead and ale, as well as the occasional hard coin that was his due. He had a private word or a jest for every man who came to deliver his taxes, whether he was a lord's chamberlain riding ahead of a pair of laden ox carts or a local farmer carrying a wicker cage of rabbits on his back and a sack of flour in his arms.

Yet soon enough he left the taxes to his highly efficient staff and decided instead to make a small progress among his vassals. There were many lords that he hadn't seen since the spring at the great feast of Beltane, and he liked to keep a personal eye on potential squabblers and grumblers. He had another reason, as well: to look for some likely parcel of land, at least ten farmsteads worth, to bestow on Rhodry's woman, Gilyan, Cullyn of Cerrmor's daughter, along with letters patent of nobility. Although, with a good half of his demesne wilderness, finding the land would be easy, enticing the free farmers to work it was another matter indeed. What counted now, though, was that Jill have land and a title of her own; the income would be superfluous once she was married to Rhodry and he'd been installed in Aberwyn.

Since his wife, Canyffa, was pregnant, Blaen left her behind to rule dun and rhan in his stead and took only some twenty-five men of his warband along as an honor guard. They rode north first, stopping at Cae Labradd and the dun of the tieryn, Riderrc. To celebrate the gwerbret's visit there was a great feast one night and a hunting party the next day, but on the third day Blaen told the tieryn that he wanted merely to ride around the rhan on his own. With only five men for an escort he set out in mid-morning, but rather than viewing the tieryn's fields and woods, he rode straight for town.

Just at the outskirts of Cae Labradd, on the banks of a tributary that flowed into the Canaver a few miles on, stood a brewery that was known as the best in all Cwm Pecl. Set behind a low, grassy earthenwork wall was a cluster of round buildings, freshly whitewashed and neatly thatched, the brewer's living quarters, the malt house, the drying house, the brewing house proper, the storage sheds and, off to one side, the pigsty and the cowbarn. When Blaen turned off the road and led his men toward the brewery, they all cheered him, quite spontaneously and sincerely.

Over the door of the main house hung a rough broom of birch twigs, scented with strong ale, a sign that customers could buy a tankard or a tun as it suited them. When Blaen and his men dismounted, a stout gray-haired woman with a long white apron over her blue dresses hurried out and curtsied.

"Oh my, oh my, it's the gwerbret himself! Veddyn, get out here! It's the gwerbret and his men! Oh my, oh my! Your Grace, such a great honor, oh you must try some of our new dark and there's a cask of bitter, too, oh my, oh my!"

"Don't dither, woman! Gods! You'll drive his grace daft." Tall and lean, hawk-nosed, and perfectly bald, Veddyn strolled out and made Blaen a perfunctory bow. "Honored, Your Grace. What brings you to us?"

"Thirst, mostly, good Veddyn. Do you have tankards enough for me and mine?"

"It'd be a poor brewery that couldn't serve six travelers, Your Grace. Just you all tie up those horses and come inside."

Blaen handed his captain a handful of silver to pay for the ale, ushered his men inside, then lingered briefly in the yard with Twdilla while Veddyn followed them in. Once they were alone, she dropped her dithery ways.

"I take it that Your Grace is here for news?"

"That, and to look in on Camdel, poor lad. Is he any better?"

"Quite a bit, actually, but he'll never be right in the head again after what they did to him." She crossed her fingers in the sign of warding against witchcraft. "He's mucking out the cowbarn at the moment, so I'll wager Your Grace doesn't want . . ."

"By the gods, it doesn't matter to me what he smells like. Let's stroll over, shall we?"

As it turned out, they found Camdel sitting behind the cowbarn on an old stump and eating his lunch, a chunk of bread and slices of yellow cheese laid out neatly on an old linen napkin. When he saw Blaen, he got up and bowed with a sweeping courtly gesture that went ill with his dirty shirt and brown brigga, but although his eyes betrayed a flicker of recognition, he didn't truly remember Blaen and had to be told his name. He was, however, physically healthy again and even somewhat happy, smiling as he spoke of his quiet life at the brewery. Blaen was well-pleased. The last time he'd seen the man, Camdel had been a quivering shrieking wreck, stick-thin and utterly mad from the tortures of those who followed the dark dweomer.

And now, or so Blaen had been told, his beloved cousin, Rhodry was in the hands of those same evil men. Although he generally could keep the thought at bay, at times, when he least expected it, when he was talking with some vassal or merely walking down a corridor or looking idly from a window, the memory would rise up like an assassin and stab him: Rhodry could be suffering like Camdel did. With the thought came a breathless rage, a gasp for air that seared his chest and made him swear yet one more time a vengeance vow: if these evil magicians had made his cousin suffer for so much as the length of a cockcrow, then nothing on earth, not king nor dweomer, would stop him from raising an army and sweeping down on Bardek like a flock of eagles, even if he had to bankrupt his rhan and call in every honor debt and alliance anyone had ever owed him. Since he made the vow to his gods as well as to the honor of his clan, it was no idle boast.

He would have been surprised to know that the Dark Brotherhoods knew of his rage but pleased to learn that they feared it.

The central plateau and especially the hill country of southern Surtinna, the biggest island of the Bardekian archipelago, was at that time sparsely populated, a vast sweep of rolling downs descending from the knife edge of a young mountain range. Nominally the downs came under the jurisdiction of the archons of Pastedion and Vardeth, who parceled out land grants to their supporters at whim, since the hawks and field mice who lived there never bothered to argue about it. The land owners in turn rented out parcels for farms or cattle ranches or even, in a few rare cases, for summer homes and country retreats for the rich. Although the income from the grants was sparse, the prestige was enormous. As a further benefit, the archons and the laws were far, far away, so that a grant holder could live as he pleased, rather like a Deverry lord.

Up in the heart of the hill country, right under the looming pine-black mountains, lay one particular estate that had been bought and built some seventy years earlier by a retired civil servant named Tondalo. Although it received rents from some freeborn cattle ranchers, its own slaves raised enough food and linen and so on for it to be fairly self-sufficient. Only rarely did any of its slaves turn up at the market down in Ganjalo, the local town; even more rarely did visitors come to its gates. Since the few neighbors were too busy working their own land to pry into its affairs, everyone assumed that the third generation of Tondalo's heirs were running the estate. They would have been shocked to learn that the old man himself was still alive, though by no means in good health.

In truth, of course, Tondalo could have no heirs, because he was a eunuch, castrated as a boy to deny him a family and thus limit his interests to Vardeth's civil service. Since he had a brilliant mind for detail, he'd risen high and taken an active hand in the politics of his town, becoming rich enough to buy first his freedom, then an impressive house in the city, and finally this lonely estate. Now, at a hundred and sixty-odd years old (he really couldn't remember just when he'd been born), he lived in necessary seclusion. Not only had he grown so grossly fat (a hated legacy of his castration rather than any natural result of a love for pleasure and good eating) that travel was nearly impossible for him, but he needed privacy for his work. He had immersed himself so long and so thoroughly in the craft of the dark dweomer that he was as much of a leader as their chaos-sworn brotherhood could have. To his fellow practitioners of the dark arts, he no longer had any name at all. He was simply the Old One.

Of course, most times he had no need to travel. Scrying in a basin of black ink kept him in touch with the other members of the Dark Council and also brought him direct visions of the doings of his various allies and minions throughout Surtinna. Every now and then a messenger arrived, bearing books and the necessary supplies for his various workings. (The messengers never left again, of course, at least not alive.) When the full council met, it did so in an image-temple out on the astral plane, not somewhere in the hills or cities of Bardek. Yet on occasion he sincerely wished that he could travel on important errands instead of having to trust the younger students of the dark arts to run them for him. By its very nature, studying dark dweomer tends to make a man untrustworthy in the extreme.

Such a case was this matter of Rhodry Maelwaedd. If he'd been capable of it, the Old One would have gone to Deverry himself to supervise this crucial kidnapping and the disposition of its victim. As it was, since he'd had to entrust the job to a disciple on the one hand and hired assassins on the other, now he fretted constantly, wondering if the job had been done right. He couldn't simply scry them out to see, because all the important actions had happened either in Deverry itself or on another island, and not even the greatest dweomer minds in the world could scry across large bodies of open water. The exhalations of elemental force, particularly over the ocean proper, quite simply obscured the images like a fog. If he had tried to travel across them in the body of light, the waves and poundings of this same force would have broken up his astral form and led to his death.

So he could only sit in his villa and wait and brood. What particularly worried him was the complexity of the plan. If nothing else, he'd learned from his days in government that the more complex any project was, the more likely it was to fail, and this one had as many twists and turns as a bit of Deverry interlace. If he'd had a couple of years to spend, he would have thought and meditated until he'd honed some scheme as sharp and simple as a sword blade, but time had been short and the threat too present to allow such a luxury. Over the past decades various followers of the dark path had worked hard to establish a secure foothold in Deverry, particularly in the court of the High King himself. Just when their plans were maturing, Nevyn ferreted them out and in one ugly summer destroyed much of their work. In many other ways the old man was a threat to the very existence of the dark dweomer as well as a hated personal enemy of Tondalo's. As he considered all these things, the Old One had resolved, the winter before, that Nevyn should die.

An easy thing to resolve, of course; not so easy to execute. First of all, the Old One would have to act mostly alone, because he quite simply couldn't trust anyone to help him. Those members of the Dark Brotherhood who coveted his place and prestige were more than capable of betraying him to Nevyn at the last moment simply to get rid of him. If he wanted reliable allies, he would have to pay for them in cold cash and keep his real intent secret as well. There were highly skilled assassins available for hire in the islands—at least to a man who knew where to find them. The summer before, the Old One had hired a guild of these Hawks of the Brotherhood, as they were called, to carry out part—but only part—of his plans.

Since sending a simple killer against a man of Nevyn's power would have been laughable, the Old One had figured out a way to lure him to the islands, where his powers, drawn as they were from the Deverry soul and the Deverry earth, would be greatly lessened, and he would be far from the secular aid of such as Gwerbret Blaen. By all the laws of magic, in Bardek the Old One should be striking from the position of strength, the mental high ground, as it were, especially since Nevyn always seemed to work alone and thus would most likely come alone. When he looked around for bait for his trap, he fixed upon Rhodry, who was important to the barbarian kingdom's future as well as one of Nevyn's personal friends. Although his first thought was to merely kill the lad after using him to lay a false trail, he knew that Nevyn might be able to scry on the highest mental plane and discover that Rhodry was dead. It was most improbable that the Master of the Aethyr would come barreling across the seas just to give the boy a decent burial or suchlike. On the other hand, keeping him prisoner in his villa would have been dangerous, too, once Nevyn came ferreting around on the track of the bait. The Old One had no desire to go running—or waddling, as he wryly told himself—for his life like a badger flushed out of his hole.

No, it had seemed best to bring Rhodry to Bardek, wipe his memory clean so that he couldn't simply go to one of the law-abiding archons and announce his true identity, then turn him loose, hidden in plain sight as an ordinary slave, drifting wherever his fate or his luck took him. Sooner or later, Nevyn would follow. And when he did, the Old One would be waiting for him.

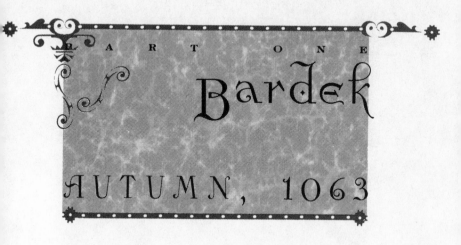

PART ONE

Bardek

AUTUMN, 1063

GORDDYAR ADAR; GWLYB TRAETH;

EGLUR NWYFRE; EHALAETH

TON. GWYW CALON RHAG HIRAETH.

A BRIGHT SKY, SEABIRDS MEWLING;

A WIDE WAVE, SOAKING THE SHORE;

A HEART, WITHERING FROM HIRAEDD.

Llwyarch the Ancestor

Although most people in Deverry thought of Bardek as one single country like their own, in truth it was an archipelago, and only the smallest islands were under the rule of a single government. The bigger ones, like Bardektinna and Surtinna, were divided into a number of city-states. Some of these consisted of only the city itself and barely enough surrounding farmlands to feed it; others controlled hundreds of square miles of territory and even other cities, either as colonies or as subject states. Myleton, on Bardektinna, was one of the biggest city-states at the time of which we speak, ruling the city of Valanth as well as a good half of the island. It was a beautiful city then, too, perched high on a cliff overlooking a narrow harbor. Walking through the gates in the pure white walls was like walking into a forest.

Everywhere there were trees, lining the wide, straight streets and covering them with a shady canopy of interlaced branches, growing thick around every house and building: palms, both the tall date-bearing variety and the squat ornamentals; spicy-leaved eucalyptus; purple-flowered jacarandas; and a shrubby variety, with tiny red flowers like a dusting of color over the leaves, known only in Bardek and called ben-ato. Flowering vines twined around the trees and threatened to smother the various wooden and marble statues scattered in the small public squares or at the intersections of streets. Among the greenery stood the rectangular longhouses with their curving roofs like the hull of an overturned ship, some guarded by tall statues of the inhabitants' ancestors; others, by pairs of wooden oars, large enough for a giant.

Sauntering down the streets or crossing from house to house was a constant flow of people, all dressed in tunics and sandals, men and women alike. The men, however, had brightly colored designs painted on one cheek, while the women wore broochlike oddments tucked into their elaborately curled and piled hair, but both ornament and paint identified the wearer's "house" or clan. Things were so safe then that the children could run loose in packs down the streets, playing elaborate games in the public spaces and private gardens alike without anyone saying a cross word to them or causing them a moment's worry.

Of course, all this splendor was paid for dearly in human lives, because Myleton was the center of the slave trade in the northern islands. With enough money and a little patience a buyer could find any sort of person there, from a scribe to a midwife to a laborer— even, on occasion, a barbarian from Deverry, though they were rare. The laws were very strict on such matters: Deverrians could be sold into slavery only for certain limited offenses against the state, such as nonpayment of very large debts, destruction of public property on a grand scale, or cold-blooded, premeditated murder. The archons of the various city-states had no desire to see a war fleet of bloodthirsty barbarians sailing their way on the excuse of rescuing some unjustly treated kinsman.

Thus, such exotic purchases were best made not in the public slave markets down near the harbor, where prisoners of war, criminals, and the offspring of state-owned slaves were auctioned off according to a registered bidding schedule, but in the smaller, private establishments scattered around Myleton. There was one such not far from the harbor, on the other side of the Plaza of Government, where a narrow, treeless alley twisted between back garden walls. As it went along, the walls grew lower until they disappeared altogether, and the houses, smaller and poorer until they degenerated into a maze of huts and kitchen gardens, with here and there pigsties, each home to a clutch of small gray-haired pigs.

Finally the alley gave a last twist and debouched into an open square where weeds pushed aside sparse cobbles and chickens scratched, squawking every now and then at the small children who played among them. On the other side was a high wall, striped in blue and red and obviously part of a compound, with an ironbound door in the middle. Although there was no sign or no name carved into the soft wood, those who knew about such things would recognize the place as Brindemo's market. Those who didn't know were best off leaving it alone.

Yet, on the inside the compound was no dark and sinister house of horrors. There was an open yard with scruffy grass and ill-tended flowers where during the day the slaves could take the sun, and clean if somewhat shabby dormitories where each piece of valuable property had his or her own bed, and a washhouse where anyone who wanted could bathe at his or her leisure. Although the food was by no means of the same high quality as would grace a rich man's table, there was plenty of it, and Brindemo and his family ate from the same batch as the merchandise. It was just that Brindemo was known in certain circles for buying slaves that other traders would refuse, slaves whose bills of sale were perhaps not quite in order, slaves who came to him drugged and unable to protest their condition—that sort of thing, perhaps legal, most likely not. Occasionally some unsuspecting beggar lad with no family to miss him had gone into Brindemo's for a handout of bread and never been seen again.

It was, then, a good measure of the strictness of the laws governing the sale of barbarians that when one came his way with a bill of sale that was less than perfect, Brindemo hesitated to sell him. Ordinarily he would have shopped such a prize around to the great houses of Myleton straightaway and asked a good high price for him, too. The barbarian was in his early twenties, extremely handsome with raven-dark hair and cornflower-blue eyes, courteous with a grace that bespoke some contact with the aristocracy, and, best of all, he already knew a fair amount of Bardekian and was learning more with a speed that indicated a rare facility for languages. He would make, in short, a splendid footman with a chance to work his way up to mayordomo someday, a valued member of the household who would eventually be given his freedom and adopted into the clan.

Unfortunately, there was that bill of sale, and the profoundly uncomfortable fact that the slave couldn't even remember his own name. Taliaesyn, his previous owners had called him, but he readily admitted that the name meant nothing to him. He could remember nothing at all, not his family, not his home city—indeed, no more than a few scraps about his life beyond the day he'd been sold. Since his previous owners had been giving him opium to keep him docile, Brindemo made sure that he had plenty of nourishing food and all the sleep he wanted. Unfortunately, this decent treatment had no effect; Taliaesyn could remember no more than he had before.

"You exasperate me, Taliaesyn of Pyrdon," Brrindemo remarked, in Deverrian, one evening. "But then, no doubt you exasperate yourself."

"Of course." The slave gave him one of his oddly charming smiles. "What man wouldn't want to know the truth about himself?"

"Hah! There are many men who hide the truth about themselves deep in their hearts, where they will never have to face it. Perhaps you are one of those. Have you done somewhat so horrible that you wipe the mind clean to forget?"

"Mayhap. Do I look like that sort of man to you?"

"You don't, though I think for all your charm you are a dangerous man. I would never give you a sword nor a dagger neither."

Taliaesyn looked sharply away, his eyes gone cloudy, as if his thoughts had taken a strange turn.

"A dagger," Brindemo whispered. "The word means somewhat?"

"Somewhat." He spoke slowly, almost reluctantly. "I can't find the memory. It just twitched at my mind, like."

Brindemo sighed with deep drama.

"Twenty-five zotars! Easily I could sell you for twenty-five golden zotars if only we could find the truth. Do you know how much a zotar is worth?"

"I don't, at that."

"It would buy ten pigs, and five of them fertile sows, even. So twenty-five zotars . . . ai!"

"My heart bleeds for you."

"Ah, the sarcasm, and how can I blame you? It is a good sign.

Your mind is coming back to life. But, I tell you, I have a guest coming tonight. He has spent many years in Deverry as a wine merchant. He might recognize you, or know somewhat to jog your mind. I cannot stand this. Twenty-five zotars, and here you sit, unsalable. It aches the heart, as you say in your country."

While they waited for Arriano to arrive, Brindemo taught the slave the proper method of pouring wine and passing a tray of cups around to guests. Taliaesyn took the lesson with a grave interest that had a certain charm, rather like an intelligent child who has decided to please his parents by doing something they want even though it strikes him as ridiculous. Yet Brindemo was always aware that he was docile only because his memory had gone. Taliaesyn moved like a knife-fighter (the professional athletes of the arena were Brindemo's only cognate for that particular gliding walk, the stance that was both relaxed and on guard at the same time), so much so that seeing him fussing over the silver tray was unsettling, as if a lion were wearing a collar and padding after its mistress like a pet cat. I never should have bought him, he thought miserably; I should have told Baruma no. Yet his misery only deepened, because he knew full well that he was in no position to deny the man known as Baruma anything.

Arriano came promptly when the temple bells were chiming out the sunset watch. Brindemo met him at the door himself, then ushered him into the main hall, a long room with a blue-and-white tiled floor and dark-green walls. At one end was a low dais, strewn with many-colored cushions arranged around a brass table. After they settled themselves on the cushions, Taliaesyn passed the wine cups around, then perched respectfully on the edge of the dais. Arriano, a wizened little man who hid his baldness under a white linen skullcap, looked him over with a small, not unfriendly, smile.

"So, Taliaesyn," he said. "Our Brindemo here says you come from Pyrdon."

"So I've been told, master."

One of Arriano's bushy eyebrows shot up.

"Talk to me in Deverrian. Oh, what . . . ah, I know. Describe this room."

As Taliaesyn, somewhat puzzled, obligingly gave him a catalogue of the furniture and colors in the room, Arriano listened with his head cocked to one side. Then he cut the list short with a wave of his hand.

"Pyrdon? Hah! You come from Eldidd, lad. I'd wager good coin on it—the Eldidd seacoast, at that." He turned to Brindemo and spoke in Bardekian. "They have a very distinctive way of speaking there. As you might have expected, Baruma was lying like a scorpion."

"May the feet of the gods crush him!" Brindemo felt sweat run down his back. "I don't suppose you recognize this supposed slave?"

"Not as to give you his real name, no. From the way he moves and all, I'd say he was a member of their aristocracy."

"What? I was thinking of him as a knife-fighter or boxer or some other performer like that."

"You forget, my dear old friend, that in Deverry, the aristocrats are all warriors. They start training for it when they're little children."

Brindemo groaned, a long rattle that gave him no relief. Taliaesyn was listening with an understandable intensity.

"One of the noble-born?" the slave said at last. "Here, this Baruma fellow said I was a merchant's son."

"Baruma lies as easily as the rain falls." Arriano said. "If I were you, Brindemo, I'd stop babbling about zotars and get rid of this man as fast as you can—but to a decent master, mind. If his kin come storming through here with blood in their barbarian hearts . . ."

"I know, I know." Brindemo could barely speak out of sheer frustrated greed. "But twenty-five zotars! Ai!"

"Will all the gold in the world sew your head back onto your shoulders if . . ."

"O shut up! Of course you're right. Baruma wanted me to sell him to the mines or the galleys, but that's out completely of the question if the man's an aristocrat."

"I should think so! May Baruma's sphincter loosen and his manhood plug itself!"

"And may diseased monkeys feed someday upon his heart! Very well, then. I'll sell him as soon as I can find the right sort of buyer. If you hear of someone, let me know—for a commission, of course."

"Of course." Arriano held out his hand. "More wine, Taliaesyn."

Even though Taliaesyn served the wine exactly as he'd been taught with all the proper courtesies, the harsh, brooding look in his eyes made Brindemo profoundly uneasy. I'd best get him out of here soon for my own sake, he thought, but ai! twenty-five zotars!

. . . .

Taliaesyn had been given a cubicle of his own to sleep in, because Brindemo was afraid to have him gossiping with the other slaves. If Baruma came back, neither the slave nor the slave merchant wanted him to know that they'd been trying to unravel his secret. Although the cubicle had room for nothing more than a straw pallet on the floor, and a tiny niche in the wall for an oil lamp, it was private. After he'd been locked in for the night, Taliaesyn sat on the pallet for a long while, considering what Arriano had told him. Even though the lamp was out of oil, he could see perfectly well in the moonlight that streamed in the uncurtained window. It occurred to him, then, that it was peculiar that he could see in the dark. Before he'd been taking it for granted.

A few at a time, Wildfolk came to join him, a gaggle of gnomes, mostly, all speckled and mottled in blue and gray and purple, quite different from the ones in Deverry, or at least, so he remembered. At the moment, he was disinclined to trust anything he "remembered" about himself. Who knew if it were real or some lie of Baruma's? He did, however, have a clear memory picture of solidly colored gnomes, in particular a certain gray one who was some sort of friend. Apparently he'd been able to see these little creatures for some time.

The ability to befriend spirits was so out of character for what he knew of Deverry aristocrats that he considered this strange fact for a good long time. Although he remembered little about himself, his general knowledge of the world seemed to be intact, and he was certain that your average warrior-lord did not go around talking to Wildfolk. Yet here was a particularly bold gnome, a dirty-green and grayish-purple with an amazing number of warts running down its spine, who was climbing into his lap and patting his hand with one little clawed paw as if it were the most natural thing in the world.

"Well, good eve, little brother."

The gnome grinned to reveal bright purple fangs, then settled into his lap like a cat. As he idly stroked it, scratching it behind the ears every now and then, Taliaesyn felt something pricking at his mind like a buried splinter trying to force its way out of a finger. The Wildfolk, the very phrase "little brother," both meant something profound, something that would give him an important key to who he was if only he could find the lock. It was a secret, a very deep, buried secret, hidden even from Baruma, perhaps.

"I wish you lads could talk. Do you know who I am?"

The pack all shook their heads in a collective yes.

"Do you know my name, then?"

This time the answer was no.

"But you somehow recognize me?"

Another yes. He wondered if he'd ever been an introspective man—probably not, if he reminded people of a warrior-lord or a knife-fighter. The bits of truth he was finding made less sense than all the lies. One of the noble-born, or an athlete, but either way, he saw the Wildfolk, and they considered him a friend. Again came that twitch at his mind. One of their friends or one of their kin? The hairs on the nape of his neck prickled as he said it aloud.

"Or one of their kin. I should know what that means, curse it all to the third hell!"

But he couldn't remember. All at once he was furious, furious with his mind, with Baruma, with the twisted fate that had stripped him of himself and dropped him here, a piece of human trash in Brindemo's market. He slammed his fist into the wall, and the pain and the rage mingled to force a brief moment of clarity out of his maimed consciousness. The Westfolk, The Elcyion Lacar, the elves. They saw the Wildfolk; they called them little brothers. He'd known the elves once—hadn't he? Hadn't he ridden to war with some of them for allies? Once, a very long time ago.

"Or one of their kin," he whispered like an exhalation of breath.

He went cold all over in the warm night. It was a hard thing, after all, for a man to realize that he wasn't completely human.

Taliaesyn stayed at the market for two more days of drowsy boredom. Although he did his best to probe his mind, he found the work hard going, confirming his own thought that he'd never been a man who paid much attention to his mind. He did, however, remember one small thing, the matter of the piece of jewelry. Although he couldn't remember exactly what it was, Taliaesyn was sure that Baruma had stolen a valuable piece of silver jewelry from him, some heirloom, handed down to him by some member of his clan or by someone he admired—he wasn't sure which. He did know, however, that having lost that piece of jewelry was a shameful thing, that he would be dishonored forever if he didn't find Baruma and get it back. The shame fed his hatred until at times he daydreamed for long hours about killing Baruma in one or another hideous way.

On the mid-morning of the third day he was sitting out in the grassy courtyard when Brindemo brought a customer to see him. He was a tall man, quite dark, with close-cropped curly black hair and two green diamonds painted on his left cheek. The straight-backed way he stood suggested that at some time he might have been a soldier, and his shrewd dark eyes often flicked Brindemo's way in contemptuous disbelief as the trader chattered on, singing Taliaesyn's praises and creating a false history for him all at the same time.

"Very polished manners, sir, a merchant's son and very well-spoken, but alas, he had a terrible taste for gambling, and fell in among bad company over in Mangorio, and . . ."

"Are you good with horses?" The customer broke in, speaking straight to Taliaesyn. "Most Deverry men are."

"I am. I've been riding all my life." As he spoke, he remembered another scrap of his earlier life: a sleek black pony that he'd loved as a child. The memory was so vivid, so precious that he missed what the customer said next while he groped and struggled to remember the little beast's name.

All at once the customer swung at him, a clean hard punch straight at his face. Without thinking Taliaesyn parried with his left wrist and began to swing back. Brindemo's horrified scream brought him to his senses. He could be beaten bloody for swinging on a free man, but the customer only laughed and gave him a friendly slap on the shoulder.

"I think you'll do. I'm leading a caravan into the mountains. One of my muleteers fell ill, and I've no time to hire a free man to take his place."

"What, honored sir?" Brindemo's jowls were shaking in indignation. "A valuable barbarian, used as a muleteer?"

"Only for a while. I'm quite sure I can resell him at a profit later on. Arriano told me that he needed to disappear, for your sake and his, and I can manage that."

"He told you what?" The trader's voice rose to a wail.

"You can trust me. Eight zotars."

"You have larceny in your heart! You wish to drive me out of business!"

The haggling was on in earnest. For a good long time they insulted each other's motives and ancestry at the top of their lungs until at last they settled upon sixteen zotars. Out came the original bill of sale, which Taliaesyn's new master read over quickly with a bitter twist to his mouth, as if he were amazed at the clumsiness of the forgery.

"I'll make out a new bill, of course," Brindemo said.

"Of course. My name is Zandar of Danmara."

When Brindemo waddled off inside the house to write out the new bill, Zandar crossed his arms over his chest and considered Taliaesyn carefully and coolly.

"You deal honestly with me, boy, and I'll do the same with you. When your relatives catch up with us, I'll sell you back for little more than I paid—provided you work hard and cause me no trouble. Is it a bargain?"

"Yes. I don't suppose free men shake hands with slaves here, or I'd offer you mine."

"No one shakes hands the way you do in your country, so don't take it as an insult. Unsanitary custom, it always seemed to me, rubbing palms with someone you barely know. You'll have a quarter-staff like the other men. Will you swear to me you won't turn it against me?"

"On the gods of my people."

"All right, then. We won't mention it again."

In spite of himself Taliaesyn felt a grudging respect for the man. He would have liked him, he decided, if they'd met in other circumstances. Zandar went on with his slow scrutiny.

"Silver dagger," he said abruptly. "That mean anything to you, boy?"

Taliaesyn felt his head jerk up like a startled stag's.

"I thought it might. You look the type. It would fit what little I've been told about your mysterious circumstances."

"So it does. Oh by every god!" He spun around on his heel and began to pace back and forth in sheer excitement as memories crowded at the edge of his mind. He could feel the weight in his hand, the perfect balance of the dagger, see the pommel with the three silver knobs, the device graved on the blade, a striking falcon. All at once tears sprang to his eyes, as he saw another picture in his mind, the grim, scar-slashed face of a man with gray-shot blond hair and ice-blue eyes, a cold man, hard as steel, but one who loved him. "I think I remember my father, and by the hells, he was no merchant."

"We were all sure of that, boy. What's his name? Think." He let his voice drop to a whisper. "Try to remember his name."

Taliaesyn felt it rising, just out of reach, tried to remember, and lost the memory cold.

"I can't." Then he felt the stomach-wrenching cold of a loss of hope. "Well, if I was a silver dagger, you don't need to worry about my kin coming to ransom me back. Doubtless they'll be glad enough to be rid of me forever."

"Many a man's worked his way out of slavery, you know. All it takes is a little shrewdness and a willingness to take on paying jobs after your duties are done."

Taliaesyn nodded in agreement, but in truth he barely heard him. He was remembering the dagger again, and he knew now what Baruma had stolen from him, knew what he had to take back at the cost of Baruma's life. Although he would never harm Zandar, he'd sworn no vow against escaping the first chance he got. Even though he would be torn to pieces as an escaped slave, he would take his revenge first, then die knowing he'd earned his manhood back again.

On the other side of the city from the harbor, Myleton sprawled along a shallow though broad river. Beside the water lay a tangle of alleys, tumbledown warehouses, and wooden jetties, where brightly colored punts bobbed in the flow. Beyond this disorderly district was a flat open pastureland where merchant caravans could camp with their pack animals. Zandar's caravan was waiting there, camped around two stone fire circles and a pair of rope corrals. It was a big caravan, too: thirty pack mules and twelve riding horses, tended by nine freemen and now, of course, one slave.

Eking out his knowledge of the language with gesture and pantomime, the men introduced Taliaesyn to his new life. The extra horses were his responsibility, as well as all the odd pieces of work unworthy of freemen: cutting firewood, fetching water, stacking gear, and serving the food at meals, though one of the other men did double as the cook. Although everyone treated him decently, no one spoke to him unless it was to give him an order. As a slave he seemed to be almost invisible, like a tool or a cookpot, hung up out of sight when not in use. When dinner time came, Taliaesyn was fed last and sat behind the others at a respectful distance. Afterwards, while they lounged talking around the fire, he scrubbed out the cooking pots and washed the bowls. Even though he'd had some days at Brindemo's to recover, he was still so weak from the long ordeal in the ship that by the end of the evening his head was swimming with exhaustion. As he fell asleep, he realized that it would be some time before he could seriously consider escape.

When the caravan broke camp the next morning, it headed out to the southeast, following the line of the river. After a few miles Taliaesyn realized why Zandar didn't seem worried about his new slave escaping. The countryside ran perfectly flat, perfectly featureless, mile after mile of small farms with only a few shade trees to break the monotony. Before noon they turned away from the river to head straight south and soon left the settled farms behind to follow a narrow caravan track through grassland. A runaway slave would have no place to hide, no food to forage, no true road to follow. Well, by the gods of my people, Taliaesyn thought, I'll have to wait and see what the mountains bring me, then.

That time of year, when winter was already howling through Deverry, the Southern Sea was so rough that the small bark was forced to tack its way across to Bardek. Of a morning it might run miles out of the direct course before a strong west wind, only to laboriously turn back in the afternoon when the wind changed. All around, the ocean stretched wintry blue and lonely, an endless swell off to a gray-mist horizon. Considering the time of year, it was doubtless the only ship out to sea. Its tattered crew of fifteen sailors grumbled at their captain's decision to make the trip south, but then they were usually grumbling about one thing or another. A rough lot, they went armed with swords and squabbled like the winds themselves, but they were quite respectful of the ship's two passengers. Whenever Salamander the gerthddyn and his bodyguard, a young silver dagger with the supposed name of Gilyn, took the sea air or stood at the ship's railing of a morning, the pirates bowed politely, left the deck to give them privacy, and made the sign of warding against witchcraft as they did so. If they had been able to see the small gray gnome that frisked along with the pair of them, they would have outright run away.

"Ah, the call of the sea!" Salamander remarked one frosty morn-ing. "The vast and windswept sea, at that, and then, far ahead of us, an exotic land and strange clime." He leaned against the rail and watched the white water foaming under the prow. "Bracing salt air, the creak of ropes and sails—ah, it's splendid."

"I'm cursed glad you think so," Jill snarled. "I'd rather have a good horse under me any day."

"Spoken like a true silver dagger, Gillo my turtledove, but you're overlooking a great advantage to shipboard life: spare time. Time to plan, to scheme, to brood revenge for the evils done our Rhodry, but best of all, time for you to learn Bardekian."

"Is it hard to learn?"

"Oh, not at all. I picked it up in a couple of weeks the first time I was there."

Salamander was forgetting, however, that he was not only half Elvish, with that race's natural proclivity for language, but also a man with a highly trained and disciplined mind. Jill found her studies maddening. Although she submitted to Salamander's endless drills, after hours of sitting in the stuffy cabin her stubbornness began to wear on him. It only took a couple of days before his patience snapped.

"Now here!" he snarled one morning. "You've got to put the adjectives *before* the nouns, you little dolt! If you say '*orno mannoto*,' you're saying 'the dogs are ten.' Ten dogs is *mannoto orno*."

"Why can't these idiots speak properly? If putting those ad-things after a name is good enough for the King, it should be good enough for them."

Salamander heaved an unnecessarily loud sigh.

"Mayhap we need a bit of a rest," he said. "I've been meaning to look over our coin, anyway. How much of Gwerbret Blaen's bounty do we have left? These pirates are both bestial and of repellent aspect, but they do not come cheap."

After Jill barred the door, the pooled their coin and counted it out. His long nose quivering, the gnome hunkered down to stare at the precious gold. When Salamander set aside the second installment on their passage, the pile left looked inadequate indeed.

"Even if we find Rhodry right away, we're going to have to stay in Bardek all winter," Jill said. "Is it an expensive sort of place?"

"It is, but men like a good tale no matter where they live. I shall ply my humble trade, but it's going to look truly humble in the sophisticated islands. The rich folk won't pay much for a storyteller, deemed fit only for farmers and slaves."

"Well, as long as we eat regularly, we don't have to live in luxury."

"*You* may not have to live in luxury." With a decidedly mournful sigh, Salamander began making the coins disappear into hidden pockets in his clothing. "Besides, if I'm not rich, how can I buy an exotic barbarian slave?"

"What? Who's going to be buying any slaves?"

"We are, my turtledove—Rhodry. What did you think we'd do? Demand him back by force or steal him with the sword? This is a civilized country. You can't just take someone's property."

"By every greasy hair on the Lord of Hell's black ass, I want revenge, not haggling in a marketplace."

"Do you also want to be arrested for armed robbery? Jill, please, for the sake of every god of both our peoples, follow my orders when we get there. If we cause trouble, we could rot in prison for years, and that won't do our Rhodry one jot of good."

Once the coins were hidden, Salamander leaned back on his narrow bunk and idly stroked the blanket with his long, nervous fingers while he thought something through. All at once he laughed, his smoky-gray eyes snapping with delight.

"I have it, my sweet, my eaglet! I shall be a wizard, not a gerthddyn." He waved a hand in a flourish, and blue fire danced and sparked from his fingertips. "Krysello, the Barbarian Wizard from the Far North!" Another snap of his fingers sent a small shower of bright red sparks flying. "Come one, come all, and see the marvels of the northern lands! Bring the children, bring the aged grandmother, and see if you can discover if it's done with powders and mirrors, or if the barbarian wizard is everything he claims to be." When he waved both hands, a sheet of purple flame stippled with gold drifted across the cabin to dissipate harmlessly against the wall. "By the hells, they'll be throwing coins at us by the handful."

"No doubt, since they'll be seeing real dweomer. But what would Nevyn say about this?"

"Does elven skin make good leather? Let us most profoundly hope that Nevyn never finds out about this little show, or the question will be put to the test. But don't you see, Jill, how perfect this'll be? Our enemies won't suspect a thing, because they won't believe for a moment that anyone would show off real dweomer in the market-place." He rubbed his hands together in glee, making a small fountain of silver flames. "Now, let's see . . . aha, you can be my beauteous barbarian handmaiden. Come see the fair Jillanna, a savage princess of far-off Deverry! See how she carries a sword like a man! You'll be a draw in and of your lovely self."

"My very humble thanks. I suppose it's better than being known as your fancy lad."

Salamander wiped his smile away and considered her for a moment.

"I'm sorry, Jill. I know your heart is sick with worry. It's a hard quest we're on, but we'll save Rhodry yet. Try not to brood."

"Not brood? Ye gods, with him in the hands of the Hawks of the Brotherhood?"

"He may not be that, remember. Snilyn the pirate was as clear as clear, they were going to leave him alive and then sell him."

"So they told Snilyn."

"Well, true spoken."

Cold fear swept between them like another wind from the sea. With a doglike shudder Salamander roused himself from what threatened to be despair.

"Let me amuse you, my turtledove. The Great Krysello had best practice his astounding repertoire of marvels."

As it turned out, with the aid of the Wildfolk of Fire and Aethyr, Salamander could put on an amazing show of true magic disguised as false. He sent balls of blue fire dancing, sheets of red flame drifting, sparks glittering down in firefalls and miniature lightning bolts shooting and blazing. In the dark, the show would be absolutely dazzling. Once he had his visual effects coming easily, he added snaps, booms, crashes, and sizzles, courtesy of the Wildfolk of the Air. At the end, he threw a golden firefall up far above his head and made miniature thunder roll as it came cascading down. As the booms died away, there came a timid knock on the door. When Jill opened it, she found a white-face pirate.

"Oh here," he said, with a lick at nervous lips. "Be all well with you?"

"It is. Why?"

"We heard them noises."

"It was merely my master, studying his dark arts. Dare you intrude?"

With a yelp, the pirate turned and fled. As Jill shut the door, Salamander broke out into howls of wild laughter.

"That's the spirit," he said between gasps. "I think me this ruse will work splendidly."

Baruma the merchant leaned onto the windowsill of his inn and looked out over the twilit city of Valanth. Far below down the hill, the last of the sunset sparkled on the broad river; here and there, lantern light bloomed in the windows of the houses or glittered among the trees of a garden. The sound of donkey bells drifted up to him from the distant streets. On this lovely evening he was inclined to be in a good mood. Not only had he successfully finished his job for the Old One, but his own affairs were progressing well. Sewn inside the hem of his tunic was a small cache of diamonds, far more portable than gold. Although he traded in goods that couldn't be displayed in any market or spoken of openly in any guild hall, they fetched a steep price for the man who knew where to sell them, and Baruma's poisons were all of the highest quality. He'd personally tested them on slaves to ensure it. While he considered which of his select group of customers to visit next, he scratched his hairy stomach, idly hunting for the tiny black fleas that were one of the hazards of traveling in the islands. It was time for him to leave Bardektinna and sail across to Surtinna; his ultimate goal lay on that island, far up in the hills where the Old One lived.

When the night grew cool, Baruma closed the shutters and turned back to his chamber, a luxurious one with white walls and a blue-and-green tiled floor scattered with velvet cushions and set about with tiny oil lamps. In one corner lay his traveling gear and two big canvas-wrapped bales, which he never allowed out of his sight. Any customs officer who went through his goods would find heavily embroidered linen tablecloths, napkins, and decorative bands for tunics and suchlike, made by barbarians in Deverry for sale to the wealthy ladies of Bardek. Unknown to those who made them, however, once Baruma brought their work back to Bardek it underwent a subtle change. He used the various traditional patterns as labels, indicating the name of the poison in which the cloth had been soaked. Put the cloth in water or wine, and there was the poison again, safe from the prying eyes of the archon's men.

In one of his saddlebags he carried Rhodry's silver dagger. He'd kept it for no real reason, more as a souvenir of those intensely pleasurable hours he'd spent breaking his prisoner's mind and will, but it did make scrying him out easier. Out of boredom as much as anything, Baruma took it out, then sat down on an enormous cushion and centered his mind by staring into the flame of an oil lamp. Since he was holding a semi-magical object of great meaning to Rhodry, the image built up fast. In the yellow dancing glow of the burning wick he saw Rhodry sitting near a campfire and eating stew out of a wooden bowl. Although he looked tired, he was far from exhausted, and he was unchained, unshackled, obviously a well-treated member of what seemed to be a large caravan. His flare of rage cost Baruma the vision. That fool Brindemo! Why hadn't he sold Rhodry to the mines or the galleys as he'd been ordered? Hardly aware of what he was doing, he drove the dagger hard into the cushion.

This lapse of control forced him to his feet. As he put the dagger away, it occurred to him that Brindemo was going to have to pay for his failure. The guilds would show the fat trader what happened to men who cross the will of the dark powers. As for Rhodry himself, since the Old One had said nothing about where he should be sold—the agony of the mines or the galleys was Baruma's own refinement—Baruma supposed the job was done well enough. Then he remembered the threat, the cold hatred in the silver dagger's eyes and voice as he stood on the deck of the ship and told Baruma that someday he'd escape and kill him. Just stupid braggadocio, Baruma told himself. Slaves can never escape here in Bardek. Yet he felt a cold sweep of fear up his spine. Rhodry was just the desperate sort of man who might risk everything for revenge, simply because he wouldn't care if he lived or died after he killed his prey.

Briefly he considered tracking Rhodry down himself, but the Old One had specifically forbidden him to kill the barbarian. If Rhodry were to die, Baruma would have to ensure that no one knew of his part in it. He could, he supposed, simply buy Rhodry back from his new master and sell him to the mines himself—but the dangers of that were entirely too obvious, considering the strictness of the laws governing barbarians and slavery. The Old One posed the worse threat. If he came to consider Baruma reckless and thus no longer completely dependable, then he'd dispose of his erstwhile student in a way that made the archons' long, slow methods of execution look merciful. He would be better off facing a loose and well-armed Rhodry than risking his teacher's judgment. There remained, however, Brindemo's insolence. Baruma could take some solace in seeing him well punished.

Down near the river in Valanth, on a narrow, dead-end alley, stood a house that was crumbling into decay. The stuccoed outer walls of its compound were peeling and cracking, the courtyard within so tangled with a garden gone riot that the ancestor statues were completely hidden. The longhouse itself had lost a good portion of the shakes on its roof, and the outer walls gapped and cracked in places. The citizens who lived nearby thought that it belonged to an old merchant who had lost both his fortune and his only son to pirates and who, thanks to the resulting madness, refused to go out or see anyone but his pair of slaves, as ancient as he. Baruma knew better. Late that night he left his inn and went to the compound, knocking on the splintery gate in a pattern of sound that few people knew.

In a few moments the gate opened a cautious crack. Lantern in hand, an aged slave peered at him.

"I wish to speak to your master. Tell him Baruma of Adelion is here, come from Deverry."

The slave nodded.

"Is he in? Will he see me?"

The slave shrugged as if to say he didn't know.

"Answer me, you insolent fool!"

The slave opened his mouth and revealed the scarred stump of a tongue long ago cut from his mouth.

"Huh. Well, I should have realized that. Are you allowed to show me in?"

The slave nodded a yes and ushered him into the weed-choked garden. They picked a careful way across on a path where the flagstones had cracked and tilted treacherously, then went into the house and down a musty corridor lined with cobwebbed statues—all stage-dressing for the neighbors and tradesmen who might come this far in. Near the back of the house were the master's real quarters.

The slave motioned Baruma into a high-ceilinged chamber, bright with lamplight, that was furnished with cushioned furniture and red-and-gold carpets laid over the tiled floor. On one wall was a fresco showing a pony and a barbarian woman engaged in a peculiar kind of sport; he was busy examining it when he suddenly realized that he was no longer alone. He whirled around to find the master towering over him. It took all his will to keep from yelping in fear. As it was, something must have shown on his face because the master laughed. A tall man, with bluish-black skin, he was wearing a plain white tunic, and over his face was a hood of the finest red silk. Tattooed around his right wrist was a striking hawk.

"If you were one of my pieces of work, you'd be dead, Baruma. Have you come to show me your wares? I'm most interested in seeing them."

"I'm honored that you are. Perhaps we can strike a bargain, then. You see, one of the little rats who scurry at our bidding has disobeyed me. I can't go back to Myleton to tend to the matter myself, but he needs to be punished. Not killed, mind—merely taught a painful lesson."

"Nothing could be easier to arrange." The master hesitated briefly. "This fool lives in Myleton, then."

"Brindemo the slave trader."

"Ah."

In the flickering lamplight Baruma could see nothing but the coarsest silhouette of the hawkmaster's face through the fine silk, but he received the impression that he was being studied. The hair on the back of his neck pricked in a perfectly reasonable fear at the thought.

"One of my men accompanied you to the barbarian kingdom," the master said at last. "I believe he was calling himself Gwin."

"Yes. I didn't realize that he was attached to this particular guild."

"It wasn't his place to tell you." There was a trace of humor in his voice. "He made, of course, a full report on what happened."

Baruma's fear deepened when he remembered the Hawk's insolence. He was painfully aware that no one in the world knew where he was at the moment, that he could disappear forever if the Hawkmaster should choose.

"I'm very interested in this Rhodry of Aberwyn." The master laced his fingertips together and seemed to be studying them. "Although

Gwin and Merryc are convinced that he was noble-born, we know little about him. I wonder why the Old One found him so important."

"I wonder myself."

There was no way of telling if the master believed him or not. After an agonizing wait of some minutes, the Hawkmaster spoke again.

"Soon you'll be completing the third ring of your studies, won't you?" His tone of voice was perfectly conversational, which was, oddly enough, more frightening than any sinister whisper or suchlike would have been. "A man like you could use a little backing in the Brotherhood."

"No doubt." Baruma picked his words carefully, wondering if he were being sounded out for a weakness. "When he walks the paths of power, a man needs to know who's walking behind him."

The master laughed, a cold sharp bark.

"I like the way you express yourself, my friend, and you're speaking the exact truth. What if I offered myself as one of your backers?"

"I'd be honored beyond dreaming, of course, but such support is far too valuable to come for free."

"Just so." The red silk rustled as the master nodded his head. "Some of us in the various guilds wonder what the Old One's up to. We wonder greatly. He is vastly old, my friend, well over a hundred at least, maybe two hundred for all we know. We wonder how the years have affected his mind. You've seen him recently?"

There was no use in lying.

"Oh yes, fairly recently. He seemed as sharp and smooth as a well-oiled scythe. Physically he's very slow, of course. But his mind still seemed . . . let us say, formidable."

"Ah. A fine choice of words, indeed. Now let me make one thing clear: I mean the Old One no harm, none whatsoever. If the blood guilds wished to dispose of him, we wouldn't bother to take the risk of bringing you into our confidence. Is that clear?"

"Very. Yet something's troubling you?"

"Oh yes. Why did he want Rhodry of Aberwyn kidnapped, then just set adrift here in the islands?"

"I honestly don't know."

"I was afraid that he hadn't told you. He's working on something, all right, something very convoluted and strange." The master got up abruptly. "I smell danger." He began to pace back and forth in front of the fresco. "And no one reaches my position in a blood guild without knowing danger when he smells it. All I want from you is this, that you go on to the Old One's villa, just as you planned to do, and see if you can find out anything about this mysterious scheme. That's all for now—just information. Later, who knows? But I promise you this, if anyone has to confront the Old One, that someone will be me, not you."

"Very good, because you know perfectly well that I could never stand against him."

"Just so." The way the hood twitched gave the impression that the master was smiling. "And, in return, we put you forward as a candidate for the Outer Circle. Our backing carries great weight, you know."

"Oh yes, and, as I say, I'm honored beyond dreaming." One thin trickle of fear-sweat ran down Baruma's ribs, but he forced himself to smile. "And I suppose someone will be keeping track of this mysterious Rhodry?"

"Of course. The man you know as Gwin, actually. He's the logical choice. He knows what the slave looks like and all."

Baruma hesitated, wondering if Gwin were really trustworthy where Rhodry was concerned, but arguing with a Hawkmaster's decisions ranked very low on his list of enjoyable pastimes.

"Excellent. I have reason to believe that Rhodry's a much more dangerous man than the Old One realizes."

"Indeed? Because he swore he'd kill you?"

The humor in the master's voice made Baruma furious, but he kept his own voice steady and light.

"I should have realized that Gwin would mention that little incident. Well, yes, partly because of that. Do you blame me? You know as well as I do that barbarians are more than willing to die if it'll salvage their precious honor. No sensible, civilized man would try to escape his owner, but Rhodry of Aberwyn is neither civilized nor sensible."

"You've got a point, don't you? You know, I think it might be safer all around to have Rhodry in our hands rather than wandering round the islands with this spice trader."

Baruma's heart pounded once. The Hawkmaster already knew a great deal more than he'd realized.

"I agree, of course," Baruma said. "I suppose it'll be easy enough for your men to take Rhodry alive. The Old One was adamant: we had to leave him alive."

"Oh, was he? That's an interesting piece of news. Very well, kidnapping it is. I'll put Gwin and some of my men on the trail on the morrow. We can probably learn a great deal simply by asking this Rhodry the right questions. He might be unwilling to answer, but then, we have ways of dealing with the recalcitrant."

"You certainly do, yes." Baruma was by now thoroughly frightened, but he knew that he had to speak the truth now rather than let the master find it out on his own later. "But Rhodry can tell you nothing. The Old One ordered me to crush his mind."

The master spun around and stared straight at him. The lamplight struck the hood at an angle, allowing Baruma to get an impression of narrow eyes and a sneering mouth. Showing fear or groveling now would be fatal.

"I followed my orders, of course. I wish you'd come forward earlier with this proposal."

"So do I." The master's tone was ironic rather than angry, and Baruma could breathe more easily. "I don't suppose there's any way to restore his memory?"

"None. No human being could possibly break the ensorcelment I put upon him. No matter how long he lives, he'll never remember so much as his own true name."

"That's a pity, but well, we'll have to work round it."

"Let me see, the man who was calling himself Merryc is still in Eldidd, isn't he?"

"Yes, and working out very nicely, too, judging from his last letter."

"And we at least know that Rhodry originally came from Aberwyn."

"You know, my friend, you and I might be able to work very well together. You think, and I like that. Curse this winter weather! There won't be another ship across in months now, and that means no news from Merryc till spring. But at any rate, what do you think of my bargain?"

Since answering too quickly would be suspicious, Baruma made a show of considering. After all, he reminded himself, gaining the Old One's backing was only hypothetical, while the Hawkmaster's offer was very real indeed—for better or for worse.

"I think that it's a crucial turning of my fate, and that I'd be a fool to refuse it." Also a dead man if I refuse it, he added to himself. "How shall we seal it?"

"The way these things are always sealed, my friend: in blood."

"Very well." Although he went ice-cold, he managed to keep his voice calm. "Whenever you wish to begin."

Zandar's caravan was working its way through hill country as they headed southwest along the spine of the island. On either side of the dusty road, field after field of dark-green vegetables nestled in the valleys, crisscrossed with tiny irrigation ditches, sparkling with water. When the caravan rode by, the bent-back farmers would look up, stretch, and stare at the long string of pack mules and horses. Riding at the dusty end of the line, Taliaesyn would stare back and envy them: farmers or not, they were free men. Toward noon, the caravan came to a river, or more precisely, to a broad gulch, littered with rocks and small shrubs, where water ran down the middle in a small, mucky stream. Out in what current there was stood a huge wooden water wheel with buckets all along the rim. As, sweating in the sun, two slaves turned a crank under an overseer's whip, the buckets dipped down, brought up the precious water, and emptied it into a wooden culvert that ran on stilts to the main irrigation ditch at the lip of the gulch. Seeing the scars on the slaves' backs reminded Taliaesyn that he was lucky.

When Kryblano, a free man working as a caravan guard, dropped back beside him, Taliaesyn asked him the river's name.

"The En-ghidal. It's dry now, all right, but soon the rains will start, and the flash floods with them. We'll be home by then, though."

That night the caravan camped downhill from a farming village called Deblis, a tidy arrangement of some fifty square white-plastered houses, each with a little wooden fence around a vegetable patch in front and a chicken coop behind. At sunset, Zandar took Taliaesyn and Kryblano in for the nighttime market. Among the flower-blossom lights of oil lamps, peddlers and local craftsmen squatted on the ground with their merchandise neatly arranged on pallets of woven rushes, but the local folk seemed to be standing around gossiping more than they were buying. Zander's goods, however, were a different thing. Once Taliaesyn got them unpacked and spread out, the village women clustered round to haggle for the little clay pots and packets of beaten-bark paper that held the precious spices.

After about an hour, as business was slacking off, Zandar sent Kryblano and Taliaesyn off to buy him some wine, and, generous employer and master that he was, gave Kryblano the money to buy himself and the slave a cup, too. After some poking around the village they found a tiny wineshop set into the side of a house, a room smoky from oil lamps where row after row of yellow clay jugs stood against the wall and patrons spilled out into the alley. While they sipped the flat cups of sweet red wine, Kryblano struck up a conversation with a pair of locals, but Taliaesyn stood a little behind him and spoke to nobody.

As they made their way back to the marketplace, Kryblano paused for a moment to slip down an alley and relieve himself in the dark. Carrying the wine jug for their master, Taliaesyn waited for him in the street, which was nearly as dark, and chewed over his continual nag of a problem: who am I, anyway? At a scrape of sandal on sand behind him, he turned and saw two men walking up to him, so purposefully and yet so quietly that he went on guard. Then he saw the bright gleam of a tiny dagger in one man's hand, and the coil of fine silken rope in the other's. Taliaesyn ducked to one side and kicked out as the steel flashed toward him, but he felt the dagger graze his arm. He threw the wine jug in his attacker's face and grabbed the rope carrier by the arm, twisting him round. When the man with the knife feinted in, Taliaesyn yelled an instinctive war cry and shoved his struggling prisoner straight onto the blade. The man in his hands screamed and slumped forward with a gush of blood. As the second turned to flee, Kryblano came running, yelling his head off, and the alley filled with villagers drawn by the shouting. As they tackled the escaping assassin, Kryblano reached Taliaesyn's side and grabbed his bleeding arm to look at the shallow wound.

Everyone was talking so fast that Taliaesyn had trouble understanding more than a few words. All at once he realized that his cut was burning and that he could no longer focus his eyes. By the light of oil lamps that shot up and wavered in great gobbets of flame, he saw Zandar forcing his way through the crowd in the company of a stout man with gray hair. It was suddenly very hard to hear the voices around him. He did hear Kryblano, shouting in alarm; then there was a gauzy gray silence and a dark.

In the dark a light was burning. At first he thought it was the sun, but as he walked toward it he saw that it glowed red like a campfire, that indeed it was a fire, but a strange one, because in the middle of the flames crouched a tiny red dragon. Around the fire stood a black man holding the hand of a white woman and a black woman standing alone. When they saw him they laughed and waved to him. Instinctively he knew that he should complete the circle, and as soon as he'd linked up the partners, they all began to dance, circling round and round, faster and faster, until all four of them blurred together in a rush of silver light, and the dragon swelled up, huge and ominous in a roar of flames, calling out to him, calling his name . . .

"Rhodry."

He said the name aloud, and he was awake, lying on a blanket in the shade of a tree at the edge of the caravan camp. By the sun's position he could tell that it was nearly noon. Although he was so dry that his tongue felt glued to the roof of his mouth, and his scratch from the night before still stung, he felt perfectly well and steady-headed, not at all like a man who'd taken a poisoned wound. When he spoke the name again, Zandar noticed that he was awake and came over with a waterskin.

"So you're alive, are you? Good."

"I've remembered my real name." Dry mouth or not, he felt his news so urgently it was like an ache. "It's Rhodry."

"Well, by the gods and all their little piglets! Good, good for you. Here. Drink first; then we'll talk."

Taliaesyn drank as much as he could hold, waited a few moments, then found he could drink some more. Zandar hunkered down next to him and watched with a commercial sort of compassion.

"There was some kind of poison on that blade," the trader said. "The village herbwoman was sure of that, but it couldn't have been very strong."

"I don't think it was poison. How about a simple drug, to knock me out and make me easy prey?"

"If so, it failed badly. The man you had in your hands is dead."

All at once Rhodry went cold all over, remembering that he was a slave.

"And will I die for that?"

"No. He attacked you, and the village headman is a friend of mine. What we all want to know is *why* he attacked you." Zandar gave him a grim smile. "Or let me guess: you can't remember if you have any enemies who want you dead."

"I can't, master. I'm sorry. I wish I could."

"Of course you do. Well, the headman's going to have the other thief executed, and that will be an end to that. Think you can ride today?"

"Oh yes. I feel fine. That's why I think it was a drug, not a poison."

"Oh." Zandar considered this for a moment, then shrugged. "Well, let's get out of this place and on the road, then. Maybe that will throw these mysterious enemies off your trail. I paid too much for you to have you slaughtered in front of me." Yet he paused for a moment, mouthing syllables. "Rhodry, huh?" He said the name strangely, with no puff of breath and barely any trill on the *rh*. "Tell the others, will you? At least it's shorter."

Some five days later, the Great Krysello and his beautiful barbarian maidservant found themselves a suite of chambers in one of the most expensive inns in Myleton. Since the innkeep had plenty of experience with traveling showmen, he demanded payment in advance, but once Salamander gave him a generous handful of silver coins, he turned servile, showing them up to the suite personally, bowing often, and muttering words that Jill interpreted as being "Hope my humble quarters are suitable" and other such pleasantries. The innkeep's boy carried up their traveling gear and laid it down on top of a low chest, then retired with an awestruck look for the pale hair and eyes of his guests, rarities enough in Bardek to be a show in themselves. Although Salamander announced that he was pleased, especially with the piles of cushions and the purple divan, Jill found the squareness of the room uncomfortable, and the echoing tile floor and stark white walls amplified every sound they made. Near the ceiling ran a painted dado of fruit and flowers, so realistically done that she would have sworn you could have plucked them off the wall. When her gnome appeared, it sniffed round the corners like a dog.

"Now Jill, listen," Salamander said. "When we go to the market-place today, you'll have to peace-bind that sword with a thong or suchlike, or the archon's men will confiscate it."

"What? The bloody gall! What kind of a place is this, anyway? What if some thief attacks us?"

"They don't have that kind of thief here, thanks to those very same archon's men. If you get your pocket picked, you see, you lodge a complaint, and the archon's men hunt down the thief for you and arrest him."

"Sounds like a waste of public funds to me, when I'm quite capable of slitting the dishonest bastard's throat for him."

"I fear me you're going to find Bardek a great trial, and doubtless Bardek will find you one in return."

"Let them. Do you think Rhodry's here in Myleton?"

"I only wish life would smile upon us so warmly, my little eaglet. I'm willing to wager that he came through here, though, because this town is the center of the slave trade. Anyone with an expensive property like our Rhodry would be insane to sell it somewhere else. I'm just hoping he went at government auction. They keep careful records of every sale, and for a few coppers we'll . . . that is, I'll be allowed to read them."

"One of these days I suppose I should learn letters. It seems like such a wretched bore, puzzling them out."

"Not once you learn, and truly, you should. Let me just see if I can pick up our Rhodry's trail now that we're back on land."

In a corner of the room stood a rectangular charcoal brazier, made of cast iron, on a solid-looking bronze stand, with a layer of kindling and charcoal all ready for a fire. Salamander lit the fuel with a wave of his hand, then stared steadily into the pale and tiny flames. Jill felt a cold trembling of fear. For all they knew, Rhodry had never been sold at all, but still suffered at the hands of the Hawks of the Brotherhood. When the gerthddyn groaned dramatically, she leapt to her feet, thinking he'd seen Rhodry dead or maimed.

"He's been sold, sure enough, to some kind of caravan leader," Salamander said. "It certainly looks like he's being well-treated."

"Oh ye gods, you chattering elf!" She felt tears misting her eyes and took refuge in anger. "Then why did you have to make such mournful noises?"

"Because they're traveling on a road through the grasslands, heading toward the undistinguished, unremarkable, and boringly bland mountains that cover half this island and a good chunk of the next, too. I have absolutely no idea where they may be."

Jill muttered several foul things under her breath.

"Fortunately," Salamander went on, "We can draw upon resources other than dweomer. We can check the aforementioned government records, and we can ask questions of the private traders, too. An expensive barbarian like our Rhodry will have been remembered."

"Good. Let's get on our way."

"We might as well, O Gilyan of the hot blood. Besides, we have to go to the market to buy supplies and to get a permit. Tonight we put on our first show."

In spite of the constant anxiety that underlay her mind like the sound of the waves in a harbor, Jill found Myleton splendid with its longhouses and painted garden walls scattered through the forest of flowering trees. When they came to the market, she was doubly impressed. The vast plaza was a sea of brightly colored sunshades, rippling in the wind over the hundreds of booths spread out around the public fountains. Here and there was a small stage where performers struggled to get the crowd's attention. Salamander told her that at noon the market would shut down while everyone slept the hot afternoon away, then reopen at twilight. They wandered around, eating cakes sticky with a white, sweet powder while they looked over heaps of silverwork and brassware, oil lamps, silks, perfumes, jewelry, strangely shaped knives, and decorative leatherwork. Salamander pawed through all the gaudiest merchandise and made his purchases; they ended up burdened with two brass braziers, packets of charcoal and resin incenses, yards and yards of red cloth, a long drape of cloth-of-gold, a tunic stiff with floral embroidery for her, and a brocaded robe of many colors for the mighty wizard to wear on stage. While he shopped he kept chattering away, but Jill noticed just how much information he managed to extract as he did so, from the best place to buy horses to the current political temper of the city and, most important of all, the names of several private slave traders along with the news that at the last public auction, at least, no barbarians had been offered for sale.

The first trader they visited informed them sadly that he'd seen no barbarians in over a year, but he did direct them to a man named Brindemo, who spoke the barbarian tongue well and was thus the private trader of choice for someone who had a barbarian for sale. After a quick stop at their inn to unburden themselves of their packages, they followed the convoluted directions and managed to find, at last, Brindemo's shabby compound. When they knocked on the door, it was opened by a slender man, too young to grow a beard, whose dark eyes darted this way and that as he greeted them. Salamander bowed to him and spoke in Deverrian.

"Where is Brindemo?"

"Very ill, my lord. I am his son. I will serve you in his stead."

"Ill? Is there a fever in your compound?"

"Not at all, not at all." He paused to run his tongue over his lips. "It was strange. Spoiled food, mayhap."

While Salamander considered him, the boy squirmed, his eyes looking everywhere but at the gerthddyn.

"Well," Salamander said at last. "Tender my humble apologies to your esteemed father, but I insist on seeing him. I know many a strange thing, you see. Perhaps I could recommend a remedy." He paused for effect. "I am the Great Krysello, Barbarian Wizard of the North."

The young man moaned and squirmed the more, but he threw the door wide open and let them into the grassy yard, where a couple of young women sat together near the well in a dull-eyed slump of despair. When Jill realized that she was seeing human merchandise, her stomach clenched, and she looked away.

"I must see if my father is awake."

"We'll come with you while you do," Salamander said.

With a groan of honest terror the boy led him round the longhouse to a side door which, it turned out, opened directly into his parents' bedchamber. Lying amidst a heap of striped cushions on a low divan, Brindemo raised his head drunkenly and stared at them with rheumy eyes, his dark skin ashy-gray from fear and fever. Her hands clasped over her mouth, his stout wife stood frozen in the corner. Brindemo looked at her and barked out one word; she ran from the room. Salamander stalked over to the bedside.

"Look at my pale hair. You know I'm from Deverry. You had a barbarian man here for sale, didn't you?"

"I did, truly." The fat trader's voice was a harsh whisper from a poison-burned throat. "I told your men already. I sold him. A spice merchant, Zandar of Danmara." He paused to cough horribly. "Have you come to kill me now?"

"Naught of the sort. I can smell the poison in your sweat, and I know what it is. Swallow spoonfuls of honey mixed with butter or some kind of fat. It will soothe the pains and sop the dregs up. Since the ben-marono plant kills quickly, and you aren't dead already, we may conclude that they gave you a less than fatal dose."

"My thanks. Ai! Baruma is one of your northern demons, I swear it."

"The son of one, at least."

With great effort Brindemo raised his head to stare into Salamander's eyes.

"You!" he hissed. "You're not one of them, are you?"

"One of whom?"

He fell back, panting from his exertion, and looked away. Salamander smiled gently.

"I won't force any truths out of you, my friend. If you mean what I suspect you mean, they'd kill you for certain. But in return, I shan't tell you one word about myself, so they won't be able to pry it out of you."

"A fair bargain." For a moment Brindemo lay still, gathering his strength to speak further. "Ease a sick man's curiosity, good sir, if you can. The barbarian lad, the one they called Taliaesyn, who was he truly?"

"He didn't tell you?"

"He didn't know. His memory was gone, completely gone."

Jill muttered a foul and involuntary oath.

"I see." Salamander turned grim. "Well, my friend, you had the honor of feeding a very important man. He was Rhodry Maelwaedd, Gwerbret Aberwyn, kidnapped and sold by his enemies."

Brindemo made a deep gurgling sound, choked, and coughed in spasms of sweating.

"Calm yourself," Salamander said. "You didn't know the truth, so no doubt no further harm will befall you. I take it you know where Aberwyn is."

"I don't." Brindemo could barely choke out the words. "Doesn't matter. Know what a gwerbret is. Ai ai ai."

At that his son stepped into the chamber, a big kitchen knife clutched in one hand and his face set in hard determination. When Brindemo muttered a few Bardekian words, he blushed in embarrassment and set the knife down on the windowsill.

"This Baruma?" Jill said to him. "Tell me what he looked like. Your father can't keep talking. He needs to rest."

"He was a fat man, you would say porklike, I believe, in your tongue. Very very strange skin, very smooth, and his black hair and beard are always shiny and oiled down. He wore a silver beard-clip, too, and his eyes were like a snake's, very narrow and glittery and nasty."

"What do you remember about the slave called Taliaesyn?" Salamander turned to the boy. "Everything you know."

"There was little to know, sir. We thought he was noble-born because he moved like a knife-fighter, and all your lords are soldiers. He remembered he was a thing called a silver dagger, but naught else about himself." He glanced at his father, who whispered out Zandar's name. "Oh truly, the caravan. It was going south. That was ten days ago. Zandar works his way through all the villages and so on to the south coast. He sells spices to the cooks." He thought for a moment, apparently struggling with the not very familiar language. "The name of the drug in your tongue, it is . . . um, opium, that's it! Baruma was giving him opium. Taliaesyn was very thin when we bought him, too."

"Baruma is going to pay for all this," Jill said quietly. "He is going to pay and pay and pay until he whines and screams and begs me to kill him and put an end to it."

"Jill!" Salamander gasped in honest shock.

Brindemo laughed, a tormented mutter.

"My blessing to you, lass," he whispered. "My humble but honest blessing."

Salamander started for the door, then paused, looking back at Brindemo.

"One last thing. Why did Baruma do this to you?"

"I disobeyed him. He said to sell Taliaesyn to the mines or the galleys. I sold him instead to the decent master."

"I see. Well, that act of mercy's cost you dear, but you have my thanks for it."

All the way back to their inn Jill burned with rage, and that burning translated itself to her vision, until it truly seemed that pillars of flame danced ahead of them through the streets. Although he kept giving her worried looks, Salamander said nothing until they were back in their chamber and the door safely barred behind them. Then he grabbed her by the shoulders and shook her.

"Stop it! I don't even know what you're doing, but stop it right now! I can feel power pouring out of you."

"I was just . . . well, seeing things again. I don't know how to stop it."

Yet the shaking and his very real fear had already snapped her mind back to a more normal state. The flames were gone, although the edges of everything in the room still shimmered with silver energy.

"Then don't start it in the first place." Salamander let her go. "Jill, you get to brooding on things, though I can't truly say I blame you, mind. But, well, how can I explain it? When you brood, you summon power, because you have a dweomer mind, deny it all you want. When most people brood over things they see pictures in their mind or hear the voice that they consider their self talking, but it all stays in the mind where it belongs. When you've got this raw power pouring into you, you begin to see the pictures and so on outside of your mind, don't you?"

"I do." She made the admission reluctantly. "I saw fire running before us down the street."

"Well, that's cursed dangerous. Dweomerfolk see images, too, and work with them, but we've learned how to control them. If you go on blundering around this way, you could go stark raving mad. Images and voices will come and go around you of their own free will, and you won't be able to stop them."

Since she could barely control them even then, she went cold all over at the prospect. With a dramatic sigh Salamander sprawled onto the cushioned divan.

"Food," he said abruptly. "Eating somewhat generally helps shut things down. It's tediously difficult to work any dweomer on a full stomach. Drink dulls the mind right down, too. But I doubt me if that's going to be enough. I've no right to do anything of the sort, but I'm going to have to teach you some apprentice tricks of the exalted trade."

"And what makes you think I want to learn them?"

"Your basic desire to stay sane and alive, that's what. Don't be a dolt, Jill! You're like a wounded man who's afraid to have the chirurgeon stop his bleeding because pressing on the wound might hurt." He paused, and he seemed to be studying the air all around her. "Well, you're too worked up now to try a lesson. How about food, indeed? The Great Krysello is famished. If you wouldn't mind assuming your guise of beauteous barbarian handmaiden, go down and ask the innkeep to send up a tray of meats and fruits. And a flagon of wine, too."

"I'm hungry myself." She managed to smile. "Oh mighty master of mysterious arts."

Salamander was certainly right about the effects of food on her visionary state of mind. As soon as she'd eaten a couple of pieces of meat and some cracker-bread, she felt a definite change, the dulling, as he'd called it, which she needed so badly. Although the colors in the room seemed unusually intense, the constant shimmerings disappeared. A couple of glasses of sweet white wine finished her involuntary dweomer-working completely.

"When are we getting on the road?" she asked. "I wouldn't mind leaving tomorrow, when the city gates open at dawn, say."

"I know your heart burns with impatience, Jill my turtledove, but we must consider what Zandar, prince of the spice trade, is going to do next. Mayhap he's heading home to Danmara, mayhap he's traveling this way and that about the countryside, unloading his goods upon the commerce-minded public. If he is, we could be going one way while he's going the other. If we go to Danmara to wait for him, we could sit around there for weeks. On the other hand, we can't sit around here either, doing naught while evil villains scheme, plot, work wiles, or even machinate. Whichever way we go, we'll have to travel slowly, stopping often to perform, like the showmen we call ourselves."

"Well, true spoken. We've got to get some coin before we go anywhere, though. I can't believe how much you've spent!"

"Good horses are not cheap in this rare and refined land."

"We haven't even got the horses yet, you wretched wastrel. Our show had best go well tonight, or you're in for it."

From a couple of jugglers Salamander had learned that any showman was welcome to perform in the public squares, provided he turned a quarter of his profits over to the archon's men. When it grew dark, they hauled their newly acquired props down to the market, which was just coming alive again in the cool. Oil lamps flickering among the gaudy sun-shades and banners cast colored shadows on the white buildings, while the merchants and their customers stood in little groups, talking and joking over cups of wine and snacks of spiced vegetables wrapped in fresh-baked rounds of thin bread. After a little asking around Jill and Salamander set up on the terrace at the top of a flight of steps leading to a public building. While Jill laid charcoal into the braziers and sprinkled it with incense, Salamander spread out the fancy carpet, then picked up the cloth-of-gold drape and began doing tricks with it, making it swirl in the air and catch the light, or suddenly turn stiff and billow out like a sail before the wind. Down below a crowd gathered to watch.

"I am Krysello, Barbarian Wizard of the Far North. Look upon my marvels and be amazed!" He flicked the drape one last time, then let it settle on the steps. "Jillanna, my beauteous barbarian handmaiden, and I have traveled far across the seas from the wondrous kingdom of Deverry to amuse, delight, and mystify you with magic that your otherwise splendid city has never seen before."

By now some fifty people were gathered at the foot of the stairs. Salamander slowly raised one arm and pointed at the first brazier. In a perfumed tower flames leapt up high, then fell, leaving the charcoal burning red and the sweet resins smoking. When the crowd gasped in honest awe, other people came running to see. Salamander waited until the crowd was steady again to light the second brazier.

"Shall I proceed with my humble show, oh good citizens of Myleton?"

The crowd laughed, dug into their purses, and flung a shower of copper coins. Jill scooped them up, then took a place out of the way as the Wildfolk of all sorts flocked to the improvised stage and clustered around Salamander. Her gray gnome appeared, did a little jig of excitement, then jumped to her shoulder and settled down to watch.

"Now behold the marvels of the north!"

Salamander pulled a long silk scarf out of midair—or so it seemed—and began to do the ordinary sort of tricks that any sleight-of-hand artist might do. First he made it disappear, then pulled it out of Jill's hair; he tossed it up in such a way that it looked like a bird, flapping down to his shoulder; he turned it into three scarves, sailed them around his head, then held them up to show that they were mysteriously knotted together. All the while he sang, snatches of a long wailing elven war chant, bits and pieces of Deverry ballads, and fragments of songs in some guttural tongue that Jill thought might have been Dwarvish. After a few minutes he switched to doing stunts with silver coins—again, just standard trickster's fare. He wanted to impress upon the crowd that he was only a showman and nothing more, to plant in their minds the idea that there had to be a rational explanation for everything he did.

Finally, when they were starting to get restless, Salamander flung up his arms and sent a glowing waterfall of many-colored sparks high into the air. As it poured down in a double rainbow, the crowd shouted and surged closer, a sea of sweaty faces in the rippling light. With a howl of elven delight Salamander drifted great red-and-blue washes, shot with silver and gold, across the stage, then followed with miniature lightning bolts and thunder growls. On and on the show went, with bursting flowers of light in many colors and purple cascades, while the crowd sighed and gasped and Salamander alternately sang and joked. When Salamander announced that he was growing weary, the crowd threw another rain of coins, and most of these were silver with here and there a gold. After some juggling tricks with hen's eggs, he gave them another good display of real magic, then announced that this time he truly was weary and the show was over. Still, a good many more coins came their way.

As the crowd drifted away, still talking over the marvels they'd seen, one of the archon's men—he had the city crest painted on his cheek—appeared to claim the official cut. While Jill rolled up the carpet and folded up the cloth-of-gold, Salamander sat down with the official near a brazier to count the haul.

"That was the best show I've seen all year, wizard. Just how do you do it? Some kind of powder in those braziers?"

"Oh, not at all. It's all true magic, as taught in the barbarian kingdoms."

"Well, it's not fair of me to pry into your secrets. It would only spoil the fun if I knew how the tricks worked. But still, I'll bet that handmaiden of yours is scattering all sorts of chemicals across the stage when everyone's watching you juggle. I see that robe of yours has good deep sleeves, too."

Salamander merely smiled, but the Wildfolk scowled and stuck out their tongues, as if wondering how the man could be so blind.

They'd racked up so much coin that Salamander gloated all the way back to the inn. Once they were up in their chamber, he danced around, humming elven melodies and dancing in the elven way, head thrown back, arms up rigid by his shoulders, as he swayed and jigged through the piles of props on the floor. Jill had to laugh with him.

"You love it," she said. "All those adoring female eyes looking up at you."

"Of course." He stopped, panting a little for breath. "Here, oh beauteous barbarian handmaid, grab a handful of those coins and go buy us a jug of wine, will you? The Great Krysello is fired with thirst, and we shall celebrate the success of our ruse."

Yet once the wine was fetched and poured, she found herself thinking of Rhodry again, wondering if he were safe, and if he would ever forgive her even if they did manage to rescue him.

"You're brooding again," Salamander said abruptly. "It's not going to do one rotten bit of good."

"Oh I know, but I don't have any elven blood, and so I can't be heartless."

"What a nasty tongue! Here, if I were truly heartless, would I be running all over Bardek looking for Rhodry?"

"You wouldn't. Ah, forgive me—I'm sorry. I'm just all to pieces."

"Of course." He picked up the jug and frowned into it. "Almost empty. In a bit I'll go buy more, but first we'll drink this up. That way, if the shop is closed or I break my neck on the landlord's unsafe stairs, at least we'll have enjoyed the final cup. That's the elven way, Jill, and is it truly heartless, to enjoy today when no man knows what evil the morrow will bring him?"

"It's not. I should be thankful that Rhodry and I had as many good times as we did, even if he heaps scorn on me when we meet."

"He's not going to scorn you! Hum, I see from your dark look that if I go on talking, you're going to strangle me, which would be a great hindrance to our plans. The Great Krysello shall make the supreme sacrifice and hold his tongue."

． ． ．

Since they'd been stopping in every town and village, it had taken
Zandar's caravan several weeks to work its way to the city of Daradion,
on the southern tip of Bardektinna. From there, Rhodry learned, they
were going to take one of the special caravan barges, more cattle boat
than sailing ship, across to the island of Martinna and their home city
of Danmara. Since they arrived at the harbor town just before sunset,
they camped outside the north gates in a public campground to wait
until the gates opened again in the morning. Although the campground was deserted when they rode up, as they were tethering out
the stock, a small caravan joined them, among them a young man,
expensively dressed in a white tunic with gold and purple vertical
stripes and a belt with a solid gold buckle. He had with him a boy
who seemed to be a personal slave and three pack mules, laden with
what turned out to be traveling gear, not merchandise. Zandar hailed
the fellow, Pommaeo, as an old friend and insisted he join them for
dinner round their campfire.

Once everyone had eaten, Zandar had Rhodry bring out a jug of
wine and serve it round. While Rhodry worked, he noticed Pommaeo
watching him, and in a few minutes he discovered why, when the
fellow turned to Zandar.

"The Deverry slave? How much will you take for him?"

"I was thinking of keeping him, actually. He's a good man around
horses."

"My dear old friend, you've never had much flair, have you? Are
you really going to keep a showy little rarity like that out in the
stable? I can think of lots of infinitely more appropriate uses for him.
I'll give you thirty zotars."

"He's not for sale."

"Fifty, then."

"I'm not haggling. I mean it."

For a moment Pammaeo hovered on the edge of sulks, all pouty-
mouthed like a child who's never been denied any trinket or toy.
Then he reached inside his tunic, pulled out a pouch of jingling of
gold, and produced an enormous coin: one of the fabled Bardekian
zials, worth a hundred zotars at face value but a good bit more than
that in a transaction, thanks to its rarity. The other free men caught

their breaths, but Zandar merely shrugged. Pommaeo's scowl darkened further.

"By the wings of the Wave-father!" Zandar gave him a smile meant to be conciliatory, most likely, but that turned out suspicious. "Just what do you want him for, anyway, if you're willing to pay that much?"

Rhodry had been rather wondering the same.

"As a gift for a very important friend of mine. I'm sure she'd be absolutely delighted with an exotic barbarian to tend her front door."

"Oh." All at once Zandar laughed. "I take it you're still courting the widow Alaena?"

"I don't see where it's a laughing matter, but yes, I happen to be going to visit her."

"And it takes a wealthy gift to snare a wealthy wife, eh?"

Pommaeo replied with a Bardekian phrase that Rhodry didn't know, though he could guess its general tenor by the way the other men both winced and snickered. With a grin Zandar got up and motioned for Rhodry to follow him as he walked a few steps away.

"It feels odd, justifying something to a slave, but I've grown to like you, boy. I'm going to take this offer because I think you'll be safer this way. Anyone can find out that I live in Danmara. For all I know, the men who want you are sitting there waiting for you to walk right into a trap. This should pretty well throw them off your track. Besides, you'll live well in the widow Alaena's household, and you'll have plenty of chances to earn tips. Just don't piss the money away on gambling and drinking, and you can buy your freedom back sooner or later." He gave Rhodry a friendly slap on the shoulder. "And good luck."

For Zandar's sake Rhodry forced out a smile, but inwardly he was steaming at the thought of being a courting gift. If his position had allowed it, he would have cursed in a steady stream.

To clinch the deal Zandar threw in the horse that Rhodry had been riding and the clothes and blankets he'd been using. As the young slave boy, Miko, helped him carry his gear over to his new master's campsite, the lad talked so much and so fast that Rhodry could only understand about half of what he said. He did manage to figure out, though, that Pommaeo was a difficult man, prone to slapping his slaves around if they didn't do exactly as they were told. He realized that if he were going to live to see this widow's household, he was going to have to keep a firm grip on his temper; striking back could get him flogged by the archon's men. Although he couldn't remember specifically why, he did know that restraining his temper was something he'd never done before in his life and that the job wasn't going to be easy.

Later that evening Pommaeo left Zandar's camp and returned to his own fire. While Miko combed the master's hair and removed his face paint for the night, Pommaeo gave Rhodry a small lecture in remarkably good Deverrian. It turned out that he'd made several trading runs to the kingdom with his uncles.

"So, an Eldidd man, I'd say, and sold as a slave in the islands? Zandar told me it was a matter of gambling debts, but I have my doubts. It doesn't matter a pig's fart, mind, just so long as you watch your courtesies from now on."

"And do I have any choice about that?"

"None, of course. Now listen, you're about to go to a fine household that makes those barbarian duns of yours look like pigsties. You'll have strict duties, and there'll be other slaves to make sure you perform them in the correct manner. If I hear of you giving the lady Alaena the least jot of trouble, I'll flog you myself. Do you understand me?"

"I do, master."

Although Rhodry bobbed his head respectfully, he was considering ways to strangle Pommaeo and leave his body beside the road. The mincing piss-proud excuse for a real man! he thought to himself. Hunting rich widows! Let's hope the poor old woman has the wit to see him for the snake he is!

"Do you know what the whole secret of the dweomer is?" Salamander said abruptly. "Making pictures in your mind. Just that and little else—making the right sort of pictures and saying the right words to go with them. How does that strike you?"

Startled, Jill looked up from her breakfast.

"Are you sure you're not having a jest on me?"

"I'm not, though I know it must sound like one. There's this book we all study—eventually you've *got* to learn to read, my little turtledove—which is known as *The Secret Book of Cadwallon the Druid*, though I've been told that it's actually a lot of short bits and aphorisms jotted down by various dweomermasters over the years. Be that as it may, there's one particular piece that springs to my mind at the moment. 'You could go to the marketplace and, like a gerthddyn, preach aloud the secret of all dweomer without one soul being a wit's worth wiser.' Do you know why? Because it's so simple everyone would sneer. Or to be precise: simple to describe; cursed hard to do."

"I'll admit to fighting the urge to sneer if all you're talking about is a lot of pictures."

"Aha, I know a challenge when I hear one. Very well." He held up his elaborately jeweled table dagger. "Look at this for a moment. Then shut your eyes. Try to see the dagger as clearly as you could with your eyes open—a memory picture, like."

Although Jill stared at the dagger for a long moment, she did so blankly, as if she could soak it up the way a bit of rag soaks up spilled ale. As soon as she shut her eyes, its image was gone, and no amount of struggling with her memory would bring a clear picture back. With an oath, she looked again, and this time she actively tried to memorize the details, but she could only retain the vaguest general impression, more of a daggerlike shape than a dagger.

"Harder than it sounds?" Salamander was grinning at her frustration.

"It is."

"By the time you're done with your 'prentice-work, you'll be able to walk into a chamber you've never seen before, stay but a few minutes, yet be able to call up a picture of that chamber so clearly that you'd swear you were standing inside it. You'll curse the work before you're done, too, because learning how to manipulate images is the most boring thing in the world. Think of it as a test, my minuscule finch. The bard tales talk about suffering mysterious ordeals both harsh and lurid to gain the dweomer, but are you willing to be bored sick with it? That's the true test of every apprentice."

"When my father was teaching me how to use a sword, he drilled me until I wanted to weep. Have you ever lunged at a bale of hay over and over in the hot sun? Some days I'd do it a hundred times, while he stood there and criticized the way I was standing or holding my wrist or suchlike."

"Gods, I doubt if you'll find me as harsh a master as Cullyn of

Cerrmor must have been. Now, let's see. It's easier to start with a picture than it is with a solid thing, somehow. We can search the marketplace for a painted scroll."

"Oh come now, you don't expect to find some rare dweomer book right out in the Myleton market, do you?"

"Of course not, but we don't want one. What we need is the sort of thing a merchant's wife would have in her reception chamber to amuse a guest, a little scroll with four or five colored drawings on it, maybe pictures of famous temples, maybe seacoast views—that sort of mundane thing. Trained slaves copy them out by the hundreds, so we should be able to find one with little trouble. You need a complicated thing to keep your mind alive while you do the wretched exercises."

"Whatever you say. What comes after learning to hold pictures in your mind?"

"Oh, extensions of the basic work. You start by maybe changing some details of the picture you're seeing mentally—adding clouds in the sky, say, or putting in a tree. Then, let's see . . . uh well . . . eventually you have to pretend you're in the picture yourself and looking around at all its various parts . . . I know we did that . . ." His voice trailed away.

"You don't really remember it all, do you?"

"You may berate me for a wretched and most frivolous elf, if you wish, because, alas, alack, well-a-day, and so on and so forth, you speak the truth. I do remember the beginning banishing ritual, though, and that's truly important for someone in your state of mind."

"Well and good then. What is it?"

"There's no time to go into it right now. If we're going to buy horses, we have to get to the market before it closes for the midday heat, so let's wait till we're out on the road. But don't let me forget to show it to you."

It occurred to Jill that, as harsh ordeals went, learning dweomer from Salamander was going to have its moments.

Before they went to the market, Salamander did his usual morning's scrying. His face all narrow-eyed concentration, the gerthddyn bent over the glowing embers in the charcoal brazier and watched as strange images moved among them. All at once he smiled and began to speak in a whisper.

"Finally! He's riding up to a city, my turtledove, so we can—now wait, what's this? Hell-ice and foul humors! Rhodry's been sold again! Curse it all! I can see him riding behind some new master." He paused for a long moment. "Ah, finally! They're going into the city gates. I can see the crest, oh joy, oh rapture, the glorious city crest! Daradion down on the south coast . . . oh ye gods! Curse them, curse me, a pox and the vapors upon us all! They're going down to the harbor! Oh dear dearest gods, not onto a ship!" He made a gargling noise deep in his throat, then watched in silence for a long while. "May the Lord of Hell's balls atrophy and fall off! This wretched fool is dickering with a ship owner for some kind of passage!" With a toss of his head he looked up, sweeping away the vision. "At least I got a chance to read the ship's name. It's the *Gray Kestrel*, so we can ask the harbormaster where it was going."

"When we get there. Ye gods, how far away is the place?"

"Well over a fortnight's ride, alas. We have the lovely choice of traveling straight and slowly through the mountains, or roundabout but a more rapid pace along the coast. I can't scry while they're crossing the sea because of the . . ."

"The blasted elemental what's-it . . . veils of astral force."

"Where did you learn that?"

"You told me yourself, lackwit."

"You needn't be so nasty. Look, at least we'll know we're on the right track. We might have been rambling, roaming, and generally tramping about to no purpose at all."

"True spoken, and I'm sorry I snapped at you. It's just that this new owner could be taking him anywhere at all . . . I mean, hundreds and hundreds of miles for all we know."

Salamander's face sank like warm wax into despair.

"Alas, 'tis true, little eaglet. Fortunately, ships sail all year long across the nicely sheltered Inner Sea, and so we shall be able to follow them wherever they go. We have tarried long enough. Let us pack up our gear and head for the market place, so we may bend our course for glorious Daradion, winged with sails and so on and so forth. Myleton has enjoyed the pleasure of our presence long enough."

· · · ·

During the slow trip across the Inner Sea to the island of Surtinna, Rhodry was quartered down in the hold in a stall next to the horses and mules, although he was allowed abovedecks to eat his meals with the other slaves. The arrangement suited him well enough, giving him the privacy to think a good distance away from Pommaeo's ill-temper. Or at least he tried to think; most of the time he slept, drowsing in the warm straw with Wildfolk heaped around him like a pack of dogs. It did occur to him once that he probably had been a soldier if his body would insist on taking every chance it got to stock up on sleep, but try as he might, he never had another flash of insight like the drugged dream that had given him back his real name.

They left the ship at Ronaton and spent another two days riding northwest to the hill town of Wylinth, where the widow Alaena lived. Pommaeo was so arrogant and demanding that, by the time they finally arrived, Rhodry had decided that the shame of being a courting gift was a small thing compared to the joy of getting away from him. All white stucco and flowering trees, Wylinth spread out over clustered hilltops behind walls of pink sandstone. After he paid the toll at the city gates, Pommaeo led his minature caravan to a long, sprawling inn in the center of town and hired a suite. The main chamber had a floor tiled in blue and green, and a marble fountain splashed lazily in the center of the room. The two slaves carried up the mounds of luggage; then Pommaeo gave Miko a string of orders, while Rhodry spread Pommaeo's embroidered blankets on the bed instead of the innkeep's plain ones.

"I'm going to the market," the master said. "Rhodry, do what the boy tells you."

Miko's orders were welcome enough. Apparently the master was going to give Rhodry away that very night, and he wanted him presentable. Rhodry was more than willing to go down to the slave's corner of the bathhouse and get truly clean for the first time in weeks. He even let the boy cut his hair for him with only a minimum of grumbling. Pommaeo returned from the market shortly after, and in a few minutes, when a slave arrived with an armful of purchases, Rhodry noticed with some interest that Pommaeo did indeed tip the man a couple of coppers. The master pawed through the bundles and tossed one to Rhodry.

"Put these on. You won't be much of a gift with horse sweat all over your clothes."

Inside was a plain but good-quality white tunic and a new pair of sandals, a hair comb, and—much to Rhodry's surprise —a good bronze razor in a plain sheath.

"Well, you'll need to shave every day," the master said; he'd apparently noticed Rhodry's surprise even if he seemed to think nothing of handing a slave a potential weapon. "You're a house slave now, and you'll be expected to keep yourself clean, not wallow with the animals like a barbarian. Speak humbly at all times, and do exactly what the chamberlain tells you. If you do one wrong thing, and I'm not here to flog you, then her brother-in-law will. And try to do something about those Deverry table manners, will you? Her other slaves are civilized people, and they'll have to share a table with you."

They left the inn just after sundown. Carrying a lantern, Miko went a few paces ahead as they walked through the wide, straight-running streets, lined with palm trees and jasmine. They passed the market square, where tiny oil lamps were flickering into life like the evening stars, then climbed a hill to a neighborhood where enormous houses stood in their compounds behind stucco walls. Although it was hard to see clearly in the lantern light, Rhodry could make out elaborate frescoes painted on every one of them. Eventually they came to a wall painted with a rural scene; set in a painted cottage was a real wooden door. When Pommaeo called out, an elderly slave opened it and ushered them inside.

In the midst of tangled jasmine and spent roses a fountain leapt and splashed in a courtyard, which was lined with the tall wooden statues of the clan's ancestors. The longhouse itself, with a pair of crossed oars in front of the door, stood toward the rear. At a tiled entranceway a maidservant bowed low, then took them down the hall into a large, airy room with a blue and white floor. The walls were painted in a cunning illusion of branches, leaves, and bright-feathered birds, as if the room were set in the treetops of a forest. Dozens of oil lamps glowed in niches and on shelves and glittered on silver oddments and glass vases of flowers. Toward one end was a low dais piled with velvet cushions. Lounging among them was one of the most beautiful women Rhodry had ever seen.

She was not very tall, but slender with coppery skin set off by curly black hair that waved tightly around her perfect oval face. Her enormous dark eyes watched Pommaeo with just the right touch of humorous disdain, while her long, slender fingers played with a silk scarf. In the lamplight she looked like a girl, but her movements and expression made Rhodry think that she must be well past thirty. Pommaeo gave Rhodry a cuff to make him kneel before the dais, then launched into a long and flowery speech, whose point was mainly that his humble gift was unworthy of her great beauty. So this is the poor old widow, is it? Rhodry thought. He found it in his heart to think better of his temporary owner. Laughing under her breath, Alaena tossed the scarf aside and sat up to look Rhodry over.

"Oh how sweet! For me? You shouldn't have!"

His arrogance dissolving into a love-besotted simper, Pommaeo perched on the edge of the dais. Alaena patted Rhodry on the head like a dog, giggled when she held up a soft brown hand to compare the color of his skin, then called to the maidserveant to bring an oil lamp. Together they stared into Rhodry's eyes.

"Look, Disna!" the mistress said. "They're blue!"

When Disna giggled and shot him a sidelong glance, Rhodry realized first that the slavegirl was almost as pretty as her owner, and second, that he might find some consolations in his captivity. Alaena turned to Pommaeo and held out her hand for him to kiss—the gift, apparently, was a great success.

Although Miko stayed to pour wine for the masters, Rhodry followed Disna to the enormous kitchen, tiled in browns and reds. At one end was an adobe cooking hearth where three women were busy preparing the meal; at the other, a welter of storage jars and wooden barrels. In between was a low table, a bit nicked but as expensive-looking as anything in many a Deverry lord's hall. Sitting there was a dignified-looking man of about sixty and a boy of twelve or so. In a flood of giggles, which drew a sharp remark from the old man, Disna explained who Rhodry was. The man got up and gave him a distant but not unkind smile.

"My name is Porto, and in Deverry you'd call me a chamberlain, I believe. Here, I'm called the warreko, and never forget it."

"Yes, sir." Rhodry knew authority when he heard it in a man's voice. "My name is Rhodry."

"Good. You give me no trouble—you'll get no trouble. Understand?"

"Yes, sir."

"Very good. Well, we've needed another man around here. Come with me."

They went up a narrow, twisting stairway to the top floor, just under the roof, where the day's heat still hung close and stifling. On one side of a hall were the women's quarters, on the other, the men's, with four narrow bunks set into the wall. Only two had blankets, but Porto rummaged in a wooden chest and brought out a pair which he tossed onto one of the empty beds. His gestures, the setting, were so familiar in a strange way that Rhodry felt his mind struggling to remember something, a place no doubt, or no, a string of places, all much the same. Finally he shook his head and gave it up as a bad job. Porto was looking him curiously.

"Don't you feel well?"

"I'm sorry. It's just the heat. I'm not used to it yet."

"Heat?" The old man paused for a grin. "It's almost winter, boy. You wait until the summer comes if you want heat."

Rhodry spent the rest of the evening in the kitchen. After the meal was served, first to Alaena and Pommaeo, then to the slaves, he hauled water from the well outside, then helped scrub pots under the cook's keen eye. He realized straightaway that Vinsima was the other center of power among the slaves. A woman of fifty, with skin so dark it was a glittery brown-black, she was tall and broad-hipped, with arms as well-muscled as a warrior's and the reflexes to match. Once, when the young boy made an insolent remark, she rapped him on the skull so hard with a wooden spoon that he cried out. The look she shot Rhodry implied that he'd be next if he didn't watch his step.

After the work was over, everyone settled in around the table to talk over the events of the day. Every now and then a little bell rang, summoning Disna to bring more wine or a plate of sweetmeats. When she returned, she would report on what was happening in the other chamber. It was obvious that none of the slaves wanted Alaena to marry Pommaeo; after putting up with the man for a few days, Rhodry had to agree. Gradually Rhodry learned everyone's name and began to sort out the hierarchy in the household. Porto and Vinsima were at the top, although Disna, who had the mistress's personal favor, had a certain independence. At the absolute bottom were the litter bearers, four young men who lived in a shed behind the house and who were fed out there like dogs. Rhodry got quite a shock over the boy, Syon, who turned out to be Porto's personal slave, bought with tips to do the jobs that Porto disliked, such as polishing the lady's enormous collection of silver animal figurines. That one slave would own another was utterly beyond Rhodry's understanding, but it was clear from the conversation that this vicarage, as it was called, was perfectly common.

Since Rhodry himself was new and therefore an unknown quantity in this elaborate scheme of things, he often caught Porto studying him, doubtless wondering if he'd turn out to be a good worker or a troublemaker. There was something oddly familiar in that appraisal, so much so that Rhodry found himself wondering about it while he tried to get to sleep in his narrow and lumpy new bed. All at once a chunk of memory rose to his mind, and with it a rush of information. Captains of warbands had looked at him that same way, when he was a silver dagger back in Deverry. He could remember several faces, several names, several duns, even, where he'd briefly stayed. The information was so exciting that he stayed awake half the night, musing over it.

Unfortunately Porto woke him just at dawn. Yawning and stumbling Rhodry went down to the kitchen, to find Vinsima kneading a vast lump of bread dough on a marble slab.

"Firewood, boy, Short lengths, about as thick as your arm, and lots of them for the baking. The woodshed's straight out the door and to your left." She pointed to a rack on the kitchen wall. "There's the axe."

To his surprise Rhodry saw a heavy woodsman's axe with a good steel head, a dangerous weapon in the hands of a man who knew how to use it. He took it outside, found the woodshed easily, and set to work, wondering as he splintered the kindling why anyone would leave a tool like that where the slaves could get it. In a few minutes Porto strolled out and stood sipping a steaming cup of hot milk while he watched. Finally he motioned to Rhodry to rest for a moment.

"You're a hard worker, I see. Good. Let me give you some advice, boy. Be nice to the mistress's friends. Smile a lot, and do whatever they ask you to. Most of them are older than her, a lot of old hens, really, and they'll enjoy tossing a few coins at a good-looking young man."

"I see. Does your—I mean, our mistress entertain a lot?"

"Oh yes, and also you're going to be her footman. She needs an escort when she goes out, and I've got too much to do here as it is."

"I'll do whatever you want, as long as you explain things to me. I don't understand all the customs of the country."

"You haven't been here long?"

"No, sir." Rhodry realized that he'd better come up with some convenient story. "I came here as a bodyguard for a rich merchant and got way over my head in debt, gambling. That was only a couple of months ago."

"Your merchant wouldn't buy the notes back?"

"No, sir. I was nothing to him, only a kind of mercenary soldier called a silver dagger. Ever hear of them?"

"No, but I take it they have no status to speak of. Well, that's too bad." He paused, looking shrewdly at the axe. "Let me tell you something, boy. Do you know what happens if a slave murders his master?"

"They hunt him down and torture him to death."

"Oh yes, but they also kill every other slave in the household, whether they had anything to do with the murder or not."

"What?!"

"They drag them out and slit their throats, except for a few that they torture to give evidence in the courts." Porto's voice had gone flat and soft. "I saw it happen once, in the house across the street from the one where I was born. The master was a beast, a sadistic animal, and everyone knew it, but when one of his men killed him, the archon's men slaughtered the whole household, dragged them screaming to the public square and killed them all, right down to the cook's babe-in-arms. I'll never forget that. I see it in nightmares still, even though it was over fifty years ago." He shook himself like a wet dog. "I can't imagine why anyone would lift a hand against our lady, Alaena, but if she accepts Pommaeo, he'll be lord and master here. I warn you, if I ever think you're so much as dreaming of violence, I'll turn you over to the archon myself. Understand me?"

"Yes, sir, but as we say at home, don't trouble your heart over it. I'd never do anything that would put the rest of you at risk."

"I think you mean it, and you know, Rhodry, I think you're a good boy at heart. Too bad about the gambling, it really is. I've always heard that you barbarians are too fond of the dice."

"Barbarians? We're barbarians, are we? Ye gods, your wretched laws sound savage from what you've just told me."

"Savage? Oh no, merely practical. Slaves who murder their masters are very very rare in the islands." And yet he looked away with a world of sadness welling in his eyes.

About the middle of the morning, Rhodry got his first taste of his new duties when Alaena decided to pay a call before Pommaeo returned to her house. Porto gave Rhodry an ebony staff with a heavy silver knob at one end and a small leather whip—the whip for the litter slaves, the staff for the beggars and other riffraff who might block the lady's way. When the litter came round to the courtyard, he finally saw these supposedly bestial dregs of slavery: four boys, not more than fifteen, who shrank back at the sight of the whip. Paler than most Bardek men, they had strange yellow eyes, oddly slit and staring. With a shock Rhodry wondered if they had elven blood in their veins. As if they'd heard his wondering, some of the Wildfolk appeared, and the boys' eyes moved, following them as they strolled around.

"They come from Anmurdio," Porto said, meaning of course the slaves, not the spirits. "It's a horrible, primitive place, lots of small islands, all infested with disease. They say the people there are cannibals." He shrugged, dismissing the island group and its inhabitants both. "Here's a rag. Take it and dust off the litter. The mistress is almost ready."

The litter itself was a beautiful thing, made of ebony like his staff, painted with floral garlands on a dark blue background. The cabinet in which the two passengers rode was fastened to the poles by cast brass fittings in the shape of monkeys, whose paws and tails joined to form the enclosing circle. Inside were more of the purple velvet cushions that the lady seemed to favor. Rhodry had just handed the rag back to Porto when Alaena appeared, dressed in a brocaded, knee-length tunic, a large number of emeralds at her throat and a scarf of green silk gauze wrapped round her head to keep the sun off her face. In the sunlight she definitely looked in her mid-thirties, but beautiful all the same. When Rhodry helped her into the litter, she gave him a little pat on the cheek. Disna followed right after, carrying a carved wooden box about two feet square but only some four inches deep. When Rhodry helped her in as if she were a fine lady, he was rewarded with a brilliant smile.

Although Porto rattled off a long string of directions, Rhodry would have been lost if it weren't for the litter boys, who seemed to have followed the route many a time. As he strode along, scowling at passersby, the closest bearer called out where they were supposed to turn in a voice shaking with fear. It occurred to Rhodry that, if they all got lost, the boys would be whipped, not him, thanks to the rigid hierarchy among the slaves. He decided to try to get them some extra food that evening; he could think of no other reward that would have any meaning in their desolate lives.

Their destination was no more than a mile away, another splendid compound whose outer walls were painted with an underwater scene of fish in a coral reef. Rhodry left the litter and the litter boys in the care of a gatekeeper, but carrying the wooden box, he accompanied the mistress and Disna up to the house. An elderly maidservant, all toothless smiles, bowed them into a house even more luxurious than Alaena's.

In a central chamber where the walls were painted with climbing roses, and four gray-and-black kittens chased each other among embroidered cushions, three women were waiting at a low table. Even though he'd never seen them before, Rhodry could tell immediately that they were a mother and two grown daughters; they shared the same beautifully shaped brown eyes and full mouths, as well as a certain way of tilting their heads and smiling. They got up to greet Alaena with a flood of chatter that was hard for Rhodry to follow, since most of it seemed to concern neighbors and friends of which he knew nothing. Then one of the daughters noticed Rhodry and gave a small, ladylike squeal.

"A barbarian, 'Laen! Where did you get him?"

"From the tedious Pommaeo, actually. He may talk about himself all the time, but he certainly does know how to buy gifts." She motioned Rhodry closer. "Look at his eyes. They're blue."

The daughters gawked and giggled while the mother merely smiled in a fond sort of way and Rhodry blushed, a response that only made them giggle the more. At last they'd satisfied their curiosity and all knelt on cushions round the table. Alaena took the wooden box from Rhodry and emptied out a set of little ivory tiles, painted with flowers and birds among other designs. With a rumbling sound like thunder the women began flipping them face down and mixing them up. As if at a prearranged signal, two servants appeared with brass trays piled up with sweetmeats and set them down at the corners of the table. When they started to leave, Alaena signaled to Disna to follow them, but an imperious wave of her hand kept Rhoodry on the dias.

"You may sit behind me."

"Thank you, mistress." Rhodry had the distinct feeling that she hadn't seen quite enough of her present, like a little girl who won't put a new doll down for a moment.

By then the tiles were apparently properly mixed, because the other three women had stopped scouring the table with them and were looking at Alaena expectantly. A few at a time, a small crowd of Wildfolk materialized to stare at the table as well, but as far as he could tell, anyway, Rhodry was the only one who saw them, even when a bold blue gnome laid a skinny finger on one of the tiles.

"Do you want to be first, Malina?"

"Age before beauty?" the mother said comfortably. "Mine always is the dullest one, so we may as well get it out of the way."

When the others laughed, Malina began picking out tiles, one at a time, and placing them, still face down, in a star-shaped pattern. Rhodry realized that what he'd been thinking a game was actually some sort of fortune-telling device. He felt a certain mild contempt, a condescension really, that these silly women would believe in this nonsense when there was real dweomer all around them. Suddenly he felt cold. What did he mean, real dweomer? How did he know that such a thing existed, how could he be more certain of it than he was of his own name? He felt like a man who, talking over his shoulder to some companion, walks himself smack into a wall—both confused and foolish. The only evidence for his certainty was the Wildfolk, settling down on the floor and unoccupied cushions to watch as Alaena leaned forward and turned the first three tiles face up to reveal a sword between two flowers.

"A lover? Well, well, well—what do you mean, yours is always dull?"

At that all four of them laughed with sharp little cries like birds in an aviary, and the Wildfolk clapped soundless hands and grinned. Alaena helped herself to a sweetmeat, a gelatinous oblong covered in a dead-white powder. She took a thoughtful bite while she studied the tiles, then turned, motioned to Rhodry, and held the sweetmeat out to him like a treat for a dog. When he opened his mouth to make a polite refusal, she popped it in and patted his cheek. Rhodry had no choice but to eat it, but it was so sweet that he nearly gagged. Fortunately Alaena had returned to her tiles and never noticed. By all the ice in all the hells, he thought, the sooner I escape and start hunting Baruma down the better! I'd rather die than be a lapdog, even for a pretty wench like this. Then he set himself to the difficult task of staying awake as the long drowsy morning dragged on.

When they left Myleton, Jill and Salamander had opted for the direct if difficult route straight south from the city, and for over a week now they'd been winding their way through the hill country. Since the traveling was slow and tedious, and the imaging exercises kept her mind off Rhodry, Jill poured herself into the work and made such rapid progress that Salamander admitted he was impressed. Before they'd left Myleton, they had indeed found a picture scroll for her lessons. About a foot high and five long, it unrolled right to left, all backwards to Salamander's way of thinking. Since she'd never read a Deverry book or scroll, to Jill the direction seemed as good as any other. She rather liked the paintings themselves, three scenes from the history of Myleton, showing the first colonists founding the new city, a famous tidal wave of some hundred years later, and finally, the election of an archon known as Manataro the Good. Each picture was crammed with small details, all cleverly arranged so that it seemed she was looking into a box, not down onto a flat surface.

Yet, after days of staring at the historically renowned tidal wave and working on seeing it as if it were real in her mind, she was heartily sick of the scroll and the practice both. The banishing ritual she found more tolerable, even though Salamander drilled her mercilessly, because she could see its direct benefit, the control of the floods of imagery that threatened to overwhelm her whenever she was angry. First she would place those images in her mind as if they were practice lessons, then banish them with the sign of the flaming pentagram. At times she still failed, and the fires of rage would seem to burn around her unchecked, but every time she succeeded she felt her skill growing, and over the days the out-of-control images came less and less often.

On the afternoon that they reached the center of the island, everything seemed to go wrong with her working. First, she stumbled over the words of the ritual, drawing the gerthddyn's scorn. Then, when she tried a new picture from the scroll, she could get only the barest trace of the image of Archon Manatero, and it seemed that all her hard work had gone for naught. When she complained to Salamander, he smiled in his most infuriating way.

"You don't dare give this up, you know. Or do you want to go slowly but inevitably mad?"

"Of course I don't! And I'll follow orders, just like I always followed orders when Da was teaching me sword craft. I just don't understand why these blasted pictures are so important. I mean, with Da, I always could figure it out—this exercise strengthened your arm, or that one worked on your grip, but this is all too peculiar."

"Ah. Well, what you're doing is indeed like your da's exercises; you're just strengthening mental muscles. Here, when the bards sing about dweomer, they always talk about strange powers, don't they? Where do you think those powers come from? The gods?"

"Not the gods, truly. Well, I suppose you just get them. I mean, it's dweomer, isn't it? That's what makes it magical." She suddenly realized that she was sounding inane. "I mean, magical things just happen."

"They don't, at that, although that's what everyone thinks. All those puissant powers and strange spells come out of the mind, human or elven as the case may be. Dweomer is a matter of mental faculties. Know what they are?"

"I don't."

"When you learn to read—and I think me we'd best start lessons in that, too—I'll find you a book written by one of our Rhodry's illustrious ancestors, Mael the Seer himself, called *On the Rational Categories*. In it he defines the normal mental faculties for humans, and most of them apply to elves, too, such as seeing, hearing, and all the other physical senses, as well as logical thinking, intuition, and a great many more, including, indeed, the very ability to make categories and generalizations, which is not a skill to be taken lightly or for granted, my petite partridge. These are, as he calls them, the rational faculties, open and well-known among elves and men, although the elves have a few faculties that humans don't, such as the ability to see the Wildfolk. Every child should develop them as he grows; if some-one's blind, say, or simply can't remember things, we pity them and feel they've been robbed of part of their birthright.

"Then there are the buried, hidden, or occult faculties that exist in the mind like chicks in a new-laid egg. While every elf and human possesses a selection of them in potential, very few are born with them already developed. You can call these faculties 'powers' if you wish, though it sounds perhaps too grand for perfectly natural phe-nomena. Do you understand the idea of a category of the natural? As opposed to the supernatural?"

"Uh, what? Well, uh . . ."

"The Maelwaedd's book becomes a necessity, I see."

"Very well, but what do these rotten picture exercises have to do with all this grand-sounding stuff?"

"Oh. Truly, I did ramble a bit. Well, if you want to awaken these sleeping powers, you use pictures, mostly, and names and sometimes music to go with them. Once you've awakened them, you can use them over and over. Perpend—once you've learned how to be logical, can't you reawaken that faculty whenever you've got a problem to solve? Of course. Just so, after you develop the scrying faculty, say, you can open it with the right images and words any time you want. A great master like Nevyn doesn't even need the names and images anymore, for that matter. For him the occult faculties have become manifest."

Although his small lecture was so difficult to understand that Jill felt like a half-wit (as the organizing faculties go, Salamander's were far from being the best in Annwn), everything he said resonated in her soul, with a hint more than a promise that here was a key to open a treasure chest.

"But I'll tell you what, my robin of sweet song, you can try a new exercise if you'd like. Instead of using the scroll, make up your own image and try to realize it clearly in your mind. I don't mean draw it or suchlike—we don't have any ink, anyway—just decide on some simple thing and try to see it, like an inn you once stayed in, or your horse Sunrise, he who now eats the king's bountiful oats—somewhat like that."

"Well and good, then, I will. As long as it's all right to jump around like this."

"Oh, by the gods! This 'prentice-work isn't truly even dweomer. You're just learning some useful tools. I can't imagine that the least harm could come of it."

On his final night in Wylinth, Pommaeo and Alaena quarreled. Since he was waiting on table, Rhodry heard all of it; they seemed as indifferent to his presence as they were to that of the furniture. As soon as he'd laid out the meal and poured the wine, he retreated to the kitchen, where he found Disna and Vinsima listening at the door to the distant sound of lifted voices.

"It looks good," Rhodry blurted out. "She's refusing to give him a promise of any kind whatsoever, and he's accusing her of having other suitors. Does she?"

"Only one and he's seventy-odd years old," Disna said. "So it looks very good indeed."

"I'm not breathing easy yet," Vinsima said. "What if they make things up with lots of kisses? Well, the dessert needs serving, boy, so you've got a good excuse to go back in."

When Rhodry brought in the gilded plate of small sugared cakes, they were the only sweet thing in the room. Straight and stiff on their cushions, Alaena and Pommaeo glared at each other from opposite sides of the small table.

"Take those cakes away!" Alaena snapped.

"Yes, mistress."

"They happen to be my favorite kind," Pommaeo said with ice in his voice. "Bring them here."

Rhodry hesitated.

"I said go!"

"Yes, mistress."

He hurried out just as Alaena was informing her guest that he had no business giving any orders at all to one of her slaves. Some half an hour later the doorkeeper came rushing into the kitchen to announce that Pommaeo had left in a violent temper. Yet first thing in the morning Miko appeared with a long letter from his master, one that was full of sweet apologies, or so Disna said, because the mistress had read it aloud while her hair was being combed. Much to Disna's disgust, Alaena had written a conciliatory note in return.

"And now I'm to hurry to his beastly inn and deliver it before he leaves. Oh well, at least he'll be gone all winter. He's not the type to travel in the rain."

"Our mistress can read and write?" Rhodry was honestly amazed.

"Of course she can." Disna wrinkled her nose at him. "That barbarian kingdom of yours must have been awfully primitive, that's all I can say. You're surprised by the strangest things."

"Well, so I am. I hope you don't think too badly of me."

Disna merely gave him a slow smile, hinting of many answers, then hurried off on her errand.

That afternoon Alaena summoned Rhodry to her side. Dressed in a simple white tunic, she was sitting cross-legged on a cushion at the low table and frowning at her fortune-telling tiles when he came in. A pair of warty brown gnomes materialized at his entrance and grinned at him.

"There you are. Now that I'll have the time, we're going to start educating you." She swept the tiles to one side, then looked up to consider him. "You don't do too badly when it comes to serving food, but you've got to learn how to carry my fan properly and other things like that. And then there's the way you talk. Your accent's dreadful, and we'll have to spend some time on correcting it."

Although Rhodry was hoping that Alaena would tire of teaching him such dubious skills as the proper way to fold scarves and arrange cushions, she took every detail so seriously that he soon realized she was quite simply bored with her life. Thanks to her inherited wealth, she had to work or wait for nothing, and while she understood financial affairs perfectly well, one of her many brothers-in-law did all the actual work of managing her properties. Twice a week this Dinvarbalo would come to lunch. Over a long feast of many elaborate courses, they would discuss her investments in land and trading ventures; she would ask sharp questions and make sharper suggestions while he wrote her wishes down on a wooden tablet covered with wax. Once he was gone, the spirit would slowly fade from her eyes again, and she would summon Rhodry for one of his lessons. Usually she would be irritable, too, slapping him across the face for the least mistake or even sending him away in a flood of insults. Yet, the next time that she called him back, she would be pleasant again, if strict.

Porto and Disna told him something of her history. She'd been born the second child of ten to a poor oil seller down in Ronaton, in poverty so extreme that she'd nearly been sold as a slave to feed the rest of the family. Her beauty, however, had saved her by catching the eye of a rich merchant who had most honorably married rather than bought her. Since he was fifty-two when she was fourteen, the marriage had been far from happy, even though her childhood sufferings had made her obsessed with being the perfect wife. More from his incapacity than any other reason, they had no children before he died at seventy-four, after a long debilitating illness during which she nursed him with her own hands. Now, although she was far from eager to bind herself to another husband, she also knew that her beauty was sure to fade, sooner rather than later. Cosmetics and herbal baths filled her mornings. She often sent Rhodry to the marketplace as soon as it opened to buy rose petals, fresh cream, and beeswax while she and Disna closeted themselves like alchemists in the bath chamber.

Much to his surprise, Rhodry found himself growing sorry for her. Although he wanted to hate her for keeping his freedom locked up on a bit of paper in her jewel chest, he simply couldn't. There came a time, in fact, when he realized an even more bitter truth about himself. With cosmetics for the mistress and spices for the cook, he was jogging home from the market one morning when the air was fresh and crisp with the scent of coming rain, and the last of the summer's flowers bloomed bright over painted walls. He found himself singing. With a shock he realized that for a moment he'd been happy, that he'd come to accept his new life. All day he noticed other things, how pleased he was when Porto praised him, how he laughed at jokes in the kitchen, how he smiled when as a sign of her favor Alaena gave him a silver piece. He realized that if he someday took Porto's place, being a trusted warreko would give him security no matter whom Alaena married.

At first he'd wondered why slaves didn't rise up in open revolt; now he was beginning to understand. For a slave with his standing, life wasn't cruel enough to take the risk. Any slaves such as the tin miners who might well be driven to desperate measures were kept branded, chained, and half-starved, and their lives were too short for long-term plans. Any slave like himself who had a firm commercial value had every necessity in life, a few comforts, even, and the possibility, though a chancy one, of someday earning freedom. If he'd remembered his former life, he decided, he would have felt differently, longing, no doubt, for freedom with a hiraedd befitting a man born free, but as it was, Deverry was a thing of shadows and patched memory to him. His only certainty was that he'd been a silver dagger, a despised outcast without clan or home, a shamed man without honor, doomed to fight endlessly in one petty lord's feud or another until an early death claimed him. There were plenty of times when being Alaena's footman seemed a better throw of life's dice.

Yet there was one memory that kept contentment from trapping him. Baruma. Every afternoon, when the entire household, slave and mistress alike, took a couple of hours to nap or at least rest on their beds, Rhodry would remind himself that he owed Baruma a bloody death, even though it would cost him his own life. *What's the swine done with my silver dagger?* The question became an obsession, as if the weapon itself, those few ounces of dwarven silver, contained his very honor the way a body contains a soul. Every now and then he dreamt of killing Baruma and taking the dagger back; after one of those dreams he would be silent, wrapped in himself all morning, and he would notice that everyone would avoid him then, even the mistress.

There came an afternoon, as well, when he recovered another memory of his lost life, one that stabbed him to the heart. After a gray morning rain broke, a chilly drizzle that set everyone grumbling. Since he couldn't work outside, Rhodry went to attend their mistress, who was as usual pouring over her fortune-telling set. For some time Rhodry merely sat beside her and handed her tidbits of dried apricots and sugared almonds when she held out an impatient hand. The rain droned on, the oil lamps flickered, while Alaena laid out tile after tile, only to sweep them impatiently away and start all over. When she finally spoke to him, he was nearly asleep.

"This wearies me, and don't yawn like that."

"I'm humbly sorry. Shall I put them away now, mistress?"

Alaena shrugged, pouting, and held out her hand. Rhodry gave her an apricot, which she nibbled while she considered.

"I know." All at once she smiled. "I'll tell your fortune. Sit round the other side and start mixing up the tiles."

He'd seen the fortune-telling game so many times now that he knew what to do. After the mix he picked twenty-one of the ninety-six tiles at random, then laid them out in a star-shaped pattern. Alaena helped herself to an almond and ate it while she studied the layout.

"Now, of course, this is all in the past, because you've never had your tiles read before. Sometimes you get several readings that refer backward before you start going forward again. I don't know why. The scroll that came with the set didn't say." She paused, thinking. "By the hem of the Goddess's robe! I never knew you were a soldier. I see lots of battles in your past."

"That's certainly true, mistress." Rhodry moved closer, suddenly interested in this game. What if she could find out other things about him, ones he didn't know?

"And you fought in many different places." She pointed a tile of two crossed spears. "This indicates you were a mercenary, not a citizen volunteer."

"I certainly was."

"How very odd, because it looks like you were born to a highly placed family." She laid a painted fingernail on the ace of Golds. "Very highly placed. But, oh yes, here it is! You got in trouble with law, and you were either exiled or you just ran away. Honestly, Rhodry, how naughty of you! Was it gambling that time, too?"

Since he couldn't remember, he merely smiled, a gesture she took for a yes.

"You never had any sense about money, that's certain. Draw two more tiles."

When he handed them over, she turned them faceup and placed them by the two of Golds.

"No sense at all," she laughed. "I see you handing out rich presents to everyone who asked."

"That's the way of a Deverry lord, mistress. They have to be generous, or they're dishonored in everyone's eyes."

"So you *were* noble-born. I rather thought so, but Pommaeo said it was a stupid idea, and I should forget it. Honestly, Rhodry, how awful, to fall so far, and all because you couldn't keep your hands off the dice." She considered the tiles again, then smiled wickedly. "There were other things you couldn't keep your hands off, as well. Look at that prince of Swords with a Flower Princess on either side. You had lots of love affairs."

It struck Rhodry as unjust to the extreme that he could remember none of them.

"Oh, look at this! You have a child back home."

"I do?" The shock made him forget his mask of servility.

"You didn't know? What did you do? March off with your army before she even knew she was pregnant, probably." She burst out laughing. "Well, Deverry men are certainly like Bardek men in some crucial respects, aren't they? I'm afraid the tiles can't tell if it's a boy or a girl." Still smiling, she took another apricot and ate it slowly while she thought. "I wonder about this Queen of Swords at the top. It seems such an odd place for her. Draw me two more."

The pair turned out to be the Ace of Spears and the Raven.

"Oh!" Alaena gasped in honest shock. "How very sad! She was the one true love of your life, but it all ended tragically. What happened? It almost looks like she got sold into slavery, too, or married off against her will to some other man."

Suddenly Rhodry remembered Jill, remembered the name to put with the blonde woman who at times had haunted his memory and his dreams, remembered with a rush of emotion his despair when he had lost her, somewhere along the long road. Dimly he could remember beginning to search for her, somewhere in dark woodlands . . .

"Rhodry, you're weeping."

"I'm sorry, mistress." He choked back the tears and wiped his face on his tunic sleeve "Forgive me. I loved her very much, and she *was* forced to go with another man."

He looked up to find her watching him with a startled expression, as if he'd just materialized like one of the Wildfolk.

"No, you forgive me. I forget that you weren't always a slave." She looked down at the tiles and frowned, then swept her hand through the pattern. "Just take that fruit away, will you? Do whatever you want until it's time for dinner."

Since he had no other privacy, Rhodry went up to his bunk in the men's quarters and lay down, his hands under his head as he stared at the ceiling and listened to the rain. Slowly he pieced together a few of his memories, but only a few. He knew that he had loved, that he still did love, with a fierceness that shocked him, this woman named

Jill, but who she was, where he'd met her, why she'd been dragged away from him—they were all mysteries still. He wept again, but only briefly, a few tears of frustration more than heartbreak.

Although Alaena never referred to the incident again, from that afternoon on Rhodry was aware of a change in her attitude toward him. At times, he caught her watching him with a little puzzled frown, as if he'd become a problem for her to solve. Outwardly, nothing seemed to have changed; he spent his afternoons with her as before, learning the protocols of greeting and announcing guests of various ranks, and none of the others seemed to have noticed anything, except, perhaps, Disna. Suddenly Rhodry noticed that the maidservant had grown cold to him; whenever he complimented her, she gave him the barest trace of a smile or even a downright nasty look. When he tried to turn the whole thing into a joke and tease her about it, she refused to answer, merely walked away fast with her nose in the air, making him wonder if all those love affairs that had appeared in the tiles were doomed to remain in the past.

After some days the rain stopped, and Alaena went out to the marketplace. Since everyone in town seemed to be there, catching up on their shopping and gossip, they left the litter on a side street, hired a shopkeeper's lad to watch it, and walked to the market itself. Carrying his ebony staff, Rhodry followed a few paces behind the mistress while she went from booth to booth, looking mostly at jewelry and silks while merchants groveled before her. Finally she motioned Rhodry up beside her and pointed at some silver brooches set with bits of semiprecious stones.

"I want to buy a present for Disna. Do you think she'd like the one with the large turquoise?"

"I have no idea, mistress. I don't know anything about jewelry."

"You should learn. It helps you judge people when you first meet them—their taste in things, I mean, not just what they can afford to spend. But I don't think these will do." She walked on, motioning him to walk at her side. "I have heaps of things Pommaeo gave me at home, of course, and some of them are quite fine, but . . ." All at once she flashed one of her wicked smiles. "No, I have a different use for them. Come along. There's another jeweler over here."

This particular jeweler was a fat man who reminded Rhodry of Brindemo. On each hand was an amazing collection of garish rings, and he wore a dozen different pendants around his neck, too. Among his collection of merchandise was one pin so different from the others that it seemed to call to Rhodry, a tiny rose, worked in fine silver, no more than an inch long but so lifelike that the leaves seemed to stir in the breeze. Alaena picked it up.

"What an odd thing," she said to the merchant. "What kind of alloy is this? It's much too hard to be pure silver."

"I don't know, oh exalted and beautiful exemplar of womanhood. I won it in a dice game actually, from a man who said it came from the barbarian kingdom."

"Indeed? How much do you want for it?"

"Two zotars only, for one as lovely as you."

"Bandit! I'll give you ten silvers."

The haggling was on in earnest. At the end, Alaena had the pin for twenty silvers, about a sixth of the asking price. Rather than having the man wrap it, she turned and pinned it onto Rhodry's tunic, near the collar.

"A barbarian trinket for a barbarian," she said, smiling. "I rather like the effect."

"Thank you, mistress." Rhodry had learned that gifts like this were his to keep, even if he chose to turn them into cash some day. "I'm flattered you'd think so well of me."

"Do you know what kind of metal that is?"

"Well, yes. I had a knife made out of it once. In the Deverry mountains are little people called dwarves, who live in tunnels and make precious things out of strange metals like this kind of silver. Some of their trinkets have magic spells on them. Maybe this one does, too, but we won't find out unless it chooses to show us."

"How charming you are when you want to be." She laughed and reached up to pat his cheek. "What a darling story! Now let's find something for Disna."

Eventually she found a pair of long gold earrings, shaped like tiny oars, that she pronounced suitable. Rhodry took the parcel and started to follow her out of the marketplace, but again she had him walk beside her.

"That was fun, but now everything wearies me again." She sighed gently. "Do you think I should marry Pommaeo?"

The question took him too much by surprise for him to think of a properly phrased answer. He gawked at her while she laughed.

"Well, I think he'd be mean to you—and far too interested in Disna," she said at last. "So perhaps I won't. Besides, he can be the most wearisome thing of all when he wants to."

At that she moved ahead and let him walk behind until they reached the litter.

When they returned to the house, Alaena closeted herself in her bedchamber with Disna while Rhodry went on to the kitchen to haul in firewood for the evening meal. In some half an hour Disna rushed in, the earrings glittering as they framed her face in a most appealing way.

"Guess what? The mistress won't marry that awful Pommaeo after all. She's going to ask Mistress Malina to find her other possible suitors instead."

The staff raised a small, dignified cheer.

"My thanks to holy Zaeos, to all the Goddesses of the Many-Starred Sky, and to the Wave-father," Vinsima said. "Any member of Mistress Malina's family is bound to be a fair-minded and generous man."

"I think," Porto said, "that we may have some extra wine with the evening meal. To toast the gods for smiling upon us if nothing else. Girl, does the mistress require anything?"

"Yes." Disna glanced at Rhodry, her smile disappearing in an oddly abrupt way. "She wants you to run an errand. She's in her bedchamber at the moment."

Rhodry assumed that he was to take a note over to Malina's, but when he came into the chamber, he found Alaena sitting, as carelessly as a girl, on the floor in front of her jewel chest. When he hovered uncertainly in front of her, she motioned for him to sit down, too, with a flick and a point of one slender hand. Beside her on a cushion lay a tangle of emerald necklaces and two heavy gold arm bracelets.

"Pommaeo gave me these. I want you to take them over to the temple of Selenta as a gift to the priestesses. They run an orphanage, and they can sell these off a bit at a time when they need coin."

"Very well, mistress. Are you going to give me away, too?"

Alaena laughed in a peal of musical amusement.

"No, I don't think so, really." She reached up and put her hands on either side of her face. "Well, come along. Kiss me."

More in shock than pleasure, Rhodry kissed her on the mouth.

"You do that much better than Pommaeo ever did. Yes, I think I definitely like the slave better than the stupid master." She glanced at the jewelry beside her. "Oh, that can wait."

The meaning was unmistakable, but Rhodry hesitated, half-panicked. All his intuitions were screaming that it would be very unsafe for both parties if a slave had an affair with his mistress, no matter how common it was for men to take their female slaves. No doubt it's worse for the slave, too, he thought; I've no desire to end up getting flogged in the public square or suchlike.

"How can you look so shy?" She was grinning at him in her wicked way. "What about all those other women I saw in your tiles?"

"They weren't as far above me as you are. You own me body and soul."

"Then you'd best do what I want, hadn't you?"

This time she reached up and kissed him. The hungry feel of her mouth, the soft warmth of her body, the way she pressed herself against him, all conspired to made him forget that he'd ever thought this a dangerous idea.

From that time on, Alaena would often summon him to her bed-chamber on one excuse or another or even tell him to slip out of bed at night and join her. Yet most of the time, she treated him exactly as she had before, as an exotic servant who often needed a good slap to teach him a lesson. Although he was glad enough of the sexual comfort she was giving him, Rhodry honestly wished that the affair had never begun. On the one hand he felt that his lovemaking was just another of the well-trained footman's duties; on the other, he knew that it threatened his secure niche in the household. What if she tired of him and decided to sell him off to remove an embarrassment? Although Alaena realized his reluctance, it amused rather than an-noyed her. She liked ordering him into her bed, and once he was there, he could never refuse her.

Since at night he was creeping out of the room they shared, he had no doubt that Porto knew what was happening in the mistress's bedchamber, just as Disna did, though neither of them betrayed a thing, not by one word or gesture or giggle. Once or twice, though,

Rhodry overheard Porto making a sharp remark to one of the other slaves that was obviously designed to keep the scandal within strict limits. Finally Rhodry was sick enough of feeling shamed to bring the matter out into the open. He was restacking the woodshed one afternoon when Porto came out to tell him that there would be guests for dinner that night.

"You've done a good job on the shed, boy, and I'm afraid it really needed it. I'm getting too old for that kind of thing. You do all your work well."

"Thanks. Yes, I'm sure I do. All of it."

Porto stiffened, his eyelids flickering.

"Oh by Zaeos and all your gods!" Rhodry burst out. "Do you think I like these goings-on? I'm scared sick."

"You're sensible, boy. More so than our poor little mistress."

"Tell me something, will you? How much trouble is there going to be over this? I don't want to be beaten to death in the marketplace just to set a good example for every slave on the cursed island."

"Now, now, I doubt it'll come to that. Alaena's so rich that no one's going to interfere, not even that brother-in-law of hers. Without the commission she pays him he wouldn't live very comfortably. But there's going to be nasty talk if this gets spread around, and somehow or other, things always do get out, don't they? No matter how careful we all try to be." He sighed, shaking his head. "You'd best pray to all the Holy Stars that Pommaeo never hears of this. A clever man, of course, can help the goddesses answer his prayers."

"By keeping his mouth shut and watching every step he makes?"

"Just that. And by making himself well-liked. If any of the mistress's friends tip you, you might consider spending part of it on Vinsima."

"Very well. And Disna's never going to carry a heavy load upstairs again, not while I'm within reach of it."

On a day sticky with a cool drizzle Jill and Salamander arrived at the harbor town of Daradion. Since it was too late in the day to question the harbormaster about the *Gray Kestrel,* they found a room in an inn, then went down to the evening market as soon as the rain stopped. Jill found the wet weather such a pleasant change that she was shocked to hear the citizens complaining bitterly about the cold and damp. The market was nearly deserted, with over half the stalls empty and only a handful of customers hurrying along on brisk business.

"Well, there won't be much use in putting on a show tonight, will there?" Salamander remarked with a certain gloom. "I'd forgotten how the Bardek folk carry on about the weather."

"You'd think we were in for howling snows, truly." She paused to grab her gnome, who was splashing through a filthy gutter puddle. "How are we doing for coin?"

"We've got enough to pay our passage over to Surtinna, but we can't go first class."

"That hardly matters."

"It does. Cursed if I'll spend days and days crammed into the common hold with merchants and other riffraff."

"Then you'd best think up a show you can do in daylight, hadn't you?"

"Now that, oh beauteous handmaiden, is an excellent idea. Hum. Colored smokes might work. And I could have some sylphs carry a scarf through the air—it'd look like it was flying of its own accord. People would think I was doing that with black wires, no doubt. And how about mysterious music from unseen sources? Possibilities—truly, I see possibilities."

For the rest of that evening, Salamander brooded over his new show. Every now and then he would make some alarming noise, or fill their inn chamber with vast illusions of red and green smoke, but mostly he left Jill to her work. By then, she was gaining a remarkable degree of control over images, enough so that she was forced to admit her natural aptitude for the craft. Once she snapped a remembered object into her mind, she could turn the image this way and that, looking at it from all sides and moving it so that it seemed she was seeing it first from above, then below. That night she stumbled across a particularly interesting trick. She was visualizing the small leather sack in which Salamander carried their coin, and in her mind she laid the open sack on a table so that she could peer inside it. All at once she felt that she was only a few inches tall, standing on the table and looking into the yawning mouth like a cave. Startled, she lost the image immediately, but it seemed important enough for her to disturb

Salamander, who was producing an effect of sunset clouds on the ceiling. He let the illusion dissipate and listened carefully,

"This is real progress indeed, turtledove. You're beginning to get to the important part of the work, so don't lose heart now."

"Oh, don't trouble yourself about that. This is the most interesting thing I've ever done in my life."

He let his jaw drop in honest surprise.

"You think it's interesting? Ye gods, you *are* marked for the dweomer sure enough!"

"Well, not the exercises themselves. I can see how they must have driven you absolutely mad with boredom. It's the whole thing, truly, everything that's happened to me this summer. I'm beginning to see where . . . where what? It's so cursed hard to put into words! But where doing things with my mind like this might lead, and it's . . . well, it's like the day my Da came and took me from our village. There was a whole world just down the road, and here I never even knew."

By the morrow morning, the rain and the clouds were gone when Jill and Salamander went down to the harbor, a semicircular bite out of cliffs that dropped straight down to a narrow stretch of white beach. Along the cliff-tops, radiating out from an enormous wooden longhouse with statues at either end, was a crowded scatter of booths and stalls.

"Is that a temple?" Jill pointed at the longhouse.

"It is, to Dalae-oh-contremo, god of the sea. Actually, he's the god of all sorts of other things, too, including for some odd reason unjustly treated slaves."

"There's some provision in the laws for that, then?"

"Of course. Don't Deverry bondsmen have rights that their lord can't cross?"

"Well, but bondsmen aren't slaves."

"Oh come now!" Salamander snorted profoundly. "They can't be sold away from their land or their families, true, but free? You jest, my turtledove. Of course, there aren't many bondsmen left in Deverry anymore, so no doubt you've never thought much about them."

"Well, I haven't, truly. Here, were there once a lot of them?"

"On every lord's manor, or so I've been told. Now it's pretty much only the King who holds bound-land. I don't know why things changed, but I'm blasted glad they did. Do you know why slavery is such a bad thing, my turtledove?"

"Well, it's cursed unfair."

"More than that. It makes men grow used to being cruel and to justifying their reasons for being cruel. That way lie the paths of evil."

He spoke so quietly, with none of his usual jests or affectations, that Jill was forced to remember the real power underlying his jokes and foppery.

Since the departures and arrivals of all ships were publicly posted outside the harbormaster's office, they found out easily enough that a ship called the *Gray Kestrel,* owned by a certain Galaetrano, had just returned from a run over to Ronaton on Surtinna. After some searching they found Galaetrano himself, an enormous bronze man with a shock of straight black hair, sitting with some of his crew in a wine shop at the edge of the marketplace. He was returning to Ronaton on the morrow, with plenty of room for two more passengers and a couple of horses, especially if the passengers wanted to pay for a first-class passage. Salamander bought wine all round, told a couple of his less-than-delicate stories, and got everyone talking at great length about life in general and the shipping trade in particular. Almost at random, or so it seemed, the captain himself began telling them about someone named Pommaeo, a regular passenger who had made his last trip over with a rare barbarian slave.

"He paid twice what the man was worth, too, he told me, just to get him for a courting gift. As far as I can tell, this woman he's after inherited a fortune."

"Oh, so that's why he'd go all that way just to find a wife," Salamander said, carelessly. "She must live right down in Ronaton, huh?"

"Well, no." The captain suddenly laughed. "You know something? He never did tell us where she lives. Just realized that myself. A sly dog, that one. If you know a rich widow, you keep her to yourself."

"I don't blame him, no, but it's too bad." Salamander glanced ever so casually at Jill. "We could use a Deverry man in the show. It would look good on stage, especially if he were another blonde."

"Oh, this slave had black hair," Galaetrano said. "But I see your point about the effect. You know, it's odd. You're the second man who's asked me about barbarian slaves lately."

"Indeed?"

"It was before my last trip to Ronaton, but this other fellow was from the islands. Let's see, I don't think he ever did mention his name, actually, kind of odd, now that I think of it. But anyway, he was only interested in buying for resale. He came from Tondio, I think he said. He didn't take passage with me, anyway, so I didn't think much more about him."

After more wine all round, this time at the captain's expense, Salamander announced that he and his handmaiden had to prepare an evening's show, invited everyone to come see it, and left on a general wave of good cheer. Jill managed to keep smiling until they reached the street—no longer.

"May this Pommaeo freeze in the third hell!"

"I'll admit to being vexed, miffed, and in general annoyed with our gallant. Even worse, however, is the captain's other bit of news."

"That so-called slave trader who was asking about barbarians?"

"I like that 'so-called,' turtledove. It shows you were listening with crafty ears. I don't like this at all. Of course, it might be some sort of coincidence."

"Just like it was a coincidence that Brindemo was poisoned the day before we got to Myleton."

"Entirely too true spoken, alas. You know, when we get back to the inn, I think I'd better have a look around."

"What? If you want to look around town, why go back to the inn?"

"At times there are better ways of traveling than using one's feet, my sweet sandpiper. Haven't you ever seen Nevyn go into trance?"

"Well, so I have. You mean you can do that, too?"

"I can, and soon, no doubt, you'll be learning how yourself. It's one of the basic techniques."

Jill went cold all over, partly in fear, but partly in excitement. She'd been assuming that Nevyn's ability to work in the trance state was the mark of a highly exalted master, not of a mere journeyman. Yet Selamander's trance was certainly nothing exciting to watch. With Jill kneeling to one side, and a crowd of curious Wildfolk at the other, he lay on the divan in their inn chamber and crossed his arms

over his chest. In a moment he seemed to have fallen asleep, his eyes
shut, his mouth a little open, his breathing slow and soft. For some
time Jill watched him, then let her mind wander, so much so that she
yelped aloud when he abruptly sat up and started talking.

"I don't like this, Jill. I don't like it at all."

"What happened?"

"Naught. But there were . . . oh, how can I describe them? I can't,
truly. Call them traces or tracks—that will have to do. And I saw one
particular spirit that could only be associated with a dark master, a
pitiful twisted thing." His face darkened with rage. "I wanted to help
it, but it was so frightened I couldn't get close to it. It obviously
associated human and half-human souls with pain and naught more.
Oh ye gods, how I hate these swine!" With a toss of his head he
stood up, stretching, then smiled, slipping back under his mask of a
sunny-natured idiot. "Is there wine, oh beauteous handmaiden? The
wizard's worked up a powerful sort of thirst."

"I'll fetch some, but are you telling me that the dark masters are
here in Daradion?"

"Naught of the sort, turtledove. Only that one or two of the lesser
slimes oozed through here some days ago. I think me, though, that
we'd best be as sly as sly from now on."

When she went to bed, Jill lay awake for a long while, her mind
drifting on the borderlands of sleep. She happened to remember the
Dark Sun, the elven goddess whom she and Salamander had called
upon to witness their vow of vengeance against Rhodry's tormentors.
It seemed years ago, not a matter of months, when back in Cerrmor
they'd pledged death with goblets of mead. The goddess had death
wolves, or so Salamander had told her, and the vow invoked those
beasts to run ever before them on their bloody hunt. She liked that
vow, liked the image it called to mind, of a goddess standing tall, an
elven longbow in her hands, quiver at her hip, and at her feet the two
crouched black wolves.

In her mind one of the wolves turned its head and looked right at
her. With a little yelp she was wide awake, annoyed with herself for
letting her mind play tricks. Yet she could remember the picture
perfectly, and when it was time to do her exercises with mental
images, she chose the wolf—but without, unfortunately, telling Salamander what she was doing. Since it was an ancient nexus of power

on the astral, the image built up remarkably fast, and since it was so easy to work with, she decided to go on using it for a while in her practice.

Just after dawn on a chilly wet day the *Gray Kestrel* left her dock at Daradion and wallowed out to sea. Since they had a favoring wind, in about an hour or so the lumbering ferry-barge was out of sight of land, and the tedium—to Jill's taste, anyway—of a sea voyage settled over her. While Salamander regaled crew and fellow passengers alike with his stories, songs, and juggling, Jill spent most of the uneventful voyage working with her wolf image. Finally, on the last night aboard, she felt for a moment that a giant wolf lay beside her on her bunk, and it seemed that she could almost see it. Although she made the usual banishing gestures at the end of the practice session, the wolf seemed curiously reluctant to go.

They reached Ronaton in the middle of a sunny morning and left the city straightaway by the main road, running southwest along the coast. They rode for about two hours, until, just at noon, they came to a stand of trees and a spring, deepened then lined with stone for the benefit of travelers by the archons of Ronaton, where they stopped to make an early camp to rest the horses and mule, who were still nervous and stable-weary from being in the ship. While Jill unloaded the stock and let them roll, Salamander wandered away a few yards and stood staring out to sea. When he returned, he was shaking his head in frustration.

"Well, I scried Rhodry out, for all the good it's going to do us. He was down in some sort of cellar, arranging big clay pots of what looked like pickled food and even larger amphorae of wine against a wall. There was an older man with him who seemed to be in charge of things. Ye gods, I hope they don't stay down there all day!"

By then both of them were used enough to the Bardekian custom of the afternoon nap to spread out their bedrolls and lie down for a couple of hours. Although Salamander went straight off to sleep, all of Jill's rage came to a head that afternoon. She was thinking of Rhodry, as she so often did, and she burst into tears that were more frustration than grief, a baffled rage at all the dark and magical events that had pulled them apart. Once her fit of weeping had run itself out, she gave up trying to sleep and began to think of her wolf image. It built up fast, and she imagined the shaggy creature lying at her feet.

As Salamander had taught her, she used all her senses in building the image, imagined she could smell it, could feel its weight across her ankles and its warmth through the thin blanket. All at once, she felt something snap into place in her mind. Right where she'd imagined it, the wolf appeared, a bit misty and thin, to be sure, but the image actually seemed to be there, living apart from her will. She worked on bringing it into focus, made it appear more substantial, thickened its glossy coat, imaged the teeth and the panting tongue. When she noticed it was wearing a gold collar of elven design, she was suddenly afraid, because she'd imagined no such thing. The great head turned her way, and the dark eyes considered her. Only then did she realize that a thin, misty cord seemed to connect her solar plexus with that of the wolf; yet whenever she tried to look directly at the cord, it faded away.

With a stretch like a real dog, the wolf got up. Although she started the banishing ritual immediately, her words and motions had no force behind them, because frightened though she was, she was fascinated with her creation. The wolf ignored the ritual, anyway, merely sniffed Salamander and his blankets with a remarkably real-looking wet black nose.

"It's a pity you're not real, you know. I could send you tracking Baruma down."

It swung its head and looked at her. She found herself talking to it, then, a confused babble of all her hatred, all her scraps of knowledge about Baruma, what he was, what he looked like, but she somehow knew that his physical appearance was of little moment to the wolf. With a toss of its head it leapt over her, trotted into the trees, and disappeared.

At that point she woke up, or so she thought of it. All at once she felt a jarring sensation, as if she'd dropped flat on her back from a few inches up, and her eyes were open to the sunlight flooding the camp. Oh by the gods and their wives! she thought irritably. So that was just a dream, was it? Perhaps it's for the best. She got up, and as she was rummaging for food in her saddlebags, she forgot the whole thing. Although she was so exhausted that she felt drained of blood, she put it down to the long months of strain.

In a few minutes Salamander woke, muzzy-eyed and yawning, and stumbled over to the spring. He knelt down, plunged his head into the cold water, snorted, coughed, and swore for a moment, then looked up grinning with the water streaming from his hair to drench his shirt.

"Much better," he announced. "I'm going to try scrying out Rhodry again. He's got to leave that wretched cellar sooner or later. Come join me — see what you can see."

Through a break in the pale stone the water welled up noiselessly and rippled out, splashing a little against the side of the basin before it ran out the overflow pipe. When Salamander put his arm around her and pulled her companionably close, she was aware not of his physical touch but of his aura, raw power welling up from his very being as the water did from the earth.

"Concentrate on the ripples and let your eyes go a bit out of focus. Then think of Rhodry."

For a long while she saw nothing but the glassy surge of water against stone. Then, all at once, she saw a dim, broken picture on the ripples: Rhodry making his way through what seemed to be a marketplace. To her imperfect vision the stalls and peddlers waved and fluttered as much as the cloth banners, but Rhodry's image was solid and steady. At first he looked perfectly well, tanned and fit, striding along and even smiling as he greeted the occasional person that he seemed to know. As she stared at him with hungry curiosity, she had the sensation of moving in closer, until it seemed that she hovered beside him. Then, when he turned his head so that he would have been looking right at her if she'd actually been there, she saw the change in him, a subtle thing, truly, a certain slackness about the mouth, a certain bewilderment in his eyes. Even when he smiled, something was missing. Where was the life that used to burn in his eyes, the grin that could set a roomful of men laughing in answer? Or the half-toss to his head, and the proud set to his shoulders that said here was a warrior, dangerous but a man of honor, born to command? She felt gut-wrenching sick when she realized that his mental injury was as clear and palpable as a physical wound.

"I know this place," Salamander whispered. "All that stucco and pink stone, and that view of the mountains from the marketplace, it's . . . Wylinth, by the gods!"

His crow of triumph broke the vision. He let go of her, sat back on his heels, and gave her a grin which disappeared abruptly at the sight of the look on her face.,

"Salamander, he's going to recover, isn't he? We can do somewhat for him, can't we? We can cure him. Can't we?"

His mouth as slack as his brother's had been, he was silent for a long moment.

"Salamander!"

"I don't know, turtledove. I truly don't know. If naught else, we can get him home to Nevyn, and there's Aderyn, too—I'm sure he'd come to Eldidd to help." Again the heavy silence. "But I don't know."

Jill dropped her face to her hands and wept. When they rode out, vengeance shared her saddle.

Although Wylinth was only some sixty miles away, about three-day's ride, Salamander decided that they'd best approach it by a roundabout way. That first afternoon they headed dead west, following the river to the small town of Andirra, which sported only two inns, both, much to Salamander's horror and Jill's relief, of medium price and quality. Their performance, however, was a great success, as few traveling showmen came through Andirra. The head of the local merchant guild even invited them to meet some of the leading townsfolk at his house for a lavish supper, the perfect opportunity for Salamander to ask casual questions about the availability of exotic barbarian slaves. Although the merchant knew of none, he did remark that a slave trader, passing through on his way to Tondio, had asked him that very question just the week before.

Once they were back in the privacy of their inn chamber, Jill asked Salamander whether he thought this mysterious trader was the same man whose trail they'd crossed in Daradion.

"I'd wager a goodly sum, truly. But how odd this is! If he's asking questions of merchants, he can't know how to scry. Unless, of course, he never saw Rhodry before, but why would the Dark Brotherhood send someone like that?"

"Maybe he is just a trader. He might not be from the Dark Brotherhood at all."

"Then what about that poor little spirit I saw in Daradion? Oh, I don't know, Jill! Ye gods, I feel like a farm-wife chasing chickens into her henhouse. Two pop out again for every blasted one that goes in!"

. . .

The first time that Baruma saw the wolf, he thought nothing of it, because he was staying in an inn whose owner kept a pack of hunting dogs. He was by then traveling through the mountains in northern Surtinna, working his way closer to the Old One's isolated estate but taking his time to allow the blood guild to recapture Rhodry, and he'd stopped for the night in a small town some miles east of Vardeth. Just at twilight he was crossing the courtyard on his way to his chamber after a dinner out, when he saw, on the far side of the compound, a large black dog standing and watching him as he went upstairs—an event of absolutely no moment, or so he thought at the time. Later that evening, he heard a paw scratch briefly at his door and a canine whine, but he ignored it. Sure enough, in a few minutes he heard human footsteps come down the hall, and at their approach, the scratching stopped, as if the dog had gone off with its master.

The next time, however, he realized the truth. He had reached Vardeth and was staying in an expensive inn right down in the center of town near the Plaza of Government, the kind of establishment where large dogs are most unwelcome. Again at twilight he was crossing the walled garden when he saw the black creature drinking at the tiled fountain. This time he saw clearly that it was no dog, but an enormous wolf. When the beast raised its head to look at him, no water dripped from its jaws. Immediately Baruma threw up his hand and sketched a banishing sigil, but the wolf ignored it. Throwing back its head in a soundless howl, it loped toward him, snapped at him, and vanished as silently as it had come. Shaking a little, Baruma hurried to his suite. He was just barring the door behind him when he looked around and saw the wolf lolling on the divan.

"Get out!"

Here in the privacy of his chamber he could work a full banishing ritual, and this time the wolf did indeed disappear at his final command—only to come back with the dawn. When he opened his eyes, he found it standing on his chest and growling soundlessly into his face. With a barely stifled scream he sat up and began sketching the ritual. The wolf was so heavy when he threw it off that he knew it had been sent by someone with real skill in the dark arts; the thought-form had been ensouled with a great deal of magnetism. He was sure that it had been sent by one of his enemies in the circles of initiates and would-be initiates that buzzed around the dark dweomer like flies around manure; after all, his rivals had to try to remove him from competition just as surely as he had to best them. He concentrated on doing a thorough banishing this time, and when he was done, he set astral seals over himself as well.

Yet at twilight the wolf came back. Over the next few days it dogged him wherever he went, ignoring his mighty curses by the Dark Names and his threats of demons and annihilation. Although it never tried to do him physical harm, still it frightened him, popping up at every corner, it seemed, or padding after him down dark streets. At times it invaded his dreams; at others, his dweomer practices. Finally it occurred to him that the wolf might be something of a spy, sent by yet another faction of the continually squabbling members of the Dark Brotherhood. If the Hawkmaster wanted to know what the Old One was up to, others might, too. That night he took out his jug of consecrated black ink, poured it into the special silver basin, marked round with foul sigils, and set himself to contact the Old One and tell him of this unwelcome companion.

Although Baruma had yet to become a member of the Outer Circle, he was no rank beginner, and he made the contact almost at once. On the surface of the pool of ink the Old One's face spread out, trembling a little from the palsy that afflicted him in cold weather. While Baruma told his story, the Old One listened with half-closed eyes.

"You were right to report this," he said at last. "I've suspected for some time that someone else's been tracking Rhodry down, and this confirms it."

"Indeed?" Baruma went a little cold—he should have known that not even a Hawkmaster could hide treachery from the Old One. "Well, it's reasonable that they'd be the same ones who sent this wolf, then."

"It may be a wolf, but *they* are dogs—puppies, even." The old man seemed to be chuckling to himself. "They misjudge me, my friend, because I look like a fat slug on a garden leaf, and they think I spend my days crawling in the slime. Huh. A man of power still lives inside this loathsome casing, as no doubt they'll discover, soon or later."

"Er, sir? You don't think this wolf could come from our old enemy, our 'no one,' do you?"

"No, no, no, you fool! The idiots who follow the mincing dweomer of light would never do such a thing." His mind-touch oozed contempt. "Them and their petty little strictures, fit for women and slaves and nothing more! But enough! If we have enemies, we'd better not risk being overheard. Come to me soon, but make sure nobody's following you. I'd rather wait to see you than have the wrong people follow along after."

"Of course. I'll be very very discreet."

Once he broke the vision, he allowed himself a smile. Be cautious, eh? The Old One himself had just given him a good reason to delay his trip to the villa. He was feeling splendidly smug until he turned around and saw the wolf, gnawing on one of his traveling bags. With a little hop like a skipping lamb, Baruma yelped aloud.

Jill and Salamander arrived at Wylinth late in the next afternoon, with just enough time before sunset to rent a suite in the best inn that the place could offer. That evening, when they went to the marketplace to talk with the archon's men about setting up a show, Jill kept a constant watch for Rhodry. Although she wanted to go door-to-door and ask for him at every house in the city, Salamander insisted that she be patient.

"I have a scheme, turtledove, most subtle, recondite, and, or so I hope, foolproof."

"Listen, elf! I've had some experience of your wretched schemes, and they always take forever to unwind."

"Not forever. Merely a decent interval of time. Jill, trust me yet once again, will you? If we rush, we could ruin everything. So far we don't have the slightest reason to think the dark dweomer is aware of our presence in this esteemed archipelago, while we've been warned of theirs. The longer such remains the case, the happier, indeed the healthier, we shall all be."

"Well, true spoken. But if we haven't found him in an eightnight, then I'm going to start asking around."

"Fair enough. An eightnight it is."

·   ·   ·

At least twice a week one or another of Alaena's women friends
would invite her over to tell fortunes. Although all the women in her
set dabbled in astrology, the tiles, and other forms of divination, only
she had any talent for it. The women took these sessions in deadly
seriousness, even though Alaena foretold mostly small events such as
a letter from an old friend or a visit from a relative. They were hoping
she'd see the possibility of a romance, because in Bardek wealthy
married women often had sentimental love affairs and no one thought
the worse of them for it, provided that they never deserted their
children or flaunted their lovers in their husband's face. Since these
affairs were their chief entertainment, they would crouch for hours
over the tiles as Alaena studied them for omens of romance.

One afternoon Malina did try to read Alaena's tiles for her, out of
fairness' sake, when they were lunching with another friend, Eldani,
a matron of about Malina's age. After Alaena picked her tiles, the
older woman frowned at them for a long time, then began saying a
few chopped phrases, obviously memorized whole by rote.

"The Prince of Birds is good fortune, but it's next to the Three of
Spears, so it's flawed. I'm sorry, Alaena. I just don't have your gift."

"It takes practice, that's all, and you've got to make a story out of
them. You can put in things you know about me, you see, to fill the
story out a little."

Malina frowned at the tiles again, spoke a few more hesitant
clichés, then sighed.

"I just can't find any story. I feel so selfish. Here you always do
ours, but you never get yours done. Or can you give yourself a
reading?"

"Not very well."

"Maybe that marketplace wizard tells fortunes." Eldani broke in.
"Have you heard if he does?"

"I didn't even know he existed," Alaena said.

"His show sounds like lots of fun. My husband saw it last night,
when he was on his way to the guild meeting. He's this funny-looking
man in a long red robe, but he can do all sorts of amazing tricks."

"I heard about that," Malina said. "Cook was quite excited when
she came home from doing the marketing. The wizard could make

fire leap out of his hands, she said, and lights of all different colors. It's clear he's doing it with some kind of powders and chemicals, but she says that the effect was quite lovely."

"At night it certainly would be," Alaena said. "Maybe I'll go down and watch."

"Alaena!" Malina was scandalized. "You can't go down there with the common crowd at night!"

"Why not?" Eldani's smile turned entirely too limpid. "Our 'Laen loves to be daring."

Alaena smiled in return.

"Why not? I'm much too young to paint mats day and night like you do, dear."

Malina leaned forward with a flutter of hands. "Maybe we should all go see this wizard, and take escorts, and then it won't be daring at all."

"Well, I suppose," Eldani said. "Or will Alaena bring her footman?"

Rhodry felt as if he'd been kicked in the stomach. Malina's expression turned so fierce that Eldani shrank back.

"If nothing else," Malina went on. "It will give us something new to think about."

"Yes, of course." Eldani forced out a normal sort of smile. "Or I know—what if we gave a party and hired the wizard to perform?"

"Wonderful idea!" Malina snatched at the change of subject. "If it doesn't rain, he could do his show out in the garden, and it would be absolutely lovely among the trees. I'm sure he'd come if I offered him enough."

"It would certainly give dear Tannilan something to think about," Alaena said. "Do you remember those awful acrobats she hired for her last party?"

"I certainly remember the airs she gave herself afterwards."

The tiles forgotten, the three women leaned forward over the table and began to plan.

"It's driven me half-mad, that's all!" Even though he was trying to project a calm self-control, Baruma knew his mental image was snarling. "Every time I turn around I see that demon-spawn wolf, growling at me."

"Can it hurt you?" the Old One thought in return.

"I don't know. It resists all my banishings."

Floating on the pool of darkness the Old One's image grew thoughtful.

"It was sent by a man of power, then, not one of your rival journeymen. I was afraid of this. Some of my rivals in the Brotherhood know I've got an important piece of work on hand, and obviously they're meddling. Well, when you come back, we'll do a working and follow this wolf to its den. Finding out who lives nearby should prove very interesting. In the meantime, think of it as a test of your courage."

With a flick of his hand, the Old One broke contact, and nothing that Baruma could do would bring him back again.

For some days messages from Malina had been arriving at Alaena's house. Yes, the wizard would perform; yes, he did do fortunes; by the way, Malina was going to wear a blue dress, so if Alaena would wear another color, it would be sweet. The day before the party, the mistress sent Rhodry down to the market to refill a vial with her usual perfume. As he made his way through the booths, he heard a lot of people talking about the Great Krysello and his wondrous show.

"Hanged if I know how he does it," the perfumer said. "He has a maidservant, though, who seems to be more a partner than a slave, and two big braziers belching incense. He's got to be using chemicals."

"I'm sure of it," said the fruit seller in the next stall. "You can find some strange things for sale if you go to the big markets on the coast, they say. It's really amazing, though, to see him shoot blue flames right out of his fingertips. It's got to be a pretty risky process when you think about it."

"I wouldn't mind seeing that," Rhodry said. "He must be doing pretty well for himself."

"Oh, by the Wave-father's beard! How well is he doing? Him and his barbarian girl are staying at the Inn of the Seven Lamps, that's how well!"

Properly impressed, Rhodry whistled under his breath, then happened to glance down to see a gray gnome a few feet away. The little creature was staring at him, and when he moved away, it followed, hesitantly at first, then with a rush to grab the hem of his tunic and dance up and down. Rhodry glanced around, saw no one looking his way, and hunkered down on the pretense of adjusting the ties of his sandals.

"You look familiar, sure enough, little brother. Didn't I last see you in Deverry? I don't remember where, though."

The gnome clutched its head in distress, then disappeared.

At sunset on the night of the party Rhodry escorted his lady's litter to Malina's compound. Five other litters were already there, with their bearers hunkered down beside them under the watchful eye of Malina's gatekeeper and one of her footmen. Although Rhodry would have preferred staying with them and away from the prying eyes of society women, Alaena ordered him to come inside with her. Malina had outdone herself for the party. All through her lush garden tiny oil lamps glittered, and clusters of braided ribands augmented the last flowers of the season. Here and there people were wandering around, talking and laughing, or were already seated on little benches near an improvised stage, hung with red-and-gold banners, where two brass braziers stood in readiness. When he noticed more than a few of the guests giving him a good looking-over, Rhodry became profoundly nervous, wondering if his mistress would insist on his ecorting her like a free man. As they passed a group of the curious, though, she made a point of telling him, in a clear and carrying voice, that he was to go help Malina's cook with the dinner. Before she could contradict herself, Rhodry, went straight to the refuge of the slaves' quarters.

The kitchen was a madhouse fogged with delicious-smelling steam. In one corner two slaves were frantically rolling out rounds of bread and slapping them onto a crackling-hot bake-stone; at the hearth huge pots of spiced vegetables simmered while the cook rushed back and forth to stir them, tasting one pot here, adding something to another there, and yelling orders over her shoulder the whole while. Other slaves were chopping fruit, filling condiment bowls, sugaring little cakes and arranging nuts and sweetmeats on platters. Just outside he could see a couple of men roasting a whole hog at an open fire. The cook glanced at Rhodry, pushed sweaty hair up off her forehead, and pointed to a four-foot-high amphora near the door.

"The dippers are on that little shelf. Take the wine out to the serving table. The cups are already there."

With the help of a young boy, Rhodry wrestled the amphora outside and got its pointed bottom planted in a flower bed near the table. Guests promptly appeared, holding out eager hands. For the next hour he was kept too busy serving wine to worry about proprieties. He did have time to notice that a whole horde of Wildfolk had materialized around him. They seemed hysterically excited about something, leaping up and down, pulling on his tunic, dashing back and forth under the table and even occasionally pinching one of the guests. Once the meal was laid out and everyone served, he filled a silver pitcher with wine and wandered around the garden to refresh the guests' cups. He found Alaena talking to her brother-in-law and his wife. While he poured, she barely glanced his way, holding out the flat, stemmed wine cup with an automatic hand. The Wildfolk danced around him as he continued on.

All at once a gong sounded. With a bemused smile, Malina's husband stepped out on the stage and announced that the Great Wizard, Krysello of the Far North, was ready to begin. Laughing and scurrying, the guests found seats. Rhodry went back to the serving table, which had a close if sideways view of the stage. He poured himself a cup of wine, then perched on the corner of the table in a crowd of Wildfolk just as the red-and-gold drapes parted and a slender man in a long red robe appeared. His hair was so moonbeam pale, his eyes so smoky a gray, that Rhodry swore aloud.

"By the gods," he whispered in Deverrian. "He's half an elf at the very least."

The Wildfolk nodded their agreement and clustered close as a whole flock of their kind materialized on stage, so suddenly and dramatically that Rhodry glanced around, half-expecting that everyone else would have seen them, too.

"I am Krysello, who, great wizard though he is, is but a humble beggar compared to the exalted and lofty status of this assembled company." The showman bowed deeply. "I am honored beyond dreaming that you would so graciously allow me to present my little marvels in your presence." He straightened up and waved a hand at the first brazier. Red flames shot up and towered before sinking back to a pink glow. A woman yelped, then stifled her scream. "Do not fear, exalted one. You behold merely a barbarian display of small, small magicks from the far, far north." He waved his hand again, and the second brazier plumed gold fire. "And now, let me present my beauteous barbarian handmaiden, the Princess Jillanna."

To a scatter of applause the red drapes parted, and out stepped a blonde woman, wearing a gold-brocaded tunic clasped in by a sword belt, from which hung a very real-looking sword and a silver dagger. Rhodry recognized the hilt the moment it winked in the lamplight. His breath was gone, his head strangely heavy as he forced himself to look at her face. Somehow he had known, he realized, that it would be her, that Jill would be standing on stage, smiling vacantly at the crowd as her sharp blue eyes searched desperately, smiling always smiling at the magician's little speeches as he juggled scarves this way and that, but she was turning now, looking right at him—and for a moment her smile went rigid as she too caught a painful breath before she looked away, smiling still.

Rhodry began to shake. He could no more stop shaking than he could have told anyone who this woman was or why he loved her whether he remembered her identity or not. With the shakes came a cold sweat, running down his back. The Wildfolk gathered round, patting him, stroking him, their twisted little faces all gape-mouthed concern as he carefully slipped off the edge of the table, staggered back to the garden wall, and sat down on the ground where no one would see him tremble. He was just getting himself under control when a burst of light from the stage made him look up. Krysello was dancing and weaving round the stage, his arms flung over his head, and above him burst streaks and bolts and firefalls of colored light, reds, golds, purples, ceruleans, all shot with silver sparks and blinding white barbs. The crowd was gasping and sighing like children while Wildfolk skipped across the stage in time to the wizard's music, the high-pitched wailing chants of elven war songs.

Although Rhodry began to shake again, he was mesmerized, feeling that he'd been turned to stone with his eyes forced eternally to this tiny stage where elven dweomer swelled and flooded the world with artificial stars and massive rainbows, sheets of pure-colored mists and opaque-tinted fogs while miniature lightning shot and thundered. He heard a voice screaming in his mind: it's real, it's all of it real dweomer! Don't these fools know what they're seeing? Apparently not, because the crowd was laughing and clapping, calling out words of praise and giggling while the wizard danced and wove his spells, the stage now an inferno of illusionary flames all red and white-hot gold. In the midst of it all Jill stood unmoving, her arms crossed over her chest, her smile gone, her mouth set in barely suppressed rage as she stared across the garden, apparently at nothing. Once he saw a gigantic wolf prowling beside her; then the beast disappeared in a gust of turquoise smoke. Rhodry could watch no longer. He lowered his head to his knees and merely trembled until at last the show ended in a deafening howl of laughter and applause.

As the clapping died away he heard voices, irritable voices, demanding wine, demanding service, but all he could do was clasp his arms tighter round his knees and shake. In his terror he was remembering another night that he'd crumpled into this posture and shaken this way. While he knew that he'd nearly died for Jill, that somehow defending her from insult had nearly gotten him hanged, the details were far beyond him. Then close at hand he heard a woman's voice, one full of concern.

"Alaena, come here!" It was Malina, hovering over him. "Your footman's been taken ill. Here, boy, tell me where it hurts. Is it your stomach?"

The idea of his having a stomachache was so preposterous that it broke the spell. Feeling cold sweat run down his cheeks and neck, Rhodry managed to raise his head and look at her.

"I'm not sick, Mistress Malina." His voice was a dry rasp. "Don't you see? That was real magic. It was all real."

"Oh by Baki's toes!" A dark male voice burst out laughing. "The poor boy's scared stiff! He thought one of his barbarian witch men was making big magic up on stage. Don't worry, boy. We won't let him throw fire at you."

When everyone laughed, Rhodry tried to struggle to his feet, but Malina pushed him down with a surprisingly strong hand.

"Don't mock the boy, Tralino! He'll never get over it if you're all laughing at him. Oh good, there's Prynna. Oh, Prynna, can you hear me? Come over and pour wine, girl. The guests are waiting. Now Rhodry, there's no such thing as real magic, so you're perfectly safe."

"Yes, you silly!" It was Alaena, smiling down at him with her wine cup in her hand. "You just rest for a while. We'll be going home soon, anyway. There's no danger at all."

"My dearest guests, do go get some wine and some dessert." Malina's voice snapped with command. Once the guests had dispersed, she turned to Alaena and whispered. "The poor boy! I wonder what caused this? Has he ever shown any signs of falling sickness?"

"None. I . . ."

There was a waft of incense and perfume, and the rustle of long silk robes as the wizard Krysello swept into their circle. His pale hair gleamed, slicked back with sweat.

"My dearest ladies!" He was all smiles and bows. "You look distressed! What's happened? Aha, I see a man from Deverry, and the poor fellow looks terrified! He knows true magic when he sees it."

"Oh by the Goddesses themselves!" Malina snarled. "Don't start him off again, will you! Tell him, *please*, that you were merely playing tricks up there!"

"Madam, I shall do better than that."

When the wizard knelt down beside him, Rhodry looked him straight in the face and spoke in Deverrian.

"Are you the man who took Jill from me?"

"So," he answered in the same language. "You remember somewhat, do you? I'm not. I swear to you on the gods of my people that I'm only a friend of Jill's and naught more. Now, you're going to forget about Jill for a little while. You'll forget until you see the sun tomorrow. Then you'll remember everything. Everything."

With a limpid smile Krysello placed one long-fingered hand on Rhodry's forehead. Rhodry felt warmth, a palpable thick warmth that seemed to seep into his mind through the space between his eyes, then spread, flowing down his neck, his spine, and across his shoulders. The trembling stopped, and he smiled, wondering what could possibly have upset him so badly. With a satisfied nod, Krysello took his hand away.

"Mistresses, forgive me," Rhodry stammered. "I don't know what came over me."

"Terror, boy, and superstition." Malina gave him a motherly sort of smile. "If you believe something long enough and well enough, it becomes real to you. No doubt your mother filled your head with stories of witches and sorcerers, and in your primitive country they must have seemed quite plausible. Alaena, I really must go make sure the desserts are being properly served."

And she marched away fast, no doubt to prevent herself from wondering just how a fake wizard could have calmed the slave down in such a magical way. Alaena, however, stayed, clutching her wine cup tightly in both hands as she stared at Krysello. In a rustle of silk he bowed to her.

"Madam, I am informed that you are greatly desirous of having your fortune told. Shall I attend you on the morrow morn?"

"Yes." Her voice was back to normal, with an edge of cool amusement at total variance with her awestruck eyes. "Two hours before noon would do splendidly, if it's convenient."

"Madam, waiting upon the merest whim of a woman like you is my definition of convenient." He bowed again, then turned to glide away into the crowd.

For a moment Alaena stood staring after him, then turned to Rhodry.

"Can you walk now?"

"I think so, mistress. I truly am sorry for . . ."

"You don't need to apologize." Her voice lost its sophisticated edge. "I was frightened myself. I believe you, Rhodry. I think that was real magic, too. I just had to pretend in front of Malina."

His surprise brought him to his feet. He realized, then, that the wizard's cure had worked so splendidly—he felt not in the least tired from his long terror—that he was more sure than ever that the man's magic was genuine.

"You certainly were a strange ship to come hoving into view," Alaena went on. "Bringing all sorts of even stranger things in your wake." She glanced around, saw that the party had receded to the other side of the garden on one of those tides that parties have, and reached up to kiss him on the mouth. "I want to go home."

When she kissed him a second time, her hungry excitement was as much frightening as arousing.

"As you wish, mistress, of course. Shall I go get the litter ready?"

"Yes. And when we get home, don't wait too long to come to my chamber."

"Please, don't say that kind of thing here."

"Don't be tedious." She slapped him across the face. "Get the litter. I'll meet you at the gate."

By the time they reached her house, only the drowsy gatekeeper was still up and waiting for them. Rhodry sent him off to bed, then got the litter boys locked in for the night and put his ebony staff and the whip away in their cupboard in the kitchen. For a moment he stood in the darkened room, watching the dim glow from the banked fire and catching a moment's peace before he went, slowly and reluctantly, to his mistress's chamber.

The sight of her took away some of his reluctance. Wearing only a shift of white silk gauze, she was perched on the edge of the bed and running an ivory comb through her curls. In the oil lamps her coppery skin glowed like fire itself. When he shut the door she looked up, smiling, and tossed the comb onto the floor.

"Do you think I'm beautiful, Rhodry?"

"Of course I do." He felt like a man in a ritual; every time they made love, she asked him the same thing. "I've never seen a woman as beautiful as you."

He sat down next to her, caught her face in both hands, and kissed her on the mouth. She laced her hands together behind his neck, gave him a slow and calculated kiss, then suddenly pulled back a little to study his face. He could have sworn she was frightened by something she found there.

"What's wrong, mistress?"

"Nothing, oh nothing." Yet she hesitated, glancing this way and that before she spoke again, a breathless burst of words. "Rhodry, I need you so much. I've been so lonely. I worry, too, about what could happen to us, but I need you so much."

He realized that at last he was seeing not her carefully arranged surface, but her self.

"Well, here I am."

This time, when he kissed her, all his reluctance vanished. In his arms she turned into a greedy little animal, teasing him, pretending to fight him, while he laughed and kissed and finally caught her.

Afterwards they fell asleep in each other's arms. He woke just as the oil lamps were guttering themselves out and realized that it was only an hour or so until dawn. Even though everyone in the household knew of the affair, he had no desire to be in the mistress's bed when Disna came in first thing of a morning. Carefully and slowly he worked free of her lax embrace and slid out of bed, grabbing his clothes and sneaking out like a thief to dress in the hall.

By then he was wide-awake and troubled by a sense of unease that had nothing to do with his dangerous love affair. Walking silently on bare feet he went to the kitchen, got the heavy staff, and slipped outside to take a turn round the compound. In the graying light nothing moved out in the garden except a shiver of cool breeze through the silvery eucalyptus; there was no sound at all on the street or from the sleeping neighborhood. Yet when he came to the gate, Wildfolk appeared to shake the hem of his tunic while they looked up with distressed eyes.

"Is something dangerous outside?"

When they nodded a yes, he tossed the staff up onto the flat roof of the gatekeeper's kiosk, jumped onto an ornamental planter, and scrambled up. The kiosk was just high enough for him to lean on folded arms onto the top of the thick outer wall. Across the street, in the shadows of a pair of trees, stood a man, wrapped in a light cloak and watching the house. Rhodry was so sure of his status in the household by then that he called out without thinking twice.

"You! What are you doing there?"

The man turned and bolted down the street, whipped into an alley and disappeared. Although Rhodry's first impulse was to start shouting and raise an alarm that would bring the archon's men, he decided to rouse Porto first and ask his advice. He realized, too, that there was something familiar about the man he'd seen . . . Gwin? Gwin, by the gods! He went cold all over, thanking his luck that he hadn't just opened the gates and chased after. Then he jumped down and ran into the house to wake Porto and tell him what had happened without, for some reason that he couldn't put into words, telling him Gwin's name. Yawning and stretching, the old man got up slowly and stood thinking for a moment.

"Well, whoever he was, he's probably far away by now," Porto said at last. "And the archon's men are just going off watch, too. I'll go down to the guardhouse later and report this to the watch captain, and tonight they'll have a patrol swing by here at regular intervals. Let me see, what's happening this morning? Any visitors?"

"That wizard from the marketplace is coming to tell our mistress's fortune, about two hours before noon. She invited him last night at the party."

Porto groaned in distaste.

"It's her money, but why doesn't she just throw it into the gutter if she wants to waste it? I'll go down to the archon's when he comes. I can't abide that sort of nonsense. You stay close at hand the whole time he's here, boy. I don't want to find any of the silver missing after he's gone."

"I'll stay right by the door and keep an eye on him."

"Good. Well, dawn's breaking. You go start chopping the firewood for Vinsima, and I'll wake the others."

Rhodry went outside through the kitchen. As soon as he stepped out the door, the rising sun cast a wash of light across his face. Blinking and swearing, he turned his back and remembered. Jill. He had seen her, she had been there at the party, the woman he loved, the woman he'd lost, somehow, long ago, in Deverry—in Cerrgonney. To that piss-poor excuse for a noble swine Lord Perryn, when they were both fighting in some lord's blood-feud. He was a silver dagger, then, and he'd been trapped in a siege. First Jill had ridden with the army that relieved it; then they'd gotten separated. How? Why had he left her in Tieryn Graemyn's dun? Because the King's herald was coming! He'd ridden out with his hire, Lord Nedd, to greet the herald, and when they'd ridden back, Jill was gone, stolen, or so they said, by Nedd's cursed ugly cousin. With a toss of his head he laughed aloud, jigging a few steps of a dance right there near the woodshed. He remembered finding Perryn, too, and the exquisite joy of beating him senseless. Then he'd . . . and then he'd . . . the fog within his mind rose again and shut away all memory of what had happened after he left Perryn bleeding on the ground by a cowshed wall. No more could he remember anything before he and Jill had ridden up to Lord Nedd's crumbling roundhouse on a sunny day— how long ago? He had no idea.

"Rhodry!" Vinsima's bellow cut through his brooding. "Where's that kindling? What's wrong with you? Don't you feel well?"

"A thousand apologies! I'm on my way right now."

While he worked, he went on brooding about what he'd remembered. There was something especially important about the King's herald, but try as he might, he couldn't bring it to mind and eventually gave it up as a bad job. He was going over and over the rest of the precious new memories to fix them in his mind when it occurred to him to wonder why they'd come back to him. Only then did he remember the wizard Krysello announcing that he would remember "everything" when he saw the sun again.

"Oh by the gods, so I did."

A few at a time Wildfolk materialized around him, two brown and purple gnomes, a delicate pale sprite with needle-sharp teeth, and the gray gnome he'd seen down at the marketplace.

"Jill's gnome!"

The little creature leapt into the air, danced a few steps in victory, then disappeared, taking its fellows with it. Rhodry began to tremble. All at once, he could smell freedom, and now that he'd seen Jill, freedom had meaning again. He realized then that somehow an entire identity had died along with his memories, that what we call a man's character is little more, at times, than the sum of his memories. The thought gave him a cold feeling on the edge of panic, and he shied away from it like a horse who sees an adder in the road.

The man who was using the name Pirrallo was short, pale, and pudgy, with a thick neck and full cheeks that would, with age, swell and sag to make him look like a toad. He had a face full of pimples, too, that would, with time, scar and leave dark marks much like the blotching on a toad's skin. The man known as Gwin was surprised at how much he hated Pirrallo. He had, after all, looked upon many a thing more loathsome in his thirty-two years, but perhaps it was because he knew that Pirrallo was as much a spy as a partner. The knowledge that someone was watching their every move and using magic to report it back to the Hawkmaster would have terrified most initiates of the Hawks; Gwin found it only irritating, because he didn't care if he lived or died. Another thing that surprised him these days was, in fact, just how little he did care. Although he could have committed suicide at any time, the effort seemed too great for the uncertain reward of being dead, just as the dubious joys of being alive were too little an incentive to make him suck up to the man sent to judge his trustworthiness. He was even willing to make the possibly fatal admission that he'd quite simply failed his assignment back in the farming village of Deblis, rather than whining and making excuses the way most Hawks would have done, but only so long as he admitted it to the Hawkmaster himself, not to a toad like Pirrallo. It was a matter of pride, the small sort of pride that was the only thing he had left in life.

After catching sight of Rhodry, Gwin left the city and rode north, rejoining his allies some three hours past dawn only to find the toad still asleep. They were camped some twelve miles outside the city walls of Wylinth with the small caravan that provided the rationale for their traveling around the islands. Although Pirrallo sometimes claimed to be a slave trader, keeping actual slaves with eyes to see things and mouths to blab them would have been far too risky; instead, they had a string of twenty-odd horses for sale or trade and two stock handlers who were in fact lesser initiates of the Hawks. Gwin himself was supposed be to Pirrallo's property, just because owning one barbarian gave the toad a reason for asking to buy another, a ruse that rankled, because the stigma of having been born into slavery stuck to him wherever he went, even among those who followed the dark paths. Until the summer before he'd faced or fought it down when he could and took a perverse pride in it when he couldn't, but his brief trip through Deverry had turned his views on life and his self upside down. He'd spent a long time thinking about this change in himself, and he decided that simply from living among free men had brought it about, but, of course, deeper levels of the soul and memory were working on him, more deeply than he could know. Although Gwin was no true barbarian—his father had been a Bardek man though his mother, a Deverry girl—he'd felt in some odd way that Deverry was home, that he'd been trapped all his life unknowing in a foreign exile, and that, of course, the exile would continue without hope.

His one comfort these days was knowing that the other two Hawks hated Pirrallo as much as he did. After all, Brinonno and Vandar stood to die, too, if their toad-spy turned the Hawkmaster against them. That morning, the three of them sat at the cold campfire and ate stale bread and last night's vegetables while Pirrallo snored in his tent on the other side of the campground. Vandar even said aloud what all of them were thinking, that he hoped the fat fool would do something stupid and get himself killed or arrested when they reached Wylinth.

"Not too likely, unfortunately," Gwin said. "He knows his work, all right."

"You don't suppose he's scrying us out right now, do you?" Brinonno said with a start. "And listening to what we're saying?"

"I doubt it very much." Gwin allowed himself a twisted smile. "You know what his big flaw is? He loves himself so much that it never occurs to him that other men hate him."

"I'm willing to bet he doesn't have much power for scrying, anyway," Vandar put in. "Always bragging, yes, but why are we wandering all over, playing out this elaborate hoax, if he can really scry for Rhodry? I know he's never seen the barbarian himself, but you have, and a real master can work through someone else's eyes."

"Only if that someone's willing to let him crush his will." Gwin felt his voice turn flat. "By the Clawed Ones themselves, if he tried to put his toad's paw on the back of my neck, I'd knock him halfway to Hell, and I think he knows it." Then he laughed in self-mockery. "Not that it's fear of me that's holding him back, mind. No, when he arrived, he announced that there were fresh orders from the Hawkmaster. He had reason to think that it would be dangerous to scry too much, or use much dweomer for anything, for that matter. Pirrallo didn't tell me why."

"Probably the master didn't tell him," Brinonno said.

"Maybe not." Vandar stood up, stretching. "But the little pig-bugger was probably lying, too. Well, I'm going to water the stock. It's shaping up for a warm day, now the rain's gone."

When the two walked off together, Gwin sat by the fire and considered them. Doubtless they would tell the Hawkmaster everything he'd said, especially if it would save their own skins later, but he was sure they'd let nothing slip to Pirrallo. Since in his own way Gwin was a good judge of men, he knew honest hatred when he saw it.

"Salamander?" Jill said. "Can you tell fortunes?"

"I can, but I wouldn't use true dweomer for such a stupid game."

"I was wondering about that."

"These tiles that Bardek women play around with? All they do is focus your intuition. I shall make up some highly colored, titillating, and thus satisfying blather for the Lady Alaena that more or less fits when I intuit about her, and into this spicy stew I shall weave all the bits of information I picked up about her at the party."

"Weave things into a stew?"

"Not my best turn of phrase, truly." Salamander waved the lapse away with a languid hand. "I wouldn't tell fortunes at all, except it's such a perfect way to get into her house. It would be wretchedly rude of me to just go marching up to her door and ask if she'd sell me her exotic slave. First I'll get her confidence; then, most cleverly, dripping with guile, I shall work the talk round to my pressing need of another barbarian for our show."

"Very well, then. You've been right enough so far."

"I'm always right," Salamander lolled back onto the cushions and saluted her with his wine cup. "But what particular occasion of my rightness earns your praise?"

"Finding Rhodry, of course. I owe you an apology. I thought it was daft, staying in the best inn, playing up to rich women, and here you were right all along."

"Ah. Well, who else could afford him but some wealthy house?"

"So I see. Now."

Salamander smiled, then gestured at the elaborate breakfast of cold meats and spiced vegetables.

"Eat, my turtledove."

"Can't."

"Try. Anxiety is like worms—it thrives in an empty gut."

In spite of herself Jill had to laugh. She took a slice of spiced pork, wrapped it in a round of bread, and forced down a couple of bites.

"But what if she won't sell him?"

"I'll think of somewhat, never fear. Now eat! We are due at her palatial residence in but an hour or so, and we must bathe and dress in our very gaudiest finery. After all, we have reputations as barbarians to keep up."

When, wearing red-and-gold silk and brocade, and smelling of roses and violets, Jill and Salamander presented themselves to Alaena's gatekeeper, the old man seemed more amused than impressed, but he did show them straight into the garden, where a pretty young maidservant was waiting to take them to the reception chamber. Even though Jill normally didn't care for the Bardekian style of art, when she saw the airy trees and the brightly painted birds, she was charmed. The feeling the wall decorations gave her was somehow familiar, too, and all at once she found herself remembering the painted tents of the Elcyion Lacar. Before she could ask Salamander about the similarity, Alaena came through a side door to join them.

Dressed in simple white linen, set off only by a chain necklace of what looked like solid gold, Alaena greeted them with great courtesy and had them join her on the dias. After they'd settled themselves on velvet cushions around a low table, the maidservant brought in plates of dried fruit and sweetmeats and cups of sweet wine.

"And the box of tiles, too, Disna," Alaena said.

"Yes, mistress." The girl went over to an ebony cabinet. "They're right here where Rhodry usually puts them."

At the mention of her footman's name, the mistress's expression grew oddly strained, and she glanced at Salamander in a manner that was almost furtive before a bland smile blossomed. Disna brought over the box, set it down, and took off the lid.

"You may go now," Alaena said. "Tell the cook to make orangeade. This wine is too strong for morning."

"Her exalted loveliness is most kind to a humble wizard," Salamander said.

"The humble wizard is most kind to come at her request. Disna, I said go."

As the girl, who'd been hovering all a-twitch with curiosity, scurried out, Alaena dumped the tiles out of the box and began mixing them in a well-practiced thunder. She had lovely hands, Jill thought, slender and graceful, with long fingernails that had been stained a tasteful orange-red with annatto seeds and polished to such a glossy perfection that Jill found herself hiding her own calloused fingers and bitten nails in her lap. She also noticed that Salamander was watching the lady with a warm sort of appraisal of his own, approving of more than her hands as she laid out a selection of tiles in a star-shaped pattern.

"Aha." Salamander leaned over the table. "I see many things, dark, hidden, recondite, a time for pain followed by rejoicing, laughter followed by tears, shafts of sun breaking through clouds, storms followed by sunsets of peace."

With a delighted little shiver, Alaena stared at the tiles.

"I see you standing at a crossroads in life, oh favored one of the Star Maidens. Look at the Flowers blooming among Spears. The Raven is crying out, but he will be silenced. First of all . . ." He paused to lay one finger on the Ten of Flowers. "You have many loyal friends who care for your welfare. They have been worried about you, worried to see you fretting and listless, no doubt, over the question of whether to remarry soon or to wait and see what the waves of Life wash up on your shore. Always you must worry about being loved for yourself. There are some suitors who would marry your investments and your connections with the great trading houses."

"That's exactly right!" Her breathy voice held a note of childlike excitement. "Some are so blatant about it, good sir, why, you'd hardly believe their lack of tact!"

"Alas, I fear me that I'd believe it all too well, knowing as I do the hearts of men." He frowned at the tiles for a long, dramatic moment. "I see a young man from another island here, a handsome man, but arrogant."

"Why, yes!"

"His youth tempted you, and his virility, because a great sorrow in your life is that you've never had children."

"Yes." Her voice wavered with real pain. "That's true, too. But he had other flaws."

"I can see them quite clearly. Fear not—you made the right decision. But now, alas, you wait, your mind running first one way, then another, while you wonder if your life will simply peter out, like a stream spent in the desert that buries itself in the sand. Yet few would pity you, because of your wealth."

"I find it hard to pity myself, good sorcerer. I've been very poor in my life, and I know just how lucky I am now."

"And yet, something gnaws you, an emptiness. Hum, I see that it makes you desperate at times. Now what's this? I see a great threat of scandal, but I can't seem to divine its cause."

At that exact moment Rhodry came in with a tray of glass goblets and a glass pitcher of orangeade. He glanced at Jill, then at Alaena in a kind of tormented desperation, and blushed scarlet.

"Terrible, terrible scandal," Salamander was saying. "Do you see the Queen of Wands? You must be like her, so full of righteousness that none can impugn you, so strong that you can dismiss enemies with the flick of a single finger."

Rhodry put the tray down, backed noiselessly away, and fled the room. Although Alaena never acknowledged his presence, Jill was certain that only an iron self-control kept her from blushing in turn. She looked up and waved a vague hand at the pitcher.

"Jillanna, would you pour? I simply can't stop listening to Krysello's reading."

"Of course, my lady." Jill would rather have slit her throat, but she smiled, and smiled again as she passed the goblets round.

"Now, after the trouble passes—and it will pass, I promise you this, oh vision of feminine perfection—I see happy times ahead. There are those who would love you for yourself alone. One man I see, shy, filled with humility, whose feeling of unworthiness is all that keeps him from speaking. Wait! I see two such—one barely known to you; another who is an old friend. The friend travels for the winter, far away it seems, although the tiles cannot tell me where. The new acquaintance hovers closer at hand than you would ever think."

"By the Stars themselves! I wonder who . . ." Alaena bit her lower lip and thought hard. "Do go on, good sorcerer."

Salamander managed to stretch out the reading for a good five minutes by the judicious selection of platitudes and vagaries. After Alaena had asked a few questions, she turned the talk to his travels throughout the country. As usual Salamander reveled in the chance to tell a long and involved tale, most of it embroidery, some of it lies, especially since she listened with a flattering intensity.

"But don't you have some home of your own," she said at last. "Back in the barbarian kingdom?"

"No, oh pinnacle of charm and graciousness. All roads are my home, and the swelling sea. I have my Jillanna here to cheer my lonely hours and share my labors."

"I see." Alaena gave her a perfectly friendly smile. "Do you find it a hard life?"

"Oh no. I love to wander."

"It's a good thing." The mistress turned her attention back to the wizard. "But it must be sad in a way, always packing up and moving on."

"What it is, is a lot of hard labor, actually. I've been thinking about buying a slave now that my career is progressing so well, a strong young man to load up the horses and so on. Of course, what I really need is a fellow barbarian."

"You can't have mine!" Her voice was a child's snarl; then she looked absolutely stricken. "Oh, forgive me! I'm so sorry I was rude! It's just that everyone's always trying to buy my footman from me, and I simply won't sell." She managed a smile. "It just gets so tedious, having everyone always ask."

"It must be, and truly, I would rather have your harsh words than some other woman's blandishments. Anyway, what I was wondering is where you bought him. That trader might have others from time to time."

"Rhodry was a gift from that arrogant young man you saw in my tiles, so I don't know where he came from. One doesn't ask, with gifts." She picked up the pitcher with a perfectly calm hand. "More orangeade?"

They chatted for some time longer before Salamander announced that they had to take their leave, because after the noon meal and the afternoon nap they had appointments at other houses round town, as more than one fine lady had wanted her fortune told. When they left, a good bit richer thanks to Alaena's generosity, Jill was wondering how she was going to be able to stay awake, sitting in perfumed rooms and listening to his blather. She said as much to him once they were back in the privacy of their suite in the Inn of the Seven Lamps.

"Blather, indeed!" Salamander looked sincerely wounded. "I thought I put on one of my best performances ever this morning."

"Well, she certainly was impressed. Did you pick up most of that stuff at the party?"

"I did, truly. Odd, isn't it? People who pay to have their fortunes told never seem to realize how easy it is to learn all about them beforehand. That scandal, however? That came straight from the tiles, practically off the little scroll of meanings you get when you buy a box. I figured that any woman as beautiful as she is would be bound to have at least one scandal in the offing."

"No doubt, the frothing bitch!"

"Jill!"

"Well, ye gods, are you blind? Of course she's up to her neck in scandal! Or does polite society in the islands honor women who bed their slaves?"

Salamander's face went through a spasm of puzzlement, modulating to outright shock and finally a sly sort of glee.

"She's been rumpling her blankets with my dear brother? How perfectly splendid!"

Jill grabbed a wine pitcher and heaved it straight at his head. With a squawk he ducked barely in time, and the silver pitcher cracked a tile on the wall and fell dented to the floor.

"A thousand apologies, oh fierce eagle of the mountains. I seem to have forgotten how the thing would look to you, of course." His voice was a bit shaky. "Uh, you do accept my apology? No more flying tableware?"

"Oh of course, but I'm sorry I missed, you heartless dolt!"

"It's not a question of being heartless but of scenting victory. Don't you see? This is the exact lever we need to pry Rhodry out of her household. Well, well, well—scandal indeed, and also a great relief to my ethical sensibilities. By winkling her exotic barbarian out of her household, I'm but doing her a favor—getting him out of town before said town can talk of naught else but the lovely widow and the footman!"

"True spoken, but how are you going to convince her of that?"

"A good question, my little turtledove. A very good question indeed. While I ponder, brood, and meditate upon it, how about fetching us the noon meal? I can never think properly on an empty stomach."

Some hours before sunset they presented themselves at the door of Malina's compound. Since the afternoon was warm and still, the mistress of the house and her two daughters received them out in the garden, at a table under a bower of pale pink bouganvillea. While Salamander predicted that the daughters would make splendid marriages and hinted of possible suitors, Jill half-drowsed over a cup of wine. Once their fortunes were told, Malina sent the girls away so the wizard could read her tiles in private. After a few platitudes, Salamander struck.

"Now, I don't like the look of this, my dear lady, the Four of Swords so near to the Two of Flowers. I greatly fear that some friend of yours—no, closer than an ordinary friend—some dear and treasured companion will be touched by painful scandal."

Jill was suddenly wide-awake and all attention. Malina had gone a bit white about the mouth.

"The tiles also tell me that you've been worried about something distressing. May I guess that the two things are related?"

"It would be a clever guess, yes. Um, I don't suppose you'd tell anyone what you saw in someone else's tiles?"

"Normally, no, but I felt very sorry for Alaena."

Malina winced.

"She's so vulnerable, isn't she?" the lady went on. "And the city's full of envious snips who love to say terrible things about her. Her life would have been so different if only she'd had children. Her husband was much older than she, you see. Oh by the Fire-mountain herself! If you could only have seen her when Nineldar brought her home! Just fourteen years old, a child who should have been playing with dolls, and as thin as a stick. It made me weep to see the beautiful face on that skinny little stick of a body, like a flower on a stalk. Nineldar wasn't a bad man, only so lonely, and he honestly pitied her when he found her for sale. He brought the child to me and begged me to teach her how to be a wife."

"Doubtless the marriage was far from . . . shall we say, satisfying?"

Malina slapped her hands palm-downward on the table.

"Just what are you implying, my fine showman?"

"This is no time for fencing, is it? I heard distressing rumors, and I dismissed them as that, too—just rumors. But when I saw a horrible scandal in her tiles, well, I wondered if they sprang from more than envy and wagging tongues."

"Rumors about what?"

"That handsome barbarian boy."

Malina wept, a thin scatter of tears that she controlled almost at once.

"Nineldar spoiled her, trying to make things up to her. She's gotten used to having anything she wants, even if it's something forbidden."

Salamander looked her full in the face with an expression so sincere that Jill nearly believed him herself.

"I tried to buy the boy from her for my show. She wouldn't sell him. That's what made me wonder if the rumors were true."

Malina looked away, her mouth a little slack as she thought things through.

"I'll go speak to her," she said at last. "And I'll talk long and hard. There are several other things that we haven't even touched upon yet, have we, my dear sorcerer?"

"I'm afraid I don't understand."

"Now, *that* I simply don't believe. But have it your way; I don't blame you for wanting to keep your own scandal buried in decent silence. I'll send one of my slaves to your inn with a message, one way or another. You may leave me now. The sooner I speak to her the better."

All morning, after the wizard left, Alaena paced round the garden. Every now and then she would call for Rhodry; when he came, she would look at him so intently that he wondered if she were trying to memorize his face, then either give him a kiss or a slap and send him away again. Finally, when the household retired for the afternoon nap, she insisted he spend his with her.

"Mistress, it's really not safe, here in the middle of the day."

"Who do you think you are, to be arguing with me?"

"I'm only trying to spare you grief. That wizard saw a scandal, didn't he?"

This time she slapped him hard enough to make his face sting.

"You and your rotton wizard!"

Then she burst into tears. Since he couldn't think of anything else, to do, Rhodry picked her up and carried her, kicking and protesting, into her bedchamber. After he made love to her, she fell asleep in his arms, so soundly that he could slip away and go up to his own bed in the slaves' quarters. Although Porto made a great show of snoring, Rhodry was sure that the old man had been waiting to see if he would come in. By then Rhodry was so exhausted from all his anxieties that he fell asleep straightaway himself.

He was awakened much later by Disna, shaking him and saying over and over again that the mistress wanted him. With a sound halfway between a yawn and a groan he sat up and rubbed his face.

"She wants you to come pour wine in the reception chamber. Rhodry, something's wrong. Malina's here."

"Malina comes here practically every day."

"Oh I know, but something's really wrong. I'm worried, for your sake."

All at once he was wide-awake, on his feet without even really thinking. Disna was looking at him with tears in her eyes.

"I just hope they don't beat you."

"I thought you couldn't stand me."

"Men! Island men, barbarian men—you're all blind!"

Then she fled the room; he could hear her clattering down the stairs.

In a cold panic he followed her down and rushed to the kitchen to fetch the tray of cups and the wine. When he came into the reception chamber, he found Alaena and Malina sitting at the low table, facing each other, both of them a little pale. He set the tray down and started to back away, but Malina pointed at a cushion with an imperious hand.

"Sit down, boy. This concerns you."

When Rhodry glanced at his mistress, she ignored him, and he took the cushion.

"Very well," Malina went on, speaking to Alaena. "Do you see what I mean, dear? It's all getting out of hand, if some traveling showman can hear everything there is to hear right down in the common marketplace."

"How do you know he heard it? He could be lying."

"And why would he lie?"

Alaena hesitated, slewing half-around to look at Rhodry, then back to face Malina, whose eyes snapped like a cadvridoc's when he gives hard orders.

"You see it, too, don't you? Well, are you going to do the decent thing and sell him back to his family or not? His brother's certainly come a long way to look for him."

"I don't care! He's mine, and no one can make me sell him."

"I was talking about decency, not legality."

Rhodry was frozen by surprise. His brother? At that point he dimly remembered that he'd had several brothers, back in that other life of his. Krysello must have been one of them, if the women said so; he couldn't remember enough to argue either way. Malina turned to him.

"Well, boy, isn't he your brother?"

"Yes, mistress."

"Now listen, Alaena darling, you've simply got to sell. It's the proper thing, and beyond that, if the gossip gets all over, well, what decent man is going to marry you?"

"I don't care! I'll never marry, then. I like my slave better than half the stupid men in the islands, anyway."

"Enough to have a child by him? A lovely horrid thing that would be! The poor little creature would most likely have blue eyes, and that would be all the proof anyone would need. Do you want to see your poor boy flogged to death in the marketplace and his child sold away from you?"

"Then I'll set him free. If he's a freedman, nobody can do anything to us, and if rotten nasty spiteful people want to talk behind my back, let them!"

"That's all very well, except you're assuming he'll want to stay."

Alaena slewed round again to look him with the question clear in her eyes and her half-parted lips. Rhodry felt as if he'd been struck dumb; no matter what he said it would be wrong. His silence, however, announced everything. Alaena dropped her face into her hands and sobbed.

"I didn't think so." Malina's voice was ice steady. "Are you pregnant already?"

"I doubt it." She was sniffling rather than sobbing by then. "I'll know for certain in two or three days."

"Well, if you are, there's a sensible way of dealing with the problem, and you're going to do it."

Alaena nodded dumbly.

"And you're going to sell Rhodry back to his brother, and you're going to do that tonight."

"I don't want to sell him. I'll give him to his beastly brother. I don't want one stupid zotar for him."

"Very good. Rhodry, fetch Porto and tell him to bring bark-paper and ink. I'll write out a deed of gift right now and have your mistress sign it."

As Rhodry ran from the room, his heart was pounding in excitement, but not so much from the prospect of freedom. At last he was going to learn the truth about himself. And then, all at once, he was afraid, wondering just what that truth might be.

. . . .

"It's almost night," Jill said. "Surely that blasted message should come soon."

"I wouldn't call sunset 'almost night,' oh fretful egret of mine, but truly, I can understand why impatience blooms within your—oho! Footsteps are also blooming in the corridor."

Now that the crux was here Jill felt paralyzed. Moving faster than she'd ever seen him move, Salamander leapt from the divan, dashed for the door, and flung it open just as someone knocked. Rhodry stood there, a bedroll slung over his shoulder, a leather letter case in his hand. From her perch on the windowsill Jill watched, half-greedy at the sight of him, half-afraid she'd conjured up his image like one of her visualization exercises. Rhodry glanced her way, then merely looked around the room in a soul-weary bewilderment.

"She's willing to sell you, then?" Salamander said.

"She's not, but she's made a gift of me." Rhodry handed over the letter case. "It's an odd thing, to be owned by your own brother."

"Oh by the gods! You know, then?"

"The women spotted it, and once I had a moment to look in a mirror, I could see the same thing they did." Rhodry smiled in a painful self-mockery. "I can't lie and say I remember you, lad, but I've never been more glad to see kinfolk in my life—I guess. I couldn't swear to that, either, not to save my life. Here, do you know what's happened to me?"

"Probably better than you do, oh brother of mine. Ah ye gods, it gladdens my heart to see you free."

When, half in tears, Salamander grabbed his arm and hauled him into the chamber, Rhodry tossed his bedroll onto the floor, then all at once looked up and gave Jill a smile that came from a recognizable ghost of his old self, only a shadow, perhaps, but cast by a familiar sun.

"And aren't we supposed to be rushing into each other's arms and babbling at each other like in a gerthddyn's tales, my love? It seems cursed tame, to just walk in and hand over my bill of sale."

She laughed, and with that, she felt as if a small but ugly ensorcelment had broken in her own mind. She slipped off the windowsill and ran the last few steps to his open arms. His embrace was so familiar—the way he gathered her close, the way his hands moved on her back—that she wanted to alternately shriek and howl with laughter like an hysterical child. Instead she kissed him, and again, the feel of his mouth on hers was as companionable as the voice of an old friend unheard for too long. When something wet touched her face she looked up to find him in tears.

"I remember you, Jill. I never did completely forget you, not even at my worst—I want you to know that. And now, well, I remember more about you than I do about anything else, but by every god and his horse, I don't remember everything." He paused, sniffing like a child, and let her go to wipe his face on his tunic sleeve. "I don't even remember how we met."

"Do you remember how we parted?"

"Somewhat about it. Tell me one thing—did you want to ride off with Perryn?"

"Never! I swear it on the gods of our people!"

"That's the sweetest thing I've ever heard."

He grabbed her again and kissed her, and this time he was laughing, his old berserker's chuckle under his breath, as if her kiss were magic enough to give him back his past. Yet all at once, when he let her go, that fragment of his old self disappeared into his bewilderment like a chunk of ice melting into a puddle.

"What was Perryn?" He was looking at Salamander. "Some sort of sorcerer like you?"

"A sort of sorcerer, true enough, but not one like me, not in the least, my thanks! Come sit down, brother. We've got many a grave and grievous thing to discuss, not the least of which is who you truly are."

For a brief moment Jill was angry, feeling more than a little slighted and dismissed. All at once she realized that for months, she'd been rehearsing this scene in her mind, wallowing in guilt and planning out various ways of begging Rhodry to forgive her, only to find that of course he forgave her, that all she needed to do was tell the simple truth for him to close the matter once and for all. There would be no tantrum of recrimination, no orgy of forgiveness. She was profoundly relieved, and in that sense of relief she found her first real hope that someday he would be cured. No matter how hard he'd tried, Baruma had failed to crush the honor at the core of his victim's soul.

As they all sat down at the low table, and Salamander poured a round of wine while he thought over what to say, she realized something more: that, indeed, they had far more important things to discuss than what she might have done with another man back in Deverry or, for that matter, what Rhodry might have done here in Bardek with his lovely owner. She felt a cold ripple of dweomer-warning down her back. Finding Rhodry had so filled her mind and heart that she simply hadn't let herself see the danger. Here they were, hundreds of miles from home in a foreign land and faced with enemies who were both utterly corrupt and utterly ruthless. She doubted very much if those enemies were simply going to stand by and wave farewell while they took Rhodry home again. The same thought seemed to have occurred to Salamander.

"I hate to interrupt the touching reunion and all, but the sad and tedious fact remains that we're enmeshed in the worst toil, snare, danger, predicament, and so on and so forth, that any of us—and the Dark Sun herself knows we all have a penchant and taste for terrible trouble—have ever faced before. Sweet sentiment must hold its tongue—"

"And blather," Jill muttered.

"And blather, truly, will have to wait as well. Here, younger brother. We have the same father, but not the same mother. Do you remember yours?"

"I don't, not a scrap about our clan or my home—naught. What are we? A pair of bastards sired by some powerful man?"

"Well." Salamander paused to rub his chin. "In a manner of speaking, though among our father's clan no one cares about some tedious ceremony when it comes to claiming a child."

"Ah. He's the elf, then, not my mother."

"Oh ye gods! You've ferreted out a goodly lot of secrets, haven't you now? Scandal, indeed! Well, he is, at that, and a splendid bard among the Elcyion Lacar. The thing is, young brother of mine, no one but he, your mother, and the three of us know that he's your real father. There are most urgent and pressing reasons for keeping this particular secret, too."

"Her husband's still alive?"

"He's not, but dead, and you're now his legal heir. His only heir, most likely." He glanced at Jill. "I doubt me if Rhys is still alive. He was most cruelly injured in that fall."

At the mention of Rhys's name, Rhodry frowned a little.

"Do you remember him, my love?" Jill said.

"I don't, but the name sounds familiar somehow. Is he another brother?"

"He is, your mother's son by the man everyone thinks is your father."

"By the hells!" Rhodry laughed, one sharp bark. "What is this? I feel like I've wandered into one of those hedgerow mazes the High King has in his gardens . . . or here, have I been to the royal palace? I seem to remember a good bit about it."

"You should, because you were there quite often," Salamander said. "Your mother's husband, the man whose property you stand to inherit? He was Tingyr, Gwerbret Aberwyn. Remember what a gwerbret is?"

Aberwyn nearly lost her last heir right there and then. Rhodry choked on a mouthful of wine, nearly spat it out across the table, swallowed it barely in time, then coughed, turning bright red, while Salamander pounded him on the back in real concern. At last he stopped, and his color slowly returned to normal.

"Are you telling me that I'm Aberwyn?"

"Exactly that."

Still holding the wine cup he rose, stood dazed for a moment, then wandered over to the window, where he set the cup down and leaned onto the windowsill with both hands to look out. When Jill started after, Salamander caught her arm and motioned her to sit back down.

"Aberwyn needs you badly," the gerthddyn said. "By all dictates of honor, you're not truly her inheritor, but you're the only one she's got. If you abdicate, the fields and streets will run with blood."

"I know what happens when there's no heir for a rich rhan." He was a silent for a long moment. "But a lie's a lie."

"Rhodry!" Jill and Salamander both spoke at once.

With a shrug he turned around and leaned back on the sill, and his smile was a painful thing to see, filled with mockery and weariness.

"Listen to me, a cursed slave still, talking of honor. Ah ye gods, can't you understand? You can fill my head with all the fine words in the world, but I still don't know who I am."

"Don't you believe us?" Jill said.

"Of course I do! But it's only words. I don't truly remember one wretched thing. I don't *feel* who I am! Ye gods, try to understand that!"

"I will, my love, and my apologies."

With a toss of his head he left the window and sat back down, reaching out a hand to catch hers and squeeze it.

"You I know, Jill. And I remember exile and disgrace, and riding hungry and lying wounded, but now you tell me I'm a gwerbret—by the hells, not even a poor country lord or some landless courtier, but a gwerbret!"

"Umph, well." Salamander rubbed his chin again. "I can see where it would take a bit of getting used to, truly. But try, brother of mine. Oh by the love of every god, try, and take the blasted rhan, too, because if you don't, Death will sail into Aberwyn's harbor and ride her roads."

"True enough." Suddenly Rhodry looked close to tears. "And it's the common folk who'll suffer the worst, isn't it? When the lords take their sons for riders and trample down their crops and siege their cities, Oh truly, they'll suffer and starve and suffer again. Ah by the hells! I may be naught but a bastard born and now a slave, but cursed and twice-cursed if I'll let that happen!"

Jill frankly stared at him. Never had she heard him or any other noble lord admit such a thing; truly, for all his fine honor, she'd never seen Rhodry do anything that showed he cared one whit for the ordinary folk below him. He'd always been generous to beggars, of course, but because a noble lord was supposed to be generous, and he'd respected his fighting men more than most lords, but then, they were warriors and in his mind his equals. But the farmers, the craftsmen, the merchants, the priests even—they'd meant exactly as much to him as his horses, creatures to provide for when he could and use up when he couldn't.

"Is somewhat wrong?" Rhodry said.

"Naught. It's just been such a strange road to ride lately."

"Now that is true spoken with a vengeance." He turned to Salamander. "Here, elder brother, since you seem to know so much, how did I get to these blasted islands, anyway? All I remember is waking up in the hold of a ship in a Bardek port, and there was a man named Gwin who seemed to be my friend and a man named Baruma who was a demon-spawned enemy from the third hell. We traveled round for a bit, and then they sold me to a man named Brindemo in Myleton."

"That comely and erudite slave trader we have already met, and from him we heard some of your sad story." Salamander paused to frown into his wine cup. "Gwin, I know not, but Baruma—ah, Baruma! Jill first learned of him in the Bilge at Cerrmor, where, apparently, he had you knocked over the head and taken prisoner. Remember any of that?"

"Not a thing."

"And then they loaded you onto a ship and took you off to Slaith, a secret pirate haven in the Auddglyn. I doubt me if you remember that, either."

"I don't. By all the ice in all the hells, I don't even remember being in Cerrmor or why I went there in the first place."

"A wretched shame, too, because my curiosity's been pricking at me for weeks over that. At any rate, in Slaith you and your hideous captors took ship and sailed to Bardek, and somewhere along the way Baruma—I suspect at least that the most loathsome Baruma is responsible—ensorceled you and broke your memory into little shreds."

"I remember somewhat of that." Rhodry stood up with a convulsive, automatic shudder. "It wasn't pleasant."

"No doubt." Salamander's voice turned soft. "No doubt."

With a shake of his head Rhodry paced back to the window. Although Jill wanted to go to him, she doubted that he'd tolerate sympathy. Brooding on the pain Baruma had caused him made her rage swell and burn like fever in her blood.

"Ye gods!" Salamander hissed. "What is *that?*"

In the corner stood the wolf, quite solid-looking through glimmering, his tail wagging gently, his tongue lolling as he watched Jill's face, for all the world like a dog awaiting his master's next command. What surprised Jill the most, though, was that Rhodry could see him, too. He drew back, then shrugged and held out his hand. The wolf sniffed it, tail still at the wag, then looked at Jill again.

"Uh well," she said. "He's mine, actually. I uh, well, I don't quite know how I did it, but I sort of built him one night when I was doing my exercises."

"Well-built he is." Salamander sounded furious. "What did you feed him on, hatred and rage?"

"And why shouldn't I, after what's happened to Rhodry? I was thinking of vengeance, and the death-wolves of the Dark Sun, and—"

"I can see that, you idiot! What happened then?"

"Well, he seemed to . . . well . . . go off on his own."

"Truly on his own?" Salamander's voice held cold steel.

"Uh, well, I did sort of send him after Baruma."

At that name the wolf leapt out the window and disappeared. Salamander swore in several languages for a good long minute.

"My apologies, turtledove, because when the apprentice makes a truly ghastly mistake like this, it's the teacher's fault. Oh ye gods and all your nipples! What have I done?"

"What's so wrong?"

Salamander looked at her, started to speak several times, then merely shook his head.

"There are ethics in these things, turtledove, and you've just countered every one of them, to send a thing like that out into the world. You didn't know, mind—I blame myself, and I'll take whatever blame anyone else cares to lay on me—but it was an ill-done thing all the same. There are dangers, too, because Baruma has a blasted sight more power than you, and if he decides to follow the wolf back to its owner, well, he'll find us, good and proper."

At that Jill went cold all over. "Ethics" was a new and strange word to her, but danger she could understand. All at once Rhodry laughed, and for that moment he looked his old self, the berserker grin slashed into his face.

"Let him," Rhodry said. "Let him track us down—if he dares. When Baruma was about to sell me off, I swore him a vow, that someday I'd slit his throat for him. Here, Jill, can you forgive me? The bastard's got my silver dagger. He took it from me, and there was naught I could do about it."

"Forgive you? There's naught to forgive, but it aches my heart. Do you remember the man who gave it to you? Cullyn of Cerrmor? My father?"

"I don't, or wait—I think I do remember his face, and that I respected him more than any man I'd ever met. By the Lord of Hell's balls! Then I want that dagger back more than ever." His voice was so quiet that he might have been discussing the loan of a couple of coppers, but the smile was etched even deeper into his face. "I want it badly, I do, so let him come after us if he wants. I'll be waiting for him."

When Jill laughed with a crow of vengeance, Salamander looked back and forth between them, his eyes filled with misgiving and a touch of fear.

"You two make a fine pair, truly," the gerthddyn said at last. "And I certainly wouldn't wish either of you on some other hapless soul. The gods were provident when they brought you together."

Although all of them laughed, desperately trying to lighten the dark things they discussed, Jill felt oddly cold and weary at the jest. Of course we belong together, she told herself. I'll never leave my Rhodry again, never! And yet, deep in her heart, she wondered where the dweomer road would take her, wondered now, when it was far too late to turn back.

For some time, while the evening grew darker and the room filled with shadow, they talked, trying to piece together what had happened back in Deverry, just a few months ago for all that it seemed another century now. Talking grew harder and harder, because they were always coming up against horrible things, pain and torture and the dark dweomer itself—the worst perversion of all, truly, that someone would twist the workings of the Light into darkness and death. Finally they all fell silent, staring idly across the room, looking, it seemed, at anything rather than each other. Jill got up, started a taper burning at the charcoal brazier, then lit the oil lamps to give herself something to do, but she was close to tears, feeling that Rhodry had never been farther away from her. Yet after some moments of this queasy silence Salamander showed a tact that Jill had never suspected he possessed. He stood up, stretching in a lazy way, and announced that he was going to the tavern downstairs.

"And I think me I'm going to visit more than one tavern tonight. I don't like all these dark and dour warnings of evil dweomer all around us, but I don't dare scry, either. We shall see what eyes and ears can do, unaided by mighty magicks, to pick up news, rumors, and hints of peculiar people and sinister doings."

"Is that safe?" Rhodry said.

"It is, because I'm well-known, remember, and popular to boot, the famous and amusing wizard who's entertained the town on many a happy eve. Do you think these good folk would stand by and see me murdered or abducted? I shall gather a crowd about me wherever I go, and that will be a better shield than one any weaponer could make."

"You're right, truly," Jill said. "How long will you be gone?"

"Hours. If I'm not back at dawn, then come after me, but don't worry until then. We barbarian witch-sorcerers have been known to carouse all night."

Salamander grabbed the red cloak, lined with gold-colored satin, that matched his brocaded robes, and left with a courtly bow to them both. Jill shut the door behind him, then turned round to see Rhodry back at the window, his hands clutching the sill as he stared blindly out. For a moment she watched him in utter misery, as if he were an invalid, sick so badly and for so long that she could no longer tell if he'd recover or not. Finally he sighed and turned to face her. The silence flowed around them like water, deep and threatening.

"I don't know what to say," Jill burst out at last.

"No more do I. Ah by the hells, I've listened to enough stinking words for one evening anyway."

When he caught her by the shoulders and kissed her, she felt the distance between them close. No matter what had happened to his mind, his body remembered her, and hers recognized him, too, whether or not her mind considered him changed. As long as she was wrapped in his arms, she could pretend that nothing had ever gone wrong, and from the desperate way he made love to her, she knew that he was pretending, too.

In the morning they woke to the sound of Salamander bustling round and throwing things into saddlebags and mule packs. Although he was singing under his breath as he worked, the tune was off-key and nervous to boot. When they came out of their chamber, he greeted them with an imperious waggle of his hand.

"We'll eat on the road," he announced. "I want to get out of this town now, before our lovely Alaena changes her mind, or our enemies decide to cause trouble of some sort."

"Will we be safe on the road?" Jill said.

"Of course we won't, but then, we won't be safe here, either, so we might as well travel and see more of the glorious islands. Don't throw that lamp at me, Jill my turtledove! A mere jest, that's all. Actually I have a plan in mind, most cunning and devious. We've got to set

Rhodry free sooner or later, and that's no simple matter. There are depositions to be sworn in front of priests, and a statement to be recorded by a city scribe, and so on and so forth. In the very center of this island is a high plateau, and in the center of that is a city, the beauteous and renowned Pastedion, and in the center of that is a particularly splendid temple of Dalae-oh-Contremo, the Wave-father, he who protects unjustly treated slaves. We shall go there, beg for sanctuary, and lay a formal, legal complaint against our Baruma—for selling a free barbarian on false pretenses. The archons will be duty-bound to investigate, and while they carry out their ponderous workings, we shall be reasonably safe. Who knows? If they can find Baruma, they might even drag him into court."

"Oh might they now?" Jill said. "So these archons are good for somewhat, are they?"

"You shall see, my petite partridge, the advantages of civilized life. We'll have a strong case, because I have the original bill of sale, which looks forged, at least to my elven eyes. When we visited the lovely Brindemo in his private chambers? I saw it on the writing table in the corner, and I snagged it while you were talking to his son—the bill of sale, that is, not the writing table, which was a bit large for even an accomplished wizard to conceal."

"Civilized life indeed!"

"One small thing," Rhodry broke in, and he wasn't smiling. "I swore I'd slit his throat, and that's one vow I'll hold to even if it kills me. Do you understand? Gwerbret or not, I won't leave Bardek until I watch him die, and if the archon's men torture me to death for it, well, that's a price I've vowed to pay."

The silence in the room was profound. Finally Salamander sighed.

"You know, beloved younger brother of mine, you might well get your chance to kill him long before we reach Pastedion, if our wretched rotten luck runs true to form and our enemies catch us on the road. If not, we'll worry about reaching safety first and murdering Baruma second. Agreed?"

Rhodry did smile, then, a bitter, ugly twist of his mouth, but he said nothing. Jill decide that there was no use arguing with him, at least not at the moment.

"We'd best take a roundabout way to this place," she said. "The longer we pretend to be traveling wizards, the better."

"You are correct, my owlet. We'll head back to the coast first and perform our wonders in the harbor towns to the north. You know, I think I'm getting a feel for the wizard business. I keep getting all sorts of new ideas for the show."

The great wizard and his newly augmented crew were a full day gone by the time the news finally reached the Wylinth market place: the widow Alaena had sold her handsome barbarian slave to Krysello for his traveling show, and on one of her sudden whims, too. The conventional wisdom said that he must have offered her a tremendous amount of money, which confirmed everyone's suspicions that the performer was as rich as an archon. The local gossips were outraged, seeing their delicious scandal gone all sour; surely Alaena wouldn't have sold him if, as rumored, she'd been having an affair with the boy. For reasons of their own, of course, Gwin and Pirrallo were equally annoyed when they heard the news.

"Too bad you took your time," Gwin said with a less than pleasant smile. "If you'd only been willing to make your move as soon as I found him, we could have just bought him ourselves."

"Hold your ugly tongue! We'll catch up with them on the road, that's all, and if this stupid juggler won't sell peacefully, then he'll die."

"Oh? And I suppose you can tell me which way they went, then."

Pirrallo started to speak, then drew himself up to full height.

"Of course! But I need privacy to work. Don't you or the others come near me till I'm done."

Gwin watched him stride off in a huff and wondered why he was so sure that Pirrallo was going to lead them in the wrong direction. He wondered even more why he was pleased.

Deverry and Bardek

WINTER, 1063

OTID EIRY, GWYN GOROR MYNYDD;

LLWYM GWYDD LLONG AR FOR.

MECID LLWFR LLAWER CYNGOR.

SNOW SHROUDS WHITE MOUNTAIN PEAKS;

MASTS STAND NAKED ON SEAGOING SHIPS;

A COWARD MULLS MANY CONNIVINGS.

Llywarch the Ancestor

Outside Gwerbret Blaen's great hall the dark sky let down thick ropes of snow, swaying in the wind. Inside a thousand candles winked light off silver goblets and jeweled table daggers, the two enormous hearths roared with flame, and laughter and talk whistled round the enormous room like the wind outside. Nearly a hundred lords and ladies feasted at tables set as close to the gwerbret's as room would allow, while on the far side of the hall their escorts and Blaen's own warband dined on the same fine fare. It was the shortest day of the year, and while it was no true holiday, not like Samaen or Beltane, Blaen always held a grand feast in the sun's honor, simply because his father always had. He in turn had gotten the idea from his wife, Graeca, Lovyan's sister; as lasses the women had lived on the Eldidd border, where men had picked up a number of strange customs from the people they called the Westfolk.

Every now and then he looked over to his right, where his wife headed up a table of her own. Since by then Canyffa's pregnancy was showing noticeably, he worried about her overtiring herself, but she was chatting with her guests and laughing like a lass, very much at her ease and apparently surprised at how well everything was going, just as if she hadn't spent frantic days planning every detail of the feast with the chamberlain, steward, and head cook. To make sure that the drink was as good as the meat, Canyffa had hired a temporary servitor, too, Twdilla the alemaker. Two days before the feast, the snow had suddenly stopped, much to everyone's surprise, and Twdilla and her husband had triumphantly driven their wagonload of barrels into town.

At the moment, over in the curve of the wall by the riders' hearth, Twdilla presided over several of those by-now nicely settled barrels, dipping out tankard after tankard full for the serving lasses to pass around. Since Blaen very badly wanted a word with her, he mentally cursed the finely woven web of noble privilege that kept him over on his side of the great hall, but curse or not, he was forced to wait. After the honeycake and the last of the year's apples were served, the bard played, presenting his newly composed declamation in Blaen's honor while the guests were still overfed into quiet, then switching to the well-known tale of King Bran's founding of the Holy City when they began to chatter, and finally giving up poetry altogether as the talk rose high. With a wave of his arm, he brought in another harper, a horn player, and an apprentice with a small, squishy goat-skin drum. When they began playing, servants and noble-born alike rushed to shove the tables back against the wall to clear the space for dancing.

In this confusion Blaen could finally slip away from his guests and find the ale mistress. She was supervising a group of pages as they brought in another barrel on a wheeled handcart.

"Don't joggle it so, lads!" she was saying. "It's barely had time to calm down after its trip here. Careful, careful now!"

Blaen had to wait until the full barrel was standing safely near its empty fellows, and Veddyn had appeared to open it and take his wife's post for a little while. Together the gwerbret and the dweomermaster walked down the back corridor that curved round the great hall until they found a private if draughty niche. Although Twdilla had grabbed her shabby old cloak as they left, Blaen merely shivered and ignored the cold by force of will.

"Is there any news, good dame?"

"None from Bardek, and there won't be any till spring, Your Grace. But Nevyn says that things are . . . well, restless in Eldidd."

"No doubt. Ye gods, I wish I knew if Rhodry were alive!"

"Your Grace, I believe with all my heart that Nevyn would know if Rhodry were dead. So, for that matter, does Nevyn." She gave him a reassuring, if half-toothless, smile. "The question is, will he stay that way when our Jill brings him home in the spring? We may know Rhodry's alive, but most of Eldidd's got him buried already. The men who want his rhan are spending a lot of coin and calling in wagonloads of favors to further their schemes. How are they going to take it when the rightful heir blithely rides in to claim what's his?"

"Badly, no doubt, the weaseling bandits! What shall I do, ride to Eldidd as soon as the weather breaks?"

"It might be best, Your Grace, but then, it might also be far too early. Who knows when they'll come back across the Southern Sea? I hate to ask you to leave your own affairs only to wait upon your cousin's."

"Well, if Rhodry's inheritance were the only thing at stake, I might grumble, but it's not. Look, if Eldidd goes up in open war, the High King will be forced to intervene. What if our liege were slain or wounded or suchlike? Or what if the war drags on for years and starts bleeding him white? I'm the King's man first and always, good dame. Allow me to put myself and my men at your disposal."

"We'd all be ever so grateful if you did, Your Grace." She made him a remarkably graceful curtsey. "And Lord Madoc would be pleased if you stopped and had a bit of a chat with him, since Dun Deverry's more or less on your way and all."

"A bit less than more, but he'll see me as soon as the roads are passable anyway." Blaen paused, struck by a sudden thought. "I had hoped to be here when my lady came to her time."

"Oh, you will be, Your Grace. The son she's carrying will be born a few weeks early, but he'll be healthy in spite of it, and she'll have an easy time because he'll be on the small side."

"Well, splendid! I . . . here, how do you know . . . are you having a jest on me?"

"Not in the least, Your Grace. I was worried about the Lady Canyffa myself, so I asked the Wildfolk. They know these things—I don't know how—but they do. Trust me."

And in spite of himself, Blaen had to admit that trust her he did.

· · ·

There was a different sort of feast held that day as well, all the way across the kingdom in Eldidd and right up at the northern border of Rhodry's gwerbretrhyn in the holdings of the powerful Bear clan. Tieryn Darryl of Trenrydd was sitting down to table with two close and trusted friends, Gwarryc of Dun Gamyl, who was the younger brother of Gwerbret Savyl of Camynwaen, and Talidd of Belglaedd, and with them was a man from Bardek who'd given his name as Alyantano but who was willing to be known as Alyan here in Deverry, to make things easier all round. So important was the conversation at this dinner that Darryl's wife Amma was entertaining the other women privately up in the women's hall. Since Talidd's wife had stayed at home, and Alyan claimed to have none, Amma was presiding over an intimate meal indeed, for herself, her serving women, and Vodda, Gwarryc's wife, who was her elder sister. A sleek blonde, Vodda was one of those sleepy-eyed women who cultivate an air of sensual stupidity to cover a roiling mind. She was one of the chief organizers of the faction that was pushing her husband into making a bid for Aberwyn, but to pay her her due, her motives went far beyond some petty wish to spend its taxes on Bardek silk. Their mother, Linedd, had once led a miserable life creeping through Dun Aberwyn's corridors and chambers as the often-ignored mistress of Gwerbret Tingyr and the overmatched rival of Lady Lovyan. Although Linedd was dead—unkind wags joked that she'd died to get away from the lord and the wife equally—the sisters remembered their days in the court very well indeed.

"Lovyan was always so kind," Vodda remarked as the roast haunch of boar was served. "I think that was the worst thing of all, her kindness."

"Especially after Mam died." Amma picked up a long-bladed dagger and flipped it point upward. "Shall I carve?"

When the rest of the boar appeared at the men's table, the chamberlain sliced up a platterful and served it round, then retired to head up his own table for the noble-born servitors some distance away. The men at Lord Darryl's table ate grimly, barely tasting their food, as they went on talking.

"The thing is," Darryl said. "We'll never raise enough riders to take Aberwyn. There aren't enough men or horses here in the north."

"*If* things come to war," Talidd interposed, and he could hear how nervous he sounded, even to himself.

"Well, of course, if." Darryl shot him a grin and wiped his mustaches on the back of his hand. "What's wrong, Tal? You're the one who broke this stag out of cover. Getting worried now that the hunt is up?"

"I never thought we'd be arming a pack of cursed farmers to do our fighting for us." Talidd shot a murderous glance at Alyan, whose eyes went blank and bland in return. "I don't like this."

"My lords." Alyan rose, towering over them, his dark skin glinting bluish in the firelight. "I'm only one of the Bear clan's servitors, not one of the noble-born. Let me leave you to discuss this in private."

Darryl hesitated, then motioned for a servant to carry the Bardekian's trencher and goblet to the chamberlain's table.

"Satisfied, Talidd?" Gwarryc said, sniffing a little. He had a bad cold, and his pale gray eyes and his long rabbit's nose were both more than a little moist.

"Darro, I didn't mean to insult your man, but I meant what I said. I don't like this idea of arming a pack of rabble with pikes and teaching them to fight like the cursed islanders."

"Well, what other hope of winning do we have? You're not having a lot of luck getting us allies in the south."

"True enough, but it's early yet, early. Once the autumn's here, and there's no gwerbret in Aberwyn, then we'll see men coming over to us."

"Maybe so," Gwarryc snuffled. "But here, Tal, don't look so grieved. If I'm the only serious candidate, it's likely the Council of Electors will settle the matter nice and peacefully."

"The Council has every right to turn you down and call for other candidates."

"And will you accept the Council's vote, then," Darryl snapped. "If it goes against us?"

"I will, and I'd advise you, my friend, to do so, too. I know how much getting that territory means to you, but . . ."

"The gwerbrets hold it unjustly!" Darryl slammed his fist onto the table and made the tankards jump.

"And they have for hundreds of years," Talidd said. "So it won't shatter your clan's honor if they keep it a few more."

"Indeed? I don't hear you being so reasonable about Dun Bruddlyn." Talidd felt his face flush hot, but he kept himself under control.

"I intend to abide by the Electors' vote even if it costs me what should have been mine."

"All because of my pikemen, eh?"

Rather than answer, Talidd let out his breath in a sharp puff and had a long pull from his tankard to settle his nerves. Gwarryc blew his nose heavily into a scrap of rag.

"What I don't understand," the would-be gwerbret said, "is why we're squabbling like this. It seems to have come on suddenly, like this cursed catarrh."

"True spoken," Talidd said. "My apologies, Darro. Lately I've been as jumpy as a cat by a pitch-pine fire."

"So have I." Darryl considered the problem with a slight frown. "And my apologies to you, Tal."

"There's no use in fighting over hiring a jockey until we're sure we've got a horse race," Gwarryc went on. "I know you're both keen on seeing me in the gwerbretal chair, and my wife talks of little else these days, but I'm not convinced Rhodry Maelwaedd is dead."

"He's dead, sure enough." Darryl spoke with a quiet conviction, and his eyes strayed to the other table, where Alyan was joking with the bard. "Before he left Bardek, Alyan heard the story. Rhodry offended some powerful man in the islands, and over there, they have ways of eliminating people who offend them. There's some sort of paid guild, or so I understand."

"Bloody barbarians," Talidd muttered.

"Maybe so, but useful at times," Darryl said. "Anyway, Rhodry's death is why Alyan came here in the first place. The story of what happened to the Maelwaedd was common gossip on his island. When his enemies at home got Alyan exiled, he came to Aberwyn because he figured there'd be a lord or two who might need a proper military man's services. He had old connections there, too, and one of the merchants put him on to me as a favor, like, to both of us."

"Proper military man, indeed! Common-born men sticking the noble-born like pigs, and you call that proper?"

"Hold your tongues!" There was an impressive snap of command in Gwarryc's voice. "Naught's going to happen for months, anyway. Whether Rhodry's alive or dead, the King's decree said he had a year and a day to come claim his inheritance, and until then, the Council can't even begin meeting."

"And he had his gall, truly, the King I mean, interfering with the Council." Darryl's eyes turned dark. "Hundreds of years that treaty goes back, saying the King had better keep his greedy paws off the doings of the Council. Huh, it's galling all round, how many laws get bent for the wretched Maelwaedds. The High King always favors them."

Although Talidd couldn't think of another such incident more recent than ninety-odd years previous, he held his tongue. Once Darryl got to brooding on his clan's ancient wrongs, there was no reasoning with him. That night, as they drank silently together, Talidd felt an ugly truth pushing itself into his reluctant mind. When he'd gone scurrying around, testing feeling against the Maelwaedds just because he was so furious over the apportioning of Dun Bruddlyn, he'd raised a lot more dust than he'd intended, enough, perhaps, to choke them all.

He found himself watching Alyan, too, with his polished manners, easy way with a jest, and complete lack of airs, and wondered why the man rubbed him so raw. The Bardekian had commanded regiments back in his own country, but he knew that he was a hired drillmaster now and naught more, existing, as so many exiles had before him, on the charity of a noble lord who had some use for him. Even when it came to training pikemen, Talidd had to admit that Darryl was hardly the first desperate lord who'd swelled his ranks with spearmen when there weren't enough riders to carry his cause. When the emergencies passed, the spearmen always seemed to disband and the noble-born to revert to the traditional and honorable way of carrying out their feuds, face-to-face on horseback.

Yet, despite all these reasonable thoughts, deep in his heart Talidd despised Alyan. That night something else occurred to him. Maybe Alyan would have heard about Rhodry's death through some kind of ordinary channel since they were both in Bardek at the time. But how had he known, so far away and so late in the sailing season, that Rhodry's brother Rhys had died without an heir? Yet, Talidd's honor stopped him from following the thought down. As Darryl said, he was the one who'd flushed this stag, and he'd sworn to his friends that he'd support them in their chase after it, and that, as far as he was concerned, was an end to it.

.   .   .

As regent of Aberwyn, as well as ruler of her own large demesne, Tieryn Lovyan had more to worry about than just her missing son. It seemed to Tevylla, whenever she saw her lady for a few minutes here and there, that the streaks of gray in the tieryn's hair were getting larger and the wrinkles round her eyes deepening. Yet, harried as she was, Lovyan always had a pleasant word for the nursemaid when she saw her, and she always managed to look in on her granddaughter for some minutes every day. In fact, her brief times with Rhodda seemed to refresh the tieryn, who was not above hiking her skirts, sitting down right on the floor, and playing blocks or dolls with the child until a frantic servitor or page came rushing in with some new crisis.

Since back home in Dun Gwerbyn Rhodda had spent several hours a day with her beloved Granna, the child naturally resented the new order of things. After Lovyan had been dragged away from one of their times together, Rhodda would howl and rage for nearly an hour no matter what Tevylla did to calm her. She was beginning to wonder if something were wrong with the child—not that she was simple or half-witted, far from it. Even though she was only three, she spoke beautifully and knew as many words as an ordinary child of six or seven; in fact, she seemed to have a greedy appetite for words and was always badgering the bards and the scribes by asking what such and such a term meant and how she should use it. But along with all this precocious intellect came odd rages, and odder melancholy sulks, and times when she would tear off all her clothes, sob piteously, and say that she wanted to go live in the woods with the Wildfolk.

Tempers like that drove Tevylla to distraction, but she found that she had an unexpected ally in Nevyn. Not only did he give her good advice about handling the moods, he began taking the child for a walk at least once a day—just to talk about things, he said. Since Rhodda loved to go with him, Tevylla could hand over her difficult charge and get an hour or so alone with a clear conscience.

"I must admit I'm surprised, my lord," Tevylla said to him one morning. "I thought a learned councillor like you would be above such things."

"Oh the child has a fine mind. Her company's very pleasant after hours spent with noble-born lords."

He looked so sly at his joke that Tevylla had to giggle.

"We're going to see the gnomes today," Rhodda announced.

"Are you, dear? How lovely." Tevylla assumed that the child and the old man had some elaborate game going. "Well, while you're doing that, I'm going to go see Cook, and we'll have a gossip."

To get to the kitchen hut, Tevylla cut through the great hall, and as she happened to be passing the captain's table, a young lad, slouching at the end of the bench, caught her arm with an ale-damp hand.

"You're a good-looking woman, aren't you? How come you keep hiding away in the women's hall?"

Before Tevylla could reply or pull away, Cullyn was on his feet and moving, hitting the rider so hard across the face that tears sprang to his eyes.

"Hold your tongue, Lwc." The captain's voice was low and perfectly steady. "You're speaking to a widow and the mother of a son."

Lwc flinched back, one hand pressed over his swelling cheek, his eyes fixed in doglike apology on Tevylla's face. Cullyn made her a bow.

"My apologies. None of my cubs will dare say one wrong word to you again."

"No doubt." Tevylla dropped him a curtsey. "My thanks, captain."

As she hurried to the door, she saw two of the serving lasses watching Cullyn with undisguised longing from among the ale barrels. Since both pretty blonde Nonna and pinched-face Degwa were young enough to be his daughters, she stopped for a word with them.

"I wouldn't be staring at the warband if I were you. I'd be going about my work before someone told Cook that you were hunting dangerous game."

"Oh please, Mistress Tevva, don't tell her." Nonna put on her best winsome expression. "You've got to admit that the captain's just absolutely splendid. Look at how he defended you."

"Frankly, he rather frightens me, and he's far too old for you. Now get back to the cookhouse and leave the warband alone."

When she reached the kitchen, she told the cook straightaway about the lasses. Baena too had noticed their infatuation with the captain.

"I've spoken to the little sluts about it. I suppose it's better him than one of his young louts. Cullyn's a decent man around women, and if it was one of the warband they were after, they'd have big bellies already."

"So you think the captain's a decent man?"

"I do. Don't you?"

"I'm not sure. Here I've been spending time with him almost every day for months, and I feel I hardly know him. On sunny days when Rhodda and I go out, he comes along with us, but you know, he rarely says two words together, unless he's got news of my son to give me. Or sometimes when we've left the women's quarters he'll just pop up, like, to make sure we're all right. He moves so quietly for a big man that he can truly scare you when you're not expecting him."

"I can believe that well enough. What does the child think of him?"

"Now that's one good thing. She doesn't throw her tempers when the captain's around, I tell you. She'll start to fuss, but he'll give her one of his dark looks, and she's as quiet as quiet again. And yet she never minds him coming along with us."

"Well, he raised a daughter on his own, you know. His wife died very young, or so I heard the tale."

"Truly? Now that's a surprise! I wouldn't have thought he was that kind of a man at all. Is his lass married now?"

"It's Cullyn's daughter that's off with young Rhodry."

"Oh! I hadn't realized that."

"It's true, and I don't know how the poor little lass manages, riding all over the kingdom like that."

"It would be awful, sure enough. I do hope the King finds the lad soon, though. Our poor Lady Lovyan is eating herself away with worry."

"Well, so she is. Rhodry's always been a spoiled little beast, if you ask me. Look at him, seducing Rhodda's mother first and then poor Jill! But truly, I'd rather have him in the gwerbret's chair than some interloper who isn't even a Maelwaedd. My mother was head cook here in Aberwyn before me, and her mother before her, and we've always served the Maelwaedds. I wouldn't like to see some other clan come in here. What if they were mingy, like, or nasty tempered? You just never know with the noble-born."

About an hour later, Nevyn turned up at the door of the kitchen hut with Rhodda and the captain both trailing after.

"I've got to go attend upon the tieryn, Tevva," the old man said. "But Rhodda's nowhere near ready for her nap yet."

"We'll have a bit of a walk, then. I see our bodyguard's with you."

Cullyn shot her a wry smile. She was surprised at herself, realizing just how much difference the cook's news had made. Somehow knowing that the captain had a daughter made him seem like a human being. And what did I think he was before? she asked herself in some annoyance. A fiend from Hell?

As they made their way to the garden, they collected the equerry's four-year-old son, a leather ball, and a pair of curved sticks that would do for a pretend hurley game. As the children ran around and swatted at the ball, Tevylla and Cullyn perched on the low brick wall and watched. Although the lawn was still green that time of year, it had a sad, thin look, and the western breeze made Tevylla shiver inside her wool cloak. When she looked off to the south, she could see dark clouds massing on the horizon for an assault on the dun.

"The kitchen gardener was telling me that he thinks we're going to get a bad frost tonight," Tevylla said. "Or maybe even a bit of snow. He says the omens are right for it."

"Are they now? That'll be a cursed nuisance." All at once he laughed. "Listen to me. I've gotten soft and spoiled, living on the coast again. The few dribbles of snow we have down here are naught in a place like Cerrgonney."

"So I've heard. You truly did travel all over before you took the tieryn's service, didn't you?"

"Oh, a fair bit."

Suddenly he was silent again, staring absently across the lawn with eyes that seemed to see another view entirely.

"Did I offend you? My apologies."

"What?" He turned, his lips twitching in the gesture that did him for a smile. "You didn't, at that. I was just remembering the long road, and being cursed glad I was off it."

"I see. You must be worried about Jill now."

"I was worried from the wretched day she rode off with our young lord, but what could I do? She was always too headstrong for me to handle." This time he gave her a proper grin. "Know what my woman used to say? Jill was as stubborn as I was and twice as nasty when she wanted to be."

They shared a quiet laugh, but Tevylla felt suddenly sad, thinking of her husband, dead these long years now. At moments like these it seemed more odd than painful that at thirty, when most women were thinking of making a match for their eldest daughter, she had nothing left but one son, and him gone from her into the male world of a warband. Back when she'd been the miller's pretty daughter, life had seemed to offer so much more than the scraps it had finally thrown her way.

"Somewhat wrong?" Cullyn said abruptly.

"Oh, just thinking of my man."

"What did he die of, anyway? If you don't mind me asking."

"A fever in the blood. He stepped on a nail out in the stables, and not even Nevyn could save him."

"My wife died of a fever, too. I was riding a war, miles away, and I couldn't even be there with her."

The old pain in his voice was like the scar on his face, healed, maybe, but the blatant memento of a wound. Impulsively she laid her hand over his.

"I'm so sorry."

"So was I."

Just then, predictably enough for him, the equerry's boy fell flat on his face and began to howl. By the time she had him settled down, it was cold enough to drive them all indoors. Although it never did snow, the rainstorm dragged on and on, and they had no more walks with the captain for some days.

Out of custom more than necessity, Dun Aberwyn set a watch every night, four rotations of two men each at the locked gates and four of a dozen up on the ramparts. It would have surprised these loyal men, however, to know that another watch, and a strange one, went on at the same time up in the tower suite that Nevyn shared with Elaeno. Every sunset, when the tide of the element of Water began to flow on the astral, and at midnight, when that gave way to Earth, and again at dawn, when the Aethyr burgeoned, the two dweomermen made a magical sphere of blue light all round the dun and set it with seals in the shape of flaming pentagrams. During the day they could rest, because the tides of Fire and Air are so inimical to the dark dweomer that even its greatest masters rarely buck them. All that autumn their watch had held, but even now that winter had arrived in earnest, Nevyn saw no reason to relax it.

"I can't believe our enemies have simply fled the field after one miserable battle," he remarked one night.

"No more can I," Elaeno said. "They're trying to lull us to sleep, more like. Someone ensorceled that stable lad and set him on Rhodry's daughter, and it wasn't any flyaway spirit, either."

"Just so. But I've searched all over the blasted astral, and I know you have, too, and neither of us have found a trace of dweomer-work."

"They're lying low, that's all. When they think we've given up looking, they'll pounce."

"In the meantime they've got to be living somewhere, curse them! I've had the regent send messages to her loyal men, asking them to keep an eye out for any suspicious strangers, but our enemies aren't going to just ride into town and announce they're setting up a dark dweomer shop."

Elaeno managed a laugh at that.

"Curses for sale!" he intoned like a street vendor. "Come buy our nice hot love potions! Curses for sale! But truly, the local lords don't have the necessary eyes to ferret out our nasty little friends. We make better arrangements for this sort of thing back home, I must say. Oh, that reminds me. I think I'll pay a visit to the shipmasters' guild tomorrow. They may know if any of my countrymen have taken up residence in Aberwyn lately."

"There's no reason that our enemies have to be Bardek men."

"I know, but we've got to start somewhere, don't we?"

There was no arguing with that. In the middle of the morrow morning, once the tide of Fire was running clean and strong enough to baffle any dark dweomermen, Elaeno left the dun on his errand. While he waited for him to return, Nevyn went to see his patient-cum-prisoner up in the tower.

By then Perryn was much recovered, though far from well. In those days, treating a consumption of the lungs was a tricky business. Nevyn was having him spend all day in bed and most of the night lying wrapped in fur rugs on the roof, where he could breathe the icy air in an attempt to strengthen his lungs. Although the cure was working splendidly, thanks in part to Perryn's unnaturally high vitality, still Nevyn was keeping a close watch on him. He was also too afraid of setbacks to risk any more magical attempts to discover the man's true nature. That particular afternoon, when Nevyn entered his chamber, the first thing Perryn did was complain about being restless.

"I just can't sleep any more, my lord. It's being inside all the time like this. I'm going to go daft in here, truly I am."

"Better daft than dead, lad. I've seen cases of consumption that seemed cured for weeks, only to flare up again as soon as the patient overdid it."

Perryn sighed and flopped back against his pile of pillows to stare miserably at the ceiling.

"Er, ah, well, there's somewhat I've been wondering, truly. Why are you working so hard to save me if I'm only going to hang? Or do I have to get well just so Cullyn of Cerrmor can cut me into pieces? I won't have a chance in combat whether I'm well or ill, so he might as well do his slicing right now."

"Oh come now, don't be morbid!"

"Morbid, is it? You're the one who had me caught and locked up in here."

"Well, so I did. But the more I study you, the more I'm sure you're not a criminal—at least as far as Jill's concerned. On the other hand, you really should have known better when it came to all those horses. Stealing is wrong."

"That's what Jill always said, too." Perryn looked utterly confused. "But um, well, er, she never could explain why."

"Indeed? Well, there's lots of reasons, but consider this one, lad. When you steal a horse from someone, you may be taking away a thing they may truly need someday."

"But I only took them from lords who had lots."

"Just so, but how do you know what the future and their Wyrd might bring them? The day might come when the horse you took would be the last left to them, and they might die in battle from its lack, and that death might set off some vast and subtle chain of events beyond anyone's control. Now I admit, this all must sound very farfetched, but you never know. That's the crux of it: you never know."

Perryn looked profoundly unconvinced.

"Well, then, here's an example that should lie close to your heart.

Consider Jill and Rhodry. When you took her away, you didn't even know that Rhodry was Aberwyn's heir, did you? If he hadn't been following you and Jill all over the wretched Cerrgonney wilderness, his enemies would have had a hard time kidnapping him. Come to think of it, Jill might have been able to stop them. She has dweomer, so the Wildfolk would have warned her, or she would have felt danger on her own. In either case she could have called for help—from me, or Salamander, or simply from your uncle or another local lord."

Perryn sat straight up in bed, and his face turned pale.

"My lord, I hear the guards talking. They say there could be a war because Rhodry's gone."

"They're quite right."

"But the noble-born fight on horseback in this part of the kingdom. If there's a war, horses are going to be killed in droves."

"And men, too, I might add."

Perryn seemed deaf to Nevyn's qualification. He was staring off into space, and his eyes were filled with tears.

"All those horses," he whispered. "Ah ye gods, I'm sorry!"

"Are you? Then I suggest you think about what I've said."

It was well after the noon meal that Elaeno came back from his trip to the guildhall. Nevyn had just returned Rhodda to the women's hall after their daily walk when Elaeno met him on the stairs. The Bardekian's face was grim indeed.

"We've got to talk privately."

"You've got news, do you?"

"Of a sort. Very much of a sort."

They went into Nevyn's tower room, and although Nevyn settled himself in the cushioned chair in the window, Elaeno paced restlessly round and round as he talked.

"A man who was calling himself Alyantano and claiming to come from Orystinna passed through Aberwyn and the guild a couple of months ago. By asking a lot of questions I finally figured out who he really is. Now he's never been associated with the dark dweomer in any true sense, but he's as rotten as a beached hull nonetheless. He comes from the city of Naralion, his real name is Lerranno, and he's known as the Butcher of Vulture Pass."

"A lovely title, sure enough. How did he get it?"

"Well, he was an officer in command of a couple of regiments on what should have been a routine exercise — oh, about a year ago now, I think it was. Since I only heard the general gossip, I'm not sure of all the details. The upshot, though, was that he ordered a hundred citizen recruits across a rope bridge after he'd been warned it was unsafe. The bridge pulled free, the men all died, and he was — let me see, you don't quite have the words for these terms in Deverry, but he was tried in a special kind of malover by other army officers and found guilty of all sorts of criminal charges. Although some of the judges pressed for death, he ended up being exiled."

"And he's here now?"

"He is, and when he arrived in Aberwyn, he had an awful lot of hard coin for an exile. I'm wondering if someone gave it to him, like, to do a bit of work for them. He's in a certain Lord Darryl's service at the moment."

"Not Darryl of Trenrydd?"

"The very one."

"What does he want an exiled Bardekian general for?"

"Well, a couple of the men down at the guild seemed to think he was planning on forming an army of common-born pikemen if things came to war. It would make sense."

"So it would, but an ugly thing it would be. I wonder if that kind of army would be more or less effective against the usual warband?"

Elaeno shrugged and turned both hands palm-upward.

"A rhetorical question only, my friend." Nevyn said, grinning. "I don't know much more about warfare than you do. I'll have a word with Cullyn, I think."

When Nevyn put the question to him, the captain had a ready answer.

"Oh, the pikemen would be effective enough if they were properly disciplined. Now I've never been in Bardek myself, my lord, but from what I've heard, their spearmen drill for months before they ever see a battlefield. They carry these big curved shields, shaped like the side of a leather bottle, you see, longer than they're wide, and they march in tight formation, so they make a kind of wall across the battlefield. Now, as long as they hold their position, it's going to be cursed hard for a cavalry charge to break them, and that's where the drill comes in. Your average Deverry townsman's going to turn and run when the horses start coming, but not your Bardek professional."

"I see. What about when the javelins start flying?"

"I've heard about that, too. They don't use the war darts in Bardek, but they do have archers and sometimes slingers. So when the missiles come raining down, the men in the second row raise and tip their shields forward to cover part of themselves and the lads in the front, and so on all the way back in the formation. That way the shield wall's still solid, and as long as the men have the strength to hold their cover up, well, now, it's a fair hard line to break. They call it making a turtle."

"Ah. I suppose elven archers would stand a good chance against them, though."

"I doubt that, my lord. I doubt that very much, even with their longbows."

The dweomer-warning rippled down Nevyn's back like a shower of snow. It startled him so much that he missed Cullyn's next remark completely and had to apologize.

"What was that again?"

"I was just saying that if you want to use pikemen you've got to give them good equipment. Cheap shields made of raw hides won't turn steel blades. I wonder if Darryl of Trenrydd has the coin or the craftsmen to outfit enough Bardek-style pikemen to make any kind of difference."

"I don't know. I have the wretched feeling, though, that he intends us to find out if Rhodry doesn't get home soon."

"Just so." Cullyn's eyes turned oddly blank, as if he were bored with the subject, but Nevyn knew him well enough to know that he was covering some deep feeling. "I don't suppose there's been any news from Bardek."

"I'm afraid not. Even the dweomer has its limits, my friend, and we won't be hearing from Bardek till the spring. I only pray that Jill and Rhodry are unharmed."

"So do I. All the time, my lord, all the time."

After he left the captain, Nevyn considered that odd warning that had come to him—out of nowhere, he would have said, except for one small thing: dweomer-warnings never come out of a simple nowhere. Since they'd been talking of the elves and elven warfare at that precise moment, Nevyn could be fairly certain that the warning related to the affairs of that alien race. Precisely how was beyond him, but then, the Wyrd of the Elcyion Lacar lay out of his province. That very night he contacted his old pupil, Aderyn, through the fire and handed the problem over to him.

"I'm not certain of its meaning." Aderyn's image was grim as it floated above the flames. "But I have an idea. I'm coming to Eldidd."

"Well and good, then. When will you arrive?"

"Not for weeks, I'm afraid. We're a long way to the west at the moment, but I'll leave with the morrow dawn."

For several weeks the Great Krysello, King of the Cryptic, and his Mind-Boggling Brace of Bizarre Barbarians had traveled along the northeast coast of Surtinna, giving single shows in the villages and staying for a couple of nights in the towns, until at last they reached the city of Pardidion, lying on a narrow strip of plain between the ocean and the mountains. Since it was one of the richest merchant states on the east side of the island, they had a splendid run of three nights in the marketplace as well as a performance at a private party given by the archon himself.

"But all splendors must fade, and all suns sink in the west, alas and more's the pity," Salamander said. "I think we've played the fool enough for now. It's time to turn our faces toward the beauteous Pastedion."

"Cursed well about time if you ask me," Jill snapped. "How do we get there?"

"There's a caravan road, actually, which is why we came here in the first place. Colonists from Pardidion settled Pastedion, you see, some years back, and they trade all the time. There are some smaller towns along the road, too, which should come in handy for the sheltering of wizards."

As soon as the city gates opened that morning, they rode out, heading roughly northwest toward the town of Albara. Since she'd gotten used to the irrigated lowlands, the Bardekian foothills came as a real surprise to Jill. Although they were covered with wild grasses, they were dead-brown, so dry and bleached that at times in strong sunlight it seemed as if they rode through hills of beaten gold. In the coombs, where there was ground water all year long, grew holm oaks, their leathery leaves a green so dark that they looked like black bubbles caught in the golden dales. In some of the canyons and gulches, a thick choking tangle of shrubs and spiky things of all kinds spilled down to the flat road below, but the rest of the terrain was utterly treeless. It was hot there, too, a dry and breathless heat that set the roads to shimmering and danced on the huge sandstone boulders that poked up through the thin soil.

They stopped for the noon meal in a tiny valley, where a trickle of water, just clean enough for the horses, ran down the middle of a rocky streambed. The humans drank watered wine from a skin bought back in Pardidion.

"I think we'd better skip the usual nap," Salamander remarked. "I can't shake the feeling that someone's following us."

"Nor more can I," Jill said. "And I don't want them to catch us out here with no one else around."

"Truly. Well, we'll be safe in Albara. If we're very lucky, we might even find one last caravan heading north and join up with it, but I doubt it. It's too close to the flood season now, hard though it is to believe at this moment."

"Are there any silver daggers in the islands?" Jill said. "I mean, the same sort of man, someone you can hire for a bodyguard."

"None that I've ever heard of, alas and alack. We might have to . . . Wait! Silver dagger. Why do those words tug at my mind . . . ye gods, I almost forgot the wretched ring!"

"The what?"

"A silver ring, a present for you, younger brother, from our most esteemed father." Salamander took out the leather pouch he kept hidden inside his tunic and dumped a handful of small coins and lint into his lap. "Here we are."

He handed Rhodry a flat silver band, about a third of an inch wide, engraved with some design.

"Roses." Rhodry held it up. "Now that's a peculiar omen. What's this inside?"

"Elven writing. If you sound the letters out, it says *'arr-ssos-ah soth-ee lorr-ess-oh-ahz.'* As to what that may mean, no one knows, not elven loremaster nor dweomerwoman nor bard, and no more the human priests of Wmm, because I asked them myself and thus should know."

With a shrug Rhodry slipped the ring on the third finger of his right hand: a perfect fit.

"Why are roses a peculiar omen?" Jill said.

"Well, my lady Alaena gave me a trinket. I wonder if I brought it along?" Rhodry picked up his saddlebags, which were lying beside him on the ground, and rummaged through until he found a silver pin in the shape of a single rose. "It's dwarven silver, just like this ring and the silver daggers. It turned up in the Wylinth marketplace."

"Stranger and stranger," Salamander said. "They could have been made by the same hand, or at least the same workshop. Anyway, a long time ago a mysterious stranger gave our father that ring and said it was for one of his sons. Assorted divinations have awarded it to you. I was trying to find you to hand it over when you got yourself abducted."

Rhodry was staring at the ring in utter bewilderment.

"Do we have other brothers?" he said at last.

"One, a full-blooded elf, he is, and then we have a sister who's fully elven, and it's too bad she's our kin, because she's the most beautiful woman I've ever seen, well, present company excepted of course."

"No need to flatter," Jill said, smiling. "I'd never pretend that I could ever be as lovely as an elven woman."

"You're certainly as lovely as most, but they all envy our Mellario. And you, younger brother, had three brothers on your mother's side of the family. Two are dead for certain, alas, and the third, your elder, has most probably ridden through the gates of the Otherlands by now, because when last I heard, he'd suffered a very bad fall from his horse. If I remember correctly, the poor beast rolled on him, too."

"Well, that aches my heart." Rhodry did look distressed. "If I live to reach Aberwyn, I'll provide for his widow, of course."

"That's good of you, my love," Jill broke in. "But you know, you actually rather hated your brother Rhys. He certainly hated you. He's the one who exiled you in the first place."

"Truly? Ah, by the black hairy ass of the Lord of Hell! You can't know how blasted strange this is, hearing bits and pieces of my life like they were gossip about some other man! Here, elder brother. You're a sorcerer, and a cursed good one, too. Can't you do somewhat to mend my mind?"

"I can't, though nothing has ever ached my heart more than my incompetence, inability, and sheer lack of knowledge at this juncture." Salamander arranged a bright smile. "But fear not! We shall eventually take you to a healer of enormous art and repute back in Eldidd, a dweomerman who makes my tricks look like . . . well, like the silly tricks they are. He'll heal you right up for sure."

"You're lying." Rhodry's voice was perfectly level. "There's naught that can be done. That's the truth of it, isn't it?"

Salamander started to speak, then merely looked away with a long sigh. Rhodry got up with a defiant toss of his head.

"Let's get on the road. If you're both so sure there's enemies behind us, I for one don't want to sit here babbling and wait for them. Let's hope I remember how to use that new sword you bought me. Cursed if I'll let Jill do all our fighting."

Jill caught her breath in a little grunt.

"What is it?" Rhodry said.

"I just remembered the sword you used to carry. It had a dragon worked round for a hand-guard, and your mother's husband gave it to you, thinking you were his son."

"Well then, maybe it's better off lost. Elder brother, I'll pay you back the cost of the new one when we reach Aberwyn."

"You may not, because I'm giving it to you as a gift. Never before in my life have I felt so keenly that two swords are better than one."

When Gwin and his men left Wylinth, Pirrallo led them down a false trail to the south for several days. Even though they never met anyone who'd seen or heard of the wizard, the toad kept insisting he was right until Gwin finally told him that either they retraced their steps or he'd send him straight to Hell to meet the Clawed Ones that very night. Even though he cursed and blustered, Pirrallo finally gave the order to turn around and head north. Since Krysello had spent time performing in the various towns he'd visited, however, their little caravan caught up with his eventually, reaching Albara just a few hours behind him. When they made camp in the public ground provided for merchants, there was no sign of the wizard. In fact, they had the place pretty much to themselves, although the food and wine sellers who came out from the city to hawk their wares not only had heard about Krysello, but knew that he was staying in the city's only high-class inn. As Gwin bought supplies, he discovered that the wizard had announced a show for that very evening.

"It's supposed to be a real marvel, or so I've heard," the fruit seller remarked. "He does it with incenses and powders, but it's all very convincing."

"Oh, we'll come into town to have a look at that," Gwin said, smiling. "I wouldn't miss it for the world."

When they went into town to see the show, Gwin wore a pair of tall riding boots that laced up the front, a style influenced by but not copied from the barbarians, and cut loose to leave enough room inside for a very thin, very narrow steel dagger. He carried one in each boot. The night was cool and brilliantly clear, the stars glowing steadily, the moon an icy crescent. Even though the marketplace was half deserted, there was a good-sized crowd huddled below the terrace where the wizard Krysello was scheduled to perform, with his incense braziers and red-and-gold drapes already in place. As Gwin and Pirrallo found a spot off to one side, they heard people talking about the show in excited whispers. Some local merchants who'd seen the barbarians over in Pardidion or down in Ronaton, had brought descriptions of this "magic" home with them. One of them was standing to Gwin's left, a fat man in a red cloak, his hands flashing with rings as he gestured and bellowed at a skinny woman dressed in layers of rich silk.

Pirrallo nudged Gwin in the ribs in an infuriating way and whispered, speaking in the Orystinnian dialect, which would be hard to understand here in Albara.

"We may not be able to get close to them in this press."

"Shouldn't even try, this first night." Gwin answered in the same. "All I want to do is follow them back to their inn and see where they're staying."

"That's probably a good idea."

"Only probably?"

"I'm the one who makes the final decisions now, remember. You're very good at your line of work, but after what happened in Deblis . . ."

Pirrallo actually smiled. Gwin found it amazing, that the toad would be stupid enough to keep baiting one of the best assassins in the islands. It occurred to him then that perhaps the Hawkmaster was testing Pirrallo's competence as much as anyone's. Though the thought was intriguing, he had no time to develop it, because the wizard and his two barbarians were strolling out onto the terrace. When the crowd pressed close and clapped in anticipation, Krysello bowed with a flamboyant wave of one hand, and the girl curtsied with the bright grin of a hardened performer, but Rhodry merely stood toward the rear and glowered, as if he felt the whole thing a humiliation. Seeing him again tore at Gwin's heart.

"Welcome, welcome, oh exalted folk of Bardek, to my humble and unworthy display of barbarian marvels." Krysello bowed again before he went on. "Let me say first that I've heard crass and contemptible gossip, slanders all of it, stating that I perform my wizardry with chemicals, black wires, powders, hidden patches of glue, and other kinds of vile and vulgar trickery, unfit for your glorious eyes to behold. No, no, no, a hundred times no! Everything you will see tonight is true magic, barbarian witch sorcery as taught in the wild mountains of Deverry."

When the crowd giggled, Krysello bowed, grinning.

"He oozes sincerity, doesn't he?" Pirrallo muttered. "The man's a splendid showman."

Gwin merely shrugged; marketplace entertainments meant nothing to him. Yet, when Krysello pointed with a flourish at one of the braziers, which burst into a tower of gold fire, Gwin caught his breath just as loudly as the rest of the crowd.

"Brimstone," said the fat merchant to his wife. "You can tell by the color."

Pirrallo nodded a smug agreement as the other brazier bubbled over with yellow smoke and flickering red flames. All at once the wizard burst into a strange wailing song in some language that Gwin didn't recognize—he suspected it was simple nonsense—and began to juggle knotted silk scarves, which turned rigid in midair and flapped like birds overhead before settling back into his hands. This time the fat man prattled of the aforementioned black wires. As the song ended, the scarves disappeared, and Krysello flung both hands over his head to point at the sky.

"Behold the marvels of the far north!"

Some ten feet above him an enormous blue flower of flame burst into existence and floated briefly before dissipating. With an awestruck gasp, the crowd surged, packing tightly together. Gwin could feel the fat man's elbow poking his ribs and restrained an impulse to turn and hit him. Again the wizard flung up his hands; enormous sheets of gold-and-red fire exploded and rippled. Yet the crowd missed an important part of the show, because all at once, as flower after flower of light appeared in the midst of the flames, Wildfolk erupted into manifestation, sylphs darting back and forth, gnomes dancing and grinning all over the stage, and of course the salamanders, leaping and frolicking in the fires and rainbows that swirled around the wizard. Lightning shot; thunder rumbled; the crowd gasped and shrieked as the wizard sang and leapt about the stage, sporting with the Wildfolk as he worked his marvels. When Gwin caught Pirrallo's eye, the toad mouthed some words; even though it was impossible to hear, Gwin could guess what he was saying. Real magic. This has to be real magic. There in the sweaty press Gwin felt himself turn ice-cold.

The forces of the Light were right in front of them, dancing and singing and playing the utter fool, playing it so well that they'd followed this showman for weeks and never once wondered who he might be. As the brilliant colors swept across and dyed the faces of the crowd, Gwin felt his mind racing, turning this way and that like the twisting gold winds on stage as he desperately tried to work out a plan. Beside him Pirrallo was shaking like the contemptible toad he was. All at once the stage fell quiet and empty; Krysello made a languid bow and announced that he was too weary to go on. Laughing and calling out, the crowd dug deep in pouch and pocket and sent a silver rain of coins rattling onto the stage. While the barbarian girl picked them up, the wizard stood to one side, wiping his face on a rag and drinking out of a waterskin.

"Do you understand what this means?" Pirrallo hissed.

"What do you think I am, as blind as this stinking herd around us? I can see spirits as well as you do. You can forget using your pitiful little magicks on this man. Leave him to me and cold steel."

"Don't you insult my powers, you slave-born dog! But we're not doing anything until I contact the master. As soon as we get back to camp, I'll call him through the black mirror and make a report. He might want to come himself."

Gwin said nothing, but he was thinking that the toad-coward was probably right. Howling with laughter Krysello came prancing back to the center of the stage and flung up his arms in a shower of silver sparks. With little yelps of delight the crowd urged him on as he filled the air with plumes of orange-and-blue smoke, all glowy from within. Gwin looked round and saw Rhodry sitting near the red drapes at the rear of the terrace. Although in the shifting colored light reading his expression was difficult, he seemed to be smiling a little as he watched the barbarian girl. All at once Gwin realized who she must be, Rhodry's woman from Deverry, Jill, he thought her name was. So she'd traveled all this way to find her man, only to die when the Hawks claimed their prize again.

He didn't really want to think about what was going to happen to Rhodry once the Hawkmaster got his hands on him, whether Gwin turned him over or their guild leader came to get him himself, but of course, it was impossible not to think about it. Gwin supposed that he'd have to do some of the torturing himself, just to prove himself to the master and the guild. For the briefest of moments he felt paralyzed by revulsion; then all at once, he moved. Somehow he felt that he stood beside himself and watched as his leg jerked up ever so slightly, his hand reached down ever so unobtrusively, and the long dagger sprang into his fingers. On stage Krysello made a triple rainbow that suddenly twisted itself into the figure of a dragon. As everyone sighed and stared, Gwin raised the dagger and slid it between Pirrallo's ribs, right into the heart. He had it out again and sheathed before a thin trickle of blood even seeped through his victim's tunic.

In the packed crowd Pirrallo stayed standing, his head flopped a little back as if he stared at the dragon coiling in the sky. With a twist of his hips Gwin stepped back; the fat man automatically moved sideways to take his place and to prop up, all unconsciously, a corpse. With muttered apologies and servile ducks of his head Gwin made his way through the crowd until at last he was free, out in the nearly deserted marketplace. At first he strolled casually away; then, when he was back in dark streets, he trotted along, but not too fast, as if he were only a slave on an errand. The main road out to the public campground rose steadily, so that by the time he cleared the gates he could look back and see, at some distance down the hill, the glowing flower of Krysello's fires far behind him.

Out on the open road he slowed to a walk, strode along and thought of absolutely nothing at all until he saw the campfire of their fake caravan ahead of him. Only then did he truly realize what he'd done. Why he'd done it was still a deeper mystery to him than any dweomer, but he knew he'd have to come up with some sort of story fast.

"There you are," Vandar called out. "Where's Pirrallo?"

"Dead. I killed him."

"You what?" Brinonno leapt to his feet.

"Killed him. Knifed him, actually." Gwin paused, letting out his breath in a long sigh and rubbing his face with both hands. "The dog was lapping up wine at the show, and his tongue got loose. By the stinking feet of the Clawed Ones! There were archon's men all over the marketplace! What if they'd heard him sneering and bragging, saying that once this job was done, he'd have the three of us under his knife? He was supposed to give the Hawkmaster his report on us tonight, and I knew it was going to be bad, so I killed him."

They stared at him, simply stared for a long moment of shock.

"I'll take a horse and head off on my own. Are you going to try to stop me? Or you can come after me if you dare. Track me down, turn me in, and get a little glory from the guild—if you can."

"Don't talk like an imbecile!" Vandar snapped. "You could kill us both half-asleep, and we all know it."

"The question is why we aren't dead already," Brinonno said. "You're carrying two daggers."

Gwin laughed, but he stayed on guard.

"If you want to come into this scheme with me, I could use your help. Between the three of us we can take Rhodry on the road and strike ourselves a real bargain."

"How?" Vandar said. "I can't see the Hawkmaster deigning to talk to traitors."

"Who's talking about the Hawkmaster? There's more than one faction in the Brotherhood, isn't there?"

"So there is." Brinonno laughed, one sharp bark like a startled fox. "All right, I'll join you."

"Me, too," Vandar said. "And you know why you can trust us? Because we don't have any real choice, do we? If we don't find someone to take us on, we're going to die slowly at the hands of the guild no matter what we do."

"You're exactly right." Gwin felt himself smiling, as light-headed as a drunk. "And let's pray to all the demons in Hell that I can think of some clever way to get in touch with the Hawkmaster's enemies, or the Clawed Ones will be eating our souls for dinner soon enough."

Working as fast as they could, they packed up their gear, roped together their stock, and headed north out of Albara that very night, before the archon's men could identify Pirrallo's corpse and come asking his so-called servants questions. Since the only road through town ran east and west, and since Krysello had come from the east, Gwin knew what route the wizard would have to take. Although he was new to this part of the island, he was sure that sooner or later, he'd find a good spot for an ambush. Of course, now that he knew that this Krysello was exactly what he claimed to be—a true magician—he would have to think up some subtle plan. With only two men to help him, he wasn't about to simply charge into the middle of the road and yell, "Stand and deliver" at a dweomermaster.

As to what he'd do with Rhodry once he had him, well, he'd think of some bargain that would protect the captive as well as the captors. It occurred to him, too, that they might not have to go looking for other factions of the Dark Brotherhood. It could well be that such factions were already looking for them.

Far away, up in the mountains to the north, the Old One divined that some random factor had changed his plans. He was working in his Temple of Time that night, studying the symbols that he'd constructed on the twelfth floor, the most recent addition to the structure and the one that reflected his plan to destroy Nevyn. This temple was a curious thing. Although the imagery had acquired a certain dweomer over the years, at root it was only a conscious mental structure akin to the memory palaces used routinely by merchants and civil servants all over the islands. At the top of an imaginary hill he'd built in his mind a tall, square tower, made of white stone. One side was in full sunlight, to represent the knowable past and present; the other, in moonlight, to represent the less-than-knowable future. After years of work, the mental images were so well developed that he had only to think of the tower to see it whole and invariable; after equally long years of practice at mental concentration, he could walk in and look round as if it were a real building.

There were four entrances, and in the center was a spiral staircase of fifty-two steps that led to twelve levels, where each wall had seven windows. On the twelfth floor he'd placed symbolic statues and objects that would indicate how the winds of Fate and the Future were affecting his complicated scheme, just as a weathercock on a farmer's barn is an indicator of the wind and thus, at times, of changes in the weather. Since his long-range goal was the destruction of the elven race, he'd put four statues of elves round the staircase, two men and two women. He was hoping to see them begin to age or sicken, but so far they'd stayed stubbornly healthy and young. There were times, in fact, when he caught them laughing at him.

Near the elves were other statues, one meant to represent Jill — though of course the Old One had no idea of what she looked like — and one of Rhodry, stripped naked and shackled. Close by was a statue of Nevyn, whom he knew entirely too well for his peace of mind. Once Nevyn set foot on Surtinna, his statue would animate and undergo small changes that would enable him to judge the Master of the Aethyr's plans. Scattered round these main images were other, smaller symbols — statues of Wildfolk, an elven longbow, and various objects that had some emotional meaning for the Old One. Over the past few months, these symbols had indeed registered changes just as he'd hoped. Right before Baruma had first contacted him, for instance, a stone wolf had appeared, lolling in one corner and watching the stairs. Once he'd spoken with Baruma, he could see that it signified a spy and an enemy. Although every now and then he saw another statue — a shadowy thing, but apparently male and elven — standing near Jill's, so far he'd been unable to study it; whenever he tried, it disappeared.

That particular evening, when he went to the chamber, he found changes that disturbed him mightily. Rhodry's shackles were gone. The stone wolf was on its feet, hackles raised, fangs bared. In her arms Jill was cradling a turtledove, as if to protect it from a cat or some such predator. Of all incongruous birds! he thought to himself. Now what can that mean? Yet he gave it little thought because she was, after all, only a woman. With an imaginary shrug of his imaginary shoulders, he walked over to one of the windows on the moonlit side. Looking out the window took a certain amount of courage. At times strange creatures and stranger visions came there, because for all that this tower had started life as a simple mental trick, it had somehow attracted the astral plane—or moved close to it—or sent out a bridge to it—whichever metaphor you'd like for such a peculiar occurrence. Although this link poured power into the dweomer-workings there, it also brought danger.

When the Old One looked, he saw at first nothing but mist, swirling thick and wet round the tower. He waited, frowning in concentration as he peered out, until at last something seemed to move within the mist, to come closer, rising up like a swimmer from the sea, streaming mist like water as it formed into a recognizable shape, more or less human—but the face shifted like flames in a fire, sometimes swelling, sometimes shrinking. Greenish-brown hair burgeoned round the face like a vast tangle of leaves or long mosses on thick earth, and when it spoke he felt a blast of cold air swirl round him, even though its words sounded only in his mind.

"You have enkindled more evil than you can know, and someday you too will smoulder in its flames."

Then, before he could reply, it was gone. The Old One spun from the window and rushed for the staircase. As he hurried down, he could hear music playing in the chamber, strange discordant notes, as if the wind itself rang upon a harp.

That evening, as he considered this vision in his comfortable chair in his private study, he concluded that someone had invoked the forces of the Elemental Kings against him. The logical choice for that someone would have been Nevyn. As for Rhodry's image, it seemed equally obvious that Nevyn must be close to rescuing him—or, again, it would have been obvious, if only the symbolic statue of the old man had changed or shown some sign of life and power. Since it hadn't changed, he could only assume that some other dweomermaster had invoked the Kings, and equally, he could assume that the dweomermaster in question was one of his many rivals to become head of the guild, maybe the same one who'd sent the wolf after Baruma. The Old One knew his own strength, and he knew his magic: when Nevyn arrived, that statue would reveal his coming as surely as dark clouds announce the coming of the rain. He was certain of it. He refused, in fact, to believe otherwise, and of course, when it came to this one limited thing, he was perfectly correct.

Later he would realize just how badly those limits had cost him, when, unfortunately, there was still plenty of time to correct his mistake. For the moment, however, he put all his energies into working an elaborate method of scrying in an attempt to ferret out his enemy in the guild.

When they left Albara, the Great Krysello and his two barbarian servants traveled north toward the mountains. The road there ran along the edge of a wide, shallow arroyo, some twenty feet across and twelve deep, with a trickle of brackish river down the middle. On the second day, however, they woke to find the river clean and flowing and the sky an ominous gray. As they rode out, the tops of the hills disappeared into a thick gray wrap of winter cloud.

Although it rained all day, it was only a sullen sort of drizzle. By shaking the water from their oily wool cloaks at regular intervals, they stayed reasonably dry. Yet the river beside the road rose, spreading out at about the speed of a walking horse until it filled the arroyo from side to side, then deepening, until by noon it was swirling with white water, churning down from the distant mountains. Around mid-afternoon Jill saw an entire tree trunk rush past and part of what appeared to be a wooden fence as well. When she pointed them out to Salamander, he turned solemn.

"I think we'd best camp a good ways back from the road tonight. The winter floods are upon us good and proper, my turtledove, and I have no desire to wake up swimming."

"If you woke up in time at all," Rhodry said. "I heard a good bit about these wretched floods, and I don't like the idea of traveling in them, I tell you."

"No more do I, dear brother, but alas, we have no choice. Our one consolation is that we'll have the roads to ourselves for a couple of weeks until things reach some kind of equilibrium." Salamander looked utterly dismal. "Until then, we shall be riding wet, dirty, cold, and generally as miserable as one can get outside of outright illness. Alas, alack, well-a-day, and so forth and so on."

"I suppose we could lay up in a town for a few days," Jill said.

"There aren't any more towns between here and the central pla-teau, not ones big enough to have an inn, anyway. Besides, we've got to keep moving. Somewhat's wrong—I can feel it in my ill-starred soul."

"And how do you know that we're not riding straight into trouble?"

"There, my petite partridge, you have a very good point indeed. We'd best set up some kind of guard when we make camp tonight. Doubtless we won't be able to sleep much in this blasted muck, anyway."

Just before sunset the drizzle thickened to a sort of vertical fog, not quite a rain but too wet for mist, and the clouds seemed to hover a mere arm's reach above the road. Leaving the brown, swollen river, they led their stock up a hill to the cold and windswept grassy crest.

"This won't do," Salamander moaned. "We could all die of a congestion of the chest and spare our enemies the trouble of catching us."

"Well, there's some boulders and shrubs down over there," Jill said, pointing. "We can tether the horses in the grass and then try to find some dryish spots down in the rocks."

"Try, indeed. I like your choice of words."

Even though she was a road-hardened silver dagger, that night Jill was almost as uncomfortable as Salamander. Enormous pale hunks of sandstone, the boulders poked through the hillside and clustered on a small natural terrace about thirty feet down from the crest. Along with the prickly shrubs and tall weeds that grew in between them, these rocks did indeed provide shelter from the wind, but the level spaces between and around them were narrow, and the ground so wet that the damp soaked right through the blankets. Eventually they all decided that the only way to sleep was sitting up with blankets wrapped around them like cloaks. Although Jill wanted to do her share and stand a watch, Rhodry pointed out that while he and Salamander could see in the dark, she'd be blind as a mole on this starless night.

"Get what rest you can, beloved," he said. "I'll wake you just before dawn. We'll get an early start. If naught else, it'll be warmer once we're moving."

Once the last of the sunset faded, Jill realized that, indeed, stand-ing a watch would be a waste of her time. In the swirling mist-rain she could barely find the horizon, much less see anything in the broken country around them. Perhaps, if she were lucky and happened to be staring right at it, she might have seen a large animal or a man moving, if it were some light color and noisy to boot. Wrapped in two blankets and her cloak, with her sword in its scabbard right beside her, she wedged herself under a slight overhang between two boulders and wondered if she'd ever fall asleep. A few feet away she could see Rhodry poking around, looking for another dry spot, but only as a gray shape moving against a blackness.

"Salamander's on watch?" she said.

"He is, up near the crest so he can keep an eye on the horses."

By the rustling he was making Rhodry seemed to be scraping small stones and sticks out of his chosen spot. Finally he settled down, leaning back against a rock and sitting so still that she could barely make out where he was. Tented in her blankets and out of the wind, she began to warm up at last, and she managed to ignore the slight cramps in her legs enough to drowse off. Once she half-roused to find Rhodry leaving, creeping quietly uphill for his watch; distantly she heard what might have been Salamander whispering to him. She also realized that the drizzle had slacked off. By shifting around she got herself halfway comfortable before she fell asleep again.

Only to wake to a tug on her hair and the feel of a little paw tapping her face. With a cold ripple of danger down her back Jill was alert, unwinding herself from the blankets even as she was still recognizing the dim form of her gray gnome silhouetted against the night.

"Is somewhat wrong?" she whispered.

It seemed that the little creature was nodding a yes. Jill threw the blankets back and got to her knees, feeling for the hilt of her sword. Her fingers had just closed on it when she heard a rustle and a scrape off downhill. With one last pull on her hair the gnome vanished. She grabbed the hilt in one hand, the scabbard in the other, and slid the sword half-free. All at once, up at the crest of the hill, she heard a whicker, then the neigh of a frightened horse.

"Rhodry! Ware!"

With her yell Jill was on her feet, the sword drawn. As she started to pick her way clear of the boulders, she saw a trace of movement out of the corner of her eye and whirled round toward it. Dimly she could make out a head-shaped darkness against the dark sky, then another movement. Up on the hill horses were whinnying and plunging. Something hissed by her face like an angry insect. As she took a step forward, sword raised, something pricked her cheek, no worse than a bee sting. She dodged, raised her free hand to brush the annoyance away, and realized that her legs were giving out under her. In a rushy hiss the black world vanished into a gauzy gray silence.

His weeks in a comfortable house had softened Rhodry enough that sleeping wedged in between cold rocks was impossible. Although he drowsed for a few minutes here and there, he finally gave it up as a bad job and left the imperfect shelter of the boulders to join Salamander at the crest of the hill. In this dark a night his elven vision could no longer distinguish color or detail, but he could see outlines and shapes well enough to move with confidence. He found his brother sitting cross-legged and sneezing in the long grass and watching the horses and the mule, who stood heads down and weary, nose to tail in the drizzling damp.

"You can go and try to sleep if you want," Rhodry said. "I'm wide awake."

"So am I. Awake—and miserable. And forlorn, dejected, pathetic, dismal, bleak of heart. Ah, how I long for our father's tent, its warm fire, its soft cushions, and above all, its waterproof roof and sides! I wouldn't mind being surrounded by several hundred elven archers, either, come to think of it."

"Nor more would I. Do you think we should turn back to Albara on the morrow?"

"I'm tempted, truly. I wonder if I—here, what's that?"

They went silent, sitting as stone-still as only elves can. Very faintly, some distance away, Rhodry heard a noise, too muddled with the wind and drizzle for him to identify it. All at once the horses tossed up their heads and whickered. Rhodry and Salamander were on their feet, and Rhodry had his new sword drawn before he even realized he'd reached for it.

"Rhodry! Ware!"

It was Jill's voice, coming from among the rocks. Cursing under his breath Rhodry started toward her, just as the horses and the mule went mad. All at once they were bucking, yanking at their tethers and pawing at the air with their fore hooves. As dim shadows Rhodry could see what the animals saw: horrible, deformed Wildfolk, with huge fangs and red, gleaming eyes, leaping and dashing straight for the stock.

"Ware!" Salamander screamed.

The tethers snapped, and the horses came plunging straight for them. With a yell Rhodry knocked Salamander to the ground and rolled with him downhill and to the side just barely in time. He saw hooves flash by and felt mud spatter his face as the galloping horses parted around them and plunged off into the darkness, heading back toward the road.

"May the Lord of Hell eat their intestines and their balls both," Salamander gasped with the breath half knocked out of him. "Not the horses, I mean. Whoever did this."

Rhodry could guess who that someone had to be and the kind of danger they represented.

"Jill!"

He scrambled to his feet and ran for the boulders with a swearing Salamander following. Something grabbed at his ankle—one of the evil Wildfolk, he assumed—and he went down, rolling smoothly and bounding up in the same motion.

"Jill!"

There was no answer, no sound at all, truly, except the far distant hiss and chuckle of the floodtide river. Even the horses, apparently, were far out of earshot. Panting a little, Salamander joined him at the edge of the rock-strewn terrace, where nothing moved.

"Do you think they've got an archer or suchlike with them?" Salamander whispered. "I can make a light if it won't make us a target."

"A light in this damp? Are you daft? No one could—oh, of course, my apologies. Well, if they were going to stick us like pigs, they would have done it by now." Rhodry tipped his head back and called as loudly as he could. "Jill!"

A pale yellow light blossomed in the air above them to reveal a gleam of metal beside a heap of crumpled blankets. Rhodry raced over, stumbling a little, and picked up her sword, graved with the device of a striking falcon and running only with water now, not blood. His eyes burned tears.

"They've taken her." He could barely speak. "I don't know why, but the bastards have taken her."

"I wonder, too, younger brother, but let us not despair. You forget that we have a vast if not truly mighty army at our command."

"What? You've gone daft!"

Salamander whistled once under his breath and snapped his fingers. All around them in the golden light Wildfolk appeared, gnome and sprite and sylph, each one tiny, true enough, but there were hundreds of them crowding round, gray and brown, mottled and purplish-black, with their thin lips bared to reveal needle-sharp teeth, their eyes, yellow and red and green, gleaming with rage and indignation as they shook tiny clawed fists in the air. Although they were eerily silent, from the distant river Rhodry heard voices calling out to urge them on.

Jill woke suddenly to dim daylight and a hard floor. The side of her face stung like fire, every muscle in her body ached, and she was so cold that she was shaking, lying huddled in a corner on some kind of packed earth tiles. When she tried to stretch out, she realized that her hands were tied behind her back and her ankles lashed together. By moving very carefully and very slowly she managed to haul herself up to a sitting position and prop herself against the corner of the tiny bare room. The walls were whitewashed, and where one of them joined the ceiling was a small slit of a window. Since she could see earth through it as well as sky, she decided that she had to be in some sort of cellar, and from the smell as well as the burlap sacks lying around, she could guess it was a root cellar. Whispering so quietly that she was thinking more than speaking, Jill called her gnome. He appeared straightaway, bringing with him two large black-and-purple warty fellows with sharp teeth and big ears.

"Can you untie my hands?"

The bigger gnomes shook their heads in a mournful no, then proceeded to chew through the rope. Once she was free, rubbing her painful wrists with numb hands, her gnome and his friends disappeared again, leaving her to untie her ankles herself. For a long while she worked on her aching and complaining hands and legs, rubbing, stretching, shaking until at last she could stand up, cursing and stamping as the blood flowed back with fiery prickles. Outside the window something scuffled and scraped. She looked up to see a pack of purplish-black gnomes pushing a small bundle through the opening, something that dropped to the floor with a clatter. She pounced on it: her silver dagger in its leather sheath.

"My thanks, my friends. May your gods or whomever you serve bless you for this!"

When outside the door she heard sudden voices, she slipped the dagger out of sight into her shirt. There was a clang, and a curse or two as someone struggled with a lock; then the door opened and two men stepped in, one of them carrying a saddlebag; the other, a drawn sword. Since the fellow with his sword at the ready was a typical Bardekian, well over six feet tall with huge hands, and since the other man had a sword at his side too, she merely retreated to the far wall. The one who looked much like a Deverry man with his pale skin and straight black hair stared at her openmouthed. When he finally spoke, it was in Bardekian.

"You're untied!"

"Of course I am. Haven't you ever seen those tricks where the show master ties someone up and shoves them into a bag or chest, only to have them pop out again a few minutes later and wave to the crowd?"

Both her captors laughed, but it was a grim enough kind of chuckle.

"That's one on us, Gwin," said the Bardekian.

"I'll admit it. We'll have to keep a good watch on our clever little traveling player from now on." He hefted the saddlebag. "Now, I've got paper and ink in here. You're going to write a note, exactly as I tell you, and then we'll give you some food and water. If you don't write, you get nothing."

"Then I'll be dying of thirst, soon enough. I don't know how to read and write. I'm from Deverry, remember."

Gwin swore in some language that she couldn't understand.

"She's telling the truth, most likely. I should have thought of that." He turned back to Jill. "Can Rhodry read?"

"Who?"

"Don't play stupid with me." His voice was very quiet and soft, and it sent a ripple of fear down her back. "It isn't wise, little girl. Do you know who I am?"

"A Hawk of the Brotherhood, obviously." It took all her will to keep her voice steady. "And yes, I know what you do to your prisoners."

He smiled, just briefly, a gesture designed to frighten her, no doubt, but she made herself look him full in the face and smile in return, caught his gaze and held it, determined to stare him down and gain a small victory—the only kind, no doubt, that she'd have. For a moment he stared back, his mouth twisting in mockery. All at once, his face seemed to soften, to blur, and his eyes to change color, the black shimmering, then turning a cold hard blue like a winter sea. It seemed to her that she stood in some other room—she could almost see firelight behind him, could almost remember his real name, could almost remember why she envied him over something more important than her life itself.

"Bards aren't allowed to read and write," she said. "You know that."

With a wrench and a toss of his head he looked away, and he was the one shaking now, not her, his face an ashy sort of gray, his eyes—black again—darting this way and that as the Bardekian with the sword stepped forward.

"Gwin, what's wrong?"

"Naught." Gwin tossed his head again, swallowed heavily, and made his voice perfectly steady—but he was still a little pale. "Our hostage is a lot more valuable than we thought, that's all." So smoothly she suspected nothing, he turned, then slapped her across the face, so hard that she fell back across the wall. "What do you mean, Rhodry's a bard?"

"That's not what I said at all." She found herself thinking of her father's slaps, when he was in one of his tempers, and forced herself to stay as unmoving now as she had then. Only one eye betrayed her by starting to swell and tear. "As for the meaning of what I did say, you're as capable of puzzling it out as I am—neither more nor less."

Gwin raised his hand, then hesitated. She could see that he was frightened, and she knew in some obscure way, deep in her soul, that she had him on the run and could keep him that way if only she chose the right words. She found herself thinking of him as a man near to breaking. Around her materialized Wildfolk in a restless, hostile swarm, glaring at her captors, shaking tiny fists, opening their mouths in soundless snarls to reveal long pointed teeth. When Gwin barked out a string of words in some language that she didn't understand, some of the Wildfolk disappeared, more cowered against her in fear, but some growled boldly back at him.

"They won't obey you," Jill said. "But I'll send them away rather than let you hurt them." She raised her hand and did just that, scattering them more with her thought than with her gesture. Her gray gnome stayed to the last, snarling like a dog, until she chased him away with the stamp of a foot.

"Who are you?" It was the Bardekian, whispering under his breath, his dark face gray.

"You know."

She said it as a portentous bluff and nothing more, but Gwin stepped back sharply. Not in fear—she realized suddenly that his mouth was working in honest effort, as if he were desperately trying to remember, that he seemed, in fact, close to tears, as if she had piled shock onto some private grief until he could stand the weight no more. The Bardekian kept looking back and forth between them, his eyes narrow with confusion.

"Gwin, what is all this?" he snarled, and ever so slightly he raised his sword, ever so slightly his shoulders tensed. "I'm beginning to wonder if you've told us the truth, or . . ."

The Bardekian had his sword in hand, and Gwin's was in his scabbard, but all at once Gwin moved, steel flashed, there was a grunt and a spurt of blood. The Bardekian swayed, took one step, dropped his sword, and fell face-forward onto the floor. A long dagger smeared with blood in his hand, Gwin spun on his heel and caught Jill's glance, swung up the dagger, and glared at her over the tip. She went stone-still and stared back into madness.

"I could kill you without half-trying," he whispered.

"You could—easier than that."

He smiled and lowered the dagger, but only by a few inches. She felt a trickle of cold sweat run between her breasts and another down her back. Behind him materialized her gray gnome and two purple-and-green fellows, all three of them grinning and dancing as they pointed at the world outside the window. With a wrench of will she looked only at Gwin's face, but this time he refused to let her look into his eyes.

"You're beautiful, for a witch," he remarked, and his voice was so casual it was frightening. "But I know a trick or two against female magicks. You won't ensorcel me again."

She heard a sound, a scuff of a boot, maybe, that came from beyond the window, and spoke hurriedly to cover it.

"I never ensorceled you at all. I don't even know what happened when I looked into your eyes, truly I don't."

"Oh, now you're going to whine and weasel, are you, when I've got the better of you?" His grin was terrifying, as cold and rigid as the smirk on a corpse, but he did lower the dagger, holding it about waist-high in a relaxed hand.

"I'm telling you the simple truth. All I know is that I recognized you somehow, from somewhere."

He threw up his head like a startled horse, the mad grin gone.

"I felt that way about Rhodry, when first I saw him. Do you know where that was? In a stinking tavern in the Bilge in Cerrmor, where Merryc and Baruma had him trapped, like a stag at bay with half a dozen rowdies round him, and he was laughing. One swordsman against six, and he laughed like it was the best jest in the world." His voice had turned very soft. "It wrung my heart, somehow. Just like you said—somehow, and from somewhere." Then he shook himself, the dagger flashing up, and grinned again as he took two steps toward her. "Don't you think I hear them coming, too, girl? Do you think I'm stupid? You're going to be my shield."

With his free hand he made a grab toward her shoulder, intending, no doubt, to clutch her in front of him with the knife at her throat. Jill ducked, dropped, twisted as she came up and kicked him full in the stomach. As she came down, she grabbed his free wrist, dropped again, and flung him backwards over her shoulder to slam hard against the wall. His dagger went spinning out of reach. She pulled her own from her shirt, stripped it of the sheath, and dropped her weight to a fighting crouch as he scrambled up, out of breath but not in the least dazed from blows that would have left an ordinary man numb and gasping on the floor. To cover her sudden fear Jill laughed at him.

"I'm not a witch, Gwin, but I could have been an assassin like you."

He laughed in return, a berserker's chuckle under his breath that reminded her hideously of Rhodry.

"So you could have, and maybe I deserve to die for underestimating you like that. Let's see what happens between you and me, shall we, girl?"

When he settled into a stance of his own, knees wide, his weight perfectly balanced between them, she realized that he was a good fighter—and much more dangerous than she was, whether she had a dagger or not. From the way he smiled as he circled round, he knew it, too. They heard Rhodry, then, yelling her name, and footsteps pounding toward them, but neither said a word, merely circled, Gwin leading, nearer and nearer to his fallen knife. She felt her heart thudding as she waited for the one split-second she would have, when he stooped to grab it. Closer now, closer, and Rhodry screaming like a berserker outside—Gwin tripped, cursed, and went down, screeching foul oaths, under a heaving pile of Wildfolk. With a howl of triumph Jill sprang, straddling him from behind while Wildfolk scattered and grabbing his hair in one hand to wrench his head back. It was her dagger at his throat, now.

"Jill, don't!" Rhodry burst into the room with the door banging behind him, a blooded sword in his hand. "Don't kill him!"

Only then did she realize that she'd been about to do just that. She froze, staring at Rhodry. He wasn't begging—he was ordering her, his eyes snapping as he took another step into the room. She let Gwin go and stood, dodging free of him before he could rise.

"As Your Grace commands, of course."

At the snarl in her voice Rhodry turned bewildered.

"Ah by the hells, my love, I don't mean to order you about. It's just that you were half-berserk, and I wanted to make sure you understood me. Words don't mean a blasted lot to berserkers, you know."

"Well, true enough."

Gwin was still lying sprawled on the floor. Slowly he rolled over and sat up with a cautious eye for the Wildfolk who stood about in mobs or hovered above him in the air.

"Why not let her kill me, Rhodry?" This time he spoke in Deverrian.

"Because I owe you somewhat, enough so that if you have to die, I'll do it myself for the honor of the thing."

Gwin stared, his mouth a little open, his eyes filling with tears, and that grief was a gruesome thing to see on a man as cold and hard as he was.

"I can understand that kind of honor," he whispered. "My thanks, Your Grace. So, that lofty a title belongs to you, does it? Who are you? I never did know."

"Rhodry Maelwaedd, Gwerbret Aberwyn." It was Salamander, crowding into the room with a wince for the huddled corpse of the Bardekian. "Do you know what it means to raise a hand against a gwerbret?"

"By the dung of the Clawed Ones! I do at that, by every god-cursed demon in the three hells! That's just like the filth-sucking Old One, isn't it, to hire us to risk our rotten lives and never even tell us just how great the blasted risk is! The pig-bugger! I'll . . ." Gwin stopped, his mouth twisting in his mocking grin. "Well, I'll be doing naught that can harm him, truly, unless I come back as a haunt or suchlike." He got to his feet, slowly, keeping his hands in the air where they could all see them. "If ever I did you any favor, Your Grace, when you were in that stinking ship, I'll beg you to kill me quickly and easily. That's all."

He could force himself to smile, force himself to stand proudly, his head tossed back like a true warrior, but there was nothing he could do, apparently, that would make him stop shaking all over. It wasn't fear, Jill realized; his eyes were too dead already for him to be simply afraid to die. When Rhodry laid his sword blade alongside Gwin's throat in such a way as one flick of his wrist would kill the Hawk in an instant, Gwin merely looked him straight in the face—yet he went on shaking. Although Jill had been ready to kill him herself only a few moments before, she found herself stepping forward.

"Tell me somewhat," she said. "Would you rather live or die?"

"I don't know." Gwin smiled again, such a normal smile, filled with good cheer, that it chilled her heart. "I truly don't, and here I've been asking myself that question for days now. I'd rather die than live as a Hawk—I suppose. I'm not truly certain of that, either."

"It's time you made up your mind. If you stay a Hawk, you'll die, sure enough. Come over to us, and give us your word on it, and I'll beg the gwerbret for your life."

Gwin began shaking so hard that the sword blade nicked his skin. Rhodry moved the blade a little, then glanced her way with eyes that seemed to understand her better than she did herself. Salamander said nothing, but she could tell from the tense way he stood, half a warrior at the moment, that something of great importance was at stake. A man's soul if naught else, she thought to herself, and at the thought she went cold. All at once Rhodry lowered the blade, glanced at the old blood on it, and stooped to wipe it clean on the dead man's tunic. When he sheathed it, the sound was like a slap in the breathless room. As he stood there in his muddy clothes, unshaven and damp, with half his memories gone and his life still broken, she saw him suddenly as the gwerbret, the ruler he would be—no, that he was now, despite everything. She knew then for a surety that Rhys was dead, and that Wyrd had picked up the dice to roll a turn.

"I'm not killing you, Gwin," Rhodry said. "You can come with us as a prisoner, or as my man. Which is it?"

Gwin gave one last convulsive shudder.

"Rhodry," was all he could say, because he was weeping.

Salamander grabbed Jill's arm, but he had no need to drag her away; she was in as much hurry to get out of the chamber and leave them alone as he was. A few steps led them up to a muddy, bare farmyard between a long whitewashed house and a square building that might have been a barn or a granary. Lying near a well was another dead man, and tethered out in a meadow were some twenty-five horses—theirs among them. Overhead the sky was a low, cold gray, swirling with wind.

"That was a fine thing you did in there," Salamander said.

"Was it? If he's lying, I've endangered us all."

"Lying? Gwin? Not by a pile of horseshit, he isn't. Mayhap you've never seen a man broken down to naught before—I have. Oh, he'll follow our Rhodry to the death, he will, and see him as a god, too, after this."

The wind picked up, and Jill shivered, looking around her for the first time with eyes that truly saw.

"Where are we?"

"A farm in the hills. In the flood-time the tenants who hold isolated little places like this take shelter with their landlords in the big villas. When Gwin and his late and unlamented friends needed a place to hide, all they had to do was ride in and make themselves at home."

Jill nodded, barely hearing him. She was remembering Gwin's eyes, turning from black to blue, and the firelight that seemed to have burned behind him in her vision. Small wet fingers touched her cheek: rain, the first fat drops of a storm.

"Gods!" Salamander snarled. "Run for it!"

They dashed across the yard and ducked into the open door of the farmhouse just ahead of a drench of water.

"When it rains in this benighted country, it *rains*!" Salamander said, tossing his head and scattering the drops from his hair. "This is going to make traveling most unpleasant indeed, my wee waterfowl. We might just stay here for a day or two. Gwin and his freshly felled fellows seem to have broken the door right off its hinges, so we'll have to leave the good farmer some coins for damages anyway. We might as well leave him a few more for rent."

"I think we should get on the road and use the rain to our advantage."

"Advantage? What advantage? Maybe you see advantages in riding wet, sodden, damp, saturated, and soaking, to say nothing of cold, chilly, freezing, and frigid, or—"

"What about riding invisible?"

Salamander stopped his lexiconic recital in mid-word and blinked at her.

"I don't mean invisible to ordinary sight. You're the one who's always talking about the astral vibrations of water interfering when someone wants to scry." Jill waved her hand at the down-driving rain outside. "Well, what about all this?"

"It might work, it might indeed. At the least, they'll have a wretched lot of trouble getting clear images of trivial little details like, oh for instance, where we are and who's with us."

"Exactly what I thought. It's going to be hard on the horses, but we don't have to move fast. If we're off this road and into the mountains before they scry us out, they won't really know where we are. Remember when you were trying to find Rhodry, and all the grasslands looked the same?"

"The mountains are no more distinguished, truly—trees and boulders, boulders and trees, and here and there a charming little ravine, replete with snakes, which are rather tasty this time of year, come to think of it, and may be most welcome."

"What? Eat *snakes*?"

"What? Ride *wet*?" He grinned at her. "We are all in for an unlovely time, my little linnet, but I promise you that it'll be far more pleasant than—indeed, it'll be like living in the wondrous Halls of Bel in the Otherlands themselves compared to lying on a torture table in one of the hidden chambers of the Hawks."

"Odd—I was having thoughts that were somewhat the same. How far to Pastedion from here?"

"Um, well, if we went directly there, some four nights, maybe five, since we'll be traveling in this slop. If we keep to the mountains, it'll be safer but longer."

"Let's stick with safer, shall we?"

"I couldn't agree more. Very well, then, say an eightnight, depending on the weather and all. Let's go fetch Rhodry and Gwin. The sooner we put your plan in action, the better."

That very night Baruma tried to scry them out. For the past few weeks he'd been posing as a legal messenger so that he could travel along the coast with a proper caravan. Just as the winter rains began, they reached Indila, not far from his destination, and Baruma stayed there in a comfortable inn for two days while he debated whether or not it was time to join the Old One. Although he was afraid to go, he was equally afraid to stay away. What if the Old One came to suspect his double-dealings? He knew perfectly well that those who went to the master's villa were sometimes never seen again. Baruma suspected that the Old One had done nothing so rudimentary as merely killing the poor wretches. On the other hand, if he shirked spying for the Hawkmaster, his position would be even more dangerous. In an attempt to gather information that would help him decide, Baruma brought out the silver bowl and the black ink, unwrapped Rhodry's silver dagger to use as a focus, and sat himself down at a low table to scry. If the Hawkmaster had already taken the barbarian prisoner, he might well be too distracted to worry about Baruma's affairs.

Although the vision came immediately, it was cloudy and distorted, flickering and bobbing as if a wind ruffled the surface of the ink. He could see Rhodry quite clearly, thanks to the evil link of pain between them, and he could make out horses—a great many horses, or so it seemed from the brief glimpses he got of them. When he tried to widen the vision to include Rhodry's location, he got an impression more than a sight of rocks and a huge silvery rush of etheric force that had to be coming from a river or flooded ravine. Dimly within this mist he spotted a couple of human forms moving back and forth. Beyond that he could tell nothing.

The vision vanished. For a long time Baruma sat at the table and watched his hands shake, while he considered the fate of a grain of wheat, caught between two millstones.

Finally he was calm enough to pour the black ink back into its special bottle. He heaved one last sigh, then got up to see the wolf, lounging on his bed and licking its paws. In his frustrated rage he grabbed the ink bottle and threw it straight at the wolf's head. Although the image did disappear, he'd forgotten to put the cork back in the bottle. Swearing with every foul oath he knew, he grabbed a rag and started to sop up the mess, then decided to fetch the innkeeper to do it for him. He flung open the door that led to the outer room of his suite and found three men waiting for him there, and one of them was wearing a red silk hood.

"You keep a very poor watch, Baruma."

"I had no idea I needed to." He managed to force out a smile. "You might have knocked."

When the Hawkmaster chuckled under his breath, the two men with him smiled, baring their teeth like animals.

"I might have but I didn't. Why haven't you joined the Old One yet?"

"He suspects treachery. I've been debating whether I should go or not."

"Does he? Oh, does he? And you never said a word to me about it?"

Baruma went sick-cold with fear, but even though his stomach was churning and his hands were shaking, he tried to keep his voice steady.

"How could I have contacted you? Would you have appreciated me calling to you when anyone could hear? Should I have sent a public messenger with a letter?"

"Well, I have to give you that, yes. Besides, you couldn't know that he's struck against us."

"He's what?" Baruma heard the squeal in his voice, but by then he was shaking too hard to control it.

"He sent his confederates against my men. He has to be the one behind this, he has to! No one else would dare cross me."

As if by some prearranged signal, the other two Hawks stepped forward. One grabbed Baruma's wrists and twisted his arms round behind his back; the other clamped a hand over his mouth.

"Did you warn the Old One, little Baruma?" the master said. "One of my men is dead. I can't make contact with the others. Is it your fault, little piglet?"

Since his captor's grip was too firm for a shake, Baruma wobbled his head in a no. Sweat was trickling down his back and beading on his forehead.

"I don't know if I believe you, creature. You were trying to cram both heels of the loaf into your mouth at once, weren't you? Did you think you were clever enough to fool both me and the Old One?"

Baruma choked out a muffled snort that he meant for no.

"We're going to take you with us, piglet. We're going to make you answer our questions. I've heard you're a master at giving pain. How well do you take it, I wonder?"

The Hawkmaster reached out and caught his elbow between a probing thumb and forefinger that slid down, separating the muscle masses, then pressed—hard—the raw nerve against solid bone. Baruma's scream gathered in his throat and forced its way into his stifled mouth as a gargling spitting cough that made him spasm.

"Unless, of course, you tell me the truth. Let him speak, Karralo. He knows that if he screams for help, he'll die right here."

When the Hawk took his hand away, Baruma caught his breath in moist sobs.

"I didn't betray you. I couldn't. I went against the Old One's orders when I brought you into this, didn't I? He specifically said to sell Rhodry and let Fate take him. I wanted him dead or prisoner. Didn't I? Didn't I?"

Instead of answering the Hawkmaster reached up and pulled off his silk hood. With a shock Baruma realized that the man was handsome; his skin was the lustrous blue-black of Orystinnia, his mouth soft and full, his black eyes wide and beautifully shaped. He'd always imagined the Hawkmaster as some scarred monstrosity.

"You've seen my face now, little Baruma. Do you know what that means? The only way you'll leave my side from now on is by dying. Do you understand me? Oh, you're as pasty as spoiled cheese, so I think you do. The only reason you're staying alive is because I can use you. You've seen this mysterious Rhodry, and that means I can scry through your eyes. You've been to the Old One's villa, and that means you can take me there. I'm going to break your will like a wild horse and ride you like the beast you are. As long as you're useful, you'll live. Give me the slightest trouble, and your pain will number itself in weeks, not hours, before the Clawed Ones eat your soul."

Baruma felt hot urine spurt down his leg. The Hawkmaster laughed, then grabbed his shoulder to inflict the same sort of fiery agony as before. This time he couldn't scream, didn't dare make any noise that would attract the attention of the other people in the inn, because he knew that a cry for help was worse than futile, that the Hawks would drag him away long before help could arrive and begin their slow tortures that very night instead of in some indefinite future. As the pain ebbed the Hawkmaster looked full into his eyes, and Baruma felt the clutch of his will as the worst pain of all. It seemed to grow into his mind like the tendrils of some poisonous plant, burrowing deep into every crack of memory and thought, burning and biting as it went, yet still he could not look away.

"Obey me, and in a time, you will cease being a beast and start being a servant. This is the only hope you have. For a brave man it would never be enough, but it will keep a coward like you alive and obedient, crawling at my feet, but alive."

The drunkenness swirled round his mind, that trained and disciplined mind that he'd been so proud of, that he'd bragged about, that had seemed to him clear proof of his superiority over the common class of men. Now it was swirling and staggering, and he was staggering, too, as the Hawks let him go. He took a few steps, lurched forward, and fell to his knees at the master's feet.

"Get his gear," the master said to the others. "We'll go through it in a safer place. Get up, piglet. You'll be carrying this load to spare the strength of the real men."

Obediently Baruma rose, swaying a little, still dizzy. When he caught the edge of the table to steady himself, the dizziness passed off. Around him the Hawks were talking again; their words came and went through his mind like a barely comprehensible song.

"A dagger made out of silver—some ritual thing, I suppose—no, Deverrian—never mind that now—we have work to do tonight—a little surprise for the Old One's men? We don't know."

When the words faded into a wind-sound, Baruma realized both that he'd been ensorceled and that the Hawkmaster had left him enough mind to know how little he had left. Even though deep in that last fragment of mind he was roiling with rage, he knew that his fear of dying and the torments that went with it would make him obey. Thanks to those terrors, he would shuffle along before his master the way a top spins before the child who whips it.

Down in Aberwyn, not far from the harbor, was a tavern that existed on the very cliff-edge of respectability. If its owner, the widow Sama, hadn't worked so hard, the Three Swans would have slid over that edge years before, but she was up before dawn to mend up the fire and scrub tables, on her feet all day cooking solid meals for decent folk and serving good ale for a fair price, and late at night, by the light of a dying fire and a cheap tallow candle, she was sweeping the floor and starting the next morning's porridge to stewing. All of this exhaustion enabled her to save a handful of coins, which she'd portioned out, a few at a time, as dowries for three of her four pretty daughters, so that they were all respectable married women now instead of hanging round the tavern working for the wrong kind of coin. Everyone in the neighborhood, even the unmarried young longshoremen, honored the widow for her virtue, and even in their most drunken moments none of them would have ever considered brawling in her tavern, where they might break a precious mug or overturn an expensive table and thus add to the widow's hard lot in life.

The youngest and prettiest daughter, however, still lived with her mother, but not out of filial devotion. Although Sama had named her Heledd, everyone called her Glomer—as hard as coal at the very marrow of her bones, they all said, and why the Goddess saw fit to give a daughter like that to such a good woman we'll never know!

Even though she was sixteen and should have been married for several years, she'd turned down two decent suitors, saying the tanner's lad stank too badly and the dyer's lad had warts all over his hands. What Glomer wanted in her heart of hearts was the chance to work in the gwerbret's dun. In those days being a servant for a generous clan like the Maelwaedds was a good position for a poor lass; you had plenty of food and drink, a new dress every year, a warm place to sleep and exciting events to watch, and you shared the labor with so many other servants, taken on for the status of the thing, that the actual work was much lighter than waiting on table and scrubbing pots in a tavern.

Unfortunately, to get a place in a dun you needed to know someone who already worked there. The only person Glomer knew, a serving lass named Nonna, came mincing down to visit her family, the potters who lived across and down by the coppersmiths, about twice a month. She would wear her newest dress and bring her mother and her siblings scraps of fancy cake from the gwerbret's kitchen, then sit at their hearth like a fine lady and regale the locals with all the latest gossip and news. Every time Glomer tried to ask her to put in a word for her, Nonna would turn her nose up and make snide remarks, usually about Glomer's supposed laziness. There were times when Glomer wished she could follow her into some dark street and strangle her on her way back to the dun.

Just lately the tales that Nonna brought home had been exciting ones indeed. Early in the fall a mysterious noble-born prisoner had arrived from Cerrmor, and Nonna overheard two men from the warband saying that, by all accounts, he wasn't a man at all but a fiend in human form. Their authority for this was something that old Nevyn, who absolutely everybody said was a sorcerer, had let slip one night when he was leaving the prisoner's guarded chamber. And now everybody was also saying that the enormous Bardekian ship's captain was a sorcerer, too, because he'd captured the demon and brought him in. At any rate, not long afterward the famous Cullyn of Cerrmor, captain of the regent's personal warband, had stopped Bryc the groom from murdering Lord Rhodry's only heir. Everyone (including Bryc himself, before he went back to his father's farm in the north) said that the lad had been bewitched. Nonna was sure that the prisoner from Cerrmor was responsible.

"Probably Nevyn doesn't want to kill this red-haired demon be-cause he can use his powers—Nevyn can use this Perryn's powers, I mean, because I'll wager the old man's stronger than any wretched demon. You should see the old man, and the look in his eyes. Oooh, like ice they are, and he could bewitch anyone, I'll wager, just by snapping his fingers or suchlike. Everyone's afraid of him, well, except Cullyn of Cerrmor of course. I'll wager he's never afraid of anybody."

And everyone sitting in the potters' kitchen nodded their heads sagely and agreed.

Perhaps it was stories like this that made Glomer so suspicious of the peddler named Merryc. At first glance he was ordinary enough, a man in his mid-thirties with dark hair and the walnut-shell skin that bespoke some Bardek blood in his veins, and he had the easy cour-tesy and ready way with a jest that a traveling man had to have in order to survive by selling ribands and embroidery thread and bits of lace and beading. Certainly Sama trusted him when he told her that he needed a place to live for a few months, till the worst of the winter was over and he could get back on the road again. Of course, she always needed custom so badly that her judgment might have been blurred by the good copper coins he handed over for a week's room and board. There was just something about him that sat all wrong with Glomer—his oily little smile, perhaps, or the way he stared at her buttocks when she went past. Late at night, too, she would sometimes hear odd noises coming from his chamber, as if he were whispering orders to large rats, who scurried to do his bidding.

"I wish you'd turn him out, Mam, I truly do," Glomer remarked one afternoon when their lodger had gone out for a walk. "I swear he's out to work harm."

"Oh, listen to you! And what's he going to do, steal my fine lot of silver dishes or all our lovely jewels?"

"I don't mean harm to us. I—oh, no doubt you're right, and I'm imagining things."

The shock of hearing her daughter actually agree with her was almost too much for Sama. Muttering to herself and shaking her head she went out back to feed the chickens. But Glomer stayed in the tavern room and scrubbed tabletops until Merryc came back and asked politely for a tankard of red. When she handed it to him, she lingered briefly.

"And how was your walk about the town?"

"A bit damp, but pleasant."

"Did you go up to the dun?"

"I didn't. Naught for a man like me there."

But his answer struck her as too slick and his tone too oily, just like his smile.

Round the bend in the street, just past the coppersmith's, lived the Widow Dacra in a wooden hut. Although everyone said she was a witch, she made her living by dispensing the common sort of herbs and, on occasion, applying a combination of hot baths, mead, and slippery elm bark to induce abortions for the local whores. With the beginnings of a plan forming in her mind, Glomer filled a leather bottle with mixed ale and went round to see her on the morrow morning. She found Dacra, a handsome gray-haired woman, picking over dried hoarhound at her table while at her little fire a pot of honey and water simmered together.

"A lot of coughs this time of year," Dacra remarked. "The blacksmith's lad is bad, his mother tells me, so I'm just making up a potion."

"I've come to ask you a favor." Glomer set the bottle of ale on the table.

"Indeed? Have you found some lad to lift your skirts and then leave you?"

"I'm not with child! That's not going to happen to me, thank you very much, not until I've married anyway."

"Huh. It's the ever-so-fussy lasses like you, young Glomer, who generally find a bit of filth to roll in at the last. Think about that, will you? Before you give yourself such fine airs that you find yourself twenty years old and moaning because you've got no husband."

If Glomer hadn't needed her advice, she would have thrown the bottle straight at her head. As it was she forced out a smile.

"I'll think on it, indeed. Now, I only wanted to ask you somewhat. Suppose someone was a sorcerer? How could you tell? I mean, do they have a demon mark on the palm of their hand or suchlike?"

"What? Hardly anything so easy and quicklike, my fine lass. Why do you want to know?"

"Oh, I was just curious, like."

"Indeed? You wouldn't be stealing you mam's ale just to satisfy your curiosity."

"I didn't steal it! I'm worried about her, too."

Dacra considered her for a moment with shrewd gray eyes.

"Well, I can see you're worried, sure enough. Is it that lodger of yours?"

"It is. How did you know?"

"And who else new has come here in months and months?"

"True spoken. There's just somewhat about him that doesn't sit well."

Dacra dumped a generous handful of crushed hoarhound leaves into the pot of honey and water, then stirred down the roil, slowly and carefully, with a wooden spoon.

"Well, that's true," the herbwoman said at last. "Though I don't know what kind of man he is. A murderer, I'd say, more than a sorcerer, but you never know." She took the pot off the fire and set in on a slab of stone at one end of her table to cool. "When he came to stay, he must have brought bags and packs with him."

"He did. A peddler's pack and then saddlebags."

"Saddlebags for a man who walks for his living? Curious, indeed." Dacra gave the pot one last stir, then went to a freestanding cupboard and began rummaging through it. She brought out a tiny square of parchment. "A long long time ago an old woman made me this good luck charm. You see? It has a five-pointed star, and then this circle of writing round it. Well, the old woman told me to always hold this parchment so the star has one point upward, never two. Two points up bring bad luck, she said, and it's a sign of evil sorcery. If I remember rightly, she said that every sorcerer would have some bit of magical gear marked with the evil star."

"Merryc goes out for long walks all the time."

"Does he now? But be as careful as careful, young Glomer. Nobody wants to see you turned to stone or your soul trapped in a bottle."

Especially not Glomer. She waited until the afternoon, when Merryc went out for his usual long walk before dinner, then fetched a big basket of wicker rattraps and a handful of stale bits of bacon rind. She set several traps in the chamber she shared with her mother, and two more in the corridor before she went into his room. It was a small chamber, a slice of the roundhouse right in the curve of the wall, with a window that looked out over the street. Near the door and out of the draughts was a narrow bed and a wobbly wooden chest that had once done duty as a dower chest for her older sisters. Although she set one trap between that chest and the wickerwork wall, Glomer didn't even bother opening it. She was sure that any sorcerer was going to be too clever to hide his evil magic in such an obvious place.

She was, of course, quite right. Since she knew her mother's house so well, she discovered the hiding place immediately. The ceiling was laced together from woven wicker panels, daubed with cheap plaster and whitewashed; right at the joining of ceiling and wall one panel sagged. As a child she'd hidden coppers and other treasures she'd picked up from the streets between that sag and the thatch, and there she found Merryc's saddlebags. For a long time, though, she was afraid to touch them. She fussed around, setting the second trap and baiting both with the bacon rinds, looking continually out the window to keep watch for the lodger, and then finally summoning her courage. It would be foolish, she decided, to go to all this trouble and then not even have a look.

When she tried, however, to slide the pair of leather bags out of the cache, they stuck. It felt exactly like someone was on the other end and pulling them back. She yelped, stifled the scream with both hands crammed over her mouth, and nearly ran from the room there and then, telling herself that, after all, now she knew the worst. Still, if she were going to carry out her plan, she needed better proof of Merryc's sorcererhood than one bewitchment that might just turn out to be a bent nail snagging a seam. This time she carefully slid her hand along the bags, found the bone toggle that held the flap closed, and unwound the tie without trying to remove the saddlebags at all. Her ploy worked; she could slip her hand all the way into the bag. She took one last nervous look out the window, then went fishing in Merryc's gear.

She could feel perfectly ordinary things at first—socks, an awl for mending leatherwork such as a peddler might need for his pack on the road, a bag of small coins—then her fingers struck a metal disk that had the greasy feel of lead. Merely touching it made her feel uneasy; when she drew it out, she nearly screamed again. It was hanging from a leather strap, so that it had a clear top and bottom, and graved on it was the upside-down pentagram, the star of evil. She shoved it back in, then bolted from the room, clattering down the wooden stairs and out, running full-tilt to the public well so she could wash her hands in the open trough, over and over again even though the water was cold and she had no soap.

By the time she felt clean enough, it was growing dark. Glomer hurried back to the tavern and the light and warmth of her mother's fire.

"And where have you been?" Sama said.

"Setting rattraps, Mam."

"Well, my thanks, my sweet. I've heard them rustling about for days now."

Glomer tried to smile and knelt down at the hearth to lay the bakestones into the embers. Merryc returned not five minutes later, striding through the tavern on his way to the stairs up.

"Oh, Merryc?" Sama called out. "We've had to put traps for the rats upstairs. Be careful you don't spring them."

"I will, then. This winter weather seems to drive them inside."

"It does, truly, it does."

Even so, Glomer spent all evening in a state of nerves, wondering if he would notice that someone had touched his hidden saddlebags, but he never said a word to her.

In the morning she was faced with the most difficult part of her plan. As soon as her mother's back was turned, she left the tavern room, grabbed her old, patched cloak from upstairs, and slipped out the back alley without anyone seeing her. Once she reached the main streets, she slowed to a steady walk and made her way uphill to the gwerbret's dun. There she hesitated one last time, because men stood on guard, pacing back and forth in the open gateway.

"You, lass!" one of them called. "What do you want?"

Although she badly wanted to bolt, she made herself go over and drop him a curtsy.

"Please, sir, I'm a friend of Nonna's, who works in the kitchen, and her mother asked me to take her a message."

"Oh, well and good, then. Go on through. See the main broch? The kitchen hut's all the way round back, by the well."

Her heart was pounding like a galloping horse as she walked into the ward. Although she'd been by the gates and peered inside many a time, never before had she actually been allowed in. Yet in a way, the dun was disappointing, not much more than an extension of the city with its clutter of huts and sheds, the hurrying servants and the chickens and hogs in pens. She had a hard time locating the cookhouse, but by asking for Nonna she eventually found herself at the back door of the great hall, where, standing in the curve of the wall, her friend was polishing tankards with a rag. The great hall, with its slate floors, enormous hearths, and carved tables, did a better job of living up to her expectations, and for a moment she merely goggled at all the finery. Then Nonna saw her and came hurrying over.

"What are you doing here? Is somewhat wrong at home?"

"It's not, but, Nonna, please help me. Do you remember that peddler who's lodging with us? He's an evil sorcerer. I've seen proof. I was thinking maybe that the man named Nevyn that you're always talking about would—"

"Oh, he's not going to have time for the likes of you!"

"Well, what about the captain then?"

"I'm not going to waste his time on your wild tales."

"But if you took me to meet Cullyn, you'd have a chance to speak with him yourself, wouldn't you?"

The bribe was irresistible. Nonna giggled, glanced round the hall, then slipped her arm through Glomer's.

"Come along. He's just sitting down at table."

The sight of Cullyn, tall and fierce with his scar-slashed face, was almost enough to freeze Glomer's tongue in her head, but she managed to drop him a respectable curtsy while Nonna introduced her as a friend from down in town. Cullyn slewed round in his chair and scowled at her.

"Out with it, lass. What brings you to me?"

"My mam runs a tavern, sir, and there's this man lodging with us. He says he's a peddler, but he's really a sorcerer. I found a piece of jewelry in his saddlebags with the star of evil graved upon it when I was setting rattraps in his chamber."

As soon as she'd blurted it out, she felt like a fool, babbling of sorcerers to such an important man, but Cullyn whistled sharply under his breath.

"Oh, did you now? Come along with me, lass. We'd best go straight to Nevyn. Nonna, my thanks. Go back to your work."

Blushing and envious, Nonna did just that as Glomer followed the captain from the great hall and into a side tower. As they climbed up and up a spiraling iron staircase, Glomer was staring at all the tapestries hanging on the stone walls and the elaborately cast silver sconces—never in her life had she seen so many fine things in one place. Finally they came to a landing and a wooden door. When Cullyn knocked, it was opened by an old man whose piercing ice-blue eyes and bristling eyebrows raised in a frozen glare made the captain seem as sweet and gentle as a little lamb.

"What is it now?" he snarled. "Oh, my apologies, Cullyn. I thought it was one of the pages. They've been interrupting my work all blasted morning. What have we here?"

"A lass with an interesting tale, my lord. I think me you'd best hear it."

Nevyn ushered them inside to his reception chamber and insisted that Glomer sit in a cushioned chair by the window while he took a plain chair opposite her and Cullyn stood by the door. Since she'd never been up so high in her life, the view out and down to the harbor made her feel dizzy, and she kept her gaze firmly inside after one quick look. She started with Merryc's arrival, told them about the Widow Dacra's sure test for sorcery, and finished up with her discovering the lead disk in his gear.

"I know it was wrong of me to go through his things, my lords, but I was so frightened. I don't know why he got my wind up so badly, my lords, but he just did, and here were me and Mam all alone with him and all."

"Oh, you did the right thing, lass," Nevyn said. "No doubt about that. Captain, go fetch a couple of your lads and meet us down by the front gate, will you? I think we'd best take this Merryc under arrest."

"He really is an evil sorcerer?" Glomer squeaked.

"He is. What's this?" Nevyn smiled at her. "You didn't truly believe it yourself before now, did you?"

She shook her head no and realized that she felt very weak and strange inside. Nevyn poured a swallow of mead into a goblet from a pitcher on the table and insisted she choke the fiery stuff down. Once she stopped coughing, she felt much better.

"Very well, lass. You take me and the captain to your mother's tavern, and then leave the rest to us. I'll see you get a reward for your sharp eyes, too."

"Oh please, my lord." Here was the crux of her plan, and Glomer arranged a humble smile. "All I'd truly want for a reward is a job here in the dun. I'm good at waiting on tables and washing pots and suchlike."

"Indeed? Well then, I've no doubt I can get you one. Now let's go put our stoat of a sorcerer into his cage."

On his way out, Cullyn stopped by the armory and got a pair of stout leather thongs, then went on to the great hall and rounded up Amyr and Praedd, who'd been dicing for straws over their morning tankards of ale. He took them down to the main gates, where Nevyn and the lass from town were already waiting.

"We want this to be quiet, like," the old man said. "If you can manage it anyway, captain."

"Oh, I think we can trick him, my lord. A peddler, is he? Everyone knows they're the first ones suspected if somewhat's been stolen." He turned to the girl. "Think he'll be in your tavern when we get there?"

"He should be. My mam always serves a meal about now."

When they reached the street of the Three Swans, Cullyn left the girl with Nevyn by the public well, then sent Praedd, a strong and beefy sort, round to the tavern's back door while he and Amyr walked in the front. There was a fair amount of custom in the smokey room: a tableful of sailors drinking by the door, a couple of longshoremen eating bread and bacon by the hearth and jesting with a gray-haired woman who already looked drawn and pale with exhaustion, here an hour before noon. At a table by himself was the man who fit the description that Glomer had given. As soon as he saw two of the regent's men come in the front door, the fellow got up and started for the back—only to find it filled with Praedd, who clamped his massive hands onto the fellow's shoulders and held him while the captain made his way over. The longshoremen snickered and the sailors all leaned forward to get a better look.

"Come along, lad," Cullyn said. "A merchant over on the street of goldsmiths says someone walked off with some trinkets of his."

"Well, it wasn't me," Merryc snarled. "I know a stranger always gets blamed for every cursed thing that goes wrong, but I didn't take anything from anyone."

"I'll just be asking you a few questions. Come along nice and peaceful like, and you'll be back here by dinnertime."

Merryc allowed himself to be shoved out the back door. Although he snarled and swore when Cullyn bound his hands behind his back, he did little else to put up a fuss, at least at first.

"All right, Amyr. Go fetch Nevyn, and then go upstairs with the old man to get this fellow's gear."

Merryc howled and threw himself to one side, kicking out, desperately trying to twist free of Praedd's hands, writhing and squeaking like a rat in a terrier's jaws until Cullyn drew his sword, reversed it, and knocked him hard over the head with the hilt. Praedd laid the unconscious man down on the ground and knelt to bind his ankles together.

"When you're done, go ask those longshoremen if they want to earn a couple of coppers," Cullyn said. "Cursed if I'll carry this little bastard back to the dun."

The longshoremen were indeed willing, and once Nevyn and Amyr had retrieved the prisoner's belongings, they all set off to carry the sorcerer to justice. Since they collected curious children on the way, and a gaggle of adult loiterers too, it was in something of a festive parade that Merryc was marched into the gwerbret's dun and dumped into a stout cell in the gaol out back of the broch. Nevyn paid off the longshoremen, sent the children on their way with them, then knelt down on the dirty straw beside their prize.

"I hope I didn't hit him too hard," Cullyn said.

"Oh, he'll live to stand his trial. Fetch me a bucket of well water, will you?"

As soon as the water hit his face, the prisoner began to moan and flop from side to side, but when he opened his eyes to find Nevyn leaning over him, he went dead-still, staring at the old man like the proverbial rabbit at a ferret.

"I think me you know who I am," Nevyn said with a grim little smile. "Good. You can bargain with me, lad. Everything you know for your life."

Merryc smiled briefly and looked away to stare up at the ceiling.

"I keep my word, lad."

"I know that, and no doubt you *would* spare me—to rot in the gwerbret's gaol until my own guild came to kill me. Even if you let me go free, they'd hunt me down sooner or later. Always running, always waiting for the feel of the knife—what kind of a life is that? And it's the only one you can offer me."

"And what if we find ways to make you talk anyway?"

"Oh, and do you expect me to believe you'd lay one hot iron on me? You? The mincing milksop Master of the Aethyr? You don't have the guts, old man, and you know it."

Cullyn swore aloud at hearing Nevyn addressed so disrespectfully, but the old man merely smiled, a sad and rueful twist of his mouth.

"I don't, at that." Nevyn sat back on his heels and considered the bound man. "But it's a true pity that you can't understand why."

"Guild, he said?" Cullyn broke in. "What's he talking about?"

"Assassins. Come now, you must have heard a whisper or two about the Hawks of Bardek when you were a silver dagger."

"Well, so I did. Then he's right enough, my lord. He doesn't have a candleflame's chance in the three hells."

"Oh, I agree. It just aches my heart, that's all." The old man got up, dusting off the knees of his brigga. "I need to go talk to the tieryn. Leave Praedd and Amyr here on guard, will you?"

"I will. Have you gotten a chance to look through his gear yet?"

"Just the merest peek—but that was enough to hang him."

Before they left the cell, Cullyn untied the prisoner, and they left Merryc sitting slumped in one corner, his head on his knees like a naughty child. Nevyn wasn't content with simply barring the door from the outside; he insisted that the gaoler bring out one of his rare and precious padlocks and chain the bar to the staples. Then the old man took Praedd and Amyr aside.

"Now whatever you do, don't look him in the face, lads. He'll try to make you do it. He'll probably taunt you at first, then maybe pretend he's sick or dying, but ignore him. If by some odd chance he does die, well, he's spared us the time spent hanging him, so well and good, say I. When it comes time to give him food and water, fetch me before you open the cell. You'll have to, actually—I purloined the key when the gaoler's back was turned."

"My lord?" Amyr said. "What'll happen if we look at him?"

"He'll try to ensorcel you, of course."

Amyr's lips parted in an "oh," but no sound came.

While Nevyn went back to the broch to find the regent, Cullyn shooed the last of the loiterers out of the ward and sent the servants back about their business, too, but he did allow Glomer to wait in the kitchen hut with Nonna. It's too bad, he thought, that Nonna doesn't have half her friend's common sense and a quarter of her wits—enough to leave a man like me alone, anyway. Since he wasn't blind, he knew perfectly well that the lass was flirting with him for all she was worth. He decided to have a word with Cook later and ask her to put an end to it, then started back to the great hall.

"Cullyn, Cullyn!" It was Tevylla, running across the ward with her skirts hiked up like a farm lass. "Rhodda's gone off somewhere!"

"Ye gods! When?"

"Just now. She was playing with her grandmother when Nevyn came in, and the poor child was so incensed that our lady went off with him that she dashed out the door before I half realized what was happening. I've got every page and serving lass in the dun searching the broch for her, but I'll wager she went outside. She always does head for the open air when somewhat's troubling her."

"So she does. The stables are a good wager. She loves the horses."

Yet as they were hurrying across the ward, it occurred to Cullyn that Rhodda had once been the object of the dark dweomer's attack, and that they had a dark dweomerman in the dun.

"Come on! This way!"

He set off at a trot with her running to keep up as they dodged through the huts and sheds in the crowded ward. Just as they turned round the armory by the gaol, they saw Amyr rushing out to meet them.

"Captain! We've got to fetch Nevyn. Somewhat truly weird is happening."

"Nevyn's in the chamber of justice with the tieryn," Tevylla said, panting a little. "Hurry, lad!"

Merryc's cell was at the end of a narrow corridor. As Cullyn ran down, he could see Praedd, cursing and writhing and swatting at the air as if he were being attacked by huge and invisible wasps. The padlock and its chain were jingling furiously, slipping this way and that on the bar but not, of course, ever coming free, hedged by the staples as they were.

"Old Nevyn's a farsighted man," Cullyn remarked. Almost in spite of himself he was remembering the time when Jill was a tiny lass and used to prattle about seeing the Wildfolk. If nothing else, he decided, it was worth a try. "All right, Praedd, I'm here. Hang on a bit."

Cullyn set his hands on his hips and glared at the air right by the lad's head.

"Stop that all of you right now, or Nevyn's going to be as mad as mad, and so will I."

With one last sob Praedd slumped back against the wall.

"It's gone, captain. It just stopped. Whatever it was."

"Good. Now, come away from the door. There's naught more you can do. Go outside and wait for the old man there."

He pressed himself against the wall to let Praedd sidle past, then went down to the door. From inside the cell he heard a howl of rage, and Merryc's face appeared in the tiny barred opening. Mindful of what Nevyn said, Cullyn looked only at the bridge of the prisoner's nose and held his gaze there. After a brief moment Merryc snarled like a dog.

"You won't be ensorceling me, lad," Cullyn said, and calmly. "Now where's the child? Tell me, or I'll break you on the wheel myself, one bone at a time. I don't have Nevyn's scruples."

"What makes you think I know where she is?"

"Tell me, or your death comes in pieces, and as slow as I can make it."

"In the shed directly in back of here. It's full of sacks of turnips. That's all I can see through her eyes, but I know she's nearby."

With a sound halfway between a sob and a gasp, Tevylla rushed down the hall and out, nearly running into Nevyn, judging from the round of hasty apologies at the door. As the old man came hurrying down, Cullyn slowly and deliberately turned his back on Merryc. He could hear the evil dweomerman snarling again in sheer frustrated rage, but Nevyn was grinning.

"By the hells, captain, from what Praedd's been telling me even the Folk of the Air are afraid of Cullyn of Cerrmor!"

"Not truly, my lord. I threatened them with you."

Nevyn actually laughed, a rusty chuckle like the creaking of an old gate, then handed over the big iron key, so Cullyn could unlock the chain. When they opened the door they found Merryc cowering in a corner with his arms thrown over his face. Cullyn grabbed him by the wrists, flung him forward, pulled him round and twisted his arms

behind his back while Merryc screamed and swore in the Bardek
tongue. Then Nevyn stepped in and looked him in the face before the
man could close his eyes. Cullyn watched fascinated as Nevyn stared,
merely stared, into Merryc's eyes, but the gaze must have seemed like
a hot iron to the prisoner, who babbled and writhed and twisted in
the captain's hands like a chicken who sees the cook's hatchet lying
on the block. All at once Merryc went rigidly still, and quiet.

"There," Nevyn remarked casually. "You can hand him over to me
now. I'll take Amyr and Praedd, if you don't mind, to get him to the
chamber of justice. Bring Tevylla and the child along after us, will
you?"

"I will, my lord. No doubt Tevva's found the lass by now."

She had, indeed, and she was waiting for them outside with the
terrified child clasped in her arms. Since Rhodda was getting too
heavy for her nursemaid to carry for long, Cullyn took her and let her
sob against his shoulder as they walked slowly back to the broch.
Although he asked her a question or two, all she could say, between
sobs, was that the bad man had a long long arm and that his mind
pinched. Nevyn explained things more clearly in the chamber of
justice.

"Merryc did to her what he did to Bryc back last autumn. He
caught her by her mind, because he realized that the Wildfolk would
do her bidding. He could use her to use them, you see—or perhaps
you don't see, but that's what happened anyway. That's why I
padlocked the door. The Wildfolk can lift a bar from its staples, but
they can't pick a lock."

"Ah." Tieryn Lovyan had an odd expression, as if she were wishing
she could allow herself the luxury of hysterics. "Well, whatever you
say I'll believe, Nevyn. Oh dear Goddess, I had so hoped Rhodda
would be a . . . well, um, never mind that now. What shall we do
with this creature?"

Merryc was kneeling on the floor between a scowling Amyr and a
Praedd who looked frankly murderous, with budding bruises on his
face that made Nevyn's talk of Wildfolk all the more believable.
During the old man's explanation Merryc had never even glanced up
once, but now he slowly raised his head and looked at the tieryn.

"Are you going to beg for mercy?" she said.

"I won't, but no more will I deny what the old man says."

"Very well. I've sent for a priest of Bel, and we'll have your hearing as soon as he comes. Nevyn, does the child need to stay for this?"

"She doesn't, nor does Mistress Tevylla. Cullyn?"

Cullyn gave him a nod of agreement and carried the child out of the chamber of justice. As they were going down the long hall to the staircase, Tevylla turned to him.

"My thanks, captain."

"Most welcome, but here, call me by my name, will you? You're not part of the warband."

"Well, so I'm not." She gave him a smile that was the more charming for being shy. "Till the morrow, then."

After he saw them safely inside, Cullyn wandered out into the ward, filled with the long shadows of Aberwyn's many towered dun as the winter's day came to its early end. As he walked out to the barracks, everyone he passed acknowledged him with some gesture of respect, a nod from the noble-born, a bow or a curtsey from the servants, a muttered "sir" and a staightening of their posture from the members of both warbands, the one that had served Gwerbret Rhys as well as the one Lovyan had brought with her. It struck him that evening that if someone had refused the gesture he would have been insulted, him of all people, a man who had ridden the long road as an outcast for all those years. He had grown solidly used to having a respected place in life, accustomed to knowing that wherever he went as Lovyan's captain, he would have not only a bed to sleep in and a place at table but a certain acknowledgment that he was an important man in the tierynrhyn. Yet that evening it also struck him, and for the first time, that something was missing in his new life. A woman of my own, he thought; by the hells, that would be good to have again. When he thought of Jill's mother, dead for so many years now, he could barely remember her face.

A stout man, shaved bald and wearing a heavy winter cloak over the linen tunic of his calling, the priest of Bel arrived soon after Cullyn had taken Tevylla and Rhodda away. Although Nevyn was wondering how the man was going to take talk of dweomer, Lovyan side-stepped the entire problem.

"Praedd, Amyr, make that weasel stand up properly, will you? He can show some respect to the priest. Now, Your Holiness. This is the man who tried to murder my granddaughter this autumn. Nevyn's proved the entire thing to my satisfaction, but I need your advice on the laws."

Nevyn turned to the priest.

"Your Holiness, what's the usual punishment for such a crime?"

"Hanging, of course. Even though the child is illegitimate, she's still a blood heir, and thus any attempt against her is an act not merely of attempted murder, but of full-blown treachery." The priest frowned, rummaging through his vast memory. "The *Edicts of King Cynan* contain the most recent statement of this principle, but there are earlier precedents, the clearest, perhaps, being found in the ninth-century codification of Maryn the First."

"Well and good, then, Your Holiness," Lovyan said. "On the morrow morn I'll convene a malover. About two hours before noon, I think, would be suitable."

"Very good, Your Grace. I shall have the proper statement of precedents prepared at that time." The old man turned his shrewd dark eyes on Merryc, who was standing stiffly between his guards. "Do you wish to talk to me, my son, or some other priest from our temple? It's time to prepare your soul for Great Bel's judgment hall."

Merryc smiled briefly, then spat on the floor. Praedd cuffed him as they dragged him away.

Nevyn and Lovyan went up to the reception room of her suite, where the wind howled and banged at the glass in the windows and blew the occasional puff of smoke from the fire. Shivering in her plaid cloak, Lovyan stood by the hearth and rubbed her hands together.

"That's better," she pronounced at last. "The Chamber of Justice is so wretchedly cold this time of year. Ah by the Goddess, Nevyn, I feel so old and weary! I've never sentenced a man to hang before, and I'll have to be there to watch it, too, I suppose." She shuddered again. "Well, no one has to worry about my stealing the rhan out from under its real heir, the way so many regents have done. I shall be very glad indeed to turn it over when the time comes." Although she was trying to speak lightly, her eyes were haggard with worry. "*If* the time comes, I suppose I should say."

"It will, Your Grace. It will."

Yet he could hear the weariness and wondering in his own voice.

After the evening meal Nevyn went back to his chambers. With Elaeno to keep him company, he stood at the window and looked out and down to the distant harbor, where the foaming waves rolled in steadily and bobbed the boats around at the piers. There was a storm on the way, he supposed, but even between blows, the seas would stay high all winter long. No matter how badly he longed to be in Bardek, he was going to stay in Eldidd till spring.

"That's all there is to it, I suppose," Nevyn remarked. "Or have you ever heard of a ship making the crossing from here to, say, Surtinna in the winter?"

"Not successfully." Elaeno considered the problem for a moment. "I've never heard of anyone even trying it, to tell you the truth."

"There's folly and then there's absolute madness, eh?"

"Just so. Even if you didn't run head on into a big storm, and that's an enormous 'if,' you could knock your craft to pieces in the swells, or lose sails tacking endlessly into the bluster, or get blown so far off-course your crew could starve before you reached land. We have an old proverb at home: no man nor demon neither can command the wind."

"And a true one it is." All at once Nevyn was struck by a thought. "But asking it a favor might be a very different thing indeed."

Later that night, when the dun was asleep, Nevyn wrapped himself in two cloaks and went out into the formal gardens. As he walked across the lawns, they crackled underfoot; in the moonlight a rimy frost lay glittering on the dark mounds of mulched rosebushes and the frozen water in the dragon fountain. When he found a sheltered corner out of sight of the broch, he made a vast five-pointed star of blue light in his mind; then he imagined it so clearly that it seemed to float in front of him in midair. Very quietly, yet so intensely that it seemed his whole body vibrated with the sound, he chanted aloud the names of the Kings of Air. Although the night had been still, as soon as he finished the call, the wind came to him, pouring from the center of the star in a rush and snap of power that made his cloak flap round him. (When he glanced round, though, he saw that nothing else in the garden was moving.) Stately and shimmering on the wind's back rode the Kings. They spoke only in pictures and feelings, of course, not in words, but in a while Nevyn managed to get his request across, that for a little space of time he wanted the wind to serve him and take a ship across to the islands. With an exhalation of graciousness they agreed, lingering round him for a moment, then gusting off to leave him shivering in the hushed garden with only a sylph or two for company. Hurriedly he withdrew the star back into himself. He wanted to get back to his fireside and a tankard of mulled ale.

For the rest of that night he sat up, brooding his plans and fighting his worries, until at last, when the dawn came, he could sleep for a couple of hours, waking just in time to make his appearance at the regent's malover. In spite of her qualms of the night before, when the time came to sentence Merryc to hang, Lovyan's voice was rock-steady. The Bardekian himself was so withdrawn, so enfolded into his own mind by some dark discipline that he seemed at times to be nothing but a portrait statue of himself, as if he'd already left the present moment to stand in some hypothetical descendant's garden among the statues of their mutual ancestors. His actual death would come as an anticlimax to Merryc, Nevyn supposed, just as Sarcyn's had to him.

"It may be one of the things I hate the most about the dark dweomer," Nevyn remarked to Elaeno later. "The way it takes men with real talent and spirit and breaks and warps them to its own foul purposes. I've met more than a few of these apprentices, and every one was as twisted and ugly as those pitiful Wildfolk they keep around them."

"The men are much worse off, I'd say. It's a long sight easier to heal the poor Wildfolk."

"You're right enough. Well, I think me that the time is coming for a little revenge on our part. Once we've found Jill and Salamander, and—one hopes—Rhodry, too, we'll see about making the Dark Brotherhood pay for their crimes."

"Good. I'm going to be glad to see spring come, believe me."

"Spring? Oh, of course, I haven't had a chance to tell you yet! We're going to Bardek straightaway. I asked the wind, and it agreed to take us straight there, safe from storms and suchlike."

Elaeno started to speak, thought better of it, shut his mouth, reconsidered once again and opened it, then finally made a strangled sort of sound deep in his throat.

"Is somewhat wrong?" Nevyn said.

"Naught. Why, what could be wrong? If the wind agrees, well then, who am I to argue? I'll just hunt up my first mate and tell him to gather the crew. I take it that the regent will provision us?"

"No doubt. Hum, I haven't spoken to her yet, either, and I suppose I'd better straightaway. How long will it take you to get the ship seaworthy and ready to sail?"

"Two, three days, depending on how many men her grace details to help us."

"I'll make sure you've got everything you need, you can depend on that."

Although Nevyn of course told Lovyan the truth about their destination, she agreed that a small deception was in order. They let the rest of the court think that, in order to get a jump on next year's trading, Elaeno was sailing to Cerrmor, a tricky journey in winter though a possible one as long as a ship hugged the coast. Nevyn himself, or so the story went, was traveling with him to confer with Gwerbret Cerrmor about the vexed political situation in Eldidd. Although no close relation, Ladoic of Cerrmor was kin to Rhodry on the Maelwaedd side, and thus a possible ally in this unspoken war for the rhan.

"I shall give you new clothes to take with you, too," Lovyan said. "And one of Aberwyn's minor seal rings as well as what coin I can scrape together. You'd best go as my councillor, Nevyn, not merely my friend. They always say that every Bardek archon starts his career as a merchant, and so I'll wager they understand just how rich the Aberwyn trade is. They'll want to be on the right side of her ruler."

"Just so. Do you think some of Rhodry's men would volunteer to come with me? I can pass them off as an honor guard, and I fear me I might need a few good swords before this scrap is done. I'd take Cullyn, but you need him more. Hanging Merryc doesn't mean Rhodda will be safe. I'll wager he's not the only rat in the granary."

"I agree, unfortunately. As for the men, I doubt very much if you'll have a shortage of volunteers. You'd best take only ten, though—any more would be suspicious."

"I'll have Cullyn pick them out, then."

"Good. And think up a new name, will you, since I'm going to give you letters patent to carry and so on. 'No one' just simply won't do. Didn't you use another name around the King's herald? Was it your real name? I had the odd feeling it was."

"You were quite right. Even though my father chose to change it later out of spite, Galrion was what my mother named me."

"How antique-sounding!"

"Then it suits me perfectly, because if ever a man was a living relic, it's me. Very well, Your Grace. We'll do our best to bring Rhodry back for you."

"Not just for me, Lord Galrion. For Eldidd."

While Elaeno and his first mate worked with the crew that afternoon, Nevyn went up to the tower for one last visit with Perryn, or so he thought of it. Although Perryn's physical health was sound again, he still spent long hours lying in bed and staring at the ceiling or sitting at the window and staring at the sky. When Nevyn came in, he found the lord at the latter, watching the sullen drift of gray clouds coming up from the southeast.

"How's your breathing today?"

"Oh, er, ah, well, clear enough, I suppose."

"Good, good. You should make steady progress from now on."

Perryn nodded and went back to staring at the clouds.

"Come now, lad." Nevyn put on his best jolly-but-firm bedside manner. "You're not going to hang or suchlike, you know. It's time to start thinking about making somewhat of your life."

"But, um. I mean, er, ah, well, I just keep thinking about Jill."

"I'm sorry, but she's forever beyond you."

"I know that. Not what I meant, you see. Er, well, I was thinking about what you said, some weeks back, I mean. About not stealing things because well, ah, it's meddling and you don't know what's going to happen. Do you remember somewhat of that?"

"I do, and I'll admit to being pleased you're thinking it over."

"I have been, truly, and it aches my heart I was so stupid, about er, well, you know, um, well, about Rhodry, I mean. I hated him because Jill loved him, and here he was rather ah . . . er . . . important."

"I'm afraid it's a bit late to be worrying about that now."

"I know, and that's what aches my heart. I want to make restitution, but I don't have anything to give as lwdd. A couple of coppers, a horse—well, er, ah, he's not truly my horse, I suppose—but the saddle and suchlike are mine. It doesn't add up to a cursed lot, does it?"

"It doesn't at that. You might be able to pay Aberwyn some service, though I can't see you fighting in the war if things come to that."

"I could be a groom, or train for a farrier. I'd do it gladly, if it would help."

"Well and good, then. We'll talk about it when I come back."

"I heard the servants saying you were going to Cerrmor. Can I go, too? My heart aches with fear all the time, wondering what Cullyn would do if you weren't here to protect me."

"He doesn't even know what you've done."

"He might find out."

"Now, now, I . . ." Nevyn hesitated, thinking hard, trying to remember something that Perryn had once mentioned about himself. "Here, lad, after you met up with Rhodry, you started following Jill again. How did you know where she'd gone?"

"It's just this thing I can do. Like, er, like charming horses. I can just do it."

"Very well, but what is it that you're doing?"

"Finding somewhat that I love, like a home or my cousin or Jill. It's this feeling. When I'm pointed the right way, I feel splendid, and when I'm pointed the wrong way, I feel rotten at heart."

"Do you now? You know, this could come in very handy indeed. Tell you what, lad, you can sail with me after all."

"Sail?" Perryn's voice rose to a squeak. "In a ship? All the way to Cerrmor?"

"Just that."

"I can't do that. I'll be sick the whole beastly way. I'd rather face Cullyn than be seasick again, truly I would."

"Too bad. You were the one who was just talking about restitution, weren't you? And you'll get used to the motion after a while."

Out of simple mercy Nevyn omitted telling him their real destination. Bardek lay many more days of sailing away than Cerrmor did.

When the day of departure finally came, it dawned utterly windless. Since Nevyn had no desire to call the wind on shore where all of

Aberwyn could watch him, Elaeno badgered the harbormaster into providing a crew of longshoremen and yelled at the gwerbret's fleetmaster till he allowed the Bardekian to press a couple of galleys into service as tugs. From somewhere these harried officials found plenty of ropes as thick as a man's arm and poles the same. Once they had the necessary equipment, the Bardekian's first mate took over and showed everyone how to link the merchantman to the galleys. Elaeno and Nevyn got out of the way and stood on the stern deck of his ship, the *Harban Datzolan*, which translates out, more or less, to the *Guaranteed Profit*.

"I don't know why they're carrying on so," Elaeno remarked to Nevyn. "Every harbor in Bardek has tugs and suchlike for days like this. You can often pick up a bit of breeze out on the open sea when it's still as death in harbor."

"Indeed? Well, I'm afraid I know very little about ships and sailing."

"You don't need to. You get me the wind, and I'll get us to Surtinna. By the way, I've got Perryn tied up down in the hold. Once we're well out of port, I'll release him, but I didn't want him jumping overboard at the last minute."

Oars flashing, the improvised tugs headed out, the ropes groaning and creaking as they tightened, and the heavy merchantman began to move as the longshore crew shoved it away from the pier with their poles. Nevyn settled himself on a couple of crates in the bow and looked up at the top of the mast, where the blue-and-silver dragon pennant of the gwerbrets of Aberwyn hung flaccid in the windless cold. Elaeno stood casually in front of him, effectively shielding him with his vast bulk while he gave orders to his first mate. Nevyn shut out the sound of their voices and gathered himself, calling in his mind on the Kings of Air as he let himself sink into a state close to trance. Up on the mast the pennant stirred and fluttered as they came, announcing that they remembered their promise to the Master of the Aethyr. Elaeno glanced up, then yelled at the men on the towropes to get ready to throw them clear. Nevyn imaged the flaming pentagram and placed it far astern. Now, he thought, let the wind come!

With a roar and a whistle the squall rushed out, a channel of wind not more than thirty feet wide, streaming over the sea and striping the water dark as it ran. With a slap it hit the sails, and the ship bounded forward like a kicked dog.

"Throw those ropes!" Elaeno bellowed. "Get 'em clear, or we'll be dragging the cursed tugs to Bardek with us!"

The men heaved the ropes clear just as the ship raced between the two galleys and burst free of the harbor. Except for Elaeno, every man on board was utterly silent, staring at their arrow-straight wake or glancing furtively round as if they were afraid to look each other in the eye. In a storm of foul curses Elaeno bellowed orders and got them moving, some rushing aloft to trim the sails, others below to shift ballast and cargo. After making a few adjustments to the wind's direction and speed, Nevyn got up and stretched. Far behind, Eldidd was already fading to a smear on the horizon.

"By the Holy Stars themselves," the first mate whispered. "I've never seen a wind like this before."

"Savor it," Elaeno said. "Doubtless you never will again."

For days the storm clouds had lain like sheared fleeces over the Surtinna foothills. Even when it wasn't actually raining, a thick mist shrouded the view and clung to the wet cloaks of the Great if Utterly Glum Krysello and his sneezing band of barbarians while the wind blew steadily, so cold that Jill assumed that it must be snowing up in the high mountains. The one good thing she could say about the weather was that being miserable was keeping her mind off the Hawks. The entire world seemed to have shrunk to the constant struggle to keep moving through wet and cold. Since they were off the road the footing was next to impossible—trails that were deep mud or grassy hillsides so saturated that the sod split like overripe fruit under the horses' hooves. At times a horse would fall, and its panic would spread through the long line of stock. Calming them again would waste precious time, until Jill was ready to simply turn the entire herd loose to fend for itself. Oddly enough, to her way of thinking, it was always Salamander who insisted they keep all the horses with them for as long as possible.

The nights' camps brought no real rest or respite. It was another struggle to find decent grazing for the horses and to keep the humans' meager provisions dry. Lighting a fire was out of the question, even with Salamander's dweomer; not only would the light announce their presence to possible enemies, but there was quite simply no dry wood. At night no one could sleep properly in wet blankets; there was no natural shelter except for the tangled and thorny underbrush or the occasional stand of boulders. They all began talking less and less, since every word seemed to come out as a snarl or a snap that set off an argument.

Through it all Jill kept a strict watch on Gwin, even though his devotion to Rhodry was so doglike that it turned her stomach. Late one afternoon, as she and Salamander were tethering out the riding horses together out of earshot of the others, Jill brought up her suspicions.

"Even if he doesn't mean to betray us, how do I know the Hawks aren't still using him? Couldn't they make some sort of link with his mind and just follow him like a beacon?"

"They could, but they haven't, my dubious dove. I scrutinized him most thoroughly and found naught."

"You're certain?"

"Certain? Certain, positive, convinced, and quite quite sure." He paused in his work to look her over with shrewd eyes. "Jealous, are you?"

"Just what do you mean, you rotten elf?"

"Just what I said. Everywhere our Rhodry goes, there's Gwin, gazing at him fondly and hanging on his every word and smile like a lover. And there's Rhodry, who may or may not be flattered—but he doesn't ask him to stop."

For a moment Jill felt like hitting him, just for pointing out what she'd been trying not to see.

"I'd be jealous, too, if I were you," Salamander went on, somewhat hastily. "I'm not belittling you, mind. But here, my sagacious sparrow, ponder this. It's not Rhodry that Gwin's in love with, but his own salvation. Ye gods, think of how he must feel! For the first time in his life, he has hope, he has a future, he has honor . . . of course he's englamoured. But he can't understand that—Hawks are not trained in the subtleties of the mind, after all—so he gives our Rhodry all the credit and worships him."

"Well, truly, I see your point. But . . ."

"It gripes your soul anyhow? Please don't throw that peg at me, my turtledove. It'll leave an ugly bruise."

With the sixth dawn, the sun finally broke through the clouds. As the mist rolled back, they could see that not only did the trail they'd been following peter out into a ravine, but also that the archon's road lay only half-a-mile downhill and to the west of their camp. After a brief argument, Jill agreed that they'd better take the road and make some speed. Just at noon the sky began to clear before a south-running wind. Although everyone's mood began to clear along with it, and Jill was as glad as anyone at the prospect of getting dry, still she felt uneasy without their water-shield around them. When she trotted her horse up to the head of the line next to Salamander, she found him anxious as well.

"I'd hoped we could hide in the rain until we reached Pastedion, my turtledove, but such, alas, is not the case."

"How close do you think our enemies are?"

For an answer he merely shrugged. Although the hills rose steep on their left hand, the road was winding level here along the lip of a canyon to their right. Some fifty yards down she could see the rush of white water among the trees.

"We'll reach Pastedion on the morrow," Salamander said abruptly. "If we reach it, that is. I feel danger like a stink around us."

"So do I. I was thinking, if we could work with Gwin, maybe we could scry our enemies out."

"I like that 'we,' my most magical magpie. Well, perhaps we could, but truly, I rather dread the idea. Opening a link to Gwin's charming little mind will not be the most pleasant of experiences."

"Neither would dying at the hands of the Hawks."

"Um, well, truly. How clearly and succinctly you put things! We'll see if we can talk him into it."

"Well and good, then. We should stop for the noon meal soon and rest the horses. The poor beasts have been through an ordeal of their own this past eightnight or so."

"True spoken, but I want to make another mile or so before we stop." Salamander looked profoundly sly. "There's somewhat I want you to see."

They were traveling here through a huge, V-shaped valley, with the river churning at the bottom point of the V and their road clinging to the left side, about halfway up the hills. After some minutes Jill heard an odd sound ahead, like the buzzing of an enormous swarm of bees, which slowly grew louder and louder as they rode until it resolved itself into the pour of a waterfall. The road made one last twist and came, all of a sudden, clear of the V-shaped valley to end on a flat stretch of ground, the top of a cliff, while farther down on their right hand the canyon it had been bordering merely ended, as abruptly as if a giant had cut the cliff with a spade. Laced with rainbows the waterfall roared and thundered, plunging straight down thousands of feet to a long open valley far below. With a whoop that was half-fear, half-delight, Jill flung up her hand for a halt. Snorting and milling, the exhausted stock came to a stop and at last stood quiet enough to let Rhodry and Gwin ride up beside her. When she twisted round in the saddle, she could see half a hill behind her, the dome sliced through as if by that hypothetical giant's knife. Across the valley, partly hidden by mists, rose its counterpart, sliced just as cleanly into another steep cliff. Beyond that hill she could see mountains rising into white-glinting peaks that marched off to the horizon.

"What made this valley?" she screamed at Salamander. "Dweomer?"

"Don't know." He yelled back. "The Wildfolk say ice did it, lots and lots of ice years and years ago, but that's impossible."

Screeching at each other over the thundering water-noise, they dismounted and rationed out the last of the grain to the riding mounts and pack animals while the extra horses had to make do with scruffy grass. Frightened though she was of possible pursuit, Jill decided that they simply had to give the stock a rest, because the only way down the cliff was a switchbacked trail, not more than four feet wide, hacked—and roughly—into the living rock. She hated thinking of the government slaves who'd been forced to cut that trail; some, no doubt, had died in the making.

Munching on a chunk of stale flatbread she walked over to the waterfall and stared down at the veil of mist floating as much as falling down to the valley floor. It fed the continuation of the north-south river they'd been following, which joined another, winding roughly east to west. The valley itself ran along this second river for miles—she could see neither end of it—and while there were trees clustered all along the rivers, the rest of the valley floor seemed to be the usual Bardekian grassland. At the moment, though, the grass was greening from the roots up, so that it seemed gold gauze lay over green silk all across the valley, and the trees were rain-washed glossy, like malachite beads in the sun. In a moment Salamander came over to join her. He pointed down at the trail and grinned.

"Hope you're not afraid of heights!" he yelled.

She shook her head no to save her voice.

"Come with me," he went on at the same high volume. "Somewhat else to show you."

Back where the road emerged from the hills, the shoulder sloped gradually enough to allow them to scrabble up the shrubby grade and climb partway up the hill. As they moved slowly round to the valley view, they also angled away from the falls sufficiently to hear themselves talk again.

"Actually I wanted a private word with you," Salamander said.

"I assumed that. Is Gwin cutting up rough about working with us?"

"I'm afraid so. Apparently he sees surrendering his will, even for the briefest of moments, as a grave defeat and insult. He's not accusing us of insulting him, mind—rationally he knows he should help—but he finds the idea so revolting that I doubt if he'll be able to do it."

"That's torn it, then! We'll have to rely on the Wildfolk. They've been good about warning us so far."

"Relying on the Wildfolk, my petite partridge, is one of the better ways to suffer a bitter disappointment."

"Oh, of course, but there's naught else to do."

"Well, unfortunately, there is somewhat else, but I say unfortunate because it's incredibly dangerous." By then the steep climb was making him pant a little. "To me, that is, who's the one who'd be doing it if we do it at all."

"Scrying in a trance?"

"Worse than that. Flying. Like Aderyn."

"I didn't know you could do that."

"Well, I just barely learned. That's what makes it so dangerous."

"Without you the rest of us are doomed. This is no time for cheap heroics."

"Exactly what I'd hoped you'd say."

They shared a grin and saved their breath for the climb. At last they came to the crest, some five hundred feet above the cliff edge, and could look down the long valley to the west. Jill swore aloud at still another marvel lying there, a lake about a mile across and so achingly blue that it looked like a piece of sky trapped among the trees. It was also circular, so perfectly so that again she thought of government slaves. Salamander waved an arm in its direction and assumed his portentous wizard's voice.

"Behold the Navel of the World."

"Ye gods, is that what the Bardekians call it? Why did they go to all the trouble to dig a pond like that?"

"They didn't. It's been here forever, or so the priests tell me. The Wildfolk say it was made by a huge stone that fell out of the sky after the aforementioned ice carved the valley. That's what I mean about trusting the Wildfolk, my turtledove, or spirits in general. They mean well, but they have no wits. If they don't know the truth about somewhat, they'll make up a fantastic story just because they want to help their friends so badly."

"I see. Well, dogs don't have any wits either, but they bark loud enough when someone's at your gate."

"Now that is true spoken, and a sign of hope. And, as you say, there's not a lot else we can do. When we're making camp tonight, you and I shall ask our little friends to keep watch for us."

"If we live to reach the valley floor. That trail frightens me."

"I've ridden down it before, actually. You've got to trust the horses. They want to live as badly as we do, and they're the ones with sure feet."

"If you say so. And where's Pastedion?"

"Just beyond the lake. If it weren't so misty you could make it out, so we're not too far from sanctuary. Unless we want to lame and founder these horses, once we reach the valley floor they're going to have to take their leisure like lords for the rest of the day."

After a few minutes more rest they set out, Jill riding at the head of the line, Rhodry next, then Gwin, and finally Salamander, taking the rear—and the dust that would make seeing difficult—because he knew the trail. Although Jill had to coax her horse onto the trail, once he started he settled down, as if in his dull equine way he realized that he'd be better off getting it over with, and the extra stock that she was leading came along steadily after him. The trail turned out to be a scant three feet wide except at the switchbacks, where it widened like the scour of a river's bends to about eight feet across, just barely room enough for a clever horse to turn himself round. Occasionally the cliff face bulged out, forcing her to lie along her horse's neck as they squeezed past, because leaning out and away would have been a dangerous maneuver indeed. Yet, so long as she didn't look down over the edge, she found the going much easier than she'd expected.

At the bottom, where the trail widened into a proper road, heading off to join the river, there was a tall slab of stone covered with Bardekian writing. Jill went some yards past it, then paused her horses and turned in the saddle to watch the others, an understandable impulse that was something of a mistake. When she saw Rhodry coming down, with his horse apparently crawling like a fly on the cliff face, she felt honestly faint, sick to her stomach, and light-headed as she clung to her saddle peak and wondered what had ever possessed her to make a ride like that. She didn't look again until all three of the men were safe and Rhodry was beside her.

"I couldn't watch when you were riding down, my love," he said. "But doing it myself wasn't so bad."

"I felt the same, truly. Salamander says we're going to camp here for the rest of the day."

"Good. Ye gods, this sun feels splendid."

With a lazy grin he stretched in the saddle, turning his face to the sky with a real delight in the simple feel of the warmth. It was an elven gesture, and she realized more of the change in him, that losing his memory had stripped the perfect warlord away from his core of self in the same way that he'd throw off his armor after a battle. But what's he going to do when he has to ride as cadvridoc again? she thought, and with the thought came a cold fear, a wondering if he were still the man that Aberwyn needed. When Gwin came riding over, she almost welcomed his interruption.

"Are we going to camp by the river?" Gwin was looking only at Rhodry. "They don't get flooding up here."

"We might as well, then." Rhodry glanced her way. "What do you say, my love?"

"Sounds fine."

When she happened to look at Gwin, their eyes met, and he

arranged a hasty smile, but not quickly enough to cover an expression that she could only call murderous. I'm not the truly jealous one, am I? she thought. I'd best tell Salamander about this.

That night, just after sunset, in a suite of painted rooms in an inn some fifty miles downriver from Pastedion, the Hawkmaster was eating a meal of roast pork and spiced vegetables washed down with fine white wine. Crouched at his feet, Baruma gobbled the occasional scraps that the master threw his way. When a slice of pork fell beside him, he snatched at it only to find himself face-to-face with the wolf, growling soundlessly. This close Baruma could see that its eyes were only two glowing spheres of reddish light. He was so hungry that he would have fought a demon from the Third Hell for that bit of pork.

"Go away!" he snarled. "It's mine!"

The wolf bared white fangs and lowered its ears.

"What?" the Hawkmaster turned in his chair. "What is that thing?"

"A wolf, master. It hates me. It follows me everywhere."

"It's not a real creature, you fool. Who sent it after you?"

"I don't know." Baruma thought hard, pushing his clouded mind to its limits. "An enemy."

"I didn't think it was a gift from a friend, no." The master kicked him in the stomach, but only lightly. "How long ago did it appear?"

"Weeks. After I visited you in Valanth. You didn't send it, then? I think I remember thinking you might have sent it."

"No, I didn't. Now isn't this interesting? Did the Old One send it to spy on you?"

"He said he didn't. He could have lied."

"Just so. I think we'll find out where it came from. Eat that food, but slowly. Keep its attention. Whoever ensouled it seems to have made it behave like a real animal. Let's see how much."

When the Hawkmaster got up, the wolf turned its head and watched him, but with no malice and no real interest. Baruma took his chance and grabbed the meat. As he munched it, the wolf stared, lips back, drooling a little, but the drool vanished before it touched the floor. He could hear the Hawkmaster chanting, and to his magically engulfed sight a circle of pale blue fire appeared, running widdershins round him and the wolf both. Just as the ring closed, the wolf snarled and leapt—too late. It slammed into the invisible wall that emanated from the flames like glass-clear smoke, leapt again, howled, threw itself at the wall over and over until at last it fell back, panting, into the center of the circle. Ears down, hackles raised, it lowered its head and snarled at him, its teeth white and wet and gleaming as it took one stiff-legged step forward. Baruma screamed.

"You fool!" the Hawkmaster hissed. "It's me it wants. I'm right behind you."

Baruma heard the rustle of his tunic as the master knelt behind him and laid one massive hand on the back of his neck. With a moan Baruma felt himself slump as the grip tightened and the master's power flowed into his mind, making his consciousness dance and sway until the world shrank to the red eyes of the wolf.

"Reach out your hand," the master said. "Touch it."

"No, oh please no!"

Pain shot through his neck in a spurt of fire that made him gasp. When he reached out a trembling hand toward the wolf, the creature snapped and sank its teeth in his fingers. Although he whimpered, there was no pain, just a coldness that spread up his arm and numbed him as it spread. It touched his neck, crept up his face, and at the last washed over his eyes. The room changed, turning all blue and swimmy, and he floated above his unconscious body in the midst of a sphere of silver light. The wolf was huge, towering above him, and from its navel stretched a silver cord made of mist that burrowed through the sphere and ran some long way off. When the master spoke, his voice seemed to come through water.

"Ride the wolf."

Baruma floated up and settled onto the creature's back. When he grasped a handful of hair at the wolf's roached neck, he realized that his hand was blue and transparent. Yet his fingers seemed to touch something solid and tighten as the silver sphere faded away. With a snarl the wolf leapt, bursting through the walls of the inn chamber and out into a night made grotesque by the stars—enormous, threatening, silver stars, hanging so low to earth that it seemed he should be able to touch them, sending rays like shards of glass into his eyes. He yelped, then whimpered steadily after he looked down to see a misty-blue landscape far below him. The wolf took no notice, merely loped through the sky as it followed the silver cord that led on and on.

At last the wolf stopped, lifting its head as if it were sniffing the wind, then swooped down, its tail wagging madly, circling round as it flew down into a long valley cut by huge silver walls of trembling mist. By then Baruma was too exhausted to whine; he heard his voice babbling, describing everything he saw as they reached the earth, not far from one of the walls of silvery smokelike mist. Here everything was a bright rusty-red, the trees like pillars of flame, the grass glowing and pulsating with vegetable force. As the wolf trotted along he could see ahead a swarm of fuzzy red and yellow shapes like a swarm of bees, and not far from them two ovoids of glowing light, one golden, one red shot with black, and two enormous silver flames. Closer and closer they came, until Baruma realized that he was seeing the auras of a herd of horses, two human beings, and two—what? The shapes within the silver flames were humanlike, yet no man or woman had an aura such as he was seeing.

Suddenly, bursting upon him like arrows Wildfolk appeared, an army of gnomes and sprites, clustering round, grabbing at him, pinching, shoving, biting at him until he screamed again, screamed and sobbed and begged for mercy while the wolf loped on, indifferent to the attack. He saw one of the silver flames ahead leap up and send a huge spear of light, hurtling straight toward him. Then the sky seemed to explode. They were gone—Wildfolk, wolf, auras, flames—everything gone, and he was falling falling falling a long way down

to wake with an audible scream and a flash of pain that tore at his entire body. Writhing and moaning he opened his eyes to see the Hawkmaster leaning over him as he lay on the inn-room floor.

"You're alive? Good. You're proving very useful indeed, little Baruma." The master sat back on his heels, then reached up and took a wine cup off the table. "Drink this."

Baruma sat up and gulped the sweet wine; oddly enough, it seemed to clear his head rather than muddle it.

"Those silver flames were elven auras," the Hawkmaster said.

"But one of them was Rhodry!"

"Oh, indeed?" The master rose, reaching for the wine cup. "For that information you get another drink. Did you recognize anyone else?"

"Gwin. Gwin was there."

"I wondered if he'd been taken prisoner. I would have known if

he'd been killed. Who were the others? They have magic, tremen-
dously powerful magic, and you should be able to recognize them.
They must be Inner Circle members."

"Her. Rhodry's woman. She was there. And the other elf used
dweomer against me. He was the one who sent the spear of light."

The Hawkmaster went on refilling the cup, his face betraying not a
twitch or a grimace, but through the link that bound him to the
master Baruma could feel his fear.

"It's the dweomer of light, isn't it, master?" he whispered. "They're
not from the guild at all. They serve the dweomer of light, don't
they?"

"Shut up!" The master threw the wine cup full into his face.

Baruma began to laugh. In the last small sane corner of his mind
he wondered if he were laughing because he was going to be re-
venged on the Hawkmaster or out of simple hysteria, but either way
he gasped and howled and writhed on the floor until the master
kicked him into silent submission.

"Very well, then," the Hawkmaster said, and his voice was perfectly steady. "At least now I know who our enemies are. They
certainly weren't sent by the Old One, were they? Later I'll see if I
can arrange a parley with him, but for now, let's give Gwin's captors
something to think about. Tonight that wolf goes home to stay."

Rhodry had just come back to their cold camp from checking on the
horses when he saw a swarm of Wildfolk rise up and tear off to the
west like a flurry of dead leaves in a wind. All at once Jill yelped in
surprise and scrambled to her feet; Salamander yelled even louder
and jumped up, too, to wave his arms in the air and chant in some
strange language. When a silver ball of light blossomed above the
camp, dimly in midair Rhodry could see a horde of Wildfolk mobbing
what seemed to be the misty and ill-defined figure of a wolf, and an
even vaguer indication of something riding on its back. Then they
were all gone, and Salamander was standing with his hands on his
hips and swearing like a pirate. It had all happened so fast and been
so cryptic that Rhodry felt as openmouthed stupid as a peasant
gawking at a fake unicorn skull in the market fair. He was honestly
surprised to find Gwin white-faced and shaking.

"Here," Rhodry said automatically. "No danger now."

"Like Hell," Gwin snapped. "I don't know exactly what happened, but the Hawkmaster's behind it. I should have known I'd never get free of him, not for long."

"Na, na, na, don't fret about that now," Salamander broke in. "You'll get free of him eventually, if we have to kill him to do it, which, come to think of it, we doubtless will. Be that as it may, I wonder if he was looking for you specifically or merely scouting out the lay of the land—if indeed that was him, which I doubt, because our wolf-rider looked most unhappy, brigga-sopping scared in fact, and I doubt me if you get to be a Hawkmaster by giving in to fits of cowardice."

"Oh." Color ebbed back into Gwin's face. "But he could have sent—by the Clawed Ones, he would have sent someone else to spy for him. He's above scut-work like this."

"Since when is scrying on the etheric scut-work?" Salamander said. "Well, I suppose a Hawk might see it that way."

"For the love of every god," Rhodry snarled. "Would you two tell me what's going on?"

"My apologies, younger brother of mine. Jill and I looked up to see a more or less human figure riding on the back of a wolf whilst a profusion of Wildfolk tried to tip him off. Needless to say, we found the sight alarming, didn't we, my turtledove—oh ye gods! Jill!"

Rhodry spun round to find her standing some five feet away. Perfectly still, perfectly rigid, one hand out in front of her as if to ward a blow, she was staring down at a wolf crouched in front of her, its lips back in a soundless snarl as it stared up, seemingly into her eyes. For a moment he thought it was real; then he realized that he could see right through it. By the light of Salamander's dweomer-lantern Rhodry could also see the silver cord that ran from its navel back to hers and the peculiar waves of force that rippled like water back and forth between them. When he lunged forward, Salamander grabbed him and hauled him back.

"She's got to finish this herself. Jill! Listen to me! You've got to reclaim it. Bend your will to the cord! Suck the thing lifeless through that cord!"

She nodded, the barest movement of her head to show she'd heard him, and kept staring the wolf down. Although she never moved, it suddenly leapt up onto all fours and laid its ears down, its mouth opening in a silent howl. When it jerked itself toward her, Jill flung up a hand palm-outward and stopped it cold. For a moment they glared at each other, the wolf all fangs and lowered head, poised for the attack, she grim concentration and hard eyes. All at once its tail began to wag, just timidly, and it whined, lifting one paw, staring up, pleading with her, then flopping down to roll on its back, whining like a puppy. Rhodry saw energy flowing up the silver cord in her direction, leaching the creature's life away as it begged and fawned desperately at her feet, growing fainter, then smaller, then fading away to the sound of a whine, hanging on the air.

Jill dropped her face into her hands and sobbed. This time, when Rhodry started toward her, Salamander let him go. He caught her in his arms and pulled her close, let her keen between sobs in honest grief, but he'd never been so bewildered since the day when he'd woken in the hold of the ship to find Baruma gloating over him. All at once Jill pulled back and looked at him, her face wet and puffy with tears.

"I loved it," she whispered. "It was part of me."

Then she fainted, so suddenly that if he hadn't been holding her she would have dropped where she stood. As he knelt and laid her down, he heard his brother cursing. Salamander knelt down next to him and laid his long fingers on Jill's face.

"Ah, by every stinking demon in every stinking hell, she's cold as ice! Gwin, fetch me a blanket! My apologies, Rhoddo, but she had to kill it herself. There wasn't one cursed thing I could do to help."

"You better be telling the truth, or I'll have your hide for a saddlebag."

"I was afraid you'd take it that way. My thanks, Gwin. Go away, will you, younger brother, and leave her to me and the fresh night air?"

Fuming with reluctance Rhodry got up and stepped back as Salamander began wrapping the blanket round his patient. A crowd of anxious Wildfolk hovered, clustering round Jill, climbing all over Salamander, darting round Rhodry's head. Two sprites even perched briefly on his shoulders, but when Gwin came up behind him, the sprites disappeared with a hiss.

"He'll set her right," Gwin said. "I've never seen anyone with dweomer like your brother's, or like your woman's, for that matter."

Only then did Rhodry realize that he'd just witnessed a magical working, and that Jill had been the one to perform it. He felt as if his already shattered and unstable world had twisted under him once again, leaving him struggling to find his footing. Gwin, it seemed, misunderstood his silence.

"Look, Salamander knows what he's doing. He's pouring enough magnetism into her to heal an elephant, and out of his own aura at that."

"That's supposed to be a good thing?"

"Of course it is! Come now, you don't have to be jealous of your own brother."

This last made so little sense that Rhodry shook his head as if he could physically shoo the words away like a buzzing fly. Later, when Jill was sitting up, dead-pale but managing to smile, and his worry had subsided enough to let him think clearly, he remembered Gwin's obscure remark again, but this time it stabbed him to the heart. Jill and Salamander had ridden all over Bardek together for weeks, looking for him. He found himself watching them closely, as they sat under the magical silver light, heads together, whispering about things that he couldn't understand, and he wondered why he had never noticed before just how intimate they seemed.

If Jill had been her normal self, she might have noticed immediately that something was wrong with Rhodry, but as it was, reclaiming the wolf had left her exhausted, and realizing that the danger round them had just doubled did nothing to let her rest. All that night she slept fitfully, waking often to mull over the strange fragments of dreams that came to her, torn visions of sneering sorcerers with burning dark eyes or enormous wolves that came plunging from the air to snap at her throat. Finally, about an hour before dawn, when the sky was lightening to a pale gray, she gave it up and rolled out of her blankets, leaving Rhodry sound asleep and snoring on his back with one arm over his face. Some couple of hundred yards from the camp, perched on a pale tan boulder, Salamander was keeping watch. Stumbling a little and yawning, she joined him there.

"You should be sleeping," he remarked.

"Can't. I feel like the Lord of Hell dragged me behind his chariot for about twenty miles, but I just can't sleep."

"How do you feel? Debilitated, mayhap, infirm, unwell, feeble, ailing, or just plain sick?"

"Just tired, my thanks. Or, well ..." She hesitated, thinking. "There's somewhat wrong, but I can't quite place what it is ... not a headache or suchlike, but ... somewhat's missing."

"Missing?"

"Missing. Part of me died with the wolf, like. I still hate the dark dweomer and everything it stands for, but I don't hate it in the same way. It's all cold, now. Does that make sense?"

"It does, and it's for the better, too. Consider this, my open-minded owlet. Suppose someone went to a chirurgeon with a tumor swelling under their arm, and in his hatred of disease that chirurgeon began screaming and swearing and stabbing the wretched growth over and over with his knife. Would that be a good thing for the patient?"

"It wouldn't, truly. I see your meaning—it's better to hunt down evil with a cold mind, so you can cut carefully and deep and well."

"Just so. Just so."

Even though Salamander looked like he was about to say more, Jill yawned so hard that she shuddered. He laid an alarmed hand on her shoulder and stared into her eyes.

"Tired, indeed, my turtledove. Look thou there! Rosy-fingered dawn does chase away the ravens of night with her war darts fashio-d of the sun's rays, and I suggest we get back to camp and wake the others. The sooner we get on the road, the sooner we get a real meal."

As they were walking back together, Rhodry came to meet them. The way that he looked her over, with cold eyes and his mouth set in a thin line, made her feel uneasy.

"What's wrong, my love?" she said.

"*Is* somewhat wrong?" He turned to Salamander. "What were you doing out there anyway?"

"Keeping watch, like we agreed."

Rhodry started to speak, then merely shrugged and fell into step beside them. I'll talk to him later, she thought, I'm just so tired. Back at the camp, Gwin was rolling up bedrolls and generally collecting the gear for the day's ride. Rhodry went off to help him without a word more.

"I'll start saddling the horses," Salamander said.

"I'll help."

"Don't. Get some rest, will you?"

Obediently she followed Rhodry into camp. When she sat down on the ground by her saddlebags, he stopped work and looked at her for a moment, merely looked with a hard assessment in his eyes.

"I'm all right now, truly I am. Just a bit tired."

"How long were you out there with my brother?"

"What? Not very."

"Good." Abruptly he looked away. "Well, you need your rest, you know."

"I do know." She stifled a yawn barely in time. "We'll reach Pastedion today. By the Goddess herself, I want a hot bath and a soft bed."

"I hope we reach it, anyway." It was Gwin, strolling over. "If the Hawks know where we are, and after last night it looks like they do, they're not going to wish us godspeed on our journey and leave it at that."

"Is there a guild in Pastedion?" Rhodry said.

"Not that I know of, but then, I wouldn't, would I?" Gwin smiled, a brief twitch of his mouth. "They never tell a journeyman one thing more than he needs to know."

Jill shut her eyes and considered the problem. She could feel Wildfolk clustering round her, feel the rushy exhalation of their energy and a cool wind of some kind, blowing over her, blowing round her

picking her up suddenly to fly up high in a cloud of overjoyed Wildfolk, beautiful and crystalline forms, glinting with light and color here on their proper plane. Her own gray gnome came to her as a quivering nexus of olive and citrine crystalline lines, shot through with russet sparks, that swelled and retracted again as they flew together high above the rusty-red earth. In the silver fountain of force pouring up from the circular lake, blue and silver beings danced and soared in greeting, and the sylphs, pure light and shimmering and little else, darted here and there round them like an honor guard.

Far below them she saw what seemed to be a pile of charcoal hunks or ingots of black iron, piled this way and that at the edge of the water. Among them crawled tiny points of light, vaguely egg-shaped, in many different colors. She swooped down lower, saw the pattern of straight streets and square corners laid among them, and realized that she was seeing Pastedion and its houses of dead wood and stone. In a burst of revulsion she swept upward again, the gnome close behind her, and headed back over the valley. Down below the archons' road ran straight, a gash of ugly black through the reddish aura of the grass, throbbing with new life from the winter rains. Never in her life had she felt so free, so happy, as she swooped and fluttered through the dawn-swept sky.

All at once the Wildfolk disappeared, winking out with an exhalation of warning. Coming straight toward her was a silver flame, swelling and towering as it burned in the blue light. Out of sheer instinct she dropped straight down, heading for the safety of the earth; then Salamander's mind reached hers.

"You misbegotten thick-headed jenny-mule! What are you doing out here? Don't you realize how vulnerable you are? Get back! Get back now!"

She felt a tug at her midriff and looked to see the silver cord, tightening, shrinking, pulling her back to her body. The moment she remembered that she had a body, she felt its pull like an irresistible lust, grabbing her, yanking her from the sky, down and down

and with a sound like the slap of a hand on wood she was awake, lying on the ground and aching all over with what seemed to be a thousand bruises. When she tried to sit up, she groaned aloud. Salamander was kneeling beside her, and over his shoulder she could see Rhodry's fear-struck face.

"Apologies," she mumbled. "I never used to make a habit of fainting like a court lady. It must be the bad company I'm keeping."

"No doubt it is," Salamander said with a long sigh of relief. "And you have my apologies, because you're going to be as sore as a demon with emrods for a while. I had to drive you back into your body and fast."

She went cold, sat up slowly, studying him all the while in the hopes of finding that he was jesting, but she'd never seen him so serious.

"What do you mean?" she whispered.

"You know what I mean. We'll discuss it later. I'm sorry, my petite partridge, but we've got to be on the road. You may curse me as you ride."

Curse him she did, too, because those bruises turned out to be not some magical illusion but the very real result of her etheric double slamming into her physical body. Staying on horseback was painful in the extreme. After a few miles of riding she had no energy for anything but shifting her weight in the saddle in a vain attempt to ease her aching muscles and sore joints or to prevent the worst of the jolts when her horse made a particularly hard step or stumbled a little. Although both Salamander and Rhodry tried to talk with her, she snarled at them impartially until they gave it up as a bad job. She was barely aware of their surroundings, except to notice in a general way that they were passing through cultivated farmlands, a good sign that the city lay nearby.

After what seemed like weeks of agony, they reached Pastedion about an hour after noon. To her normal eyes the town was lovely, built mostly of pale tan stone and studded with lavish gardens. As they herded their horses down the cobbled streets, they heard a symphony of bells ringing softly in the warm and flower-scented air: the rolling boom of temple bells, and a soprano jingle from the tasseled harnesses of the little gray donkeys that many of the passersby were leading along.

"We should get one of those," Salamander announced.

"What in the names of all the gods do we need a wretched donkey for?" Jill snarled. "That's all I want—another blasted four-hoofed worry following me round."

"My dear turtledove! How nasty you've become! If you wouldn't go flying all over the landscape against your teacher's wishes, you wouldn't get bruised like that."

"If my teacher wouldn't babble so much, he might live to see the summer come."

As they walked on, they began to attract a crowd of loiterers, children, and women with market baskets. Every now and then someone would call out, in the friendliest possible way, and tell them that they were weeks too late for the big horse market. In the middle of town they found a large public square, cobbled and sporting two fountains. On one side was the archon's residence, or so Salamander said, and on the other was the temple of Dalae-oh-contremo. Behind a stucco wall, painted with pictures of what seemed to be gods sailing boats through the night sky, rose the curving roofs of a cluster of longhouses and the tops of a row of ancestor statues. In the center of this wall was a wooden door with a pair of crossed oars over the lintel. Salamander pounded on it with all the strength he could muster.

"I hope they let us in," Rhodry muttered. "We look like the scum of the earth, truly."

If the temple turned them down, there would be no sanctuary elsewhere. Jill was suddenly aware of just how filthy and road-stained they were, with Rhodry and Gwin as unshaven and sullen as highwaymen, though Salamander never seemed to grow either beard nor bad temper. Laden with filthy gear their horses were shaggy and muddy, standing all spraddle-legged and head-down from exhaustion. When the door opened she went tense at the sight of a young priest, tall and slender in a spotless dark blue robe, his thick curly hair bound round with a fillet of solid gold.

"Well, well, the tide washes many a strange thing up on shore, does it?" he said in Bardekian, and he was smiling at Salamander as if at long-lost kin. "Here's a pleasant surprise! Come in, come in! His holiness will be so glad to see you." Then he hesitated, peering over Salamander's head at the others. "But I don't know if we've got room for all these horses."

"Later we'll take them to a public stables or something," Salamander said, also in Bardekian. "But let us in right now, Brother Meranno, because if you don't give us your sanctuary, we'll all be murdered on the street."

At that Merrano raised a shout, and other young men in blue robes came running to help lead the horses into the compound while keeping them away from the floral borders and the appetizing lawn. Although Salamander and Rhodry plunged into the middle of the confusion, grabbing halters and yelling at balky stock, Jill made her way clear and stood just inside the gates out of the way. She was so tired that she felt that all her muscles had turned to water, sloshing inside her skin, and she yawned, leaning back against the wall for support. Until, that is, she saw Gwin. He was leading in the last few horses, or rather, trying to, because every time he approached the threshold, he would suddenly stop, hesitate, then back up to try again. From the look on his face he was near tears, like a tiny child who, summoning all his will, tries to turn a somersault as deftly as his older brother but falls every time.

"What is it?" Jill called out.

"I don't know. Ah horseshit, I do know. They've got wards against the likes of me. I'd have been better off slitting my throat, Jill, back at that cursed farm where you found me."

"What do you mean?" She pried herself off the wall in a sudden rush of energy. "Is someone waiting for you inside?"

"Oh, never that. The men I'm afraid of won't be going into a place like this. It's just that I can't either."

As she hurried out the gates, her gray gnome appeared, pointing with one skinny finger at the air above the outer wall. When Jill looked up, she saw nothing at first, but if she squinted she could discern what might have been a shimmering distortion, as if she looked through glass. His mouth slack, Gwin was staring at the same empty spot. Jill suddenly realized that she could use this excuse to get rid of him, send him off with the horses to an inn or stable, perhaps, where—where what? she asked herself. Where he'll be easy prey for his old guild?

"Salamander!" she yelled. "Somewhat's wrong!"

Accompanied by a flurry of priests Salamander came trotting out, saw Gwin, looked up, and cursed in a most irreligious way under his breath. Brother Merrano apparently shared his understanding of the problem if not his taste in language.

"By the oars of the Wave-father! Now I wonder what's causing the trouble? Is this a slave of yours?"

"No, a freedman. He's been marked by—well, let us say some bad company of his youth, or so I'd guess." Salamander was giving Merrano a look of intense significance. "He's reformed. I'll swear it to you on the altar if you'd like."

"That won't be necessary. The question is how we're going to get him inside."

Gwin turned sharply away, and although his face betrayed nothing, Jill could guess that he was fighting back tears.

"We can hardly do a ceremony right out here in the public street," Merrano went on.

"Why not?" All at once Salamander grinned. "We shall dispense with the billowing incense, the chanting, the fine linen robes, and the booming gongs, but a ceremony we shall have none the less. Come here, turtledove, and take my right hand. Good. Now put your left on Gwin's shoulder, just casual like, as if you were going to tell him somewhat private. Now I put my other hand on his other arm, likewise and in a corresponding manner, and there we are!"

As soon as Salamander closed the circle by touching Gwin, Jill felt a rush of power flow round and round the three of them. The hairs on her arms and the back of her neck rose and prickled; Wildfolk swarmed into manifestation and dove into the current of force like swimmers in a river; Gwin tossed his head back and caught his breath with an audible gasp. This time, when she glanced up, Jill could see the ward, a glowing sphere of force capping the temple compound, all marked with strange sigils and flaming pentagrams.

"Aha, there's the trouble," Salamander murmured. "The rotten bastards have scarred his aura!"

When Jill considered Gwin again, she could see an inverted pentagram floating in the air above his head. There was something so sour and crabbed about that blackish, murky mark that she could have sworn she could smell it as a foulness in the air. All at once it caught fire and burned, shriveling away with a singed curl and a wisp of mucky smoke.

"There," Salamander pronounced. "Well and good, Gwin. See what happens now."

The moment Jill let go his hand and stepped back, the wards disappeared from her sight, and the Wildfolk all scattered in disappointment. Gwin picked up the reins of the horses, led them toward the gate, took one deep breath, and walked on through. Brother Merrano allowed himself a small cheer. For a moment Gwin nearly did weep, but he wiped his eyes vigorously on the back of his hand instead.

"My thanks," he said to Salamander. "I'll be your man for life."

"I'd rather you were your own man, actually, but you're welcome for the favor. Brother Merrano, now that we're all here, perhaps we'd best shut these gates. I have a most peculiar, exotic, eerie, and generally bizarre tale to tell to your superior."

"Your tales generally run along those lines, yes," Merrano said, grinning. "That's why we're all so glad to see you again."

o   o   o

As soon as he walked into the temple compound, Rhodry felt his black mood lift as palpably as if someone had stripped a wet cloak from his shoulders. Even when he glanced back to see Jill holding Salamander's hand and talking privately with Gwin, he thought nothing more than that they were trying to decide what to do with the twenty-odd extra horses that his brother had insisted on keeping with them—and which were turning out to be a nuisance that he, for one, could have well done without. When the circle broke up, he called to Salamander.

"We've got them all tethered and tied. It should do for now."

Salamander waved to him and, talking with Gwin, came strolling back inside with Jill following. Rhodry was alarmed at how tired she looked, with dark circles under her eyes and a stagger to her walk. A young priest who introduced himself as Brother Kwintanno had noticed her condition as well.

"The woman with you? Is she ill?"

"Just very tired. We've had a terrible long ride of it, getting here through the mountains."

"Let's get her to the guesthouse where you'll all be staying, then, so she can get some sleep. Evan can talk enough for everybody, and he probably will."

It took Rhodry a moment to realize that by Evan he meant Salamander. He also thought, and with some irritation, that he really should have remembered his brother's actual name before this.

Although Jill tried to claim that she was perfectly well and not in the least tired, she kept her protests short and let Rhodry put his arm round her for support as they followed the priest through the maze of buildings and huts in the enormous compound. The guesthouse turned out to be a pleasant wooden building, whitewashed inside and out, with three rooms and a number of cots, chairs, and low tables scattered through them. In the central room there was even a shelf with some ten scrolls and a lectern nearby for reading them.

"You'll have the place to yourself, this time of year," Kwintanno said. "During the summer we have many guests, here on legal matters, mostly." He went to a chest and began burrowing through its contents. "Yes, there are plenty of clean blankets. Take what you want. Later you can all visit our bathhouse if you so wish."

"I do wish, and with all my heart," Rhodry said. "Jill, you'd better sleep first."

"Am I arguing with you, my love?" She sat down on the edge of a cot and yawned, rubbing her face with both hands. "One blanket will be plenty, my thanks."

Kwintanno led Rhodry to one of the big longhouses he'd seen from the street and into a typical Bardekian reception room, its walls painted with scenes of godlike beings founding cities and handing over scrolls of laws to groveling humans. Up on the red-and-blue tiled dais, Salamander and Gwin were sitting cross-legged and talking—or rather, Salamander was talking—to an elderly man dressed in a long red robe. He was very old, his dark face lined and pouched, his curly hair pure white, but he sat straight and his black eyes were full of power.

"His Holiness, Takiton," Kwintanno whispered. "Bow when you approach."

Rhodry gladly made the head priest the lowest bow that he could manage and was rewarded with a smile and the wave of a wrinkled hand summoning him to the dais. He sat down a little behind Salamander and next to Gwin, who had the tight-lipped look of a man determined not to show his terror.

"Ah, Rhodry," Takiton said, "your brother's been telling me your sad tale."

"Indeed, Your Holiness?" Since he and Salamander had discussed this story during the journey, he knew what he was supposed to say. "I humbly hope you find it in your heart to forgive me for breaking the holy laws of your islands."

"Nicely spoken, but you weren't the first and doubtless won't be the last young man to gamble his freedom away. What bothers me is this forged bill of sale." Takiton held up the by-now much crumpled bit of bark-paper to the light that came in the high windows. "Evan, you and I shall speak of this privately later. But we can start the legal procedure for freeing your brother from your ownership this very afternoon."

"My thanks, Your Holiness," Salamander said. "How long do you think everything will take?"

"Oh, some days, most probably. The archon has his way of doing things, and there are several public festivals in the offing, too, that must be properly attended to."

When Rhodry looked Salamander's way he saw him nod agreement with a bland smile, but Gwin went tenser than before, his hands knuckling white in his lap. Rhodry himself felt a cold stab of fear: their enemies were close behind them, and there they were, forced to sit in this temple and wait for them to catch up.

Day after day, night after night, the dweomer-wind blew steadily. In a symphony of creaking ropes and groaning sail the *Guaranteed Profit* ran as straight and true as a banker chasing a debt as she headed across the Southern Sea toward the port of Surat. After a few days of jesting about luck, both the sailors and the men Nevyn brought from Aberwyn had become unnaturally calm, going about their work without saying more than a few necessary words to their officers, but whispering among themselves when they thought no one could see them. Every now and then Nevyn caught some of them looking his way in a mixture of awe and sheer terror; he would always smile gently in return and ignore the way they made the sign of warding against witchcraft every time he met them head-on. Since the carrack was a small and narrow boat, their fingers must have ached from all the necessary crossing. As for Perryn, he never noticed the peculiar wind at all, merely lay in the hold and groaned between brief spans of sleep.

Toward the end of the second week Nevyn woke one morning to find seagulls wheeling and crying above the ship and strands of kelp streaming past her sides. Up at the bow Elaeno and the first mate were staring straight ahead and discussing what to do when they hit port. At the sight of Nevyn the first mate snapped to attention and went a bit pale.

"I imagine this wind is too strong for sailing into harbor," Nevyn said.

"She is," Elaeno said. "No doubt, though, she'll slack off at the right moment. We'll be in sight of land in about half a watch, say, and should make port in another half."

"I'll tend to things, then."

With a muttered excuse the first mate fled.

"Are you ever going to be able to sign on a crew again?" Nevyn said. "Once this story gets round, I mean?"

"Good question. Well, I pay good wages, and I've always been known as a fair-minded man, so that should count for somewhat. Now, here, are you sure you want to make land at Surat? It's one of the busiest ports in the islands, and most likely our enemies will be watching it."

"Perhaps, perhaps not. If they were me, they'd sneak ashore at some obscure port, so maybe we'll fool them by marching right in. It matters naught, truly. They'll know I'm here soon enough, no matter what I do."

By noon Nevyn could see the white cliffs of Surtinna, rising sharp and clear in the brilliant light. He sat down on a crate in the bow, imaged the flaming pentagram, and called upon the Kings of the Air. In a gust and flurry of breeze they came, exuding graciousness, and remarked that he might bind the wind to his purposes once again, if he wished, to bring the Dragon of Aberwyn home to his people. From the bottom of his heart, Nevyn thanked them as one prince to another. In a few moments the wind slacked, and the dark stripe of squall that had followed them for days disappeared. As they turned round a headland and headed in, the wind dropped to an ordinary sea breeze, nicely brisk and blowing exactly as they might have wished, but an ordinary breeze nonetheless. Spread out behind its wide and shallow bay, Surat lay like an emerald on the white gold of a sandy beach. At the sight the sailors began to cheer in heartfelt relief.

Nevyn got up and started amidships to find Amyr waiting for him. The young warrior was grinning as if his face would split from it.

"You seem glad to be going ashore, lad," Nevyn remarked.

"We all are, my lord, and I don't mind telling you twice. We've got our gear all packed, too. I wanted to ask you, do you want the prisoner brought up from the hold?"

"The who? Oh, Perryn! I do at that, and my thanks. See if you can get him into a clean shirt, too, will you? I'm going below to change right now myself. Don't forget: I'm now Lord Galrion, and you and the lads are the honor guard of a very important man. If we're going to pull Gwerbret Rhodry out of this wretched mess, we all have to learn to lie like thieves."

"Done, Lord Galrion." Amyr made him a passable sweep of a bow. "Shall I send one of your humble servants to take charge of your baggage?"

"That's the spirit, lad! And come to think of it, a little help would be welcome. The regent loaded me down with all sorts of fripperies."

Among these fripperies were some beautifully made pieces of clothing and badges of rank: a shirt embroidered with the Dragons of Aberwyn, a pair of brigga in the rhan's plaid, a new solid blue cloak with a jeweled ring-brooch decorated with dragons to clasp it shut. In a pair of graved silver message tubes he carried letters from the regent, and in a velvet-lined leather pouch all the coin that Lovyan could scrounge up on such short notice. There were also two small wooden caskets, containing respectively Aberwyn's second-best set of silver goblets and the absolutely best silver-gilt soup tureen, pressed into hasty service as gifts for archons. Nevyn put on the clothes, hung the pouch of coin round his neck, and consigned the rest, along with his regular clothes and his mule packs full of herbs and medicines, to the man Amyr detailed for the job.

When he came back out on deck, Elaeno made a great show out of pretending not to recognize him, and all the sailors stared openmouthed at the captain for daring to tease a man who could command the wind.

"Lord Galrion, is it?" Elaeno said, bowing. "Well, my lord, we're almost to land. Your honor guard and your tame stoat are already assembled in the stern."

"My thanks, captain." Nevyn was grinning. "Where do we go through customs? It's been a long time since I've been in Surat."

"Well, actually, I think customs are coming to us. Look out there. Isn't that a packet boat?"

It was indeed, a slim little galley with its sail shipped and rowers at the oars. At the prow sat a gray-haired man with coppery skin and the two red triangles of Surat painted on one cheek to mark his official status. When they came alongside, Elaeno's men threw down lines, and after a few precarious moments, the galley was safely lashed to the merchantman's side. In spite of his gray hair, the official was an agile man; he judged his distance and leapt from one deck to the other with the grace of someone who's spent his entire life on boats. Elaeno bowed; Nevyn bowed; the official bowed all round.

"I see by your pennant that you hail from Aberwyn, good sirs. How, by the Holy Stars themselves, did you ever manage the run across?"

"Luck," Elaeno said. "And pressing need in the gwerbret's service. May we berth?"

"By all means." The official was squinting up at the mast head, where the silver and blue dragon flag was curling in the breeze. "I thought my eyes had given out on me when I saw that blazon, I really did. Well, captain, you'll be able to dine out on this little tale all winter long."

Since, by the time the ship was safely docked and the harbor duties paid, it was too late to make a state visit to the archon, Nevyn, Perryn, and the honor guard all spent the night in a splendid inn as the official guests of the city of Surat. As soon as he wobbled off the gangplank onto the solid pier Perryn began to revive; by the time they reached the inn and were being shown to an enormous suite, he was positively cheerful. On his own initiative he took over the role of Nevyn's valet, grabbing the councillor's luggage from the more-than-willing warband and stowing it away after the innkeep, in a frenzy of pantomime and a flurry of his twenty Deverrian words, showed him the bedchamber and the wardrobe chests.

"Your poor servant seems to have been very seasick," the innkeep remarked in Bardekian to Nevyn.

"Very. The seas are terrible this time of year."

"Yes, they certainly are." The man hesitated, practically squirming with curiosity, but he was too skilled at his host-craft to pry. "I shall send pitchers of wine, Lord Galrion. Uh, about your guards? Will the wine go right to their heads?"

"I shall make sure your property is safe in every respect, good sir."

The innkeep bowed so low that he could have touched his toes, then scurried off.

At the evening meal not only did the other guests in the common room crowd round to ask polite yet eager questions about their marvelous ocean voyage, but some of the local merchants came in specially as well. To a town that lived by trading on the sea, their journey smacked of legend, the exploit of a hero, perhaps, from their own Dawntime. Fortunately, Nevyn could draw upon his sincere ignorance of things maritime to put them off.

"When we hired this captain, we were told he was the best in Orystinna, and apparently he is. There were times when I honestly thought we were doomed, but he always pulled us through. It's him you should be buying drinks for, gentlemen, and asking your questions."

He had no doubt that on the morrow, when Elaeno came on land, they'd be doing just that. He was also sure that the ship's master could lie well enough to convince them that the voyage was as normal as a terrible crossing could be.

When Nevyn returned to his chamber, he found Perryn sitting on the edge of the usual dais in the reception chamber. In the light of the oil lamps the lord's red hair gleamed, newly washed and coppery.

"They have splendid bathhouses here, Nevyn. A servant showed me where it was, and it felt ever so good to wash off the stink of that cursed ship." He fixed the dweomermaster with a reproachful stare. "But, er, well, you might have told me we were coming all the blasted way to Bardek."

"Did I forget? Well, I suppose I did, at that. My apologies, lad. There's a good bit on my mind these days."

"Er, well, at least Cullyn can't get at me here, and that's all that matters to me." He sighed, staring vacantly at the blue-and-white tiled fountain playing in the middle of the chamber. "Jill's off to the east and north."

"You're certain of that?"

"I am. It's like an . . . well, er, ah, like an itch, truly." He got up and turned slowly, like a bit of lodestone searching out the south. "When I stand like this, it's like scratching the itch, and Amyr told me that the direction I'm facing is east and north."

"So it is. Splendid, lad! You spoke of restitution back in Aberwyn, and truly, this is a grand way to pay it. If we can find Jill without my having to scry, it'll confuse our enemies no end."

"Enemies?"

"Oh, well, I seem to have forgotten to mention that, too. I must be growing old or suchlike. You see, I'm afraid that men with evil magic are trying to find Jill and Rhodry before we do. We've got to stop them, because they're vicious killers."

Perryn looked at him, started to speak, then fainted dead away. With a sigh Nevyn reminded himself to watch his tongue from now on, then went to fetch Amyr to help put Perryn to bed.

· · · ·

Some hours after midnight, when the change in the astral tides had settled down, the Old One went to his temple of time and found what he'd been anticipating for so long: Nevyn's statue was alive. The cold gray image of stone had transformed itself into an image of warm flesh, and the piercing blue eyes seemed to turn his way as he walked into the chamber.

"Very good, enemy mine," the Old One said in his thoughts. "Soon we'll have our last battle, you and I."

First, though, he had something else to attend to. Over the past few days the Old One had been using various devices and rituals to scry, ranging from geomancy on the one hand to actual astral travel on the other, in an attempt to discover just who his enemies in the Dark Council might have been. He had found nothing. Since he was far more skilled at extracting information than any individual member of the Brotherhood was at hiding it, he could only surmise that several had joined forces against him. He had also lost Baruma; every time he tried to contact his student, he received only the dimmest impression of his mind, trapped and bound under a powerful ensorcelment. Although he could probably break through that ensorcelment to scry him out, he preferred to know his enemy before he tried.

In the dead time of that night, when all the astral forces ebb and grow still under the presidency of Earth of Earth, the Old One worked a ritual in a secret chamber deep within his villa. He roused one of his house slaves and had the frightened boy bring him two fat rabbits, trussed up but still alive, from the cages out in the stable, then sent him back to bed. Carrying the rabbits in one hand and a lantern in the other, he waddled and puffed up a small stairway, worked the mechanism for a secret door, and went into the pitch-black room. Walls, ceiling, floor—all were painted black, as was the altar that stood on the north side below a tapestry of the inverted pentagram.

When he flopped the rabbits onto the altar, they struggled and squealed, driven to a pitch of terror by the very feel of that room, but he picked up the long-bladed ritual knife, reversed it, and knocked them on the head with the heavy jeweled hilt until they lay still. Later they would die; now he needed silence to concentrate. As he went round the room widdershins to light the black candles in the wall sconces, he began chanting under his breath, an evil song older than the Dawntime, a remnant of a craft known and despised long before the ancestors of the Bardekians and the Deverry folk had left the mysterious Homelands. Although the strangely mixed origin of the name had been long lost, the Old One called upon Set the Horned One to open the gates of the Otherlands and release the spirit with whom he wished to speak. Using that name for such a purpose was a blasphemy in itself.

Once the candles were lit, the Old One blew out the lantern. Its smoke mingled with that of the candles—the room was windowless, though some clean air came in round the door—and thickened to a smokey haze. Still chanting, the Old One approached the altar again, picked up the knife, and began to summon a hundred evil things and forces and symbols to his mind and to that accursed room. At last he fell still, then raised the knife high and plunged it down. As he slit the rabbits' throats and slashed open their bellies, he let their blood pour across the altar and drip to the floor. With his trained sight he saw the bleeding as the release of magnetism, the gush and rising mist of pure life-force, the goal and only reason for this cruelty.

Stoked by the candle smoke and the wisps of magnetism that the burning released, the pure etheric stuff gathered and thickened above the altar. Drawn like hungry dogs to meat came spirits of all sorts, clustering round, snatching at the food, whimpering and mewling as the Old One drove them off with mighty curses and the flash of the consecrated knife. At last a face formed above the mist, a thin face with narrow eyes glittering under peaked brows, and a cruel mouth contorted into a snarl.

"Let me drink, Tondalo," he whispered.

"Oh, gladly, *master.*" The Old One grinned at him, a parody of a servile simper. "Aren't you glad you taught me the black arts so well?"

The spirit snarled at him and darted at the mist, only to be driven back by the knife blade.

"Promise me you'll answer my questions, and then you drink."

"I promise, you ingrate hell-spawn."

The Old One snatched back the knife and let the spirit feed and batten on the life-force. As the mist thinned, the shape thickened, until it seemed his old teacher of unclean things stood on the altar and wiped his mouth on the back of his hand at the end of his meal.

"Now," the Old One said. "I have an enemy."

"Do you? What a surprise!"

"Someone is working against me. Do you remember the matter about which I consulted you? The death of the Master of the Aethyr?"

"I remember nothing but pain."

"It's of no matter. Someone is working against me. Someone is blocking all my attempts to scry him out. He must be drawing force from the places where you dwell. Who is he?"

"There isn't anyone working against you in the Dark of Darkness, not in the miserable fetid corner where you've trapped me, at any rate."

"You lie!"

"I cannot lie."

It was, of course, perfectly true — within its limits.

"No, but you can bend the truth. You've seen someone working somewhere else, haven't you? Who is he, and where?"

The spirit drew back its lips in a soundless snarl.

"I don't recognize him," it said at last. "He must have come to power after my time on earth. The way he works marks him for a Hawkmaster, but I have no way of knowing what guild. As for where he works, why not look in the usual places instead of the paths of mastery? You're still an overly subtle fool at times, Tondalo."

"My dearest master, I have to admit that I deserve the rebuke. Now begone!"

When he threw up his arms in a ritual gesture and brandished the knife, the spirit fled, whimpering and cursing, back to its trap of torment in the Dark of Darkness that abuts the evil places of the world.

The Old One banished the various forces and released the various spirits inadvertently caught by his invocations, then picked up the dead rabbits and tossed them outside the chamber for a slave to dispose of later. As he put out the candles, he realized that he could most likely identify this treacherous Hawkmaster. The only hireling — or so the masters of the dark dweomer considered the Hawks — who could know that he had some important work in hand would be the master he'd hired the year before from the Valanth guild. Now that he knew his enemy was no more formidable than the head of an assassins' guild, it would be a relatively simple matter to scry in the usual way and see if his guess were right. Probably the Hawkmaster held Baruma, too, he decided as he thought about it. The question was whether the little fool was even worth rescuing.

In the morning, when the time came to visit the archon, Nevyn took four men of the warband along for an honor guard and Perryn as well, to act the part of manservant and carry the box of Aberwyn's second-best goblets. The municipal palace was up on the highest point of the city, a flat hill that served for the law courts, temple centers, and training grounds for the militia as well as the site of the civic leader's residence. The archon, Klemiko, received them in an echoing reception chamber, tiled in blue and pale green. At one end was a dais spread with enough cushions for twenty men, and at the other, four purple-tiled fountains splashing in front of a wall painting that depicted Dalae-oh-contremo in albatross form. Like an endless tide a bustle of slaves came and went, bringing food and wine, while Nevyn and the archon chatted in Bardekian about the marvelously lucky sea voyage. At length, after the lemon-scented finger bowls and damp towels had been brought and taken away again, Klemiko dismissed the slaves with a clap of his hands.

"Well, Lord Galrion, you must have incredibly important business on hand to take a risk like this."

"Yes, I'm afraid it's more important than I care to contemplate. I know your city and ours have treaties and alliances of long standing, but still, I appreciate this hospitality to a sudden and importunate guest."

"Any service I can pay your gwerbret will be nothing but pleasure."

"I wish it could be so, Your Excellency, but I'm afraid that there may be some considerable pain involved. You see, Gwerbret Rhys died suddenly last fall."

"My heart is pierced with a spear to learn of your ruler's death. I met Lord Rhys on two separate occasions, and always he was the soul of courtesy and graciousness."

Amyr and the other riders exchanged disbelieving glances, which fortunately Klemiko didn't see.

"It was a terrible shock to us all," Nevyn said smoothly. "Even worse, he left behind him a line of succession that's tangled at best and unclear at worst. He had no sons, you see."

"Ah." Klemiko's brow furrowed, as if he were trying to remember the to-him peculiar customs surrounding an inherited office. "Oh, of course, daughters wouldn't do, either. Did he have brothers or—I believe this pertains—an uncle?"

"Not an uncle, no, but his younger brother does indeed stand to inherit his properties. Unfortunately, that brother has disappeared. He was last seen here in the islands."

"Now that's an oddity!" Klemiko allowed himself a smile. "Has the younger brother taken to commerce to improve his prospects? It's so rare that one of your lords is that enlightened."

"I only wish he'd been so sensible. No, I'm afraid I don't really know what he's up to, but I wager that it's something disgraceful. At a guess I'd say it involved girls and gambling."

"I see that your young men aren't all that different than ours." Klemiko looked away, his dark eyes turning pained. "One of my sons has a profound interest in the dance, or so he says. It extends more to the young women who perform it than the noble art itself. I can but sympathize." He sighed and turned his mind back to the matter at hand. "Do you think he's in Surat?"

"I have no idea, but I doubt if I'm as lucky as all that. What I need, Your Excellency, is some sort of paper that will allow me to travel with my honor guard. I know that the islands have strict laws about traveling openly with weapons, but I also know that my men—well, to be exact, they're the new gwerbret's men—won't want to give them up."

"Probably not, no. I've noticed that the men of your country get rather insulted if anyone so much as suggests they might disarm themselves for courtesy's sake. Well, that certainly can be arranged. Since the new gwerbret is a military ruler, it stands to reason that his honor guard would be armed as well. I can give you a selection of documents, and you can use them as you see best. Now, are you going to require horses?"

"Yes. All of these men are cavalrymen."

"Ah. Well, we'll present you with some from the city militia's stables."

"Your Excellency, your generosity overwhelms me."

"It is nothing, a mere trifle between friends." Klemiko allowed himself a smile. "Of course, if you might mention our city's name to the new gwerbret when you find him . . ."

"No doubt, Your Excellency, I'll be mentioning it many times over."

When they returned to their inn, Nevyn found Elaeno waiting, pacing up and down with a wine cup in his hand.

"How did it go?"

"Splendidly. Klemiko definitely wants to be in the new gwerbret's favor. Everyone seems to know that the High King's given Aberwyn a bigger share of the Bardek trade, and you could hear the good archon thinking 'monopolies' with every compliment he paid. I didn't tell him the truth, by the by. I made up some tale about Rhodry being too fond of gambling and women and general carousing."

"Good. No archon in the islands is going to want to hear the Hawks so much as mentioned in his presence. Might mean he'd have to take some action against them."

"Do the Brotherhoods have as much power as all that?"

"I wouldn't call it power, exactly. I mean, they're in no position to get laws passed in their favor or proper government contracts. Every now and then some archon does hire them, of course, but that's kept from the general run of voters. And some influential men use them, too, just now and again, and they wouldn't want them eliminated from the scheme of things. But what really protects the Hawks is simple terror. If you declare war on a guild full of assassins, you're not likely to live to savor victory, are you?"

"Sooner or later, though, someone's going to have to do it, or the islands won't be civilized for long."

"True enough. I thank all the gods that the guilds have never gotten a toehold in Orystinna."

"How come they haven't?"

"Our top men would rather die than be terrorized." Elaeno smiled tightly. "And the little bastards know it."

As a shipmaster Elaeno owned a large collection of maps of various islands as well, of course, as a good working knowledge of navigation. He was the one who realized how to turn Perryn's strange talent to an even greater advantage. First he had Perryn stand in the innyard and point in the exact direction which led to Jill; then he took him out the north gate of the city, some two miles from the inn, and had him do it again. Then they retraced their steps and went out the east gate for one last try. Since Elaeno never bothered to explain, Perryn was bewildered, thinking that somehow he'd failed the dweomermaster the first two times, but later, after they rejoined Nevyn back at the inn, everything became clear. Elaeno spread a bark-paper map out on the table and used the dull point of a spoon and the edge of his dagger to score straight lines, each originating at a place where they'd taken a reading off his inner lodestone. Just like magic, to Perryn's way of thinking, the lines all came together up in the central plateau of Surtinna.

"And Jill has to be about there." Elaeno stabbed at the map with one blunt finger. "Pastedion's the closest city to the point I've marked."

"Well and good," Nevyn said. "Now, tell me, Perryn. Could you tell if Jill was closer or farther away today than she was when we first landed?"

"Er, well, ah, I'd say she hasn't moved at all."

"Indeed? That's interesting. I hope it means they're in a safe place, and not that they're being held prisoner."

"Oh come now, don't be morbid," Elaeno broke in. "You'd know if the lass were in some foul danger."

"No doubt I would, or at least, I'd hope I would. At any rate, we'll we leaving tonight. What do you think, Elaeno? Sail down to Indila, and then take to the land from there?"

Perryn forced himself to stifle a groan.

"How many filthy horses did the archon give you? Twelve and then the pack mules?" Elaeno considered, rubbing his chin. "Well, I guess we can fit some into the hold and then tie the rest up on deck—if your men stay there with'em. My ship's a merchanter, not some stinking cattle barge."

"Er, ah, well, um, my lord? Couldn't we just ride and spare the captain's boat?"

"You're being a bit obvious, Perryn," Nevyn said. "If we sail to Indila we can save a night—at least—and we've got to make all possible speed. I'm afraid we'll be taking to the sea again, but it won't be for long this time."

As he began packing up Nevyn's gear, Perryn was thinking that making restitution was turning out to be a lot more painful than he'd anticipated back in his nice safe prison in Eldidd. For the first time it also occurred to him to wonder what Jill was going to say or do to him when they met again. He began shaking so badly in a tangle of terror and desire that he had to sit down for a moment and gulp for breath.

The high priest's prediction that the archon of Pastedion would take a few days to settle Rhodry's case turned out to be overly optimistic. For more than a few Jill and the others had stayed in the temple compound—languished there, or so she preferred to think of it— while Salamander and Brother Merrano trotted back and forth between the temple and the archon's palace to bribe various civil servants, arrange appointments, keep appointments, spread more bribes, and arrange still another round of meetings with this official or that. In between each stage of this complex operation, they waited for messages to come back saying that so-and-so had accepted their humble gift or such-and-such a scribe might possibly be in his office at a certain time. The one good thing about all these delays, to Jill's way of thinking anyway, was that she had plenty of time to work on her dweomer-practices. Finally, on the afternoon when Nevyn was leaving Surat for Indila, Salamander came dragging into the guesthouse with one hand pressed dramatically to his forehead.

"The Wondrous Witch Wizard of the Far Far North has a headache fit for the biggest demon in the deepest hell," he announced. "Please, oh beauteous barbarian handmaiden, pour me some wine from that flagon, will you?"

Salamander flopped onto his back on a cot and groaned until she did just that, but he did manage to sit up to take the wine cup. Although both Gwin and Rhodry looked annoyed at the display, Jill could recognize Salamander's symptoms.

"What's wrong?" she snapped.

"Well, I'm not sure if anything is wrong, actually. It's merely tedious beyond belief." He paused to gulp half the wine straight off. "We do finally have an advocate, and Brother Merrano assures me that he's the best there is."

"A what?" Rhodry said.

"A legal advocate. Someone who knows the laws and can speak for you in the archon's malover."

"Why can't I speak for myself? Or is it because I'm still a slave?"

"No one speaks for themselves in the malovers here, oh brother of mine."

"Why not?"

"Because they don't. It's the custom. You hire this man who's made a profession out of advocating, the way you'd take cloth to the dyers' guild if you wanted to change its color. Advocates know all the tricks of the trade when it comes to arguing cases and convincing people to vote their way. If we can get Baruma arrested, he'll have an advocate, too. You see, although the archon delivers the final judgment on a case, he doesn't actually try it. They pick a hundred free citizens by lot, and they sit on something called a jury and decide the merits of the case by a vote after everyone's finished talking."

"What?" Rhodry was utterly outraged. "I've never heard of anything so stupid and dishonorable in my life! Why should I accept the judgment of a lot of common-born dolts as law?"

"Because you don't have any choice, you lackwit!" Salamander finished the rest of the wine and held out his cup. "Please, beauteous handmaid, all the way to the brim. Somehow I knew this was going to be difficult."

"Well, if I don't have any choice, I don't," Rhodry went on. "But I don't have to like it."

"Just so. I only ask one thing: that you keep your noble-born outrage clasped tight in your secret heart when you talk to the advocate. He's coming here after dinner to hear our story, which means that you and I had best closet ourselves and rehearse a convincing one. Remember, never ever mention one word about dark dweomer and Hawks and all the rest of it. Such unpleasant verities are most unwelcome visitors to the ears of our esteemed islanders."

When the advocate arrived, Jill decided against sitting in on the conference, but rather than stay in the guesthouse and be alone with Gwin, she took a stroll round the temple grounds. She had just reached the flower garden by the front gates when her gray gnome appeared, waving its arms in excitement and jigging up and down.

"Has somewhat happened?"

It nodded a yes and pointed to the south and west.

"I don't understand."

Clutching its head it stamped in annoyance. When Jill knelt down on the cobbles, it trotted a few paces away, then slowly and deliberately walked toward her while it pointed to the west.

"Is someone coming here from downriver?"

It nodded yes in evident relief, then twisted up its face as it tried to think.

"Are the bad men coming?"

Apparently not, and it went on thinking.

"Friends, then?"

This time she got another yes. Since Jill couldn't imagine one person in all the islands who would qualify as a friend, she was as puzzled as it seemed to be.

"Here," she said at last. "Can you act out this person's name somehow?"

It shook its head in a mournful no.

"That's the trouble, is it? They don't have an easy name like Blaen or Rhodry that you can put a simple meaning to."

Yes, most definitely, to judge by the way it nodded.

"Is this a Bardek man or woman?"

It wasn't.

"Someone from Deverry?"

Although the gnome nodded a yes, she could barely believe it.

"How could they get here in the winter? Why, no one could—oh, of course! Do you mean Nevyn's coming?"

The gnome jumped up and down and clapped its hands together while it smiled and nodded. Jill started to cry, a helpless sob of utter relief, while the little creature clambered into her lap and patted her cheek to comfort her.

Salamander's reaction was just as strong, when, after the advocate had left, he returned to the guesthouse and she told him the news. As he sat there sniffling, she realized for the first time just how frightened he'd been, just how hard he'd worked to keep up his mask of a chattering fool. Finally he wiped his eyes and blew his nose on a silk handkerchief and arranged one of his typical vacuous smiles.

"Well and good, then, my most magical magpie. It seems we may all live to vex the gods a little longer, then. Did the gnome say how far away the old man is?"

"Things like distance don't mean anything to the Wildfolk."

"True enough. Let us hope he's close at hand, because I doubt if it's safe to scry him out. We can wait here in relative safety and let him find us, as I'm sure he will, hopefully sooner than later, and most utterly hopefully, sooner rather than way too late. Oh most rapturous joy! It seems I was correct to work my latest most clever and recondite ruse."

Jill groaned aloud.

"Oh by the Lord of Hell! What have you done now?"

"Naught new. I mean hiring the advocate and insisting on laying formal charges against Baruma. We had to have a reason to stay here in the safety of temple sanctuary for as long as we possibly could. If you want to waste a great deal of other people's time, Jill my turtledove, there's no better way than starting a lawsuit."

If the archon's men had only known it, the man they wanted to present with a writ of appearance *sub poena* was only ten miles from Pastedion, even though Baruma wasn't exactly in full possession of himself in the legal sense. Up in the hills to the east of town, the Hawkmaster and his two journeymen had taken shelter from the continual rains in a public caravansary provided by the archons of Pastedion. Since it often rained in the summer up in the central plateau, this particular public rest area also sported a shelter that was basically a very long roof, supported by stone pillars instead of walls, over a slate floor that was a little higher in the middle than at the sides so that any rainwater that blew in would run right out again. By sticking to this high ground they could stay reasonably dry. Although the Hawks were so used to physical hardship that this shelter was a luxury to them, Baruma was miserable, cramped in every muscle and exhausted. By then, however, his mind was beginning to fight back against being ensorceled.

Although he still had no will of his own in any true sense, he did possess a kernel of hatred cached in a secret corner of his mind. His sheer physical discomfort fed that hatred and kept it alive. His terror of the Hawkmaster kept it hidden. Often the master sent him out on the etheric to spy, or rather, to soar above Pastedion and the warded temple to look for traces of the barbarian party. Every now and then Baruma saw the silver flaming aura of the elven sorcerer hurrying through the streets in the company of one or two normal human ovoids, but he never found Rhodry, the woman, or Gwin. The Hawkmaster was particularly worried about Gwin—not out of some fine concern for his man, of course, but from a simple fear that Gwin would betray the guild by babbling all its secrets under torture. In the secret place of his hatred Baruma hoped that Gwin would do just that.

On a night when the waning moon rose only a few hours before the dawn, the Hawkmaster sent Baruma out farther than usual, flying round and round in an ever-widening spiral with Pastedion at its center. Here in this sparsely populated country he saw little but the wild hills, rolling in the rusty-reddish glow of the burgeoning grass up to the mountain peaks, silver-blue and grim under their eternal snow. He felt the master's will speaking in his mind, then, urging him south along the river. At first Baruma whimpered and fought. Gushing up from the water rose a silver veil of elemental force, a surging and turbulent counterpart to the flood runoff swelling the physical river below, and a real danger to a weak soul like him, flying on someone else's will rather than his own. But the Hawkmaster's whisper promised torments, and in the end, Baruma flew south.

Whenever he could, he pulled away from the threatening veil with its tendrils of mist that seemed to reach out deliberately to snare and drag him down to his death. He was so preoccupied with the river, in fact, that it was some time before he realized that he had a shadowy companion. Out of the corner of his eye, just behind him and on his left, he could see a dark misty shape following along. Whenever he turned his head for a better look, the shape dodged away and disappeared. His fear began to swell like the water veil, and he heard his own voice babbling to the master.

"You'd better come back, then." The master's hated voice had never sounded so welcome.

Baruma swooped away from the river and began to circle back, only to come face to face with a dark tower of a figure: a sweep of black robes, marked with glowing red sigils and belted with a string of severed heads, and a face barely visible in a heavy hood. When he yelped, the figure raised a shadowy hand and shoved back the illusionary hood to reveal the grim eyes of the Old One.

"So, I've found my lost little sparrow, have I?"

Baruma could only babble out a confused welter of thoughts. He could hear the Hawkmaster's voice, edged with fear, demanding to know what he was seeing, but the voice seemed very far away. When the Old One's simulacrum raised both hands, a line of grayish light appeared, stretched between them. As he worked his hands back and forth, the line doubled, then snaked out like a thrown rope to circle them both. Once it was in position, it swelled, shot up and down, and turned into a wall of dirty-colored light, glare-shot and feverish, ringing them round.

"Your captor won't be able to force himself through that." The Old One actually sounded amused. "When you return to your body, he'll question you, of course. Tell him the truth. I want him to know exactly what he's facing. I hope he squirms, the dog."

"Master, please, save me!"

"Eventually. Perhaps. You're useful where you are for the moment. Where did he capture you?"

"Indila. I was on my way to you."

"What does he want?"

"Rhodry."

"What? What does the idiot boy want with Rhodry Maelwaedd?"

Dimly Baruma knew that Rhodry's full name was important, but in his terror and ensorcelment he could only stare like an idiot himself.

"I don't know, master," he said at last. "Or wait! He wants to know what you're doing. Or something like that. I don't understand."

"No doubt he hasn't shared his heart of hearts with you, no." All at once, the face of the simulacrum smiled, a ghastly gesture, the draw of bloodless lips away from a hollow black cavity of a mouth. "Very well, little Baruma. Tell him everything you know, and tell him that the Master of the Aethyr is here in Bardek. Let him sprinkle every sharp thorn of the truth between his sheets and then have sweet dreams."

In a flash of blinding blue glare the Old One disappeared. The wall of filthy light hung steady for a moment, then dissolved and flowed away into nothingness. Standing waiting was the towering simulacrum of the Hawkmaster, the face raging and swelling above its blood-red robes.

"It was the Old One, master."

In the secret place of hatred in his mind Baruma laughed, seeing the Hawkmaster shrink—literally shrink out on the etheric—in fear. Then the simulacrum swelled again to larger than normal size, towering over him, forcing him to his knees.

"So!" The Hawkmaster's voice boomed through the blue light. "Has he opened war upon me?"

"No, master, no. He said to tell you the truth, about Rhodry Maelwaedd, about everything, about the Master of the Aethyr, too."

The Hawkmaster's image hung as still and brittle as a piece of fine porcelain.

"The Master of the Aethyr?"

"That was the plan, to lure him here and kill him. He's here now, so the plan is working. I'm to tell you everything now, master, everything. Don't torture me! Oh please don't hurt me!"

"I won't, little piglet. Come back with me, and we'll talk, long and hard."

Thanks to the help of the Kings of Air, the *Guaranteed Profit* reached Indila in an amazingly short time, much to the relief of the horses as well as Perryn. As Nevyn supervised unloading the stock onto the stone pier, he noticed his volunteer servingman surreptitiously kneeling down to kiss the solid footing and pat the stone like a beloved dog. As it did at odd moments, the question of Perryn's true nature rose to vex him, simply because he'd never seen anyone with such an instinctive antipathy to the element of water, but he put the wondering firmly aside. Such luxuries as the pursuit of knowledge would have to wait till his return to Deverry.

"That's the last of the poor beasts off," Elaeno said, strolling over. "We'll have to buy a horse for me down in the public market."

"Actually, I was thinking that you'd best stay here."

"What? And miss the fighting?"

"Naught of the sort—maybe. Listen, once I get Jill and the rest of them out of whatever trouble they're in, I intend to retreat as fast as I can. We've got to get Rhodry home first and worry about stamping out our nasty little enemies later. I've no desire to come rushing back here only to find your ship burned or destroyed some other way, and every captain in port mysteriously unwilling to give us passage home."

"I see what you mean." Elaeno laid an enormous hand on the hilt of his sword. "Me and my lads have fought off pirates before. We'll be ready to do it again if we have to."

"Good. You might. And keep up your astral seals, too. If naught else, it'll give our enemies somewhat to stew about."

Since they'd arrived soon after dawn, Nevyn decided to lead his small warband out that very day. Although they did go down to the marketplace and buy supplies, he skipped a formal and time-consuming visit to the archon of Indila, and they rode out the north gate just about noon. By then Perryn had revived enough to be absolutely certain that Jill was still in the same place, more north than east from Indila.

"This road will take us right to Pastedion, but it does run along the river," Nevyn said. "Will traveling so close to flowing water keep you from finding her?"

"It won't, my lord. Er, um, why would it?"

"Water troubles some dweomer-workings."

"Oh, but I don't have dweomer."

"You know, I'm beginning to think you're exactly right: you don't. Just what you do have is the greatest puzzle I've faced in years."

For a reply Perryn merely looked miserable, as if blaming himself for his peculiar mental structure—a legacy of self-loathing from his Uncle Benoic, Nevyn assumed, and he let the painful subject drop.

When the Old One judged that the Hawkmaster had contemplated his bitter truths long enough, he made contact with Baruma rather than go to meet his enemy on the etheric plane, where an ambush of sorts might be possible. He found his former student's mind so clouded that it was easy to take him over, even through the scrying mirror, and look out of his eyes. As far as he could tell from body-empathy, Baruma was kneeling on a pile of saddle blankets while he fed twigs into a small fire. Nearby two men—Hawks, the Old One assumed—were playing knucklebones for splinters, while a third man, the Hawkmaster that the Old One had hired the year before, was sitting cross-legged with his back to the others and staring blankly out at the rain-washed hillside beyond the rough stone shelter. He was meditating, perhaps, or performing some sort of mental exercise, but whatever he may have been doing, he was properly distracted.

The Old One made Baruma's head turn and look from side to side, but he could see nothing more of any interest, only the stone pillars and the rain. Slowly and carefully he made Baruma's body stand up, stumbling a little until he gained full control. At the movement both Hawks looked up automatically, then returned to their game. Although the master never moved, not so much as a twitch, the Old One was willing to wager that he was perfectly aware of the movement. Wearing Baruma's body like a suit of armor, he strolled down to the end of the shelter, turned back, paced a few steps and otherwise moved round to practice controlling this borrowed physical vehicle. With part of his mind he was aware of Baruma, whimpering and frightened at being so suddenly forced out into the etheric, but it was a weak distraction that he could ignore.

When he was ready, he strode back down to the fire and with a curse woven of evil names, forced the salamanders to flare up in a pillar of flame. All three Hawks leapt to their feet and swirled to face him—with sudden weapons in their hands.

"I am the Old One, not Baruma. If you kill this body, he'll die, not me."

The Hawkmaster flicked one hand; his confederates' weapons disappeared into the folds of their clothing. Slowly, with an impressive disdain, the master slipped his own dagger into a hidden sheath.

"I've heard of such things being done. Why are you here?"

"To talk. To strike a bargain, perhaps. The Master of the Aethyr's going to be a hard bird to net. I might be interested in hiring you again."

"I see." The Hawkmaster allowed himself a short bark of a laugh. "If I want to take your cursed money, anyway. Thanks to your little scheme, three of my best men are dead, and a fourth captured."

"My scheme? Did I ask you to snatch the bait out of my trap? You were following the barbarian boy for reasons of your own. Don't try to tell me otherwise. Don't blame me if something went wrong with your plans."

"Very well, then, I won't. That 'something' is every bit as dangerous to you as it is to me, though."

"If it wasn't, would I be here bargaining with you? There's another dweomerman involved in this, isn't there?"

"Exactly—the man who rescued Rhodry in the first place. And I agree that we'd be better off working together. If I'm going to kill the Master of the Aethyr on the road, I'll need the information you can give me."

"Kill the . . . ?" For the first time in years, the Old One laughed, a deep belly laugh that left his borrowed body shaking on the edge of his control. "You utterly arrogant idiot! You? Kill the Master of the Aethyr on the road just as if you were a common bandit and him some piddling merchant? I'm amazed. I'm stunned. It passes all description."

The Hawkmaster's dark face was suffused with a dangerous sort of purple.

"If I can kill an archon in the middle of his palace, when every door and window and even the god-cursed cracks in the ceiling are swarming with guards, I can cursed well . . ."

"You can do nothing against the Master of the Aethyr. Leave him to me. Come to my villa; Baruma knows where it is. We'll lay a trap for him there."

Slowly the Hawkmaster's color returned to normal, and he smiled.

"Oh, I'll come all right. But I'll bring Nevyn's head with me. I know a thing or two about traps."

"Fool!"

The Old One slipped out of Baruma's body and allowed its owner's soul to rush in just as the Hawkmaster stepped forward and slapped it across the face. Whining and groveling, Baruma sank to his knees while the Old One withdrew his consciousness and returned through the mirror to his own body, propped in its chair back in his comfortable study in the villa.

As soon as he was fully awake, he laughed again. The Hawkmaster had taken the bait exactly as he'd hoped. No matter how the battle went, the Old One would profit. If, by some small miracle the Hawkmaster did indeed kill Nevyn, then the Old One could eliminate the assassin easily, any time he chose. It was much more probable, of course, that the Hawks would only succeed in killing the old man's companions, including this lesser dweomermaster, before Nevyn was finally goaded into taking action and destroying them. By then his position would be considerably weakened; he would be alone, without allies in a foreign land, and the Old One could move in for the kill.

After the Old One withdrew, the Hawkmaster's display of fury vanished just as suddenly. So, the ancient fool thought he could be goaded into a reckless attack like a mere apprentice, did he? He was going to be very surprised when the Hawks turned up at his gates, quite unharmed and with allies at their side. For a long time the Hawkmaster paced back and forth, thinking, wondering at himself and his ambitions, while Baruma cowered and whimpered and his men watched in silent anticipation, as if they knew that great things were afoot.

He would have to be very careful, the master told himself, to make certain that his ambitions didn't exceed his grasp. For years the Dark Brotherhood had hoarded knowledge of the dweomer like some fat rich man gloating all grease-chin over his feasts and throwing only meager scraps of stale bread and gristled meat to the beggars at his door. Since the Hawks were useful to them, they received these scraps; since they were equally dangerous, scraps were all they got. But in the Old One's villa were books and consecrated implements, perhaps even captive spirits who would speak of dark magicks upon command—if the Hawkmaster owned those things, wouldn't every assassin in the islands come grovel at his feet for a share? Wouldn't they pay with gold as well as adulation to learn what he knew? And once the Hawks were learned and strong in the dark arts, then there would be no more Brotherhood—only Hawks.

Before, no one had dared attack the Old One for fear of retribution, but now he had unleashed a dangerous enemy on the islands. No doubt the other members of the Brotherhood would agree that anyone who would knowingly bring the Master of the Aethyr—and apparently one of his disciples as well—down upon them all was growing daft and senile. No doubt the Brotherhood would not agree that the Hawks should have the Old One's books, but once the books were in their hands, the Brotherhood could disagree all it wished. Its members would be welcome to try to take them back, if they dared.

There remained, of course, the problem of the Master of the Aethyr. Although the Hawkmaster had no intentions whatsoever of attacking the old man, he could ensure that no one for miles round would willingly help him and his disciple. Eventually, the Old One and the master of the Light would meet on a field of war; no matter who won that battle, the Hawkmaster would profit. Either the Old One would be dead and defeated, or a victor but severely weakened. If Nevyn did win, then the Hawkmaster would merely loot the villa and disappear. Or—and here the elegance of his plan gratified him no end—if he should kill a battle-weary Nevyn, wouldn't the Brotherhood fear him all the more and let him study the books in peace?

There was, however, one last major difficulty: what if he never found Nevyn again after that last battle? The Hawkmaster had heard that masters of magic could kill one another out on the etheric plane while their bodies were miles apart. The Hawkmaster wanted them together on the physical plane, where he could move in on the winner. To ensure it, he would have to mark a trail in some subtle way that would lead the Master of the Aethyr right to the Old One's door. It all sounded perfectly reasonable, there on the rainy hillside, reasonable and better yet, immensely profitable.

Smiling to himself, the Hawkmaster turned to his men, sitting patiently nearby.

"Take Baruma into the woods aways—no, don't hurt him! Put that knife away, you idiot! Just keep him at a distance so he can't overhear me. Baruma is very important to us. He knows the way to the Old One's villa. In fact, little piglet, I'll see to it that you get a real meal tonight, all you want to eat."

Baruma grinned and drooled, peering up through cloudy eyes. The Hawkmaster patted him on the head, then signaled to the others to lead him away. He was about to contact possible allies through the black ink—there were several outposts of the guild in this part of the island—and he didn't want to give the Old One the slightest chance of learning it.

That same night, just after sunset, Salamander came back from his day's business at the law courts with another headache. Since Gwin and Rhodry were gone, chopping firewood for the temple for want of anything better to occupy their time, Jill was alone in the guesthouse when he came slouching in and flopped down on his cot. Without waiting to be asked, she poured him wine.

"We've had a real setback, haven't we?"

"How perceptive you are, oh partridge of perspicacity." Salamander had a long swallow and wiped his mouth on his sleeve. "They're talking about summoning Brindemo to testify."

"That could take months!"

"Indeed. If our fat friend even lived to reach the court. The idea is to force us to drop the case." He finished the other half and held out the goblet to be refilled. "The sagacious archon of this fair and fountain-studded city seems most unwilling to prosecute Baruma."

"He's afraid of the Hawks, no doubt."

"Of course. I have been repeatedly assured that, if it were a simple matter of freeing Rhodry and getting on our way, our affairs could be attended to in the proverbial twinkling of an eye. There have even been hints of a substantial reduction in the usual fees, as recompense for the inordinate amount of time which we've been forced to spend on what should be—and here I get a veritable dumb show of knowing winks and significant glances from each official present—what should be a routine matter."

"Bastards." Jill poured herself a cup, too. "I imagine Rhodry would be pleased to drop the case, though. He wants to kill Baruma himself. Letting a lot of common-born folk tell him what to do won't sit well, either."

"How simple life must seem to the likes of my beloved younger brother!" Salamander was smiling, but his fingers were twining round his wine cup so tightly that Jill was afraid he'd snap the stem. "But I think me we don't have much choice."

"Why? I thought the whole point of this lawsuit was to waste time."

"Just so, but wasting time does not include wasting yet another life. If the archons send for Brindemo, the Hawks will kill him, one way or another, if not in Myleton, then somewhere along the way. And please do not even begin to tell me that Brindemo would deserve no better, because flawed though he may be, he's a human soul and a child of your gods and so on and so forth."

"He also refused to send Rhodry to the mines. That's enough for me."

"A practical soul to the core, aren't you? Well and good, then. We shall ask His Holiness to solemnize Rhodry's freedom on the morrow, and the day after that—you have to wait a full day and night, you see, which is all to the good in our pending precarious and perilous predicament—we'll register it with the archon, and then . . . well, indeed, what then? Do you think we dare take the risk of scrying Nevyn out?"

"Will the Hawks know it if we do?"

"Most like."

Jill sipped her wine and considered the grim alternatives. With a vast sigh Salamander got up and, still clutching his wine cup, wandered over to the lectern, where a candle as long and thick as a child's arm stood impaled on an iron spike in readiness. He flicked his fingers and lit the candle, frowned, flicked them again and put it out, then waved his hand in the air and summoned a candle-shape of pure golden light to hang above the scroll laid out on the lectern.

"Why are you reading that stupid thing now?" Jill snapped. "We should be thinking about the trouble we're in."

"What a nasty temper you have! I've already thought about the trouble and have reached the conclusion that there isn't one—a conclusion, that is. Like the shepherd in the ancient fable, caught twixt lion and wolf, no matter which way we run, we are somebody's dinner."

"There are times when I feel like strangling you."

"No doubt." He was bending over the scroll, but whether or not he was actually reading, she couldn't tell. "There are times, turtledove, when my blather even gets on my own nerves. This is one of them."

The first night out of Indila, Nevyn and his men had stayed, just by traveler's luck, in a little town beside the road that had a small inn and a bigger caravan yard right in the middle of its public square. For the second night, however, he had a particular destination in mind, a temple of Dalae-oh-contremo up in the hills that was more of a hermitage for elderly priests than a working temple. It was a day's ride, twenty miles, from Pastedion, far enough to ensure its residents' privacy, but close enough to the big urban temple so that the younger priests could ride over now and then and see if their elder brethren required anything.

A complex of low, rambling white buildings and big gardens, the temple stood on top of a cliff on the east side of and about three hundred yards above the river and river road, and the only way up was a switchback trail cut out of the living rock. When Nevyn and his men arrived at the bottom of this trail, it was just at sunset, and as he looked up, idly wondering how their tired horses would take the climb, the setting sun washed the buildings with a gentle pinkish light. All at once he went cold, because the light changed to sheets of blood in the sight of Vision.

"What's wrong, my lord?" Amyr said. "You're white as snow."

"I don't know yet, lad, but I'll wager somewhat's very wrong indeed. We'll leave most of the men here with the horses, but you and I are going to climb up to take a look."

"Do you think there are enemies waiting up there?"

At that a crowd of burly purple-and-black gnomes appeared at Nevyn's feet. Although they were obviously agitated, screwing up their faces in fear and leaping up and down, they shook their heads no in a silent answer to Amyr's question. Just to be on the safe side, Nevyn brought Praedd along, too. Panting and puffing the three of them climbed up on foot with the gnomes rushing ahead until at last they stood before the wooden gates of the compound and could look down, while they caught their breath, at the little figures of the men and horses beside the tiny river far below.

Yet they lingered only the barest moment. When Nevyn knocked on the gate, it creaked open under his fist a few inches to let him see an elderly man, his dark face twisted in agony, lying on the ground, one hand stretched toward the gate in a desperate attempt to reach it. A puddle of blood was drying round him and clotting in his snow-white hair.

"Ah gods!" Nevyn's cry was more of a moan under his breath. "Brace yourself, lads."

They shoved the gate open and strode into a central courtyard with flower beds blooming red and yellow round a cobbled court. Although that first dead man had almost reached the gates, two others had fallen back by the entrance to the shrine across the court. All three had been stabbed to death. With the Wildfolk to guide them,

Nevyn and his men found two more round back at the washhouse, and the last three in the kitchens, where, apparently, they'd been sharing the humble task of preparing their evening meal of bread and stewed vegetables. As they searched, Nevyn felt curiously numb, a little cold maybe, but perfectly calm.

Since he knew that the priests would have wanted to lie close to their holy altar, he had the men carry them into the narrow, white-washed shrine and lay them down on the tiled floor in front of the enormous block of polished stone. Behind it on the wall was a fresco of the Wave-father soaring serene and free over the sun-gilded ocean, just as, or so he hoped, their souls now soared in the One True Light. By the time they'd covered all the victims with blankets from their individual cells, night had fallen. When Nevyn made a glowing sphere of golden light appear above the altar, neither Amyr nor Praedd seemed to notice. Both young men were white and shaking, but with rage.

"The piss-poor whoreson bastards!" Amyr burst out. "Slaughtering old men! Creaking ancients, my lord! They stood the same chance of fighting back as a candle's got of melting the Third Hell!"

"It gripes my soul!" Praedd snarled. "Will we get a strike on them, my lord?"

"I sincerely hope so, lads. I'll wager anything you want that these men were slain just so they couldn't shelter us."

Only then did his grief hit home, grief and rage and sheer over-whelming guilt, that these wise and gentle elders had died because of him and his troubles—but not because of him alone, he reminded himself, rather from the foul evil that was infecting the islands like rot in the timbers of a ship. He knew he was trembling, his heart pounding, felt himself turn as cold and hard as a sword carved of ice. The Wildfolk of Aethyr gathered round him like a summer storm, crackling and hissing in the air, rushing up and down the walls in the blue fire of sheet lightning.

"I swear by all my holy vows, they who slaughtered these innocent souls will pay the price in blood-coin."

As his voice echoed in the silent shrine, a flash of brilliant white burst over the altar with the acrid smell of lightning. Praedd and Amyr sank to their knees in awe and terror both.

"The god has witnessed my vow. So be it!"

And with the deepest thunder of all, three great knocks throbbed and rolled through the shrine.

If he had been alone, Nevyn would have walked through the night in his holy rage to reach Pastedion, but as it was, he had men, and beasts, too, for that matter, under his care. They all spent a restless night—even the horses seemed to have picked up that something was wrong—camped with their backs to the cliff. Though everyone else managed to sleep, Nevyn stayed up, pacing back and forth by the river as he kept up a guard in more worlds than one.

In the morning no one grumbled when Nevyn insisted they make an early start. By pushing themselves they reached Pastedion well before sunset, just as it was waking up from its noontide nap and its citizens were beginning to wander down to the marketplace for a snack and a gossip. Everyone turned to stare at the party of well-armed and grim horsemen who clattered through the streets on their way to the archon's palace. They all dismounted in a tiled courtyard planted with cypresses and set with marble fountains. When a pair of harried-looking servants rushed out and announced that the archon, Graffaeo, was receiving no visitors, Nevyn grabbed the closest unfortunate by his tunic and lifted him half off his feet.

"You tell him that Lord Galrion of Aberwyn is here on urgent business for the gwerbret of said city, and that he brings horrible news to boot. The elderly priests who served the Wave-father up on the river road have all been murdered, practically in their beds. Understand?"

The slave squeaked and nodded a vigorous yes.

"Good. Then fetch him out here now."

With one last squeak the slave wriggled free and rushed off into the palace as if demons were pinching his behind. Nevyn smiled, crossed his arms over his chest, and waited.

Although normally, freeing a slave is a joyous occasion in the islands—the former master is expected to spread a goodly feast for friends and relations—Jill and the others had no appetite for celebrating after the brief ceremony that set Rhodry free. They were all sitting glumly in the guesthouse, arguing in spurts over what to do next, when Brother Merrano came hurrying in with news.

"Rhodry, there's a Deverry man at the archon's palace who claims to be one of your servitors. A Lord Galrion."

"Who?" Rhodry glanced at Jill, who only shrugged in puzzlement. "I've never heard that name before."

"It sounds like a name out of an ancient chronicle or suchlike," Salamander chimed in.

"I don't know anything about that," Merrano said with some asperity. "But he's brought a pack of armed men with him, and the archon's afraid that he'll start cutting off heads if you don't get yourself there to calm him down."

"Now that sounds like an Eldidd man, truly." Rhodry got up and grinned. "Well and good, then. Let's go greet him."

The walk from the temple to the archon's palace was only a couple of hundred yards, but to Jill it seemed to stretch forever. As they made their way through the afternoon crowds in a tight bunch, with Rhodry in the middle for safety's sake, she was sure that she saw assassins in every shadow and on every roof, all waiting for their chance to rob Aberwyn of its rightful heir. Her nerves grew even jumpier when they reached the palace and found that the archon had brought out his handful of armed guards. Two spearmen stood at the gates, and two more at the door of the magnificent stone house itself. At the sight them Gwin froze, just for the briefest moment. Salamander laid a friendly hand on his shoulder and whispered.

"Is anyone here going to recognize you?"

"They shouldn't. You never know."

"Well, if there's lying to be done, leave it to me. I'm a master of the craft."

Gwin managed a smile at that and let himself be led along into the archon's reception chamber, echoing and gaudy with purple and gold tile. Sitting on the floor below the dais were ten Deverry men, perched uncomfortably on cushions and sipping wine from unfamiliar cups. Jill caught Rhodry's arm and squeezed it.

"All these men serve you. Act like you remember them. The blond with the scar over one eye is Amyr. Make sure you call him by name."

Then she looked at the dais and all her good advice caught in her throat.

"Nevyn!"

She found herself running like a child down the long room with no thought of courtesy or protocol. With his creaky laugh the old man got up to meet her, climbing down from the dais just as she launched herself into his embrace.

"Oh, Nevyn, Nevyn, you can't know how it gladdens my heart to see you!"

"I think I can guess, child. There, there, don't weep. We'll fight this thing out and win yet."

In something like shock Jill realized that she was indeed weeping. When she wiped her eyes on her shirt sleeve, Nevyn produced one of his usual horrid old rags from his brigga pocket for her to use as a handkerchief, a thing so familiar and common that it worked on her better than a mighty talisman, radiating sober sense and courage in the midst of dark magicks. She almost hated to hand it back.

"We'd best mind our formalities now," he whispered.

Taking her arm he led her up to the dais, where the archon was standing, visibly puzzled. Rhodry's men were on their feet too, but clustering round the gwerbret, all desperate to touch him and prove to themselves that he was real, alive, and there with them, some weeping openly, most keeping silent only by a great act of will. Yet even in the midst of the confusion Jill noticed Gwin, standing off to one side, and she would always remember the pain on his face, the stricken look of someone who realizes just what an outsider, what an outcast from all that's decent and normal he is. Then the look was gone, swallowed into his usual blank lack of emotion, but at that moment she found it in her heart to pity him.

"Forgive me, sir," Nevyn said to the archon. "This is my granddaughter and the gwerbret's betrothed, and there, just behind her, is the gwerbret's half-brother."

When Graffaeo, a portly little man on the pale side, bowed to her in the Deverry manner, Jill managed to drop a curtsey. Salamander was smiling in such an arrogant way that she couldn't begrudge the archon his sour scowl.

"I am well acquainted with this male personage, Lord Galrion," Graffaeo rumbled. "But where is the gwerbret himself?"

"Here." Rhodry strode to the dais, scorned the stairs, and leapt in one smooth motion three feet up. "So. I've heard your name often enough, honored one, over the past few weeks."

Goaded beyond human limits his men began to cheer, a wordless yelp of sheer release. Caught up in the spirit of the thing the various slaves and servants joined in, applauding gracefully in their corners until Graffaeo threw both arms in the air for silence.

"I am pleased to welcome you to my humble house, Lord Rhodry of Aberwyn." His smile was a flash of wolf in a pudgy face. "And I trust, since your servants are here to escort you home, that we will hear no more of this peculiar lawsuit."

For the rest of that afternoon and long into the evening, after the slaves had lit a hundred oil lamps in the glittering room and an impromptu meal had been served, Jill was a spectator at the strangest tournament she'd ever seen, round after round of mock combats fought only with words and precious few plain ones at that. She was shocked to see just how devious, just what a master of innuendo Nevyn could be when he set himself to it, and, of course, the archon would never have been elected if he hadn't been as subtle as a greased stoat. It was some hours before she realized that this battle was being fought not over principles, but out of fear. If there had been no Hawks of the Brotherhood to threaten his life, Graffaeo would have bankrupted himself gladly to help them safely home and revenge the murdered priests, but there were, always present, always threatening, the Hawks. Not, of course, that the archon ever mentioned their name — he talked mostly of regrettable circumstances and electoral discontent. Yet everyone knew what he meant, just as everyone realized that he as well as they assumed that the Hawks were behind the deaths at the hermitage.

"Of course," Nevyn said at one point. "There's bound to be an outcry among the voters when the news of the slaughter spreads — as it's doubtless doing right now. My manservant does happen to be watching over our horses out in the stables."

"Oh, my good sir, no doubt it would have spread quite quickly no matter what either of us did." Graffaeo moved neatly to undercut the dweomermaster's small victory. "Never fear. I shall do everything I can to reassure the people that the matter is well in hand."

"Justice must be served, um?" Nevyn saluted him with a wine cup. "Even if the meal is meager?"

Graffaeo flushed scarlet.

"Justice *will* be served, sir. One way or another."

Nevyn paused with the cup halfway to his mouth and considered the archon over the brim. Under their bristling white brows his ice-blue eyes seemed strangely sympathetic.

"One way or another, indeed." He lowered the cup. "I realize, of course, that you're in a very difficult position, with so many factors and factions to weigh and balance. What a pity that someone couldn't just take this little matter off your shoulders—unofficially, of course, while the official investigation goes forward."

"Ah." Graffaeo took a dried fig from a silver tray and considered its many convolutions. "A pity, indeed. If such a thing were possible, it would of course earn my extreme gratitude."

"Of course." Nevyn had a sip of wine and looked casually away toward a fresco that depicted the Star Goddesses presenting a heroically drawn figure with a lodestone. "What a beautiful painting that is! The artist must be well known."

"Oh, he is, he is. We were lucky to get him."

"Does anyone remember the names of the apprentices who mixed the plaster and ground the colors, or the journeyman who took the artist's drawings and pounced and scored them upon the wall?"

"What? Why should they?" Then the archon smiled in gentle understanding. "Indeed, why should anyone remember that?"

"Indeed. The agents of the great are never remembered, though much of the, shall we say, less pleasant work falls to them."

"A pity, in its way." The archon picked up the silver tray. "May I offer you a sweetmeat, Lord Galrion?"

"My thanks."

When Nevyn took a handful of almonds, Jill realized that a bargain had just been concluded—though what it was, she couldn't say.

For the appearances of the thing they lingered some minutes more, but as soon as possible Nevyn made their escape in a flurry of bows and protests of mutual admiration. As they all waited out in the lamplit courtyard for the horses to be brought round, Salamander was beside himself, practically jigging where he stood.

"Oh, most brilliant stroke, Lord Galrion!" He spoke in Deverrian, as secret as a whisper up here in the hill country. "Well-played indeed!"

"Hold your tongue, you chattering elf!" Nevyn sounded weary. "Don't gloat over somewhat that could well kill us all."

"But I don't understand," Jill said. "What did you get from him?"

"His permission to go after the Hawks. If I fail, it'll be no affair of his, but if I succeed, there won't be any talk of my legal culpability, either."

"But how do you know? It was all cursed unclear to me."

"My dear turtledove," Salamander broke in. "It's no one word or phrase—the truth resides in the sum of the entire evening. Never have I seen concessions better wrung! Our Nevyn is so subtle, so recondite even, that I'm beginning to wonder if he's half an elf himself."

"I know you mean that for a compliment, but stop gloating!" Nevyn snapped. "You didn't see the slaughter in that temple."

"Well, true enough, master. I fall abashed."

In a clatter of hooves on the cobbles and the ringing of bridles, slaves brought the horses round the corner of the longhouse. At their head, all diffidence and openmouthed grovel, his red hair gleaming in the lantern light, walked Perryn. At the sight of him Jill quite literally snarled like a dog and clasped her hand over her sword hilt. When he yelped and shrank back, her disgust rose strong enough to choke her. That—that ugly creature—that skinny little beast who looked more like a gnome than a man—that wretch was what had terrified her, terrorized her rather with his peculiar and unclean dweomer! Without a single thought she strode over, slapped him across the face with one hand and punched him as hard as she could in the stomach with the other. He moaned and doubled over.

"Enough!" Nevyn caught her wrist from behind.

"But, my lord! After what he did to me! I'll kill him!"

"You won't, and because I say so. Naught that I could say would talk you out of it, so leave him alone because I order you to."

That she could accept—barely. She shook off the old man's grip and strode over to Rhodry, who was standing at the head of his warband—she could think of the men no other way, now that he was with them—and watching her with a small, approving smile.

"Do you remember that stinking little weasel?" she said.

"Entirely too well. I caught him on the road, you know, after you'd left him. The gray gnome guided me right there, and I beat the demons out of his heart and hide and the filth out of his guts. It's a lovely memory, that one."

"Why didn't you kill him?"

"I swore a vow that I wouldn't." Rhodry frowned, thinking hard. "I don't remember why now, or what god presided. But a vow's a vow."

"It is, truly. Well and good, then—I just wondered."

"As well you might. But here, my love, I've been aping a man with a memory, sure enough, but that doesn't mean I have one. That old man, Galrion, the one you keep calling 'no one'? Who by all the hells is he?"

She felt then as Perryn must have when her fist punched gut into backbone. All her despair came flooding back, a wondering if Rhodry would ever be well again, if he couldn't even remember Nevyn.

"A man you can trust with your life, and the greatest sorcerer in all Deverry, just for starters." She managed to force out a reassuring smile. "I'll tell you about his other talents later."

Since he agreed with Brother Merrano that the priests of Dalae-oh-contremo had endured enough armed barbarians within their walls, Nevyn sent Salamander, Perryn, and Praedd back to the temple to round up the gear and horses left behind, then took everyone else to an inn that Merrano recommended: a large, clean place run by a pious man and, better yet, surrounded by a high wall with iron spikes embedded in the plaster on top. This time of year, fortunately, they had the compound pretty much to themselves, and Jill, rather to Nevyn's surprise, had an amazing amount of hard coin to give the innkeep to ensure that they would continue to do so.

"Where did you get all that silver?"

"Ah well." Briefly she turned furtive. "We earned it, actually, but you'd best ask Salamander how."

"Very well, then. Here, Amyr! You and the rest of the men will be sleeping in what's usually the common room upstairs. Get them settled, then stay out here to wait for Salamander and the others. Tell Perryn to sleep out in the stable with the horses. Don't worry about him arguing—he'll prefer it."

And he'll be safer there, too, Nevyn thought somewhat grimly—from Jill, that is. When he'd brought Perryn along, he'd forgotten that Jill would be less than pleased to see the man she saw as a deliberate tormentor. While he understood her feelings, he also had no desire to see Perryn beaten to death right in front of him.

Once Salamander returned, he, Jill, Rhodry, and Gwin all crowded into the tiny reception chamber of Nevyn's suite and sat on the floor while Nevyn paced restlessly back and forth. Although he knew that they were all waiting for him to speak, he found it hard to begin, because they were expecting him to solve every problem while he knew exactly how tangled the situation had become. Finally he decided to begin with the easiest strand of this web to unwind and pointed at Gwin.

"Who are you anyway, lad?"

Licking nervous lips Gwin only looked at Rhodry.

"He was a Hawk, my lord," Rhodry said. "But he's my man now, and I'll vouch for him."

Nevyn turned to Gwin, caught his glance when the man tried to look away, and switched to the dweomer sight that could bore deep into a soul. For a moment other eyes flickered before his—blue and hard and cold, but at root somehow bewildered—and with the snatch of vision came the sound of a man crying, one who hadn't mourned in years. Then it faded, leaving him puzzled and Gwin terrified, shrinking back into his corner of the tiny room, trying to speak but only mouthing soundless words.

"I won't hurt you, lad. If Rhodry says you've changed allegiance, then I'll believe him."

Gwin swallowed heavily, sighed once, and found his voice.

"I'll tell you everything I know about the Hawks. I was only a journeyman, not a master, but everything I know, I'll tell you gladly."

"Good. Later we'll have a small private chat, you and I. Oh come now, don't look so frightened. It'll be a good bit easier than your initiation was, I'm sure." Suddenly weary, Nevyn sat down on the edge of the miniature dais. "I can see that I need more information before I can make the hard decisions I have to make. Rhodry lad, let's start with you. After that stupid Cerrgonney feud wound down, what happened? Why did you head for Cerrmor?"

"I can't tell you, my lord. I don't remember. Oh, of course, you don't know yet. They took my memory away. I only remember bits and pieces of my life before they brought me to Bardek. A Hawk called Baruma—"

"He's no Hawk!" Gwin snapped. "A member of the cursed foul Dark Brotherhood, but no Hawk."

"Well and good, then," Rhodry went on. "This slime-gut demon's spawn called Baruma took me prisoner and broke my mind to pieces—as far as I can tell, anyway."

He said it so calmly that it took some moments for Nevyn to realize the significance of what he'd said. Then he swore, and all the rage he'd felt at the sight of the murdered priests boiled up again, as fresh and hot as the spew of a volcano.

"Oh, have they now?" His voice came out as a burning whisper that made everyone in front of him shrink back. He took a deep breath and made himself speak in a more normal tone of voice. "Oh, did they? Then that tears it. That's enough. I've taken all I'm going to take from these people. I'll need all of your information before I can plan the attack, but I've made my decision. Once you're all safely on your way to Eldidd, then I'm taking up the archon's little commission and coming back here to wipe these scum off the face of the earth."

"Begging your pardon and all, my lord," Rhodry said, and there was the steel of command in his voice. "But I'm not leaving until I've helped you do it. I swore a vow to kill Baruma, and kill him I will, even if I die for it and Aberwyn goes up in flames for the lack of me."

Nevyn opened his mouth to argue, then hesitated. With a ripple of dweomer-cold he realized that he was going to need help on this self-appointed mission. He also could recognize a waste of time when he saw one coming his way.

"Very well, and I suppose none of the rest of you are going to run, either, no matter how long I argue with you. But remember, Rhodry lad. You may be Gwerbret Aberwyn, but I'm the Master of the Aethyr. This is my war, and I'm the cadvridoc. You ride at my orders or you don't ride at all."

"Done, then. You have my pledged word."

It was getting on toward dawn before Nevyn slept that night. First he heard what Salamander, Jill, and Rhodry had to say about their time in Bardek; then he shooed everyone out and closeted himself with Gwin for hours. Although Gwin had never risen far in the hierarchy of the assassin's guild—he had little talent for dweomer though a lot for killing—he had spent most of his life as a Hawk, ever since he'd stumbled onto the guild's existence as a runaway slaveboy of ten. He knew names, and places, and secret signs and rituals; he'd overheard scraps of plans and details of feuds within the Brotherhood; he was also willing to spill every one of them, searching through every corner of his well-trained memory as he sat on the floor in Nevyn's chamber. He had made his change of loyalties as ruthlessly and scrupulously as he would have carried out a mass murder before, yet Nevyn could see that the change had nothing to do with honor and precious little with moral principles. Gwin only knew that his whole life had been a tangle of suffering, and that his love for Rhodry, a feeling both blind and wise, was his one last chance to cut that tangle and win free. Nevyn was more than willing to use any weapon that would get anyone free of evil, just as he would never scorn a medicinal that would save a patient just because it didn't happen to be mentioned in the best herbals.

"Now this is the most important thing of all," Nevyn said finally. "Do you know where the Old One lives?"

"I do and I don't. They don't tell lowly journeymen like me all the details, but I know he got that estate from the archons of Vardeth."

"Ye gods! It can't be all that far away!"

"Just that. You know, my lord, I keep thinking that he drew us here, like. That we've been thinking we're as clever as clever, but all the time he's been drawing us in like a spider that's got a wrapped fly on a thread."

"You've been spending too much time around Salamander and his lurid imagination."

"Maybe. It's just that you hear all these rumors about the Old One. Even my master back in Valanth used to say that half of what you heard couldn't be true, but he didn't know the false half from the real one. But then, the stinking Brotherhood never told us more than the bare bones of what we needed for a job."

"You know, I hadn't realized just how much the Hawks hated the Brotherhood. Back in Deverry we always assumed you worked hand in hand."

"Only when we were paid to, my lord. They say that the Brotherhood founded the Hawks, hundreds of years ago, back when there was plague in the islands and everything was a proper mess and the archons were too frantic to worry about a dark lodge or two, but I don't know if it's true or not. If it is, they parted company soon enough."

"That was probably inevitable."

"Probably." Gwin looked up, his eyes brimming pain. "My lord, can you cure Rhodry? Can you undo what that swine did to him?"

Nevyn considered—briefly—telling some reassuring lie.

"I don't know. I won't know until I try, and I won't be able to try until we've disposed of the Old One. I'll need time, and I'll need to concentrate. Wondering if assassins or evil dweomermen are going to drop out of the sky upon you tends to ruin a man's ability to pay attention to his work."

Gwin smiled, a twitch of his mouth with no real humor in it.

"Gwin, you must have seen what happened. I take it Baruma was mostly using physical pain to break down Rhodry's defenses."

"He was, but he tried to use shame for a weapon, too. He started torturing Rhodry when we were still in Slaith, and all the pirates would stand around and watch. They thought it was a bit of fun to see just how much pain the silver dagger could take." His voice was so conversational and ordinary that it was chilling. "They were laying wagers, you see, on how long he'd last."

"Was Rhodry aware of that?"

"He was. He taunted them—ye gods, my lord! He had the guts to lie there and jest with them, telling them to wager high, because he was going to make them rich by outlasting anything Baruma could do to him. I think that's when I fell—when I realized I—well, that I couldn't stand what they were doing to him." Gwin's face turned bleak. "Baruma never did much torturing at once, an hour here and there throughout the day. He wanted Rhodry to think about what was going to happen to him, and he wanted his fun to last, too. But then I realized that the little pig-bugger was afraid of me. So I'd sit where he could see me and just stare at him, and he'd get so nervous that he'd make the sessions even shorter. Once we got on board ship and away from Slaith, he really began to sweat. After he'd broken Rhodry down, he wanted to go on entertaining himself, but I told him I'd kill him if he didn't leave Rhodry alone. I wanted to kill him anyway, but the ship was crawling with pirates, and he was the one who was paying them. I want you to know that, my lord. I really would have killed him if I could have."

"I believe you."

"My thanks. If they'd killed me, they would have killed Rhodry, too, and so we wouldn't have gained anything." He looked away again. "Do you think I'm mad? Jill does."

"I think you've lived a life that would have driven most men mad, but that you've come to sanity's gates."

"Fair enough. And it's up to me whether or not I open them and go in?"

"Just that. You learn fast, Gwin."

"It's being around Rhodry, most like. Well, and all the dweomer round me, too." This time when he smiled his eyes came alive, too. "If I can speak frankly, my lord? Hearing Jill and Salamander talk about you chilled my heart, because I've never seen power like theirs, but here they kept saying you were the real master."

"Flattering of them. So, you could see that Jill has power of her own?"

"Who couldn't, my lord? I mean, anyone who has a little knowledge would have to be blind to miss it. Like the way she ensouled that dweomer image of the wolf and sent it after Baruma—or did she tell you about that? It was a fair lovely trick, I thought, but Salamander didn't seem all that pleased with her for doing it."

When he understood what Gwin meant, for a moment Nevyn couldn't speak out of sheer hurt feelings. Here Jill was studying dweomer at last, and she'd never even told him! Gwin winced, taking his silence wrong.

"I never meant to tell you somewhat Jill didn't want known, my lord, truly I didn't."

"It's not that." Nevyn grabbed his hurt with mental hands and shook it into submission. "It's just that she did a truly dangerous thing. Salamander's not much of a teacher, I'd say. What's wrong, lad? You look distressed."

"I don't understand how you run things, that's all. Do you want me to inform on them?"

"What? I don't indeed! My apologies! I forgot how an idle question would sound to someone who used to be a Hawk. Here, I'll take the matter up with Jill herself, but I'm not angry with her or with Salamander, and truly, what they may do or not is no affair of yours."

"My thanks. It ached my heart, wondering what I was supposed to say."

"No doubt. Here, you'd best get off to bed. I've kept you up late enough, haven't I? If you remember anything else about your old lodge, you can always tell me in the morning."

In truth, of course, Nevyn wanted to be left alone with his hurt, which, though subdued, was alive and snarling in its chains. He was surprised and more than a little disappointed in himself, that he would feel like a jilted lover. It seemed to him that he'd spent hundreds of years preparing a splendid gift, some intricately carved and polished gem, say, only to have Salamander nip in and hand her a duplicate he'd picked up in a marketplace without even realizing its worth. Don't be a fool! he told himself. What counts is the Light, not the servant who brings her to the Light. Yet he went to the window, threw open the shutters to the night, and stood looking out for a long time, watching the moon and thinking of little but his hiraedd.

With a tap on the door Jill let herself into the chamber. He knew it was her even before he turned to see her, hastily dressed and yawning in the last guttering light from the oil lamps. When he tossed up one hand and made a ball of golden light, she blinked like a sleepy child.

"You're unhappy," she said. "I just knew it, somehow. I meant to tell you about studying dweomer earlier, but there was no time."

When he felt tears stinging in his eyes, he cursed himself for a doddering old lackwit. She hurried over and laid one hand on his arm.

"What's so wrong?"

"Oh naught, naught."

"You used to be better at lying."

"Humph, and that's a nasty way to put it!" He cleared his throat and rubbed his eyes dry on his sleeve. "Forgive me, child. I know it's empty vanity, but I always wanted to be the one who taught you about dweomer."

"Well, don't you think you were? If I'd never known you, and Salamander came babbling to me about magical ensorcelments and suchlike, I would have laughed in his face—if I didn't slap it for him. Ever since that first summer we met, you've been trying to show me what I could have, if only I had the wit to want it. It took a horrible thing to make me look where you were pointing, but I finally have."

Hiraedd broke and shattered like a dropped jug. Although he

considered the idiotic grin that he felt spreading on his face unworthy of them both, he couldn't stop himself from smiling.

"Truly?"

"Truly. All Salamander's done is give me the practices I needed and tell me a few principles and suchlike. I'm truly grateful to him, too, but you know, he's a wretchedly scattered sort of teacher. Nevyn, you said once that I could always ask you for help. Did you mean that? Would you teach me more, when all this is over?"

"Of course! Child, nothing would please me more than to teach you everything I've learned, to pass it on and keep it safe for the future, if naught else." Even in his delight at this moment of triumph, so long postponed, he felt his duty pricking at him. "In fact, let's start right now. What's all this I hear about a dweomer-wolf?"

Jill winced and looked hastily away to gather her excuses. They talked till dawn, going over every half-aware step she'd taken both in creating the wolf and destroying it until she saw every error she'd made, but although she did her share of squirming under his inquisition, her attention never wandered. Her mind had been forged into a formidable weapon indeed, he realized, to some extent by her natural talent but even more by her father's harsh training in weapon craft and the dangerous life she'd led.

Much later, in the middle of all the confusion of packing up to leave the city, it occurred to him, almost casually, that he'd finally fulfilled his vow. Soon, he would be free to die. He felt the dweomer-cold grip him like an evil spell as he wondered just how soon it would be.

"By the way, oh younger brother of mine, what are we going to do about the other horses? The ones that used to belong to Gwin's obnoxious expedition."

Rhodry stopped packing his saddlebags and sat back on his heels to consider Salamander, who looked sincerely vexed as he squatted down next to him.

"Leave the wretched beasts here for the stable owner to sell," Rhodry said. "They've been naught but a cursed nuisance."

"What? We can't just leave twenty-four perfectly good horses behind."

"We can, and we are."

"But that's like throwing gold into gutters!"

All at once Rhodry understood.

"We are not, oh elder brother of mine, out on the grasslands. You don't need to hoard every spavined nag that comes your way."

"I don't care. If we leave them here, can we come back for them at some point later?"

"When, you stupid dolt?" It was Nevyn, striding into the room. "For all I know, we're riding to our deaths, and you're worrying about extra horses? Ye gods!"

"But what if some disaster falls upon us, and we need remounts?"

"No doubt we can buy them in some town or other. You and Jill seem to be dripping with coin. Which reminds me. Just how did you two earn all that money, anyway?"

"Oh, um, performing in the marketplace." But Salamander had gone dead-white. "I'm a gerthddyn, after all, and Jill was a good draw just by being a blonde barbarian lass."

At the word "marketplace" a crowd of Wildfolk materialized: sprites swooping through the air, gnomes leaping and dancing, and in a shuddering curtain of purple light the Wildfolk of Aethyr made their presence known. Faint thunder boomed.

"You didn't!" Nevyn turned as grim as a berserker.

"Er well, I can't lie. I did."

"May the Great Ones rend your soul! You stupid chattering elf! Real dweomer in the marketplace?" Nevyn stopped talking and started sputtering in sheer rage.

"My lord?" Rhodry broke in. "But it saved all our lives. Gwin told me that the Hawks never even suspected who Evan was until it was too late."

"And that statement, Rhodry lad, has just saved your scapegrace brother's life—from me. Still, I've more to say on this subject. Salamander, come with me, will you?"

Since Nevyn grabbed his arm and hauled him up with a grip as strong as a blacksmith's, Salamander had little choice about it. Berating him all the while Nevyn dragged him out into the corridor, and Rhodry could hear the old man's voice for a long time before they moved out of earshot.

When he finished packing, Rhodry went down to the inn yard,

where Amyr, Gwin, and the rest of the warband were milling around, waiting for his orders. Although Rhodry still didn't recognize the men from Eldidd, with Jill's coaching he'd learned their names and enough small things about them to hide his lack of memory. Amyr, in particular, he had reason to remember, because according to Jill that young rider had helped save his life in battle some years back—not that Rhodry could recall a single thing about it. Yet oddly enough, although he remembered no concrete details like names or places or battles, he did remember being a lord, just as he remembered how comfortable and masculine it was to wear brigga rather than a tunic now that he had a pair of trousers back on. Since he was heading a warband again, and every man in it was treating him with utter deference, all the feelings of leadership returned to him, from the easy pride to the hard worrying about their safety, as well as a way of standing and holding his head, a way of smiling even, that Rhodry the slave footman would never have dared allow himself, indeed, that he would never have recalled. When Amyr came forward to bow to him, he smiled and raised one hand in a gesture that felt familiar even though he couldn't consciously remember learning it. No doubt, it occurred to him, he was aping his mother's husband, the noble-born man who'd raised him, in some way.

"Do we ride out today, my lord?" Amyr said.

"We do. Amyr, you're going to be the captain for this ride, and always remember that we're heading for the strangest battle of our lives. If you notice anyone acting strange, brooding, maybe, or saying things that don't make sense, tell Nevyn straightaway. From what Jill's been telling me, our enemies can work on men's minds from a long way away."

"I'll stay on guard then, my lord. Shall I get the men saddled up and ready to ride?"

"Do that."

As the others hurried off, Rhodry noticed Gwin, standing a little ways apart and looking a little bewildered, as if he had no idea of how he fit into this new order of things.

"Gwin? I've been thinking. There's no reason for you to ride with the rest of the warband—you don't truly belong there. Will you be my bodyguard from now on?"

Nodding his agreement, Gwin studied the ground for a moment, then looked up and smiled at him with an affection that went far beyond the deference of a rider to his sworn lord. Rhodry knew that Gwin loved him; he was touched at times, embarrassed at others, but always he had more than one reason to be grateful to him—of that, he was painfully aware. He gave Gwin a friendly slap on the shoulder.

"Come ride next to me, will you?"

"I will. My thanks."

"Welcome enough. You've got to be at the head of the line if you're going to keep an eye on me."

Gwin smiled again, and for a moment they stood there together, savoring each other's company and little more. Then Rhodry glanced up to see Jill, Nevyn, and a much-subdued Salamander coming down the outside staircase together. He felt an odd guilt at the sight of his betrothed, as he thought of her these days, but even more, a resentment, to see her in the company of sorcerers. At times he felt that she was drifting away from him, floating out to a measureless sea on a cryptic tide, inexorably sailing farther and farther away beyond his power to call her back.

"What's wrong?" Gwin said. "You look half-sick about somewhat."

"Naught, naught, just thinking. I've been penned up too long. It gets on my nerves."

With Salamander and Jill in tow Nevyn swept over to join them, and the old man was grinning like a berserker himself.

"Are you ready to ride, lads?"

"We are," Rhodry said. "But do you know which way we're going?"

"I do—in a general sort of way. The Old One's villa is to the east of here, up in the high hills, and a good ways away. I finally thought of the obvious and asked the Wildfolk. They know it well—to avoid it."

"Oh by the Clawed Ones!" Gwin burst out. "Can they lead us straight there?"

"The Wildfolk have never led anyone straight to anything. I'll do my best to think up something better, but for now, they're the only guides we've got."

·   ·   ·

Although it wasn't very wide and neither graveled nor drained, there was a road of sorts that ran roughly east and west through Pastedion. To the west, or so the priests told Nevyn, it dwindled to little more than a goat track before it ended at an insignificant village, but to the east it wound all the way through the mountains past Vardeth to Wylinth far across the island. If Salamander had taken that road after rescuing his brother from slavery, he might well have led Rhodry right to the Old One, Nevyn realized—provided, of course, that the Old One's villa did indeed lie to the east of Pastedion but the west of Wylinth. On the material plane, the Wildfolk are easily confused; such abstract concepts as east and west are beyond them, to say nothing of true abstractions such as distance or time, and, without abstractions, they can only follow routes that they've traveled before, even if those routes are the longest possible way to their destination. For all Nevyn knew, the gnomes who were trying to help him had once started out to the east, then wandered off in another direction, or doubled back, or simply gone skipping from hilltop to hilltop all over Surtinna before they'd ended up near the Old One's villa. If he'd been trying to find an ordinary person or place, he could have sent the Wildfolk out on random hunts over the countryside, but he refused to let them near someone as dangerous as the Old One, anymore than he would have sent Salamander out flying in his newly learned and unstable bird-form.

"By the way," Nevyn asked the gerthddyn that morning. "When you fly, what bird are you?"

"You're going to laugh."

"What?"

"Well, you don't exactly get to pick the bird whose shape you want to assume. The dweomer itself finds one that reflects your nature. It's rather like freezing water in a clay pot. When you break the pot, lo! ice in a pot-shape!"

"True, true, but what bird do—"

"I might as well admit it and get it over with, oh Master of the Aethyr. Try though I might to take a nobler form, I always end up a magpie."

Nevyn laughed.

"See? Everyone laughs."

"My apologies, Ebañy. A magpie can fly with the best of them."

"How kind. Yet true, truly though alas. I'm willing to shapechange if you need me to. Mayhap the Old One would never suspect a giant magpie of possessing dweomer. Then again, he might be laughing too hard to harm me."

"Now there's a wager I wouldn't lay a copper on. I doubt me if the Old One's laughed in fifty years. I'd go out on the etheric myself before I'd let an apprentice do such a dangerous thing."

"It would be more dangerous for you just because the Old One's going to be watching for you."

"I'll take that risk, if I have to. And it may come to that."

"Let us devoutly hope it won't. You know, they say here in the islands that anyone who makes a pact with the Clawed Ones always gets betrayed in the end. Maybe they'll lead us right to their ancient servant. Or—sorry. I can see by your face that my feeble attempt at a jest wasn't funny in the least."

"It's just my mood. I was thinking of somewhat that Gwin said earlier. He was afraid that the Old One was making us come to him by some magical means."

"He's not, then?"

"Oh of course not! Don't be a superstitious lackwit! Now, wait a moment. That's an interesting thought. Suppose he wanted to draw me here for some reason—to kill me, most like, knowing him. Wouldn't our Rhodry be the perfect bait?"

"He got you here, sure enough."

"Huh. I'll have to think about this. I've been racking my brains, wondering where Rhodry's political enemies could have found a guild of Hawks to hire, and here I may have maligned them. I never could make sense of this whole thing. I'll talk to Gwin again later and see what his exact orders were."

"You know, oh exalted master of our mutual craft, there's somewhat I've been meaning to ask you. Here's Gwin, who's probably murdered dozens of men and women too for all we know, and yet he strikes me as pathetic. Then there's Perryn, who did indeed rape Jill, but unwittingly, at enormous cost to his own health, and without so much as bruising her—yet he strikes me as utterly repellent. Is it because Jill's my beloved friend, while Gwin's victims remain hypothetical and abstract in the extreme?"

"Partly, but mostly it's because you share Gwin's humanity, for all that you're half an elf, and while Perryn may have a human body, his soul isn't human in the least."

For the first time in all the years he'd known him, Nevyn had the satisfaction of seeing Salamander speechless. He left him alone to think and guided his horse up to the head of the line, where Gwin and Jill were riding on either side of Rhodry.

"Gwin, come with me a moment, will you? There's somewhat I want to ask you."

Gwin did indeed remember the orders he'd been given when he and the man called Merryc had been sent to Deverry. It was clear from the beginning, as far as he could tell, that the Old One had sent Baruma to hire the guild, not that anyone knew exactly why. More and more Nevyn was sure that he could guess. He sent Gwin back to Rhodry's side and rode on alone, getting about half a mile ahead of the line of march but never out of sight of the dust cloud that told him where they were. If the Old One wanted a strike at him, he was willing to let him try. Before they'd left Pastedion he'd set astral seals over the entire party to hide them from the Old One's scrying, but there was always the possibility that their enemy would risk traveling on the etheric in the body of light in order to track them down. Although he couldn't be sure that they were being watched in this way without going into a full trance, he could open himself up to the slight whispers and warnings of danger that the Old One's presence would induce.

For the rest of that morning the road wound through an endless roll of greening hills and the dark slashes of the tree-choked valleys. Every now and then a gaggle of sylphs or mob of gnomes would pop into manifestation and point frantically to the east, then disappear again. It was well into the afternoon, however, before anything untoward happened. When he crested a particularly high hill, he realized that he'd put a dangerous distance between himself and the others—dangerous to them. What if the Old One chose to attack those least capable of defending themselves! Cursing himself for a shortsighted fool, he turned his horse and trotted back to fall into place beside Jill at the head of the line.

"Has anything untoward happened while I've been gone?"

"Naught. Or, well, I suppose this isn't truly anything."

"Out with it."

"I just keep feeling like we're being watched."

"No doubt someone's trying to scry us out. I've set seals that should frustrate the Old One good and proper."

"Splendid. Tell me somewhat. Will the same seals keep out the Hawkmaster? The one who used to own Gwin?"

"They should. Why?"

"I don't know. I told you how he sent the wolf back to me. I just can't believe that he packed himself off and went home after that."

"No doubt you're right. Well, we'll just have to deal with him, too."

Yet even as he spoke, Nevyn felt the dweomer-cold run down his back, a warning against arrogance. As he considered its implications, he realized that he might be drawn into a situation where he would have to do something that he abhorred above all else: use violence to kill on his own authority, not that of the laws. Or would he have to offer himself as a sacrifice, now that his time was finally drawing near? The thought brought him close to tears, that he would lose Brangwen so soon after bringing her to her Wyrd, but he knew that he would always put the Light before all else, even the woman he'd loved for four hundred years, and that he would obey its will.

Yet even so, the decision lay heavily upon him, and it was nothing that he could share with Jill or even Salamander. That night, when the camp was asleep except for a trio of armed guards, he went a little ways away to the top of a hill and sat down cross-legged in the long grass. Above him the night sky was so clear that the great drift of the Snowy Road seemed to hang just an arm's length away. As he slowed his breathing and let his mind calm of its own accord, the Wildfolk came to cluster round him, especially the gnomes, who patted his arm with timid paws and climbed into his lap as if they wanted to comfort him.

"I'm afraid there's naught you can do, my friends. If there's a sacrifice to be made, it's mine alone."

He felt their distress as an exhalation of sadness, wrapping him round and mingling with his own melancholy until he nearly wept. Then, with a toss of his head, he threw the feeling off: he had work to do, whether it cost his death or not, and he would do it.

"If I die, so be it," he said aloud. "Now, let's see if we can find the

Old One. You guard my body, my friends, and wake me up if anything goes wrong."

As soon as he transferred his consicousness over to his body of light, Nevyn knew that he wasn't alone; the feeling of another magical presence was so strong that it sent ripples through the blue light, like a stone thrown into a pond. In the swirling blue waves of the etheric plane he rose high above the hilltop, then let himself drift, turning this way and that as he tried to see his enemy. Up higher, far above the sleeping camp, he saw a pentagram, a silver shape floating in the light, and all his blood ran cold, because this was no construction of the Old One's demented mind, but a talisman of beauty, with the single point upright as is natural and holy, glowing in the center with a golden light that streamed from some plane far beyond the simple etheric. As Nevyn rose toward it, he was trembling with awe, so badly that he had to exert all his craft to keep his body of light from breaking up and dropping him unceremoniously back to the physical plane.

There, arranged in all their splendor round the pentagram, were the Kings of the elements: Aethyr, Fire, Air, Water, and Earth, each a pillar and a blaze of many-colored light pulsating at a point of the star. In the center was a presence, impossible to see in the spill of golden brilliance pouring from the center—if indeed he had anything so concrete as a form to be seen. Even though Nevyn felt the presence as masculine and thus still linked to the worlds of form, they were too far apart to communicate in words or concrete thoughts. It seemed to him that the presence spoke—a clumsy word, but the one that's available—to the Kings of the Elements, and they in turn spoke to him in waves of feeling and imagery, with here and there a snatch of thought. But even though he couldn't know how he heard, he knew that he knew what had been spoken, a rebuke and a promise. Pride, his wretched princely pride had once again tripped him up and sent him stumbling into unnecessary pain. Who was he to think that he would be the sacrifice, the one whose ever-so-noble forfeit would rescue all those around him? And who was he to think that he stood alone, the only rescuer? He was needed, yes. There were things to be done that only a man like him could do. But there were other things that would be done for him. The very Kings of the Elements pledged their word on that.

As soon as he accepted their pledge, the star vanished, winking out suddenly into darkness, but the Kings remained, beckoning to him to follow them through the blue light. In the safety of their company he flew a long way east and slightly north, until they came to a little town called Ganjalo, or so the King of Earth named it. They swooped wide round the town, as if warning him to avoid it, then led him to the north until he saw an enormous walled compound below him. His companions sent out such a wave of loathing that he knew he'd seen the Old One's villa. As he returned to his body, he also knew that he could find it again, and soon, because they were no more than two-days' ride away.

The Old One stood in his Temple of Time and considered the images on the twelfth floor. Overnight they'd multiplied so fast and taken on so much life that he knew his plans were rushing toward their crux. At one window stood Nevyn, grown huge and towering; round his feet like so many toys huddled the figures of a dozen men on horseback, and at their head was Rhodry, about twice as large as the rest. Off to one side, and a normal life-size, were Jill and the image of a man he didn't recognize, though he was willing to wager a guess that it was Nevyn's disciple. At another window across the room stood the enormous image of the Hawkmaster, and again, at his feet crouched a huddle of followers, Baruma among them. Since he was planning on defeating Nevyn out on the etheric plane, where armed men would be of no use to either side, it was the Hawkmaster's followers that particularly interested the Old One. When he'd scried through Baruma's eyes, he'd seen only two other Hawks with the Master. Now there were twelve. Treachery? Perhaps. The Old One was willing to consider that the Hawkmaster might merely have summoned reinforcements against the master of the Aethyr. He was not, however, willing to ask him directly.

He returned from the temple, banished the mental construct, and opened his eyes. He was sitting in his favorite chamber below a ceiling painting of the zodiac and in front of a desk heaped with scrolls and sheets of bark-paper. In the midst of the litter stood a small bronze gong. When he rang it, Pachela, the middle-aged slave woman who ran his household, opened the door and stepped in.

"Do you wish food, master?"

"No. What are you doing, tending my door? One of the boys is good enough for that."

"I have accounts for you to look over, when you have time."

"They'll have to wait, probably till tomorrow. Send someone up here to keep everyone out. I have important work to do."

She bowed and slipped out, shutting the door softly behind her. He waited until he heard the slave come take up his guard, then brought out his consecrated mirror of black enamel to scry. As soon as he sent his mind out searching for Baruma, he saw the image of his erstwhile student flickering on the surface. Since Baruma was asleep, it took him only a few moments to steal his body for his own use. Once he'd gained control, he made a show of waking up, yawning and stretching as he opened the body's eyes.

He found himself sitting on the bare ground in a little valley. Off to one side, not far away, was a campfire; sitting near it were a handful of men, armed and grim. To the other, the Hawkmaster was walking up and down while he talked to someone that the Old One not only recognized but hated with all his heart: Dargo, the Hawkmaster who ran the Indila guild. His hatred for this particular master was one of the reasons, in fact, that the Old One had hired his assassins from another island. Secrecy, of course, was the other, but as he listened, he realized that the two Hawkmasters were discussing everything they'd gleaned about his plans, and that they knew a very great deal indeed.

"I've been laying a trail to lead Nevyn right to the Old One's villa. If we get there first, so much the better."

"Yes, indeed," Dargo said. "If the Old One's dead or weakened. A cave's a good place to lay an ambush, but not if you're sharing it with an angry bear."

So it was treachery, then. His wave of rage broke the Old One's concentration and threw him clear of Baruma's body. Once he transferred his consciousness back to his own, he snarled like the bear of Dargo's figure of speech and dug his fingernails into the wooden arm of the chair. So. They thought they'd hang around like jackals at a hunt and pick up whatever spoils the lions left them, did they? They would be very surprised when they felt the power of the Clawed Ones unleashed upon them. The Old One decided that he would destroy them first; it was the easier job, after all, and one he could do through ritual.

For a long time that night he sat and brooded, while the room slowly darkened as the oil lamps burned down and the glittering zodiac above lost itself in shadows. At last, some hours before dawn, when the tide of Earth was running deep out on the astral, he roused himself and rang the gong. Once the slaveboy had fetched him a lantern, he hauled himself out of his chair with the boy's help and made his slow way to his ritual chamber, but he dismissed the slave before he opened the hidden door into that black pit of a room. As he waddled in, a wave of scent, stale incense and long-dried blood, washed over him with comfortable familiarity.

As soon as he'd set the lantern down on the altar, he knew that something was wrong. He and his various students had worked so much magic in this room over the years, and so many human beings, to say nothing of animals, had died in it, that it normally had a malignant life of its own. Any person sensitive to such things would feel, walking in there, as if the very air quivered with the hope that he'd spill both blood and power. In a sense, the Old One's workings had turned the entire room into a talisman, vibrating with and radiating back all his evil lusts. Yet that night he felt that it had gone dead, as lifeless and spent as any other broken talisman—a smashed crystal, say, or melted bronze disk. It was merely a black chamber with odd marks on the walls, filthy and smoke-stained, reeking of sour perfume and the memories of death—nothing more.

"Nevyn!" he snarled. "It has to be Nevyn!"

No Hawkmaster would have either the power or the knowledge to exorcise a ritual chamber at all, much less from some great distance. In fact, the Old One had absolutely no idea of how Nevyn could have done such a thing, and with good reason, since the job was impossible for any human or elf, even one of Nevyn's power and learning. For a long time the Old One paced back and forth and swore with the pettiest foul oaths of the marketplace and gutter until at last, shaking and out of breath, he stood before the altar and stared up at the banner of the reversed pentagram on the wall behind it. In the flickering lantern light the star seemed to swell and glimmer. All at once the Old One was afraid; he felt power gathering around him of a kind that he had never invoked. In the central pentagon of the evil star a point of light gleamed, spread itself into a thin glowing mist, and as he watched in horrified fascination, images appeared in that mist.

They were persons of some sort, but nothing so earthly as human beings or elves or as otherworldly as pure spirits, presences rather that had form and shape but no true bodies. Since he was, after all, a master of magic in his twisted way, he knew that he was seeing only reflections or perhaps projections of these beings from some plane as far removed from the astral as the astral is from us, and that trying to communicate with them directly would be a waste of power and nothing more. At first he assumed that they must be beings of great evil, since they were appearing on a ground prepared for the working of evil, but then he remembered that his ritual room was dead and empty, and the goat-star banner nothing but a barren sign as well. In an electric stab of fear he gasped for breath.

At that precise moment three great knocks boomed out, rolling through the room and shaking the walls. The altar on which he was leaning cracked from side to side with a noise like the stroke of an enormous gong, and stone dust plumed in the trembling air. With a shriek the Old One pitched forward, but such was his presence of mind and true strength of concentration that he grabbed the lantern as he fell and blew out the flame, or the room would have caught and burnt with him in it. In the midst of the rolling thunder of the knocks, he heard or thought he heard a voice, a single word that was another crash of thunder in itself.

"Unclean!"

Lying in the dark the Old One shrieked again, wallowing from side to side as he tried to rise, as trapped as a tortoise turned onto its back. He could feel his ancient heart pounding, the blood throbbing in his neck and temples, and for a moment he thought his death was bursting out from within him the way a plant bursts open its seed. Then the door, which he'd never properly shut, was flung open, and slaves came rushing into the room. Light blossomed from other lanterns; he could hear Pachela's voice giving orders as well-trained hands grabbed him and hauled him to his knees.

"Earthquake," he gasped. "Must have been an earthquake."

"Yes, master." She sounded panicked and puzzled all at once. "We all felt it. Can you see?"

He realized, then, that she thought he'd had a stroke.

"Yes, yes. It was just the shock."

With the slaves' help he got to his feet and realized in a kind of horror that half his household was there and that they'd all seen the forbidden chamber. They would have to die, but without Pachela to care for him, what would he do? He also realized that, although the slaves were frightened of what they took to be a natural disaster, none of them showed the slightest trace of that screaming panic which the room used to induce in its victims. Still gasping and muddled, he smoothed down his tunic and shook off the hands that held him. Though he swayed, he managed to stay on his feet. When he looked around, however, he nearly fell again in a panicked faint. Not only was the altar lying in pieces, but the tapestry of the pentagram was gone—not merely torn, or shriveled, or ripped from the wall, but gone. Only an oblong of scorched paint, already cold, showed where it had hung.

And with a cold stab of certainty, the Old One knew that he had already lost his war. All that remained was to make his enemies pay high for their victory.

"Here, master." With clumsy fingers Baruma fumbled through the saddlebag and found Rhodry's silver dagger. "This was his. I used it to scry him out. It made it easy."

The Hawkmaster took the dagger and hefted it, then peered at the graved falcon on the blade.

"What's this? Some sort of magical symbol?"

"No, master. It's probably his mark. The barbarians can't read."

"Ah." The Hawkmaster flicked a thumbnail against the blade, which rang ever so softly. "Well, it's certainly an alloy you won't find in the islands. Good, little piglet. This will do splendidly for our last clue." He waved to one of the Hawks. "Take this into the Ganjalo marketplace and sell it. Make sure the buyer remembers you."

Once the runner was on his way, the Hawkmaster turned his attention back to Baruma, who was squatting by the dead campfire and shoving food into his mouth with both hands. He was drooling and gobbling so loudly that the Hawkmaster nearly killed him then and there, but he restrained himself. That pleasure would come later, after they'd taken over the Old One's villa.

"Stop stuffing yourself for a minute and answer me. How far are we from your master?"

"Is it sunset or dawn now?"

"Dawn."

"We ride all day. Then we're there."

"Good. We'll wait in the hills until the Master of the Aethyr's nearby, and then we'll spring our trap."

It took all day and well into the night for the Old One to recover. As he lay gasping and wheezing on his bed, he realized that his body was reaching the end of its unnaturally prolonged endurance, that even if he could kill all his enemies, Nevyn and the Hawks both, he would die soon anyway. At first he raged and swore; then he wept and trembled; finally he lay still, his feelings spent, and considered the situation. The Clawed Ones were deserting him, he supposed; they always did desert a master of his craft, sooner or later, as one last test to see if that master could stand without them. Only then could he pass into the life that was death.

Regret it though he did, it was time for him to die. No doubt his enemies thought that his death would mean the end of him and his power; no doubt they thought that they'd be rid of him forever once they killed this loathsome husk that weighed him down. He knew that he was only going to another place, where he would live on and find unlimited power to take his revenge.

"Fools!" he whispered. "Someday soon I'll suck their souls dry."

"Nevyn?" Jill said. "You seem to know exactly where we're going."

"I do. I'm afraid I was being a stiff-necked dolt, trying to do everything in exactly my way and in my own time. Fortunately, I had the wit to accept help when it was offered."

"From the Wildfolk?"

"From their kings and their lords. Those are beings with a full consciousness—a very different sort than ours, but a true consciousness all the same. They stand in the same relationship to the Wildfolk as the Great Ones do to us."

"I don't know why, but whenever you talk about the Great Ones, I feel terrified."

"Why? Because you're a sensible sort of person, that's why. They're not all cozy and comfortable, you know."

They were riding at the head of the line, a little ahead of the others so they could talk privately. That morning when they broke camp, Nevyn had led them off the road with the remark that he didn't see any reason to give Ganjalo the scare of its life and then taken them straight through the wild hills. Now they were following a stream, running full and wild from the floods, that would—or so Nevyn said—take them right to the Old One's estate.

"Why isn't the Old One trying to stop us?"

"I don't know, but I suspect that he's getting ready to run for his life. Or, truly, that's not quite the right way to put it. Listen, Jill, you'll find out soon enough. I only ask one thing from you: whatever I tell you to do, do it. I don't care how badly it aches your heart—do what I say."

"Of course. I promised, and I will."

Toward noon Nevyn called a halt. While Jill fretted, pacing back and forth and wondering what he was up to, he went alone to the top of a nearby hill and sat in the grass for close to an hour. When he returned, he announced that the Old One's compound lay just ahead. As they rode that last few miles, Jill noticed how quiet Nevyn was, slumped a little in his saddle as if he were lost in thought. At that moment he reminded her of her father; he looked every bit as bored and distant as Cullyn did when he was about to charge into a battle against bad odds. At the crest of one last hill they paused their sweaty, blowing horses, and Nevyn rose in the stirrups to shade his eyes and look out.

"There it is."

Like a piece of jewelry in the palm of a hand, the villa lay in a green valley. White stucco walls set off the gardens and the buildings—a main longhouse, a stables, a scatter of square sheds—which were all roofed with the usual Bardekian shakes of reddish wood. From their vantage point Jill could see nothing moving, not so much as an animal.

"Nevyn?" Jill said. "Are there wards over the compound?"

"You *have* been studying, haven't you? There are indeed, but I'll just do somewhat about that now."

Nevyn clutched his saddle peak with both hands, shut his eyes, and went limp, bowing toward his horse's neck. For some minutes nothing seemed to happen; then his head jerked up—though his eyes stayed shut—and his whole body twitched and shuddered.

"There." All at once, he was awake again. "Well, I was right about one thing: the Old One's gone. Finding him again could be a problem, I suppose."

"Do you mean we've won?"

"I only wish. There's a small army of Hawks down there, all hidden and waiting."

"Do we charge the gates, my lord?" Rhodry guided his horse up closer. "Me and my men are ready."

"Your men, and Gwin and Perryn, too, are going to stay up here with the horses. You may come down with me and Jill and Salamander, if you promise not to get in the way and to leave the fighting to me."

"What? Have you gone daft?"

"Not in the least. There's a thing in that villa that I absolutely have to have if I'm going to track the Old One."

"Walking right into a nest of assassins and asking for it sounds daft to me."

"No doubt, but I won't exactly be asking, bargaining, more like."

"Nevyn," Jill broke in. "I feel cold as ice. There's danger all around us."

"Of course. I'll admit it's somewhat of a gamble. If I thought they'd kill us the moment I opened the door, I wouldn't go, but they'll want a look at me first, to gloat if naught else. You see, I'm willing to wager that they're as sure as sure that I'm helpless against armed force. Those of us who study the dweomer of light would generally rather die ourselves than cause another man's death and these stupid piss-poor excuses for sorcerers have always taken that for a sign of weakness." Nevyn actually laughed, a rusty-sounding burst of good humor. "Now, Rhodry, are you staying here or are you coming on my terms?"

"I'm coming to guard Jill if naught else."

"Well and good, then. Remember your orders."

Nevyn dismounted, tossed his reins to the startled Gwin, then strode off downhill, leaving the others to follow as fast as they could. By the time everyone caught up with him, he was knocking on the front gate as calmly as a peddler with trinkets to sell. Jill began to think that Rhodry was right and the old man's wits were going.

"Er, my lord?" she said. "I doubt me if they're just going to answer as courteous as you please."

"I wasn't putting that kind of knock on the door."

Nevyn raised both hands over his head, held them there for a moment, then slowly brought them down in one smooth sweep until his fingers pointed right at the ironbound double gates of the compound. With a roar and a gust the wind rose and slammed into them like a battering ram. Wood splintered, iron bands snapped, one gate shattered right then; the other flew open and shattered against the wall behind it. Over the roar and the pounding Jill heard screams, prayers, and the sobs of terrified men as well as women.

"Well, come along," Nevyn snapped. "No need to dawdle."

As he strode through the broken gates, they crowded in after him. In the lush garden trees still quivered and rustled from the wind; ancestor statues lay broken on the ground. Out in the middle square of lawn huddled the Old One's slaves while all around them, as if standing guard, clustered a veritable army of Wildfolk. Jill had never seen so many—big burly gnomes standing grim and attentive, hordes of sprites hovering like wasps in the air, smaller gnomes dancing and baring their needle-sharp teeth.

"Flee, all of you!" Nevyn called out. "Run for your lives and now! Run to the town and beg for help, go hide in the mountains—but run!"

When he waved his arm, illusory lightning plunged and thundered among the trees. Screaming, shoving each other, the slaves bolted and raced ahead of him, panting and yelling and sprinting round the longhouse toward the back gate. In a swirling pack the Wildfolk followed, pinching, poking, biting the poor souls to keep them moving out to safety. Nevyn walked up to the front door, shoved on it, found it open, and flung it aside. Jill gasped, half-expecting an arrow or knife to come flying out. Nothing moved; the rustling trees fell silent; there was no challenge, no taunting, nothing.

"Very well, then we'll go in after them."

As they walked down the long corridor, the Wildfolk came back, materializing in midair and drifting down like drops from a leaky roof. Jill was so sure they were walking into a trap that she could barely breathe when they stepped into a modest reception chamber of the usual sort, the walls painted with fading flowers, the dais tiled in restful blues and hung with blue-and-purple silk drapes. Sitting in a low-backed chair on the dais was an enormously tall man with the dark skin of Orystinna; around one wrist he wore a tattoo of a striking hawk, and his face was masked with a red silk hood. Crouched at his feet was a Bardekian whose black hair and beard were so slick that it looked as if they'd been oiled.

"Baruma," Rhodry hissed.

When the Bardekian raised his head, Jill saw that he wore a collar and a chain. The other man jerked the chain and smiled at her, as if he'd read her mind and was underscoring her point.

"Greetings, Master of the Aethyr," the Hawk said in Bardekian. "How sad that we meet only to say farewell."

"Oh come now!" Nevyn answered in the same. "Do you really think your paltry brigands are capable of killing me?"

"What's to stop them? You've left your only hope up on the hill. Slaves may run from your tricks with the wind, but my men won't."

"No doubt, no doubt. And truly, you must be far stronger than I thought to chase the Old One out of his hole." Nevyn glanced around the room. "I never thought he'd have such good taste in furnishings. I was expecting something gaudy and morbid. Rather like your taste in hoods."

The Hawkmaster hesitated, then shrugged.

"Bluster all you want, old man. You followed my bait and walked right into the trap. You've got to admit that—you tracked me exactly like I wanted."

"Nothing of the sort, actually. My spirits showed me where the Old One lived, and you were a mere incidental. But come along, if you'd go to all the trouble to lay some sort of abortive trap, there must be somewhat you're after. Let me guess—if I do some thing for you, you'll let my companions go."

"That was the bargain I had in mind, yes. I'll even make sure that they reach their ship without anyone else giving them a moment's trouble. You know, when the Hawks bargain, they keep their word. We're not like the Brotherhood. No one would hire us if we reneged on our contracts."

"I've always heard that, and I believe you. What do you want from me?"

He sounded so calm, like a farmer haggling over cabbages in the market square, that Jill wanted to scream just to break the tension. On either side of her Salamander and Rhodry had gone as still as the statues in the garden outside, and both of them were a ghastly sort of pale, too, looking at that moment more elven than human from the wild fury in their eyes. The Hawkmaster smiled and lounged back in his chair to cross one ankle over the opposite knee.

"It's nothing that will even trouble your conscience, Master of the Aethyr. You came here to kill the Old One, didn't you? Well, so did I, but he's escaped. Tell me where he is. Which way he's running will do. You can die content, knowing that we'll finish the job for you."

"Well, that certainly sounds like a fair bargain."

"Nevyn, no! You can't!" Jill felt all her hard-won strength slip away like a doffed cloak and leave her sniveling and shaking. "I'd rather die than see you—"

"Whist!" Nevyn snapped. "Every man comes to his time, child. Mine is now. Get Rhodry back to Eldidd—I enjoin you, I lay this task upon you, I insist upon it in the name of the Holy Light itself. Will you promise me?"

Through a blinding scald of tears she nodded her agreement. When Salamander opened his mouth to argue, Nevyn silenced him with a black look and threatened Rhodry with a slap across the face. Then he turned back to the Hawkmaster, and at that moment he seemed taller, young and proud and straight, standing in an unearthly light as the Wildfolk came to cluster around him and lend him their strength and wildness.

"Very well. I'll find the Old One." Nevyn even smiled at the Hawkmaster. "But do you have somewhat of his that I can use for a focus? Some thing he worked dweomer with?"

"It's right here, all ready for you."

When the master snapped his fingers, Baruma picked up a bundle wrapped in black velvet and shuffled to the edge of the dais. Whimpering all the time, glancing Rhodry's way in abject terror, he handed the bundle to Nevyn, then in a clank of chain rushed back to his master's feet. Although Rhodry's eyes followed him, his expression of utter impassive blankness never changed. Nevyn unwrapped the bundle to reveal a silver chalice, engraved with a welter of peculiar symbols and sigils and crusted, just here and there among the engraving, with drops of dried blood.

"The Old One's slaves were careless when they cleaned the silver." Nevyn wrapped it back up again. "This will do splendidly."

"I have some small knowledge of these things." The Hawkmaster smiled as if at a compliment. "You best had send your companions away."

"I'll just walk with them to the door."

In a silence that seemed as thick and cold as seawater, Jill and the others followed Nevyn down to the chamber door. Just outside, blocking the corridor, she could see two men, armed and at the ready. Nevyn bent down and kissed her on the cheek.

"Kill those men without any compunctions," he whispered in Deverrian, then raised his voice and changed his language. "Farewell, child. Remember me in your heart."

Hope stabbed her very soul.

"Always, my lord," she said. "And may the gods go with you on your last journey."

"Well spoken, isn't she?" The Hawkmaster called out, "Very well, all of you. Get out of here, fetch the rest of your men, and get on your way to Indila. No one will harm you. I've given my word, and I keep it. Nevyn, as for you, come back here. It's time to perform your last little trick."

"Oh, gladly." Nevyn turned to face him and raised one hand, a gentle gesture as if he were about to point out some small error of discourse. "What about a trick with fire?"

The draped silk caught with a hiss.

"You may keep your word." Nevyn smiled gently. "But I never swore mine. I'll find the Old One after you're dead."

Flames leapt to the walls, crackled, and spread in the dweomer-wind that rose and charged across the dais. The Hawkmaster dropped Baruma's chain and jumped up, screaming, his tunic blazing as he ran panicked for a side door in a stream of sparks that fell to fire the scattered cushions. Tiles began to crack and burst from the wall with booms and explosions like in one of Salamander's shows. Just as the master reached the door, Baruma rushed after. He held his own chain in both hands and swung it hard, lashing the Hawkmaster across the head and knocking him sideways into the flaming wall. The enormous assassin grabbed the burning curtains and fell, pulling them down with him into a writhing, blazing heap. With a shudder the side wall collapsed on top of him.

"The ceiling will go in a minute," Nevyn yelled. "The Wildfolk are firing the upstairs chambers—anyone hidden up there is beyond help, so let's get out of here."

As Jill turned and raced out through the billowing smoke, she was drawing her sword. Screaming out curses the two assassins charged, but she spun to one side, let her man overrun his mark, and slashed him across the neck as he tried to catch his balance. Grunting he went down, folding into death at her feet just as his fellow dropped on top of him. With a bloody sword in one hand Rhodry grabbed her shoulder with the other.

"Baruma!" he screamed over the roar of flames. "Where's Baruma?"

"No time! Let's get out of here! Look, Nevyn and Salamander are already gone."

When he took out running down the long corridor, Jill followed, thinking that he was heading for the gates out of the compound.

When the flames on the floor above began scorching the ceiling of the reception chamber, Nevyn and Salamander raced across the room and out the side door, which led into a big disorganized courtyard in back of the house itself. Nevyn clutched the precious scrying focus with both hands as they dodged through sheds and storage huts, rounded the empty stables and ran across the kitchen garden to the back gates, which were standing wide open from the earlier flight of the Old One's slaves. Nevyn glanced around to make sure that the Wildfolk had followed his orders to carry or chase to safety all the various animals that were bound to be part of an estate like this, then led the way out the gate. Beyond the villa walls lay the wild grassy hills, rolling away to far-distant mountains. As they ran, heading far away from the burning compound, Nevyn seemed to pick out something moving among the hills.

"There he is! Can you see him?"

"Not one thing," Salamander was panting for breath. "And I'm the elf."

Only then did Nevyn realize that he'd already slipped into a light trance, that he was seeing the small group of men, carrying some large and lurching thing up a hill, only in his mind.

"It's Tondalo in a litter. This hideous chalice is practically throbbing in my hands, it's so linked to him. Well and good, then. You guard my body while I go into full trance. If this wretched fool thinks he can escape me as easily as he fooled the Hawks, then he's stupid as well as evil to the core."

Panting and gasping under the weight of the litter, the slaves staggered up the hill. Inside, thrown this way and that, grabbing at window frame and curtains indiscriminately to steady himself, the Old One was already making his mental preparations. Across from him Pachela moaned as she clutched a padded box with one hand and the litter frame with the other. Her gray hair was slipping from her coiffure in big wisps. Suddenly the motion of the litter eased somewhat as the slaves reached the crest of the hill.

"Stop here!" the Old One called. "Put me down here."

The litter jerked to the ground, and the door flung open of its own accord. Pachela scrambled out first, then helped the Old One haul his bulk free and stand up. Far down below him the smoke from the burning villa rose in an oily plume. The Old One turned and found the slaves huddled together by the tipped litter.

"As of now you're all free, for all the good it will do you. Pachela, get out the bottle of the poison. I brought a wineglass, too. If it hasn't broken, I might as well die in proper style. The rest of you, run away now! Fast! Head to town and tell everyone that brigands have fired the villa. If you're lucky, they'll believe you before the Hawks get you."

Half-slinking, half-scrambling they hurried off downhill. The Old One lowered himself to the grass and patted the ground with one hand. It was such a distasteful feeling, the ground hard, the grass slick and somehow oily on his parchment-dry skin, that he realized with some surprise that he hadn't been outdoors inside his own body in over fifty years. Shaking with fear, Pachela opened the prepared poison, dissolved in wine, and poured it out. The Old One held up the glass goblet and swirled the dark red wine, a Myleton vintage, raw and brash enough to cover the acrid tinge. Far below the greasy plume of burning had climbed to the sky.

"Pachela, you may go now. I see that Nevyn's worked my revenge for me." He took the first long swallow of wine. "The Hawkmaster is—was—a very stupid man, good with knives, no doubt, but not with his wits."

As he sipped the second dose, he looked round to note the details of this early spring day: the view of the mountain peaks far away, pure and shining in the warm sun, Pachela herself, once a beautiful girl with ensnaring dark eyes instead of this thick-waisted matron with gray hair, who was walking slowly, with dignity, down the hill toward the burning ruin of the only life she'd ever known. No doubt she was glad that he was dying. Here in the soft sun, with the wind picking up cool and flower-scented, he couldn't begrudge it to her.

"Everything changes," he mumbled. "It's the curse of the world: everything changes. But I—I go beyond all that."

Although his hand responded slowly and trembled all the way, he got the goblet to his mouth and gulped down the last of the wine. A dribble ran from the corner of his mouth, but when he automatically tried to wipe it away, his hand spasmed, tossing the glass against the earth to shatter there.

"It is time."

His eyes shut of their own will, but he stayed conscious, his mind alert within the dying lump of flesh. Even though his body of light would be useless in a few minutes, he summoned it as a bridge to the etheric and transferred his consciousness over to the simple thought-form, a slender man in a plain tunic. The relief of finally being free of his huge and deformed body was so great that he swooped up to the sky and fluttered once round the hilltop. He could see Pachela, a dim shape inside her pale aura, making her slow, proud way along through the waist-high waves of grass. When he flew off to the north, he glanced back to see that the silver cord joining him to his body was growing very thin and pale. It was time to change levels while he was still somewhat alive and in firm command of his mind.

He pictured a circle divided into quarters, each a different color:

olive, russet, citrine, and, in the bottom quadrant, black. He held the image in his mind until it stayed clear and solid, then slid it out so that the circle seemed to hang like a vast curtain before him. Just then, he felt the silver cord snap. Like pieces of unstitched cloth, chunks of his body of light slithered and fell away, leaving him a naked bluish form hovering amid the billowing energy waves of the etheric plane. He bent all his concentration to the circle, which now changed from a painted-looking figure to a solid disk. The blackness was swirling within its bounds like trapped smoke. In thought only, the Old One called out the names of the Lords of Husks and Rinds, but there at the gate between worlds the thoughts seemed to boom like gongs. On that quiver and rage of sound he slid forward into and through the swirling blackness into the Earth of Earth, the lowest point of the world that knows the Light.

He felt it more as a smell than as a space, a thick mustiness of decay, yet perfectly benign, like leaves crumbling to enrich good soil, perhaps. As he burrowed his way deeper in, he felt pressure, as if the earth grasped him with firm hands. It became harder and harder to move, even though he was now pure mind scrabbling molelike into the astral plane. A desire filled his being, a lust for sleep, for resting there forever in the clingy dark, but he had trained his will for a hundred years in preparation for this exact moment. As he clawed onward, he envisioned himself going down, pictured in his mind that he was digging his way through to a darkness that lay below the universe and that touched it only at this one point. Earth of Earth began to fight him, as if its King had somehow discovered his evil intent. The dark turned crystalline and hard, gleamed briefly with an oily copper light, formed into vague faces and hands that clutched him and whispered with voices that all cried, "Go back! Go back to the Light!" Yet raging and cursing he smashed his way on, hammering at the faces and crushing the little hands with the huge steel clubs he visualized for weapons.

With one last howl of rage he broke through. Since his mind was still bound by earthly concepts, he saw everything very concretely. He was a tiny naked human figure clinging by its fingers to the bottom of a vast black sphere. Below, storm-tossed and infinite, spread a black sea. There were no stars, only currents of greater darkness, no true forms, only shifting pale images that alternately beckoned and menaced. The Old One felt his terror like a biting cold, smelt it as an acrid stink. This was the gate to the Dark of Darkness, the world of Husks and Rinds. Here, if he could claw and fight his way to power, he would exist forever as a separate soul, beyond all judgment of the Great Ones, beyond death though beyond all life as well. During every moment of his unnaturally long life, he had trained and planned and longed for this moment, but now he hesitated, stunned by the loathing that welled up within him.

For those moments beyond time he wanted to turn back. Earth of Earth would receive him; even as he had the thought, he felt his grip upon the sphere grow more secure, as if something had reached out and caught his wrists to steady him. Yet turn back to what? Nevyn? That meeting, perhaps, he could have faced, but behind the barbarian dweomermaster stood the Great Ones and their ultimate threat: the utter annihilation of a soul as unclean as his. Besides, he had a certain stubborn dark honor of his own. All his life he had longed for the manhood stolen from him by the slaver's knife, longed for power to replace it and longed, too, for vengeance. What was he to do now? Crawl back to Nevyn like a whimpering puppy and grovel before the Lords of Light?

"Never! I swore that from evil I would forge my good, and I hold myself to that vow!"

He let go the sphere and dropped. Yet, even as great black waves lapped up to receive him, he saw, plunging out of the storm-tossed sky a figure of shining light, and as it plunged, it threw before it a gigantic shimmering net. With a howl of rage the Old One tried to dodge to one side, but too late. The net caught him, spread out, and wrapped him round. In the gust of triumph that echoed over the sea, he recognized the touch of Nevyn's mind. Sea, storms, the sphere itself—they all vanished in a blaze of light as he felt himself swung round and round then slung clear of the net in an arc like a cry of triumph. On and on he tumbled through the silvery billows of the astral light to fetch up at last in some uncertain place.

He stood at night on a strangely familiar hilltop and looked out over a misty valley. A full moon hung overhead, but it was bloated to an enormous size and burned with an eye-slashing silver glare. The moon was watching him. He was sure of it, suddenly, that it had turned into a single malignant eye. His terror made his flash of loathing at the Dark of Darkness seem like a child's pleasurable shudder over a ghost tale. He was doomed. Nevyn had anticipated him, gone to meet him, trapped him, and now turned him back into the world where there was no escape from the Great Ones. He would have no endless life of working evil as he crept through the dark. He would have no life at all.

In a spasm of screaming panic he wrenched himself around and saw, looming nearby, his magical Temple of Time, but now everything lay in moonlight, not half in sun. He ran or rather flew toward the white tower, and as he swooped into the open door he saw all his symbolic figures lying smashed and broken. He rushed for the staircase, raced up and up, pausing at each floor only to see the same chaos, his work smashed and reduced to strewn rubble. At the top floor he had his greatest shock, because it was empty—not so much as a splinter left—except for the statue of Nevyn, gazing out the window where he'd left it. The Old One stood at the top of the staircase and tried to steady himself, because in his mind he still had a body of sorts, while he wondered about the significance of this one last symbol. When Nevyn turned from the window and smiled at him, he screamed.

"I've been waiting for you. Ask for mercy, and you shall have it."

With another scream the Old One flung himself down the stairs, tumbling and swooping out the tower door just as the temple collapsed with a silent—utterly silent—shimmer of destruction. He rushed down the hill and staggered into the mists, but although he tried to run, he merely drifted this way and that. He realized then just how far gone in dying he was. With one last spasm of strength, he seemed to rise up and catch a draught or current in the light, and slowly it bore him up and away. It seemed to him that he was a boy again, a young slave in training for the clerkship. Ahead of him stood the school, built round a pleasant stucco scriptorium in the midst of gardens. He'd been happy there, well-fed and well-treated for the first time in his life, good at the work, praised by his master, courted by the other boys. He saw, then, the scriptorium, the arched doorway leading into the long, white room, all glowing with little oil lamps.

In the slender form of an adolescent boy, the Old One skipped toward the doors. He could feel his sandals slapping on the tiles and smell the scented oil. Once he reached those doors, he would be safe.

Master Kinna would never let anyone harm his best pupil. He faded through the doors and out into the long room, where plain little writing desks stood in tidy rows and oil lamps flickered golden against the rising dark. Up on the dais someone was standing at the lectern and contemplating a draped scroll.

"Master Kinna! It's Tondalo. I'm back."

The figure raised his head and pushed back the hood of its robe: Nevyn. The scriptorium vanished. They stood face-to-face in the white mist.

"Tired of running?" The sculpted face of Nevyn's thought-form wore no expression at all, not a snarl, not a smile, nothing. "Go where you will, but every road will lead back here to me."

The Old One felt as if he still had a body and was slowly sinking to his knees. The room spun in a swimmy blur, a whirlpool, a murky vortex of gold-shot white light.

"You have one last chance." Nevyn's voice spun round the vortex to reach him. "Forswear the Dark and submit to the Light."

"Curse you! Curse you and all your wretched kin!"

Nevyn vanished. The Old One knew only movement, felt himself to be one tiny point of consciousness that was swirling, rising, caught now in the whirlpool, choking, spinning, fading, always spinning—

Then nothing at all.

"You want to know what happened to the Old One?" Nevyn said. "Where does a candle flame go when you blow it out?"

When he realized that he understood, Salamander shuddered in his very heart. By then the flames were swarming and swirling over the entire villa and the compound around it, the greasy smoke spreading through the sky and staining the light into a hellish parody of sunset. Yawning and sighing like any old man waking from a nap, Nevyn sat up, stretched his arms over his head, then clambered to his feet.

"Let's find the others and get on the road. When those slaves reach town, the archon will send men out to investigate. I'm in no mood to be arrested just yet."

"Quite so, oh exalted master. Ye gods, you gave me a turn in there! I honestly thought you were going to die to save our miserable and unworthy lives."

"You're not the only one who can put on a good show for the marketplace. Look—there's Gwin and the warband riding for us. No doubt they've been a bit worried. But—oh by the Goddess herself! Where are Jill and Rhodry?"

Salamander swore and went cold all over again as he counted up the riders and realized that his brother and his pupil were nowhere among them. Without even thinking he began running toward the black and flaming ruins of the villa. Cursing a steady stream under his breath, Nevyn followed.

When Jill and Rhodry rushed out of the house into the garden, they found the wooden ancestor statues already burning, licked with leaping flame like huge logs in some giant's hearth. Smoke poured around them and billowed down from the blazing shake roof in a swirl of darkness while the heat parched and trembled the living trees and flowers. Through the crackle and roar of burning Jill could hear men screaming, trapped in the upper rooms of the villa. Choking and coughing she dashed for the gates in the outer wall only to realize that she'd lost Rhodry. She spun around to see him turning round the corner of the house and racing down the narrow passage between it and the outer wall on his right.

"Rhoddo! Stop! Come back!"

"He went this way!" Rhodry kept running. "I heard his chain clanking."

For the briefest of moments she stood crippled with fear. With the roar of a thousand demons a plume of fire burst free from the roof and towered in a spew of golden sparks.

"Rhodry!"

Cursing him in her mind Jill ran after him. Dodging sparks, choking on smoke, stumbling at times and leaping over a clot of burning debris at others she raced down the passage and burst free just barely in time into the clutter of sheds behind the house. Already roofs were smoking and charring as the Wildfolk swept among them in an orgy of ruin. Through the smoke she could just make out Rhodry, hesitating by the back wall.

"Come on!" she screamed at him. "Out the back gates!"

"Won't. He can't be far." Rhodry suddenly burst out laughing, his old berserker's howl of harrowing delight. "Baruma! Remember my promise!"

Wailing in joy he took off again, racing round a shed and heading away from the back gates and safety. In an unthinking rage Jill dashed after. Behind her the empty stables collapsed with a rush of fire and spewed embers out across the yard. A shed caught in a shriek of dweomer-wind. Blackness shot with burning filled the yard. Still Rhodry ran on, with Jill right behind him, screaming curses and begging him to come back. Finally, as she put on a last burst of speed, she saw Baruma up ahead, panting and blowing as he tried to run with his heavy chain. With a banshee howl Rhodry took out after him just as Baruma ducked through a little gate. Although Rhodry plunged right after him, Jill hesitated and looked back. The plastered walls on the far side of the compound were collapsing in a pour of smoke as their supporting timbers caught from the sheer heat in the yard.

"Rhodry! Come back!"

Her only answer was a swirl of smoke and fire as the roof of the house fell in. She turned and ran after him, batting at the drift of sparks with both hands as she charged into a walled garden. Already fire crept through the parched flowers that edged it, and in the far corner a tree blazed like a torch. Heat danced and shimmered along the soot-stained walls; she could feel heat grabbing her face like a clawing animal. Ahead in the smoke Baruma crouched at bay, his only weapon the heavy chain that he swung in both hands, back and forth in a desperate arc to keep Rhodry and his sword out of reach. There was no time to let Rhodry wear him down with fancy footwork. Jill drew her silver dagger, caught it by the point, aimed, and threw. As straight as an elven arrow it sailed home and bit into Baruma's right eye. Screaming and blind he dropped the chain and staggered back as Rhodry pounced and struck, slashing his throat open in a howl of laughter.

"Rhodry, come on! Now!"

He pulled her dagger free and swung around just as the wooden gate behind them went up in a blaze of flame. They were trapped. She could see the berserker fit leave his eyes as he realized it.

"Oh ye gods! My love, I'm sorry!"

The dagger in his hand was blazing with dweomer-light as its spell responded to his elven blood. She had one maddened thought that at least they'd die together; then her newfound strength welled to the surface of her mind. With a howl of her own she flung both arms over her head.

"Lords of Fire! In the name of the Light, attend me!"

She felt as much as she saw them, vast and towering shapes of light in the flames, a steady presence when all else around them was leaping and flickering, a rush of power and majesty like a cool wind billowing out of the smoke.

"Lords of Fire! In the name of the Master of the Aethyr, save us! I beg you as a servant of the Light."

The presences swelled with the leap of flame, and for a moment she thought they would refuse her. Then came a wind, hissing and gliding as it parted the flames like the prow of a ship parts the sea. The foaming wake turned gold and red as the burning chunks and embers of what once had been the gate boiled to either side and a smoking path appeared between.

"Rhodry, follow me. Don't stop and don't look back. Lords of Fire! Your hands hold our lives."

Jill took a deep breath of air turned suddenly pure and ran, knowing instinctively that the safe path could only hold for a few brief moments no matter how much the Lords wished otherwise. Over the roar and crackle of the blazing house she could hear nothing, had no way of knowing if Rhodry were behind her or not, but she could spare not a second to look back and see. The world had shrunk to a tunnel that opened in the solid blackness of smoke. She burst out of the walled garden, dodged through the burning sheds, raced for the fire-free breach that suddenly appeared in the crumbling outer walls while around and above her the sparks and floating chunks of burning flew back as if invisibile hands knocked them away. Her lungs were seared from heat, and the air was poisonous again, but in one last burst of will she leapt free and stumbled, staggering up and careening like a drunken woman across the grassy ground outside.

Something caught her hand, and she looked down to see her gray gnome, dancing in glee and pulling her onward. Through a waft of smoke shapes appeared ahead: more gnomes, all sooty and triumphant.

"Rhodry!" she gasped out. "Are you . . ."

"Right here." He was choking and hacking. "Right here and safe."

The gnomes clustered round and grabbed his hands to drag him forward. In a crowd of Wildfolk they staggered up to the crest of a hill and flopped down, coughing and gasping for breath. When Jill looked back, she saw the compound walls collapsing inward in a rush of greasy black smoke. Even though the tall grass grew all round, and sparks and great slabs of burning debris blew through the air, not one blade of the green ever caught, nor did the fire reach them. She turned to Rhodry and burst into hysterical laughter, because even in the midst of all these vast dweomer-workings, these mighty magicks drawn from the soul of the universe, her dagger still faithfully glowed to warn her that an unreliable elf was close at hand.

"Oh, I wish Otho could see this!" She was choking and laughing and sobbing all at once. "Never trust an elf, he told me. They'll get you into trouble for sure, he said. Ye gods, he was right! He was right!"

Rhodry stabbed the dagger into the ground to douse it and threw his arms around her. Alternately choking and laughing they clung together until Nevyn and Salamander came pounding up the hill.

"Are you hurt?" Nevyn said.

"We're not. Singed, no doubt."

"You don't have any eyebrows that I can see. And as sooty as the inside of a charcoal brazier, both of you." Nevyn's voice shook so badly that it was hard to tell if he were close to tears or hysterical laughter. "Can you ride? We'd best get out of here."

Rhodry scrambled up, then caught her hand to pull her after him. When she stumbled and nearly fell, she realized just how exhausted she was, and not in any normal way. Only then did she realize something else as well, that there in the burning garden she'd worked dweomer, not done an exercise or accidental trick, but performed an act of magic, and a mighty one.

Late that afternoon Rhodry led his ragged line of frightened men and spooked horses up to the grassy crest of a low hill. Down below he saw a sheltered valley where a stream ran over clean rock, and holm oaks grew in a scattered grove. Although it was a perfect place to camp, when he turned in the saddle he could still see the smoke of the burning villa, a black though distant streak on the sky. Nevyn rode up next to him.

"It's time to camp for the night."

"We can't stop here. We're still in danger."

"Well, so we are." Nevyn's voice seemed to trail away in exhaustion after every phrase. "The rest of the Hawks are bound to discover what's happened sooner or later."

"That's not what I meant, my lord. Those slaves you drove off? They must have reached a town or another villa by now. The authorities will round up the local militia. The smoke from that fire's like a beacon, and once they get to the villa, they'd have to be blind to miss our tracks."

"Just so. That's one reason I set the wretched fire in the first place. Gwin's got you thinking like a Hawk, Rhodry lad. Once we're under arrest, we'll be safe." The old man patted the leather bags that hung from his saddle's peak. "I have letters from the archon of Pastedion to show around as we need them. Come to think of it, I've got some from the archon of Surat, too."

For a moment Rhodry wanted to yell at the old man. It was a physical thing, sharp and bitter—he wanted to snarl at Nevyn and announce that he was in charge here and that they'd blasted well camp when he wanted to and not a moment before.

"Jill's got to rest," Nevyn went on. "She's so utterly spent that she can't even stay in the saddle much longer."

Hearing the old man mention her name infuriated him further, especially since he hadn't thought to check on her himself.

"Very well," Rhodry said. "I'll call a halt."

Rhodry jerked his horse's head around and rode back along the line, shouting orders as he went, until he reached Jill, who was riding next to Salamander. For a moment Rhodry felt so jealous of his brother that he wanted to slap him across the face; then he realized that it wasn't Salamander who was making him suspicious, but Nevyn. He nearly laughed aloud. Don't be a dolt! he told himself. Why, the old man must be eighty if he's a day! Yet later that evening, when he saw Nevyn and Jill sitting at a campfire and talking in whispers, their heads bent together and the Wildfolk all around them, his jealousy bit as deep as if she'd been flirting with the handsomest man in all Deverry. He went over, sat down next to her, and took her hand in his. Nevyn smiled at him so warmly and openly that he suddenly felt like a fool, especially when Jill moved close to him and leaned her head on his shoulder with the ease of a long intimacy. Of course I'm the one she loves, he reminded himself, and he wondered all over again why he had to keep doing that reminding.

"Is somewhat wrong?" the old man said. "Or truly, that was a stupid question, after everything we've been through!"

"All this magic gets on a man's nerves, sure enough," Rhodry said. "Though I don't know why I'm surprised anymore at one single thing you do."

"It does take some getting used to." Nevyn sounded comfortably smug, like a house-proud wife. "Even for a man who's traveled the kingdom the way you have."

All at once Rhodry remembered something that had been obscurely nagging at his mind all day, waiting for him to have the leisure to attend to it.

"Oh by the hells! My silver dagger!"

"What of it?" Jill raised her head and looked at him.

"I never found it, and here it was your father's. I swore I'd get it back."

"Well, my love, if it was in that house, it's naught but a puddle of silver by now."

Rhodry swore so foully that most of the Wildfolk vanished.

"Don't ache your heart," Nevyn said. "Cullyn wouldn't care. To him it was only a mark of shame."

"Mayhap, but I swore a vow I'd get it back."

Nevyn glanced at Jill's gray gnome.

"Do you know where it is?"

The gnome shrugged a no and began scratching its armpit.

"Did it melt?" Jill said. "Wait, I can see you don't understand that. Did the silver turn into water and spill?"

This time the no was definite.

"Then what, by the hells and horseshit, did they do with it?" Rhodry growled.

The gnome shrugged, then disappeared.

"Do you think he's gone to look for it?" Rhodry said.

"I doubt it, my love. I don't think he has the wits." Jill considered, thinking hard. "If you're meant to have it back, it'll find its way home."

"And what is that supposed to mean?"

"I don't know. Just what I said, I suppose." She yawned with a little shudder. "I've got to lie down. Right now. I've never been so tired in my life."

All that night Jill had strange dreams. Although she could never remember them clearly afterwards, she did recall walking down jeweled corridors into enormous rooms that blazed with colored light as palpable as gems, while she talked with splendid beings, clothed with gold and wreathed with silver fire, who may have been either spirits or men and women—she was never sure which, just as she could never consciously recall the amazing secrets they told her. She would always remember, however, waking up suddenly to find the sun shining in her eyes and a soldier squatting beside her, a tall black man, wearing a cuirbolli breastplate and leather skirts over his tunic and dangling a plumed helmet in one hand. With the other he was steadying himself by leaning on a long spear whose businesslike steel point winked in the sun. When she bit back a scream, he grinned at her.

"Forgive me for startling you, girl, but you're safe now. As far as I can tell, we're rescuing you from something or somebody."

"Oh? Well, then, thank you and all that, but ye gods!" Yawning and rubbing her eyes she sat up, looked around, and found their camp full of armed men. "How did I sleep through all of this?"

"I was wondering that myself, to tell you the truth. Have you been drugged?"

"No, not at all."

Yet when she started to stand, she felt so dizzy and sick that she had a brief moment of wondering if Nevyn had given her some sort of sleeping draught. Since she couldn't remember drinking one, she could only assume that her clumsy and desperate dweomer-working of the day before had left her dangerously exhausted. The soldier—she still wasn't sure if he were captor or rescuer—gallantly caught her elbow and steadied her.

"Your grandfather's over there, talking with the officers. He must be an important man, huh?"

"Very important." She ran hasty fingers through her hair to smooth it down. "Where's Rhodry?"

"The black-haired barbarian? With the officers. Are you going to be able to ride?"

"Of course. Where are we going?"

"As far as I can tell, we're escorting you down to Indila and the archon's law courts. Except for your grandfather and you, everyone's under arrest."

With so many riders, horses, and foot soldiers along, the march down to Indila took three days. Since the officers had decided that Jill and Nevyn were victims, while everyone else was a criminal, she had no chance to speak to Rhodry or Salamander during the journey, not so much as a simple "Good morning." Even from a distance, though, she could see that Rhodry was wrapped in one of his black moods, and she didn't envy Salamander the job of cheering him out of it. Finally, some two hours before sunset on the third day, they reached Indila and found a surprising welcome. Although Jill was afraid that Rhodry and his men would be marched off to prison, instead the archon himself was waiting at the gates with a token escort of city guards, and with him was Elaeno, wearing all the fine clothes and gold jewelry that were his due as the owner and master of a merchant ship.

"I contacted him when we were first arrested, you see," Nevyn murmured in Deverrian. "He has influence in the islands, after all, and I decided that he might as well use it."

That influence combined with Nevyn's various official letters worked a dweomer of their own. Instead of the archon's prison they were escorted to a splendid inn down near the harbor—quite conveniently near Elaeno's ship, in fact—and told that the expense would be borne by the state, because they were possible criminals under investigation, and the prison was very small—a line of reasoning that ignored the inconvenient fact that the supposed criminals were being quartered with their supposed victims. There was nothing feigned, however, about the city guards who stood in fours at every door and pairs at every window, nor were the innkeeper's bitter complaints an idle masquerade. That very evening, as well, the archon's personal scribe appeared to summon Nevyn and Elaeno for a conference with various officials. Jill walked downstairs with them to the walled courtyard around the inn.

"Will you be hiring an advocate, too?" Jill said.

"We will," Nevyn said. "But only for show. Don't look so alarmed, child. Things are going our way, whether it looks like it or not."

"If you say so. It's just hard to believe we're truly safe, and everything's all over."

"Oh, I didn't say that! We've got to get home, for one thing, and for another, I've got to see if there's anything I can do about Rhodry's memory."

Jill had been so sure that Nevyn could cure Rhodry as a matter of course that she felt as stunned as if he'd slapped her. He cast an anxious glance over his shoulder at the secretary, impatient in the doorway.

"We'll talk later—I've got to go right now. But Jill, I did try to warn you."

"You did, truly. I'm sorry."

After the guards escorted them out to the street, she went back to the common room of the inn, where oil lamps flickered, flashing points of light off the tiled floor and painted walls. At a table in one corner Rhodry and Salamander were playing dice while Gwin and the men from the warband stood round and watched, wine cups in hand. In time, she supposed, Rhodry could relearn most of what he needed to know, such as the names of the important men in his rhan and a working knowledge of common law. But something valuable beyond words would still be missing, the extravagant capacity for life and feeling that had always made him as attractive as a roaring fire on an icy night. Although she would still love him, his subjects were going to find him curiously changed and perhaps disappointing. He's going to need me at his elbow all the time, she thought, and with the thought she felt as though a cold hand clenched her heart. If she were going to continue her dweomer studies, she would need time to herself—hours upon hours of time, and all of it alone. If. She had to continue. She knew it better than she'd ever known anything, that if she stopped studying the dweomer now, her soul would shrivel into something dead and ugly within her just from her own bitterness at being forced to lay her studies aside. She loved the dweomer as much as Rhodry, or was it more? That simple little word seemed to burn in her mind. Until that moment she'd never thought that she could love anything more than Rhodry, her wonderful handsome Rhodry who needed her so badly now. I'll never leave him, she thought, never!

And yet she knew that she could never leave the dweomer behind, either, not now, not after she had at last found her heart's true craft.

Although Nevyn was dreading the official visit to the archon's palace, His Excellency, whose name was Gurtha, entertained them so lavishly that it was obvious, without a direct word being said, that he felt they'd done all Bardek a favor by firing Tondalo's villa. By the time they could make their escape from the feasting, drinking, and music, the waxing moon was hanging low in the sky. Although Nevyn normally slept no more than a few hours a night, he fell into bed as soon as he got to his chamber and stayed there until the noon sun came glaring in through the cracks round the shutters.

It was Jill, in fact, who woke him with a timid tap at his door. When he called out a drowsy "Come in," she did just that, carrying a tray with a plate of warm soft flatbread and a wooden tankard.

"Ale! They've got ale here, Nevyn. It's not very good, but it's ale."

"Splendid! Hand it over, and my humble thanks."

The ale was weak and oddly sweet both, but as Jill said, at least it was brewed from barley rather than grapes. He sipped it slowly, making it last, while he nibbled at the bread. After Jill threw open the shutters to let in the warm spring air and sunlight, she sat down cross-legged on a pile of cushions.

"I've been putting some hard thought into what's wrong with Rhodry," she said. "He's told me things that you and Salamander might not know."

"Ah, I thought he would."

"But it doesn't match up with what you and Salamander have told me. Salamander, in particular, thought he'd never recover, but here he's actually gotten back a good many memories all on his own."

"What?" Nevyn felt his first real hope. "Tell me everything he said—Rhodry, I mean. Certainly not Salamander; we don't have a whole fortnight to waste."

"Well, first of all, there was his name. Baruma gave him a false name, but Rhodry remembered his own in a dream—a drugged dream, actually, he said, because the Hawks tried to poison him. And then, when Salamander and I finally caught up with him, Salamander tried ensorceling him and telling him that he'd remember who I was when the sun came up the next morning, and by the gods, he did. And then just a few days ago, after he killed Baruma, he remembered Aberwyn and Rhys and what his mother looks like—or used to look like, I should say, because the way he described her Lovyan sounded about thirty years old."

"Splendid! Oh, truly splendid! This drugged dream? Did he tell you about it?"

"It was somewhat about dancing in a ring with three other people around a fire that turned into a dragon."

"Red or black dragon?"

"Red. Does it matter?"

"It does, and I can't tell you how glad I am that the beast wasn't black. White would have been best, but red will do well enough."

"Nevyn, you think there's hope, don't you? I can hear it in your voice."

"Well, I do, but let's pray to every god that I'm not wrong. Baruma must have been a fumbling apprentice at this hideous line of work. Now, it stands to reason that, when Rhodry killed the man who'd ensorceled him, he'd free a certain amount of energy and heal a small amount of damage, but he never should have recovered any memories at all while Baruma was still alive."

"Baruma was no fool or amateur." Jill's voice went cold and flat. "Gwin made that clear. He was known for breaking people down. That's probably why the Old One sent him."

"No doubt. I'm sorry you have to think about these terrible things, child."

"Why? If I don't face them now, I'll be thinking about them every day I'm married to him."

"Just so, and my apologies. But I don't—oh, of course! Ye gods, I should have seen this before! I think we can assume that Baruma never knew that Rhodry's half elven."

"That would make a difference?"

"A very great difference indeed. But I'm not promising anything. For all I know, I still won't be able to heal him. But why don't you just hunt up His Grace and tell him I want to see him? It's time we tried to clean up this wretched mess."

It was some minutes before Rhodry came in, and Nevyn knew that something was wrong immediately, just from the arrogant set to his shoulders and the grim look about his mouth. It was the first time that Nevyn quite simply had had the leisure to realize that Rhodry neither remembered nor trusted him. He felt as hurt as a father with an ingrate son, even though rationally he knew that Baruma's ensorcelments were to blame.

"Rhodry, I can help you if you let me."

"So Jill said. Why wouldn't I let you?"

"I don't know. Why, indeed?"

"No reason at all."

"Indeed?"

Rhodry shrugged and paced over to the window. In the strong sunlight he looked impossibly weary, as if he'd aged ten years instead of one since he'd left Deverry, and dark circles shadowed his eyes.

"I first met you when you were about eight years old," Nevyn said. "I doubt if you remember. And then once when you were about sixteen, you were very ill of a fever, and I cured you—just with herbcraft, though, not dweomer."

"I don't remember that either."

"Of course not. All I'm saying is this, that if you did remember, you'd trust me more."

"Who says I don't trust you now?"

Nevyn merely looked at him. In a moment Rhodry turned from the window, strode to the door, hesitated, then turned back and leaned against it.

"Jill's going to marry me."

"Of course, she is. What's that got to do with anything?"

He shrugged again and looked down at the floor.

"It's the dweomer you're jealous of, you young dolt! Not me or Salamander either!"

When Rhodry blushed scarlet, for a moment Nevyn thought he was going to turn and bolt, but he looked up instead and even managed to force out a crooked smile.

"Well, maybe so." For one last moment Rhodry hesitated on the edge of leaving; then he let out his breath in a sharp sigh. "Can you heal me, Nevyn?"

"I can't, but I can help you heal yourself. I've been thinking, lad, about Baruma's botched job. His ensorcelment's unwinding itself, and with time, who knows? It might unwind all the way and disappear."

"I don't have a cursed lot of time, not if I'm going to rule in Aberwyn."

"Just so. And even if his magic was flawed, Baruma left you scarred, sure enough. What did he do to you?"

"I don't remember."

"You don't want to remember."

"I can't!" Rhodry looked up in a flare of rage.

"Indeed? Then you'll never reclaim the rest of your life. Baruma planted a hedge of thorns in your mind. You've got to break through it and trample it down."

"I can't, I tell you!"

"You're afraid of remembering all that pain. I don't blame you, mind. I'd be afraid myself."

The rage in his eyes turned murderous.

"It's the honor of the thing, Rhodry lad. Are you going to let him win this battle?"

"I'd rather die."

"Ah. I thought so." Nevyn held out his hand. "Come sit down, lad. I'll be here with you every step of the way."

After Rhodry went up to Nevyn's chamber, Jill tried waiting in the common room, but the noise and the laughter, the simple sight of Rhodry's men enjoying themselves over dice games and Salamander's tall tales, drove her outside to the relative silence of the inn yard. When she wandered up to the front gate, the guards warned her not to go into the streets without an escort, all in the friendliest possible way, but she wanted to scream at them—no doubt she could take care of herself in a strange city better than they could. She went back to the little garden provided for the guests and sat down on a bench in the shade of one of the innkeeper's ancestors while she wondered what Nevyn was doing to Rhodry or if indeed there was anything he could do. In the silence it seemed she could hear them talking or at least receive the impression of words. Although she went as still as a hunted hare to listen, the meaning escaped her, but she could sense feelings, waves of emotion that quite clearly came from outside herself: pain and bitterness, an overwhelming terror, and more pain, the shadows of an excruciating physical agony. Once it seemed she heard Rhodry sobbing like a child, and it took all her will for her to stay where she was and not go running up to Nevyn's chamber to interfere, and all to spare herself as much as Rhodry. Finally she remembered her lessons; in her mind she drew the circle of protection and sealed it with pentagrams. Once she had it visualized outside and around her, the whispers and the pain-shadows stopped.

With a sigh of relief she looked up to find Perryn staring at her from some twenty feet away, lurking—or so she thought of it—between a pair of eucalyptus trees.

"What do you want, you sniveling little stoat?"

"Er, ah, well, um . . ."

"Out with it, or I'll slit your throat."

"Jill, I'm sorry! That's all."

She found that she had risen, and that she was holding her silver dagger. Only the memory of her promise to Nevyn made her sheath it and sit down again.

"I never meant to hurt you," Perryn wailed. "I loved you."

"Horseshit! Listen, stoat-face. Do you know why you're still alive? Nevyn ordered me to leave you alone. Otherwise I'd kill you. Understand me?"

With one last wail like a haunt at dawn, Perryn turned and fled, running—as far as she could see—for the refuge of the stables and his beloved horses. She felt her rage as fire, beating to the sky, lapping at her magic circle and threatening to break through. With a wrench of will she called it back and re-imaged the pentagrams to fence it round. Once the circle held firm again, she could realize that she was no longer afraid of Perryn but of what she would do to him if she let herself go. She saw the change as the most satisfying gift she'd been given in years.

For an hour or so more Jill stayed in the relative privacy of the garden. Although she tried to do her dweomer-exercises, she was quite simply too distracted; every few minutes found her wondering about Rhodry. Finally she went back to the common room, where Salamander was entertaining the crowd, even the sullen innkeep, by telling one of his bawdy stories while he juggled eggs and oranges. Although most people would have thought him heartless, Jill could tell from the very brightness of his chatter that he was worried sick about his brother. She sat down in a corner and watched him without truly listening while her mind wandered to Rhodry and Nevyn. Since she'd broken her circle, she could feel their minds working, but the pain had subsided, leaving a bitter emptiness. As the afternoon dragged on, she would at times pick up other flashes of emotion or hear the ghosts of words, but their intensity subsided until at last, when the sun was low and the innkeep busy trimming wicks for his lamps, they vanished altogether.

After one last jest Salamander left his audience. He fetched a flagon of wine and two cups, then sat down beside her with an exaggerated sigh. Jill poured for both of them.

"Is the Great Krysello weary?"

"Oh, do hold your tongue, beauteous barbarian handmaiden. After the things Nevyn said to me I never want to hear that name again." But he did flash a grin. "But it was a splendid show, wasn't it?"

"It was, truly. I miss it, in a way."

"So do I. Ah well, it's back to the humble gerthddyn's trade for the likes of me." He saluted her with the cup, then drank deep. "I wonder what Nevyn's doing up there. By the Lord of Hell's furred behind, it's taking forever."

"I think the worst is over. I could sort of feel things happening, but they've stopped."

"Sort of? Things? Well, I probably don't want to know more."

"I don't think we do, truly."

The innkeep was lighting the oil lamps with a long splint from the hearth when Rhodry came into the common room. When he stopped just inside the door, Jill got up, thinking that he would somehow need her physical support like a man recovering from a long illness, but she hesitated, suddenly frightened, as the uncertain light from the lamps grew and flared around him. She had never seen a man in such a rage. His anger poured out like light from the burning oil in one of the lamps, hot and dangerous yet somehow pure as it burned.

"I think me he remembers what they did to him," Salamander said with the trace of a shake in his voice. "And I don't think he's pleased about it."

As Rhodry stared round the room, everyone fell silent, the men turning to look at him, then hastily looking away again, until at last he moved and released them all. He strode over to Jill, acknowledged Salamander's presence with a nod, then snatched her half-full wine cup from the table.

"I'm making a vow, my love." His voice was a growl. "Once I've been invested with Aberwyn, I'm raising a fleet and burning Slaith and every stinking pirate with it." He raised the cup over his head. "May the gods be my witnesses! That hellhole burns to the ground!"

Then he turned and threw the cup into the hearth so hard that it shattered. Although the wine hissed on the burning coals, paradoxically enough the flames leapt up high and flared. Towering among them Jill could see the Lords of Fire, accepting the vow.

Every morning, Cullyn and Tieryn Lovyan were among the first people awake in Dun Aberwyn. Yawning and drowsy, he would usually stroll into the great hall just as she was coming down the spiral staircase. While a sleepy page brought them both bowls of spiced milk and a servant mended up the fire in the hearth, they would sit at the table of honor and discuss the official business of the dun. After she gave Cullyn his orders for the day, Lovyan would always make the same remark.

"Nevyn's been gone a long time now, captain."

"So he has, Your Grace," he would answer. "But spring's on the way, and the weather will be good sailing soon."

"Well, true spoken. It's all on the knees of the gods now, anyway."

And the regent would nod with a wan sort of smile and dismiss him.

On this particular morning, since Lovyan had no pressing orders, Cullyn wandered down to the gates of the dun and stood chatting with the guards. Although the day was warm, the sky was marbled with clouds, easing in from the south—a sign of coming rain, as he remarked.

"Sure enough, captain," said a guard. "Seems like it's been a long winter this year, but maybe that's just the waiting. Do you think Lord Rhodry's still alive?"

"I do."

"Well, I certainly hope you're right, sir. We all do, truly. When

Gwerbret Rhys was still alive, we had to hate anyone he hated, like, but now things are different."

"Are they? I'd wondered."

"They are. If Lord Rhodry's gwerbret, well, we'll all follow him to the death. If naught else, at least he's a Maelwaedd."

"Sure enough, and it gladdens my heart that you can see things so clear, like."

"I—here, who's that?"

Cullyn looked where he pointed and saw a pair of travelers coming up the hill, an old man wrapped in an ordinary cloak with the hood up and a young man wearing a short cloak and a floppy-brimmed leather hat. They were leading a pair of beautiful riding horses, both the golden color of fresh-dug riverbank clay, as well as a sturdy chestnut pulling a laden travois.

"Oh, by the Lord of Hell's hairy ass!" Cullyn muttered. "Well, this should prove interesting. All right, lad, see that old man? You treat him with all the respect due a prince, because he's a friend of Nevyn's and the same sort of man—if you take my meaning. As for the fellow with him, well, now, you and everyone else in the dun are in for a bit of a surprise." He waved to the approaching pair and jogged off to meet them. "Aderyn, my lord, it gladdens my heart to see you again. Calonderiel, if this isn't a welcome thing! What are you doing so far from your cursed grasslands?"

"Guarding the Wise One from you wretched round-ears." Grinning, the elf gave him a friendly slap on the shoulder. "He wanted to come alone, but I wouldn't hear of it."

"I wouldn't have either, if I'd been in your place." Cullyn turned to Aderyn. "What brings you to us, my lord?"

"Oh, a small matter of my own. Can you get a page to take these horses, Cullyn? I need to talk to Nevyn straightaway."

"But he's gone, my lord. He sailed to Bardek weeks ago."

"He what?" Aderyn's open-mouthed surprise was close to comical.

"Sailed off for Bardek with Elaeno, the Orystinnian captain. Didn't he tell you, my lord? I mean, I've always thought you had ways of sending messages that were faster than horses."

"So we do, so we do, but he never did contact me. I assumed there was some sort of danger, but apparently that wasn't the case. Oh ye gods, Cullyn, he must have simply forgotten! I'm beginning to wonder if the old man's slipping a bit, I truly am."

By then they'd gathered a small crowd of the idly curious. Cullyn handed the horses over to one servant, sent a page off to warn the tieryn, and ushered their guests inside the dun. When he realized how glad he was to see Aderyn, he had to laugh at himself. Only a few short years past he would have mocked any man who claimed to believe in sorcerers, and now here he was, outright relieved to have a dweomermaster in the dun again. When they came into the great hall, the tieryn rose from her place at the head of the honor table and turned their way. For a moment she looked terrified, but as they walked over to kneel in front of her, she relaxed and greeted the pair with a gracious smile.

"Calonderiel, isn't it?" she said. "For a moment there I thought you were someone else. And who, good sir, may you be?"

"My name is Aderyn, Your Grace. Perhaps Nevyn has spoken of me?"

"He has, and truly, you're more than welcome in my dun for as long as you wish to stay. Page! Run and tell Cook to prepare refreshments for our guests. They've come a long way. Bring mead, too. You'll have to get out the best goblets, by the way. The usual ones are—well, never mind that now."

"Her Grace is very kind," Aderyn said. "And truly, if she has any need of me whatsoever, I'm at her service."

Lovyan's eyes filled with tears of relief, but she brushed them away and arranged another smile.

"I shall take your offer with humble thanks, good Aderyn. After you and your friend have rested, perhaps we can have a private talk in my chambers." She glanced at Cullyn. "Maybe now we can get some news. I've been driven to distraction, wondering what Blaen's been up to. Do join us, captain. I know that Calonderiel is a friend of yours."

As they settled themselves at the table of honor, Calonderiel remembered his manners and took off the leather hat, dropping it casually on the table just as the page returned with a tray of goblets and a flagon of mead. The lad frankly stared at his long ears, curled to a delicate point like a seashell, and at his violet cat-slit eyes, too, until Cullyn leaned forward and intervened.

"You've got work to do, lad. Go do it."

The boy fled. Calonderiel picked up his goblet and had a sip of mead.

"Sweet and light, but good, Your Grace," he pronounced, saluting the tieryn. "My thanks for your hospitality, but don't you think I'd better leave now that the Wise One's safely here? It appears that I alarm your subjects."

"They'll have to get used to you and your people sooner or later, good sir." Lovyan sounded oddly weary. "I have the distinct feeling that my son is going to welcome you in his court once he returns to claim his rhan."

"No doubt," Aderyn broke in. "Your Grace, grave matters are afoot, beyond, perhaps, what any of us could know."

His words made Cullyn feel strangely cold and solemn. For as long as he lived, he would remember that moment at the table of honor: Lovyan, leaning forward, her blue eyes deep and shadowed with some private thought; Calonderiel, his lips half-parted, the goblet clutched in his hand as he turned to her as if in support; Aderyn himself, with his white hair swept up from his forehead in two peaks like an owl's horns and his enormous dark eyes that seemed to look far into a future that none could see but him. Yet, at that moment, Cullyn had an odd instinctive glimpse of that future, and the even odder feeling that someday he and the elven warleader beside him would play an important part in it.

"So great things are on the move, are they?" Cullyn said to the dweomerman.

"They are. We'll talk later, captain, but I'm going to need your help."

"You'll have it, of course." With a nod to the tieryn, he rose, then made her a bow. "My lady, with your permission, I've somewhat that needs attending to."

"By all means, captain."

"My thanks, my lady. Cal, I'll see you in a bit. Come sit at my table for dinner, will you?"

"Gladly. I'm an archer, not a horse soldier, but I feel more at home in a warband anyway."

Cullyn strode off, heading for the stairway up to the women's hall. Soon, he knew, he'd be riding over half of Eldidd on Gwerbret

Rhodry's business, and there was something he wanted done before he left. He'd only gotten to the first landing when he met Tevylla coming down with Rhodda clinging to one hand and a basket in the other.

"I was just going to look for you," she said. "Rhodda and I were thinking we'd have our noon meal outside."

"Good idea. I'd best come with you, then."

Since the day was sunny and warm enough if you were out of the wind, they took the chunks of sweet bread and pot of soft cheese in the basket out to the sheltered rose garden in a curve where two half-brochs met. Although the roses were still naught but mulched sticks, the lawn there was green again, and Rhodda was happy to sit on the grass and pretend to share her meal with her imaginary friends, the ones she called gnomes. Cullyn and Tevylla sat down on a stone bench nearby. Now that the crux was here, Cullyn found himself utterly tongue-tied until Tevylla gave him an opening.

"How's my Merddyn these days? I never seem to see him anymore, except from a distance."

"He's been working hard, and I'm pleased with him, though I'll ask you not to tell him I said that. He's got a good hand for a sword and the right amount of courage—enough to make him fight, but not enough to make him do stupid things in a scrap."

She winced.

"Well, my apologies. I don't suppose any mother wants her son to go for a rider."

"None that I know of, truly. I think you bewitch your young men, Cullyn. They all want to be just like you, and they never think once of what you risked to become the man you are."

"That's true spoken, and it aches my heart. But lads are like that. You never think that you could be the one to die in battle, not till you're twenty or so, and by then, well, all you know is the warband. But here, I didn't mean to trouble your heart about his future."

"Tact's never been a weapon in your armory, has it?" But she was smiling at him.

"It hasn't, at that. I've never been much for words. Somewhat of a pity, now."

"Indeed? Why?"

He shrugged to gain a little time, wishing that he could think of some elegant or flowery phrase, wishing that he'd asked one of the bards for advice. Women were supposed to like it, weren't they, when you said fine words to them? She was watching him with her head tilted a little to one side.

"You know," he said at last. "That widow's black doesn't suit you."

"Indeed? Well, it's not truly my choice to wear it, you know."

"If you were the captain's woman, you could have it off and be done with it."

She went stone-still, her lips half-parted, as surprised as if he'd barked at her like a dog. Since he'd been counting on her answering, one way or another, he began to feel a little desperate.

"Ah well, think you could put up with me?" he went on. "We wouldn't make such a bad pair, you and I. We've both been through too much to babble about love and suchlike."

"So we have, truly."

For a long moment they stared at each other, half-listening to Rhodda as she sang to the Wildfolk. Cullyn struggled to find something to say, then broke off a bit of bread and offered it to her, the way a man would do to his wife. She hesitated only briefly before she bent her head and took it from his fingers. He smiled and felt that the sunlight had just turned a little warmer.

"I'll be asking the tieryn for permission to marry this afternoon, then," he said. "I wonder if I can find a jeweler to sell me a brooch for you straightaway. We're going to have to be quick about it. Spring's almost here."

"Do you think there's going to be a war in the rhan?" Unconsciously she laid one hand on her throat.

"I don't know. There's a lot of powerful men working to keep the peace. I just want to make sure that nothing gets in the way of us marrying, one way or the other."

"I see. You know, in its way that's more flattering than any fine words or poetry I ever heard."

He grinned, thinking that he'd made the right choice for a certainty.

Although Tevylla had always considered the captain an efficient man, she was surprised at the ruthless speed with which he got them married. That very afternoon Tieryn Lovyan called her into her private chamber to congratulate her on the coming wedding.

"We'll have to get a lass to help you with Rhodda," Lovyan said. "You'll need time for your husband now, too."

"My thanks, Your Grace. What about that new lass, Glomer? She struck me as a clever sort."

"More clever than you know, actually. She's a very good choice indeed. Speak to her about it today, will you?"

"I will, my lady. Oh, do you know where Cullyn's got to?"

"He's down in town, talking to the priests about the wedding."

"I see." Tevylla dropped her a curtsy. "I'd best go find Glomer. I'll doubtless be needing her soon."

After some searching, she found Glomer out in a storage shed by the back wall. Balanced precariously on a pile of wooden crates, the lass was untying onions from a long garland and filling a basket with them. She was more than pleased to come down and hear about her new job, which she greeted with a shriek of delight.

"I'll get to work in the broch itself? Oh, that's so splendid, Mistress Tevylla! I promise I'll work truly hard."

"Good. Let's go tell Cook, and then you can come up to the women's hall and meet Rhodda. I've left her with the serving women, and she's probably driven them daft by now."

As they were walking round to the kitchen hut, they saw Calonderiel, rubbing down his golden horse with a twisted swatch of straw. At the sight of him a big-eyed Glomer stopped and made the sign of warding against witchcraft. Since Tevylla had been born and raised in Dun Gwerbyn, she'd seen elves before, but she couldn't deny that they made her nervous.

"Tevylla?" Glomer's whisper was barely audible. "Is that one of Nevyn's demons?"

"It's not, but a man of flesh and blood. Very real flesh and blood for that matter. Now listen, lass. I don't know why myself, but a lot of women fancy the Westfolk men the way a cat fancies catmint, and the Westfolk men have absolutely no honor where women are concerned. You leave him strictly alone, or we'll end up with another babe to watch over."

Tevylla slipped her arm through the girl's and led her firmly away, but once or twice Glomer looked back, furtively, reluctantly, as if she couldn't quite help herself. Tevylla could only hope that Calonderiel hadn't noticed.

When Cullyn returned, late that afternoon, he brought two things with him. One was a silver betrothal brooch, made of two wires so cunningly interlaced and spiraled that they looked like a single strand. The other was a priest of Bel, who announced the betrothal that very evening in the great hall, as the warbands and the servitors were lingering over their ale. When the captain pinned the brooch on her dress, his men started cheering, and everyone else joined in, making Tevylla blush like a lass. Cullyn, however, seemed oddly distracted, his face impassive, his eyes distant while he watched his new wife take off the black headscarf and toss her head as if she were physically shaking off the burden of widowhood. Later, when she grew to know him better, Tevylla would remember that look of profound boredom and realize that he was brimming with feeling like a goblet about to spill over with mead.

"If any man or woman either has reason to speak against this wedding," the priest called out, yelling over the general noise, "let them step forward now or come to me in private at the temple on the morrow morn. Otherwise the wedding will proceed at noon."

"Noon?" Tevylla blurted. "On the morrow?"

"Why not?" Cullyn said. "I'm not a little lad who needs to say farewell to his mam."

At that she could laugh, and she felt much better. Yet, as soon as she decently could, she made her escape and went out to the kitchen hut to talk with Baena, who was cracking parched oats on a quern for the morrow's porridge. Automatically Tevylla picked up a wooden scoop and began transferring the cereal into a kettle as they talked.

"I'm so happy for you, Tevva, I truly am."

"My thanks. Our Cullyn certainly doesn't waste any time once he makes up his mind about somewhat."

"True enough. He's a good man, though. I'm happy for him, too." Baena paused, laying down the heavy stone grinder so she could tuck a wisp of hair back under her headscarf. "The regent called me in earlier. We'll have a nice feast on the morrow."

"Oh, you shouldn't have to go to all that work. It seems silly to make a fuss over a second marriage."

"Not to me, it doesn't, and I don't mind the work at all, I don't.

Everyone needs a bit of fun to lift their spirits these days, and that's the truth."

Since she had to instruct Glomer in her new duties, the following morning passed quickly for Tevylla with hardly a thought of her coming marriage. Yet, as she watched the lass playing with little Rhodda, she found herself remembering her first wedding day. Since her father had picked him out from another village, she'd barely known her husband, and she'd spent the whole morning alternately vomiting or giggling hysterically. Now, when Cullyn appeared in the doorway, she merely smiled at him.

"Time to go?"

"It is. No use in keeping the priest waiting."

As she followed him down the long spiraling stairs, she had a brief moment of doubt, yet when they left the broch and he held out his hand, she took it as trustingly as Rhodda always did.

"Shall we walk down?" he said. "I can get my horse if you'd rather ride."

"Oh, a walk is fine. It's a lovely morning, isn't it?"

It was warm and clear, as if the threatening clouds of the night before had left to make them the present of a splendid day. Down in the harbor the turquoise sea was at low tide, rolling slow breakers onto the pale beach.

"Tell me somewhat," Tevylla said. "Do you want another child? We might well have one."

"Well, I do, at that. Ah ye gods, I don't think I've ever wanted anything as much as I want a son. I suppose it's because I'm getting old. I'm not saying I'd turn up my nose at another lass, mind, but you'll have to stop me from spoiling this one rotten."

"I'll do my best, but you don't seem like the sort of man who likes to be argued with."

"It might be a good thing if I learned to put up with it."

"Good, because you'll have to."

When they shared another smile, Tevylla felt that they were married. The ceremony before the priest was only a formality.

Yet, when they returned to the dun, they had a surprise ahead of them. With a howl of laughter and shrieks like battle cries, both warbands came bursting out of the broch and swept across the garden. A horde of young men mobbed them, slapping Cullyn on the back, grabbing Tevylla's hands and kissing them. Then Calonderiel shoved his way through the mob with a goblet in his hand.

"Let the lady breathe, lads!"

As Tevylla made her way clear to the group of women standing near the main door, Calonderiel flung the mead in his goblet straight into Cullyn's face. At the signal mead seemed to come from everywhere and drench her new husband like a summer storm. With a whoop, the warband grabbed the struggling, swearing Cullyn and carried him bodily toward the ornamental pond round the side of the broch complex. Laughing and calling, the women hurried after, their brightly colored dresses billowing and streaming in the wind.

With one last howl the warband dumped Cullyn into the pond and ducked him a couple of times when he tried to scramble out. When they finally let him go, he was soaking-wet but laughing, taking mock swings at his men and vowing that he'd chop them into dog meat. In a great pretence of terror they danced back out of reach. Laughing herself, the tieryn appeared and began calling for order.

"Let the captain go change his clothes," Lovyan said. "We've got a feast on the way, you know, and mead all round."

The men spontaneously cheered the lady who was their lord.

Although the evening meal included an entire roasted hog and other fancy dishes, there was, all in all, as little fuss as Tevylla wanted. When Cullyn fed her the first bite from the trencher they shared, the warband did cheer, as they did again when they shared a goblet of mead — or at least, she took a few sips and let him finish the rest. At the end of the meal, she was planning on retiring with the other women and letting him drink with his men, but when she left the table, he came with her, taking her hand as they walked to the staircase.

"The warband can drink itself sick without me," he remarked.

She was so pleased to hear him say it that she suddenly realized just how much she wanted him. Yet with her wanting came a shyness, a sudden feeling that she hardly knew him, a last reserve about letting him close to her in such an irrevocable way. Her early fear of him, she saw then, was a fear that she might love this man too much, if she let herself, a warrior whose craft might take him away from her for long months at a time, whose death might claim him at any moment. And now she had gone and married him, right when the province was on the brink of open war. In her mind she heard her mother's weary voice: have you no common sense, lass? No, she answered, and I'm proud of it.

In her chamber, strangely silent without Rhodda there, his wet clothes lay in a puddle on the floor. She picked them up, glad of the excuse to keep from looking at him, leaned out the window to wring the worst of the water from the clothes, then draped them over the sill to dry.

"My apologies," he said. "I was just in such a cursed hurry to get back downstairs."

"Oh, I don't mind."

"You're rid of Rhodda for the night, and so you need someone to play the nursemaid for."

When she forced herself to turn around and face him, she found him smiling at her, his hair half-silver, half-gold in the candlelight, with such good humor that her shyness vanished.

"Nursemaid? Oh, I wouldn't call it that."

He caught her by the shoulders and kissed her openmouthed, just once before he let her go—the first kiss he'd ever given her. She untied her kirtle and laid it down on the table carefully, smoothing the elaborate needlework. While she took off her overdress he unbuckled his sword-belt and slung it onto the table, the scabbard lying golden and heavy across the embroidered flowers. She felt weary, as if at an omen. Ah well, she thought, we'll have our good times before I have to wear black again. Cullyn looked at her so solemnly that she thought he was about to speak, but he picked her up like a child and carried her to their bed.

At the Inn of the Flying Fish, down near the harbor in Indila, Jill had spent the past three days working harder than she ever had in her life. Not only was Nevyn's idea of mental exercises a good bit stricter than Salamander's, but the old man set her to memorizing lore as well. While she struggled to remember the names and characteristics of the ten secret levels of the universe and the thirty-two paths between them, Rhodry and his men spent their time drinking and dicing down in the tavern room with Salamander to entertain them. What Perryn may have done, she neither knew nor cared.

Finally, on the morning of the fourth day when the archon summoned Nevyn to his palace, Jill went with him, mostly as a reward for her hard work. Gurtha received them in his private chambers and had his slaves spread an elaborate meal and pour the best wine. Lunching with them was a huge and ominous man introduced as Hanno, captain of the city guard. After some polite talk of civic affairs, Gurtha remarked that the date for the trial had been set.

"It's not for two weeks, I'm afraid. The courts are always busy this time of year, because the winter weather gives people the leisure to invent lawsuits." Gurtha glanced at Hanno. "Two weeks is a long time. You must be very careful, captain, that the barbarian prisoners don't escape."

"Of course, sir. Why, how could they escape, with my men guarding the inn? I've got them posted all round."

"True. On the other hand, tonight, just when the tide is full, there's going to be that procession in honor of the Star Goddesses. You'll need to reduce the guard at the inn."

"Hum, so I will. We'll have to leave a few men there, though."

"But what if they started drinking out of boredom and became wine-muddled?"

"Never happens. Not with me there to watch them."

"Ah, but you might become distracted."

"That's true." Hanno smiled at Nevyn and gave Jill a wink. "What an awful thought."

"So it is, so it is." Gurtha shook his head sadly. "But you can't blame human beings for making a mistake now and then, can you?"

"No, you can't," Nevyn said. "Happens to the best of us."

That night, while they waited for the tide to turn, they had a feast of sorts in the inn. The innkeeper hovered nervously near the table, while outside the archon's men prowled back and forth, occasionally sticking a head through a window to see if it were time yet for them to neglect their duty and let the prisoners escape. Since all of the other customers ate in their chambers to avoid sharing the common room with criminals, they had the echoing tavern room to themselves. In this far from festive atmosphere Rhodry hurried through his meal, then left the table to go stand in the door and chat with the captain of the watch. He needed to be seen by a passerby or two if anyone was going to believe that he had somehow managed to distract the formidable Hanno in order to escape.

While he picked at a bit of bread, Nevyn went over a last few logistical arrangements.

"We need to sell or return those horses that the archon of Surat gave us. Oh, and that reminds me—we never could go back for all those wretched horses we left in Pastedion, as I remember telling a certain gerthddyn was most likely. Well, when the archon confiscates them, they'll repay him for some of his trouble."

"Begging your leave and all, oh master in this craft of ours," Salamander said. "I should like to have them as well as the stock we've got with us."

"Whatever for?"

"So I can pose as Evan, traveling horsetrader from the faraway barbarian kingdom, renowned for steeds. You are all sailing for home on the morrow, but my work here, alas, is not yet done."

"What?" Nevyn seemed torn between annoyance and curiosity. "What stupid scheme do you have in mind now?"

"A scheme not of stupidity but of compassion, or so I may hope. During our travels, I ran across someone who showed a certain basic talent for dweomer but who never had the least chance to develop it. Since she's much addicted to fortune-telling, I fear me she may come under the influence of certain unscrupulous types unless she's given some way to tell gold from mica. She's rich, and aforesaid types are bound to come flocking round her. But since at the time the Hawks were stooping to impale us all upon their blood-soaked claws, I had no leisure for long and civilized conversations on the subject."

When Jill realized whom he must mean, she was profoundly glad that Rhodry had already left the table.

"Um, well, I see your point," Nevyn said. "If she's got money to attract lying fools and tricksters, this woman could indeed come to a great deal of harm. Well and good, then, but please, don't get yourself embroiled in more mischief over here. I shan't be asking the wind to bring me over just to bail you out of trouble."

"You have my promise, oh Master of the Aethyr, that I shall be circumspection itself."

Jill looked up to see one of the archon's men waving at her from the window.

"I think they're going to start being drunk on duty now," she said. "Salamander, you'd best go upstairs and get out a window or suchlike if you're not coming with us."

"I shall, my turtledove." He got up, bowed to the table, then strolled over and kissed her lightly on top of the head. "We shall meet again. You'll forgive me for not coming to sing at your wedding?"

"I will. But be wary as you ride, won't you?"

"You have my promise on that." He hesitated, looking stricken. "Say farewell to my brother for me, will you? I shall vanish while his back is turned and save us both a nasty scene."

When she started to speak further, Jill found to her surprise that her throat was choked with tears. Salamander waved and trotted over to the staircase, hesitated, turned to wave once more, then hurried up and disappeared.

The rest of them gathered up their gear and slipped out the back way through the kitchen. They passed only one guard, and he was busy drinking down an enormous cup of wine to ensure that Hanno could smell it on his breath later. Even so, Jill found herself hurrying through the dark and twisting streets and chivvying the others along, too. The sooner that there was an ocean between them and the Hawks, the happier she would be. Finally they reached the harbor and found the right pier. Pacing back and forth on deck, Elaeno was waiting for them with a lit lantern.

"Just in time," he boomed. "The tide's about to turn, lads. Let's get aboard and be on our way."

Even though Rhodry protested, Elaeno insisted on giving his private cabin to the gwerbret. It was tiny, of course, with a narrow bunk on one side, a bench built into the wall on the other, and a sliver of table bolted to the floor in between, but Elaeno was so large that what was a single bunk to him could actually hold two people provided they did love each other very much. That first night, when they were cramped in together, watching the hanging lantern throw wild shadows as it swayed, Jill realized that they had more privacy in this wardrobe of a room than they'd had in weeks. It was time to talk of important things, she supposed; yet she was afraid to voice even her smallest doubt, lest the rest all come rushing out like one of the Bardekian floods.

Rhodry himself was in a melancholy mood, and simply because it was easier to listen to him than to talk about herself, she asked him what he was thinking.

"Oh, just some cursed strange thoughts, my love, about the long road and all. You know, I'm going to miss it—just a bit, mind, but miss it I will."

"What? I never thought I'd hear you say that, after the way you used to moan and groan about your exile."

"True spoken, and I owe you an apology for making you listen. But we were free, weren't we, riding where we liked, and never seeing the same town twice if it didn't suit us. And we never had to mince and bow and pay court to men we hated and who cordially hated us, or be even so politic and careful to curry favor with men who might support us, and all the rest of it." All at once he laughed. "Ah, curse Rhys anyway—it's just like him. He never could do anything right, not even live to a ripe old age!" He paused, smiling, his fingers stroking the embroidered dragon on his shirt. "Oh, the dragon has me in its claws, sure enough, and you along with me, my love. From now on it does all the flying, and we follow in its wake."

For a moment Jill hated him, just for his wretched elven eloquence that had voiced her worst fear better than she ever could have put it herself.

"Here, my love, you look sad."

"It's because I agree with you, I suppose. After all, I've never known anything but the long road, traveling with my Da like I did and all. Well, except for those miserable weeks before you got exiled. Rhodry, I hated being at court."

"But then you were only my mistress, and truly, I hated to put you in such a terrible position. Now, my love, you'll be my wife. Oh, things will be different now, just you wait and see. When Lady Gilyan comes into a room now, no one's going to sneer and look down their long noses. Oh, that they won't! Instead it'll be bowing here, and if it please Your Grace there, and everyone clustering round to see just what her ladyship requires or thinks or wants, because you'll have more influence over the gwerbret of Aberwyn than any other person, human being or elf alike, in the kingdom. In some ways, my love, you'll be Aberwyn, especially when I'm off on a campaign or suchlike."

Jill's stomach clenched cold, but she smiled, just because he so badly wanted to please her.

"But Rhoddo? There is one thing we've got to talk about. You know that I've started studying dweomer, and . . ."

"Well, who's to say one wrong word about that, even if they do find out, and from what Nevyn's been saying, you're supposed to keep it secret anyway, if you're an apprentice. My love, you don't understand. The only person in the world who can tell you what you may or mayn't do is the High King, and judging by what Nevyn told me, the High King knows how blasted useful the dweomer can be."

"That's not what was worrying me. It's the time."

He stared at her, blinking a little.

"I've got to have so many hours a day to do this work. Time and privacy, where I can concentrate and not be burdened with entertaining your guests or having pages barging in to ask what sort of bread to lay on table and that kind of bilge."

"Oh. Um, I see." He considered for a long moment, chewing on his lower lip. "Well, we'll just have to make sure you have your privacy then, in the evening watch after dinner, say, or suchlike. It might be hard at first, my love, but soon enough, things will settle down, particularly in the winter months."

She wanted to cry out, to scream at him: that's not good enough! But she bit back the angry words, because she knew that once started, they wouldn't stop, and they would lead her inexorably to the decision she refused to make. I won't leave Rhodry, I won't! She thought it over and over, like a prayer to the Goddess. And in the golden lamplight he looked so beautiful, grinning at her now, glowing with honorable pride at finally having come into his own, that her love for him swelled and wrapped her round until it seemed that she would simply die without him.

That particular evening, while Tevylla was putting Rhodda to bed, Cullyn climbed up to the catwalk round Dun Aberwyn's walls and leaned onto a merlon to enjoy the view. Far away to the west the last of the sunset hung over the fields and farms, while down at the harbor to the south the waves rolled in all silver in the fading light. Although the night was chilly, and he was wrapped in a good wool cloak, it wasn't truly cold, either. Spring would come soon, and good sailing weather. He wondered if the regent would be able to endure waiting patiently for Nevyn or if she'd send a galley with marines across the Southern Sea. If she did, he intended to be on it, for all that it would ache his heart to leave his new wife behind.

"Cullyn? A word with you?"

He turned and looked down to find Aderyn and Calonderiel at the bottom of the ladder.

"Of course, my lord, any time."

As agile as a page the old man climbed up, with the elven warleader right behind him. When Aderyn sniffed the wind and held up a licked finger to test its direction, Cullyn found himself remembering, even though he would have preferred to forget it, that the dweomerman could turn himself into an enormous silver owl and fly when he felt like it.

"I've had news," Aderyn announced. "From a reliable source. Gwerbret Blaen of Cwm Pecl is on his way to Eldidd."

"Rhodry's cousin?" Cullyn said. "Now that's interesting."

"Interesting and a half, truly. He's leaving Cerrmor by ship for Abernaudd tomorrow. I want to meet him there and head him off. It may not be politic for him to come marching into Aberwyn just now."

"Darryl and Gwarryc would take it wrong. They'd think he was the king's spy, most like, and go all touchy about it."

"Just so, especially since Blaen's got a warband with him. And another thing—when Rhodry does get home, it might be better if he landed at Abernaudd or even in some quiet little harbor like Morlyn rather than sailing right into a wasp's nest. Which brings me to the main point. I was wondering if you'd come with me? We need to take the rest of Rhodry's men along, too, if the regent will allow. We might need them."

"We might, at that, and of course I'll come if my lady allows." He turned to Calonderiel. "Now, I'm not sure what we'll do with you while we're gone. Lock you up, maybe. My wife tells me that her lass Glomer finds you too interesting for her own good."

"The child has splendid taste in men." Calonderiel grinned at him. "But I'm coming with you. I know that Abernaudd will shriek at the sight of me, but I want to be there to greet Rhodry when he lands.

Think of the effect it'll have—a man of the Westfolk hailing our Rhodry as gwerbret and ally."

Cullyn whistled under his breath.

"Effect, indeed," Aderyn said, and he sounded oddly grim. "Well, *if* Rhodry lands, anyway. I wish to every god that there was some way to get reliable messages across this cursed ocean! I'll have to try to think one up. Blaen is going to want to know where his cousin is, too, and the gwerbret is not the sort of man you like to keep waiting."

Although Blaen knew that traveling incognito would be impossible for a man of his rank and renown, he was trying to keep his arrival in Eldidd reasonably quiet. Under the king's peace a man had the right to travel anywhere in the kingdom that he chose, whether he was a commoner or a gwerbret, but in practice gwerbrets were a good bit more limited than commoners, especially if they brought an honor guard of twenty-five men along with them. Blaen had no desire to offend Ceredyc, Gwerbret Abernaudd, by bringing armed men into his demesne; on the other hand, he refused to travel without them, because he couldn't predict what sort of welcome he'd get in Aberwyn. If Rhodry were indeed dead, then Blaen would need to leave Eldidd very quickly, and someone might well be chasing him. Long before he left Cerrmor he sent a messenger to Ceredyc to make it clear that Blaen expected absolutely nothing in the way of ceremony or gwerbretal pomp and that he would only be staying a short while in Abernaudd, at the dun of a cousin, Lord Sibyr, who lived about two miles outside the city proper.

He was surprised, therefore, to see a small crowd of men who were obviously riders from a warband waiting when the coaster came gliding up to the main pier in Abernaudd, and even more surprised when he realized that they were wearing the red-lion device of Dun Gwerbyn. With his captain, Comyn, trailing after, Blaen walked up to the bow of the ship while the sailors were tying her up to the bollards.

"That's Cullyn of Cerrmor, isn't it?" Blaen remarked.

"Wouldn't know, Your Grace. I've never seen him."

"Ah. I have, and I'd swear that's him. Much older, of course, than the last time I saw him. He's been Tieryn Lovyan's captain for some time now. What's he doing here?"

The mystery was solved when the gwerbret disembarked and Cullyn came hurrying over to kneel before him.

"It gladdens my heart to see you, Your Grace. A friend of Nevyn's sent me to meet you."

Sorcery again. Blaen sighed, resigned and, now that he thought of it, rather accustomed to the whole idea as well.

"Well and good, then, captain. You may rise. Where is this friend of Nevyn's?"

"Staying at an inn down in town, Your Grace, and waiting until you have a moment to speak with him."

"Well, that best be as soon as possible. I'm about to go impose upon my cousin, Lord Sibyr, who lives just off the north-running road. Go fetch your sorcerer, captain, and bring him to me . . ." Blaen paused, glancing up to check the sun's position. ". . . about noon, I'd say. We should be finished with all the formalities by then."

"Done, Your Grace. Oh, and if I may be so bold, congratulations on the birth of your son. The King's herald came through Aberwyn with the news about three weeks ago."

"My thanks." Blaen allowed himself a small smile. "I'll admit to being pleased myself."

Lord Sibyr's dun was small and fortified only in the sketchiest sense; a low earthen wall enclosed a stone broch and some outbuildings standing on about two acres of land. Since Sibyr owed direct fealty to the gwerbrets of Abernaudd and thus would retreat to his city in time of war, and he also received his income from properties scattered all over the rhan, he didn't need to live in a stronghold. In fact, the dun reminded Blaen of some merchants' holdings: the graceful tower, made of imported pinkish stone, was flanked by two equally graceful half-brochs and set round with beautiful gardens. As the gwerbret and his men dismounted in the cobbled court in front of the main broch, Blaen was wondering if he should offer to go stay in an inn just to spare his cousin the trouble of housing real warriors. Yet when Sibyr hurried out to greet him, his welcome was warm enough. A tall, slender man with a fringe of gray hair round his well-shaped skull, Sibyr shook Blaen's hand vigorously and yelled for pages to come tend his men.

"Come in, cousin, come in!" It gladdens my heart to welcome you to our humble little home. Haven't seen you since your wedding, eh?"

"Has it been that long? Well, truly it has. I suppose you've heard . . ."

"About the new heir? I have, and my congratulations indeed."

Sibyr's great hall was as luxurious as his gardens. Its floor was covered with mosaics in the Bardek fashion, and its walls were hung with tapestries from the islands. They sat down in cushioned chairs at the table of honor and drank white wine served in blue glass goblets.

"There must be a quite a lot of the Bardek trade coming through the city," Blaen said.

"There is, and a boon it is to everyone. Of course, in this new charter the High King's granted Aberwyn a bigger share of it."

"Ah. That must irk some of your local merchants."

Although Blaen was only speaking casually, Sibyr went tense, cocking his head to one side to study his cousin as if he were wondering just what his implication might be.

"No offense meant," Blaen said, all cool courtesy.

"None taken on my part, but there are some who might. It's more than the merchants in Abernaudd who prosper on the Bardek trade."

Blaen smiled and had a sip of the excellent wine. So—there were some lords who might welcome trouble in Aberwyn. The question was, would they actively support it or merely look the other way? It was not a question that he cared to ask openly, especially not of a man who'd made him welcome at his table.

"And how long will we have the honor of sheltering you?" Sibyr said.

"I honestly don't know. Not long enough for me to become a nuisance, I'm sure. Actually, I'm waiting for news, and it should be arriving here about noon. I took the liberty of telling the news-bringer that he could find me here. I hope that's acceptable?"

"Of course. Treat my house as your own."

Just at noon Cullyn of Cerrmor strode in, bringing with him a small man with snow-white hair that rose above his forehead in two peaks like the horns of a silver owl. Although Sibyr most courteously offered them seats at the table of honor, Blaen managed to find them a private spot, just up the central stairway and round a corner of the landing, where they could talk without being overheard.

"This is Aderyn, Your Grace," Cullyn said. "A trusted friend of Nevyn's indeed."

"I'm honored to meet you, then, good sir." Blaen made the old man a half-bow. "What news do you have for me?"

"Not much as concerns Rhodry, Your Grace. I have the strong and distinct feeling that he's safely on his way home, but I can't be sure of it. As far as the situation in Eldidd goes, well, things are very vexed indeed, but I don't think that this is the place to discuss it."

"No doubt you're right. Just where can we discuss it, though? I suppose I could come to the tavern room where you're staying."

"That might be politic, Your Grace. We just arrived here ourselves, you see, and I'm hoping that on the morrow I'll have more to tell you about Rhodry, too."

"Suppose he is sailing home right now. Is he coming directly into Aberwyn? Will we get some advance warning before he lands?"

"I hope he'll land here, Your Grace, and as for the warning, well, I've figured out a way to get us some hours' notice."

"A few hours? A night and a day would be better."

"Of course, my lord, but this is going to be tiring enough." Aderyn looked pained, as if over an insult. "I'm not as young as I used to be, you know."

It seemed to Jill that during the trip from Bardek the *Guaranteed Profit* had traveled not across the ocean but through a crowded city. Not only was the dweomer-wind full of sylphs that swarmed round the mast and played among the sails, but gnomes and sprites thronged the deck, and sea undines clustered round the hull and in the wake like a mob of citizens lining up to watch a parade. At night the spirits of the Aethyr settled on the mast in a glow and flicker of blue fire. When she wasn't with Rhodry or working on her dweomer-exercises with Nevyn, she would sit in the bow for hours and watch the Wildfolk. Usually her gray gnome came to sit in her lap or run up and down beside her like a restless child.

Early one morning, when Nevyn had taken it upon himself to lecture Rhodry about the various political problems in his new rhan, Jill was sitting in her usual place in the bow when she saw a particularly large flock of sylphs. Some hundreds of yards ahead they wheeled and dipped and circled around some unseen center like seabirds above a shoal of fish. She got up and stood shading her eyes with one hand. As she peered at the flock, it seemed she could see an enormous bird at its heart—an albatross maybe? No, it was too large and too silver a gray. In fact, it looked like an owl, but no owl would ever fly out to sea.

"Aderyn!" She began jumping up and down and waving her arms. "Aderyn! Here we are! Over here!"

With a weary sort of flap the owl circled round and glided straight for the boat. As it came closer, she could see that it carried a cloth sack in its talons. Winging lower it passed overhead, dropped the sack safely on deck, then settled gracefully after it, perching onto a coil of rope.

"Aderyn, Aderyn, I'm so glad to see you! Can you talk in that shape? I don't remember."

"Somewhat." His voice was a flat distorted squawk. "Fetch Nevyn."

As Jill turned and headed for the hatch, she realized that a number of sailors had seen the owl, too. Their faces a pasty gray, they jumped back and rushed to the stern to huddle around the helmsman, who was looking at the sky with the expression of a man engaged in furious full-speed prayer. Apparently Nevyn had heard her yelling, because he climbed up on deck, with Rhodry right behind him, before she reached the hatch.

"Aderyn's here." Jill was jigging in delight. "He'll have news."

When they all trotted back to the bow, Aderyn was not only human again, but he'd already put on the pair of brigga he'd been carrying in the sack and was slipping a shirt over his head.

"That's better," he announced. "This wind is cold, I must say. Did you invoke it, Nevyn?"

"Merely asked, actually. It most certainly gladdens my heart to see you. What's the situation in Eldidd?"

"Vexed, very vexed, but not blood-spilling dangerous—yet. We need to talk to your captain here, because it would be best to land in Abernaudd, not Aberwyn herself. Rhodry, Blaen's in 'Naudd, waiting for you."

"Is he now?" Rhodry broke into a grin. "It's going to be cursed good to see him again."

"Well, you will and soon, because you're not all that far from land. Ye gods, my arms hurt! I've been flying out from the coast every day." He began rubbing his right arm with his left hand as he talked.

"We've got to be quick about this, because I've got to head back and warn Blaen you're coming."

"You can ride the dweomer-wind back in," Nevyn said. "Ah good, there's Elaeno now. Let's go talk to him."

When the others hurried off below decks, Jill stayed where she was. She sat down on the coil of rope, picked up her gnome and settled him on her lap, and wondered at herself, that she felt sad to the point of tears that they were reaching land. Sylphs and sprites settled around her, touching her face with little hands like puffs of wind and trying to comfort her, but all she could think was that she would lose them all if she didn't fight to keep them. If court matters took her over, the Wildfolk would slip away, a few at a time, until she never saw them again.

Before Aderyn left, Nevyn rubbed a rubifacient mixture into his old pupil's aching arms and shoulders, and a great silver owl reeking of mint and camphor flapped wearily off to Abernaudd. Jill waved farewell until he was out of sight, then turned back to find Nevyn standing behind her. Rhodry and Elaeno had apparently gone below.

"Nevyn, you will be coming back to Aberwyn with us, won't you? I mean, you'll live at court, won't you?"

"If my lady requests it, of course I will. Don't forget, child, you're the one in command now. I can't give you orders or even ask too many outright favors anymore."

"Oh, by the black hairy ass of the Lord of Hell! Then I most humbly beg you, Lord Galrion, to come be my personal councillor at my husband's court."

"My thanks, my lady. I shall be most pleased and honored to serve you." Nevyn made her a courtly bow, but he was grinning. "And my first piece of official advice is to stop swearing by the Lord of Hell's nether anatomy, especially in mixed company. Neither you nor Rhodry can afford to have you sounding like a barracks' brat. Which reminds me. Along with all the other fripperies Tieryn Lovyan packed up for me, she sent some dresses and jewelry for you. I suggest you put them on for our arrival. Blaen and all sorts of notables will be there to greet us, you know."

"And how, pray tell, am I going to jump off this wretched boat in a pair of dresses?"

"You can't. Rhodry will have to lift you down."

"Oh, stuff that!"

"My dear Lady Gilyan!"

"My apologies. But what if he drops me?"

"He won't. From the time he was a little lad, they trained him to do this sort of thing, you know, like helping a lady dismount from a sidesaddle or feeding her at a formal dinner."

"I don't care! He'll just have to wait to practice on me, that's all. I'll dress up when we're going to Aberwyn proper, but cursed and blasted both if I'll do it now."

"Oh come now, do all these trivial little matters truly ache your heart so much? Or is it somewhat else?"

"Well, there's a lot of things, but . . ." She hesitated in sudden and profound embarrassment. Oh, come now! she told herself. No matter what else he is, Nevyn's a physician and a healer. "Well, um, I was thinking, and well . . ." Suddenly her words came out with a rush. "Nevyn, do you think I'm barren? After all these years, first with Rhodry, and then with that stupid horse thief, too—but neither one of them ever got me with child. What if I'm barren, and then Rhodry has to put me aside someday for Aberwyn's sake? I'd die rather than be humiliated like that."

"It won't ever come to that because I'm sure you're not barren at all. Consider the life you've led, child, riding all over the kingdom, training like a lad in swordcraft, fighting battles, sleeping on the ground, eating catch-as-catch-can and the cheapest tavern food as often as not, and running for your life half the time, too, once you and Rhodry were together—your womanly humors must be utterly disrupted! All the fiery humor's been engulfed and overwhelmed by the cold and watery ones, just for a start. And as for the time with Perryn, well, my dear Jill, I would have been very surprised if you'd conceived his child. He's not truly human, you see, and much much less like a human being than an elf is. A boarhound and a sheepdog can produce perfectly good puppies, but consider a cat mating with a rabbit. You wouldn't get kittens with long ears, would you?"

"What a revolting way of putting it!"

"My apologies for your tender feelings." The old man was grinning at her. "I didn't realize my lady was so delicate."

"Oh, don't tease!" She could feel her face blazing with a blush. "But do you truly think I can bear children?"

"I most sincerely do. Once you've had six months or so in the dun, with a soft bed to sleep in, and plenty of warmth and leisure, and the best food to eat and clean water to drink—you wait and see. You'll be carrying an heir for Aberwyn soon enough."

"Oh. How wonderful. I, um . . . that gladdens my heart."

Nevyn raised one bushy eyebrow and looked her over with questioning eyes. She turned her back on him, studied the water foaming under the bow, and refused to answer. In a few moments she heard him sigh and walk away.

Jill did compromise, however, for the landing at Abernaudd. Since they were nearly to land, Elaeno let her commandeer the last of the fresh water on board to wash her hair and as much of the rest of her as the supply would allow. Although she refused to wear a narrow and constraining underdress, she did put on a regular dress over her brigga and even kirtled it with a length of the red, white, and brown plaid of the Red Lion, Lovyan's clan, which the regent had thoughtfully sent along. Since her father served the tieryn, that plaid would be Jill's until her marriage. By hitching the crisp gold-colored silk up around her waist, she could leave the ship on her own terms and ride astride once they were on land, too. At the jewelry she balked, because every piece of it, ring brooch and armlet and medallion, had the dragon of Aberwyn worked into its design. Wearing it would have made her feel branded.

Once she was dressed, Rhodry went out of his way to tell her how lovely she looked. Even though she knew that he was only trying to make her feel better, she was furious with him.

Just before noon Nevyn released the dweomer-wind, and on a normal breeze the *Guaranteed Profit* glided into Abernaudd's harbor with the strangest cargo it had ever carried. Once they were well within the funnel-shaped bay, Elaeno took over from the helmsman to bring his ship in. From her place in the bow, Jill could see a crowd on the main pier. In a clean shirt, with the plaid of Aberwyn pinned at one shoulder by an enormous ring brooch, Rhodry came up beside her and slipped his arm around her waist.

"There's Blaen, my love. Can you pick out him out? There in front with the red-and-gold plaid."

"I can just barely see him. You're the elf in the family."

"You know, we're going to have to stop making jests about that, aren't we? It would ruin everything if anyone found out who my father was."

"True enough. I'll keep a watch on myself from now on. By the Goddess herself there's a lot of people there! Who else can you see?"

"Aderyn. Ceredyc, Gwerbret Abernaudd. And—it's your father, Jill! Cullyn's here!"

She nearly wept out of sheer joy. As the boat eased itself into dock under Elaeno's expert piloting she was as impatient as one of the Wildfolk dancing around her in the bow. Yet when they were finally secure and tied up at the pier, she had to wait upon ceremony. Nevyn went ashore first to announce Rhodry's presence to the other two gwerbrets in attendance and to ask Ceredyc's permission for his lord to land. Once that was given, the men of Rhodry's warband came off to form up as an honor guard before Rhodry could jump down to the pier. Even though Jill started to clamber over the side of the low-riding merchantman herself, he insisted on catching her and lifting her down beside him. As Blaen stepped forward, all the men in attendance—and there was Rhodry's full warband of twenty-five, the twenty-five Blaen had brought with him, Ceredyc's and Sibyr's escorts and a miscellany of captains and on-lookers—began to cheer, calling out Rhodry's name and that of Aberwyn. Laughing his berserker's howl, Rhodry flung up his arms for silence, and in a moment or two, they gave it to him.

"Welcome home, cousin," Blaen said.

"My thanks, Your Grace. It's been a cursed strange road I've been riding. Tell you about it some time."

"Do that. Our mutual cousin here has offered you his hospitality, by the by."

"My thanks, Lord Sibyr." Rhodry turned to him. "It gladdens my heart to see you."

"And mine to see you, Your Grace."

There were bows and smiles all round, and Jill curtsied as best she could whenever anyone bowed to her, but all the while she was looking over the crowd for Cullyn. When she finally found him, off to one side, he winked at her, a gesture that made her feel calmer than she had in days. At least I'll have Da there, she thought to herself; I can go through with this. Just then the crowd parted to let a man with gleaming-pale hair make his way through. It took her a moment to recognize Calonderiel, dressed as he was in more finery than she'd ever seen on an elf: knee-high boots and fitted trousers of the finest white buckskin, a linen tunic stiff as leather with floral embroidery in swirling vivid bands, the quiver at his hip gleaming with solid gold appliques, the bow he carried obviously a ceremonial weapon, inlaid as it was with gold and gems. Everyone around goggled and gasped as he bowed to Rhodry and held out his hand.

"My name is Calonderiel, Banadar of the Eastern Border. I've come to offer my friendship and alliance to Gwerbret Aberwyn."

Rhodry grabbed the offered hand in both of his and squeezed it.

"Rhodry, Gwerbret Aberwyn accepts with all his heart and soul. Cal, you bastard! A banadar, are you? And here you never even told me before!"

"Wasn't any reason to." Calonderiel turned to Jill and grinned at her. "I'll explain later, but by the Dark Sun herself, it's good to see you."

"And it gladdens my heart to see you. I always thought I'd be riding west one day. I never dreamt you'd be riding east."

"No more did I, but it just proves the old saying: who knows what Wyrd will bring you?"

As if at some prearranged signal Blaen and the other noble-born men swept in and surrounded Rhodry and Calonderiel to lead them away in an important mob, all serious talk and grim expressions as they bent their heads toward each other and shut out the common world. For a moment Jill hesitated, caught between them and the warbands, but Cullyn appeared at her side and slipped his arm through hers.

"Come along, my sweet. There are horses waiting."

"They can wait a bit more. Oh, Da, it's so good to see you."

"And you can't know how it gladdens my heart to see you." He caught her by the shoulders and grinned at her. "You've got your cursed gall, Jill, running all over two kingdoms for three long years and never even sending your old da a letter."

She started to laugh, then flung herself into his arms and wept while he held her tightly. Her tears were brief, though when she looked up, she found his eyes suspiciously moist as well. As the crowd broke up, and the men hurried to fetch their horses and fall into line behind the noble-born, they strolled after slowly, arm-in-arm.

"Has it really been three years, Da?"

"And a bit more. It's a stupid thing to say, but I've got to say it, anyway: you've changed, my sweet, changed a fair bit, and I don't think it's just the passing time."

"It's not. Da, there's somewhat I've got to tell you. I'm studying the dweomer."

She'd been expecting some dramatic gasp or oath, but he merely nodded in a thoughtful sort of way.

"Can't say I'm surprised."

"Truly?"

"Truly. You were always such a strange child, Jill, talking to the Wildfolk, having strange dreams, seeing omens in every wretched cloud or fire." He shuddered a little, remembering. "But this is no place to talk about that. There's Lord Rhodry, mounted already and waving at us. We'll have a bit of a chat later."

Yet, with all the confusion of arriving at Sibyr's dun and getting so many riders settled for the night, it was after sunset before Jill got a private moment alone with her father. By then the evening meal was over, a patchy affair that was little more than a cold promise of a feast to come, and she'd been to her chamber to strip off her dress and put on her comfortable old shirt. Borrowing a tin lantern from the porter, they went out to the earthwork and climbed up to sit on the grassy mound in the mild spring night. For a long time they said nothing, merely enjoyed each other's company in the silence.

"Your old da's got somewhat to tell you," Cullyn said at last. "I've married again."

"Da! How splendid! Who is she? What's she like?"

"Her name's Tevylla, and she's in the tieryn's employ. She was widowed a while back—her first husband was a blacksmith, but he died of a fever—and she's got a son that I'm training for the warband. He's a good lad. Tevva's a sensible sort, strong-minded, but then, she needs to be since she's gone and married me."

"Is she pretty?"

Cullyn considered for a moment, smiling a little.

"She·is," he said at last. "Truly, you could say so."

"I'm so happy for you."

"You do sound it, truly." He turned a little to study her face in the flickering lantern light.

"Did you think I wouldn't be?" For a moment she was puzzled; then she realized his drift. "Well, truly, once I would have been writhing with jealousy—I'll admit it—when we were still on the long road together and all, but not now. After all, I'm about to marry, too."

"So you are. You know, my sweet, it's an odd thing. I've heard you mention that marriage a couple of times now, and . . ." He let his voice trail away.

"And what?"

"Ah, you won't be wanting your old father's advice anymore. None of my cursed business. I've got to learn to keep my long nose out of your affairs."

"Come on, tell me. What is it, Da?"

"You never sound very happy about it, that's all. There's just somewhat in your voice."

Tears threatened, hot and shaming. He threw his arms around her and pulled her close, her same old comfortable father, smelling of sweat and horses like he always had.

"Are you frightened?" he said softly. "All those fine ladies mincing around, waiting to get their claws into the gwerbret's favorite? Or is it the intrigue, the noble lords and their feuding and jockeying for favor and all?"

"Both. I'm not like Lovyan or Blaen's wife. They were born to all this. I wasn't. But . . . but . . . it's not that I'm frightened." Safe in his arms she could think clearly for the first time in weeks. "It's that I'm going to hate it. Courtly affairs look so petty, Da, after you've started studying dweomer. The noble-born are just children squabbling over toys, and smashing things when they don't get their way, and them all with their noses in the air, thinking they're the favorites of the gods themselves." She drew a little away so she could look up at him. "Do you remember Tieryn Braedd, and the war over pig food, all those years ago—the first summer you took me with you?"

He thought for a long moment, then laughed.

"I do at that," he said, chuckling. "You know, my sweet, you always were a cursed lot like me. I hope it's your boon and not your bane, I truly do."

At first she laughed; then she went a little cold as she realized that he wasn't going to contradict her, that, in fact, he agreed with her opinion of court life. She would have said more, but all at once he let her go and listened, his head cocked to one side. She'd spent so many weeks living in fear of assassins that she automatically reached for her sword, but it was only Nevyn, calling to them as he hurried out to the earthwork wall.

"Cullyn, Jill, is that you up there?"

"It is, my lord," Cullyn called back. "Is aught wrong?"

"Maybe, maybe not. Have you seen Perryn?"

"Not since the evening meal." Cullyn glanced at Jill, who shook her head in a no. "No more has Jill, my lord. Here, we'll come down. Has the little bastard escaped?"

"It certainly looks like it, although I wouldn't call it an escape. He isn't a prisoner anymore, not as far as I'm concerned."

"But did he know that?" Jill put in.

"Most likely not. It would be just like him to slip away in the night like a cursed weasel!"

For about an hour the three of them hunted round the dun, but they never found a trace of him or his bedroll. Finally Jill thought to check the postern gate, and sure enough, it was standing open, unlatched from the inside and never shut again. A quick check by an equerry and a head groom showed that a horse was missing, too.

"Well, that's torn it," Nevyn said in some disgust. "He was free to go, of course, but he might have given me a few more days to study him."

"Good riddance, say I," Jill muttered under her breath.

"You know," Cullyn said. "I never did know what charges had been laid against him."

"Well, he was a horse thief. At one time I thought him a spy from the dark dweomer." Jill answered him to spare Nevyn the lie. "But I was wrong. He's just a man of no importance." All at once she smiled. "Truly, now, of no importance at all."

"News, all sorts of news," Blaen said abruptly. "Things are moving fast, cousin, now that you're home."

"Good," Rhodry said. "The sooner this matter's settled, the better for Aberwyn."

Ceredyc, Sibyr, Nevyn, Calonderiel, Aderyn, Cullyn, a couple of minor lords that Rhodry didn't recognize—all the men at the table of honor nodded gravely. After much too heavy a breakfast for Rhodry's liking, they were all sitting in Sibyr's sun-streaked great hall and drinking ale while they discussed the troubled situation in the rhan of Aberwyn.

"It's time for you to ride home, and this message is as good a reason as any." Blaen held up the thin roll of parchment that had arrived some hours earlier. "Four days from now Lord Talidd's holding a tourney, and every single one of the would-be rebels will be there. In this letter Lord Edar says he'd be honored to shelter me and mine if I should choose to attend, and I wouldn't be surprised if he were glad to see you, too."

Rhodry tossed back his head and laughed.

"Never have I been more pleased with an invitation, cousin. Good old Edar! Let's see, his dun's about sixty miles from here, if I remember rightly. Three days ride—perfect."

"You'd best not take all of these men, though," Sibyr put in, leaning forward. "You want to prevent a war, not start one."

"Just so." Rhodry nodded his way. "Just twenty-five apiece for me and Blaen, the escort we're entitled to under the holy laws, and Calonderiel, too, and Gwin, and a few other retainers. The rest can go on to Aberwyn and wait for us there."

"Sounds like a solid plan to me," Blaen said. "One last question. Do you want to go openly or try to keep things quiet?"

"Quiet, I'd say. For all I know, our would-be rebels have spies all over Eldidd, but if they don't, I wouldn't mind giving them the surprise of their ugly little lives."

Whether or not the rebels had spies, Lord Peredyr and Lord Sligyn, two of Rhodry's most loyal vassals, certainly did, though they were hardly the professional sort who pop up during long wars. Peredyr's head groom had a brother who worked a free farm near Belglaedd, and Sligyn had blood kin himself in that part of the rhan. Through the fast-flowing channel of gossip, both lords learned about Talidd's tourney at the same time and decided to attend, just to scrape Talidd's conscience raw if nothing else. In a rather clumsy attempt to pretend that they weren't acting together, they also decided to arrive at separate times, Peredyr first and quite deliberately, while Sligyn would pretend that he'd been visiting his kin and just happened to hear of the tourney.

Since his sister's husband's dun was some miles from Belglaedd, it was an hour or so after noon when Sligyn and his escort of five men arrived. As they rode up to the dun, which was set on a low artificial hill, they found Peredyr waiting for them outside the gates.

"Ye gods, it's disgusting!" Peredyr burst out without even a good morrow first. "Wait till you see Gwarryc, prancing around as if he were gwerbret already, with the flatterers there to lick his hands."

"Oh, is he now? Listen, man, I promised you I'd hold my tongue, and I'll do my best, but—"

"And if we get cut down here, there's two fewer loyal men to fight for Aberwyn. Can you remember that? This tourney is swarming with rebels."

"You're right enough, eh? Very well, I'll hold my tongue."

Even in his state of rage, Sligyn had to admit that Talidd had outdone himself on the tournament. The dun itself was hung with Belglaedd's banners of silver and yellow, and there were more banners, in the colors of the various noble guests, hung from trees or mounted on poles in the area set aside for the festivities. The area around Belglaedd was known for its beautiful ash trees, and there was a particularly fine grove in back of Talidd's dun, where a small stream wound through a broad meadow. Among the trees the servants had set up table after table of food: sliced spiced meats, cheeses, fresh bread by the chunk and stale bread turned into puddings, pickled vegetables in the Bardek manner, roasted glazed larks and squabs, and as a centerpiece an entire roast boar. There was ale by the barrel and mead by the skin, and no one was turned away, not even the scruffiest beggar in Talidd's village, which had come in force not just to eat, but to watch the combats. Sligyn even saw a couple of silver daggers mingling with the crowd and helping themselves to the lord's bounty without anyone saying a harsh word to them.

Across the meadow, a good safe distance from the spread, were two combat grounds, marked out with ribands of green and gold—Gwarryc of Dun Gamyl's colors, interestingly enough. On one ground the main series of mock combats had taken place that morning, fought by riders from the various warbands, mostly, though a couple of impoverished younger sons of the local nobility had put aside their pride and taken a place in the series. The three hosting lords had put up generous prizes, trophy daggers and silver coins for the winners of every round, and for the grand prize a beautiful bay gelding, battle-trained, with some Western Hunter blood in him to judge by his deep chest and long legs. By the time Sligyn arrived, though, all the preliminary rounds of this splendid contest were over.

"They'll fight the final round on that other field," Peredyr said. "They've kept it untouched, so the finalists will have perfect footing. Then any of the lords who want to show off can join a mock tourney. No prizes, but it should be amusing to watch."

Sligyn snorted in a puff of disgust.

"Amusing? Only if the right men break their necks, eh?"

"If we say the right prayers, maybe the gods will take a hand. Gwarryc's in the lists, of course. I think me the idea is for him to come off the victor. The man's a splendid swordsman, mind, without any help, but I wouldn't be surprised to see some of his opponents staying their hands a bit. Just to ensure the show goes their way, like."

Although Sligyn had been given to fits of blustering, cursing, arm-waving anger all his life, never before had he felt cold fury, that preternaturally calm state where all the world seems very clear yet very far away, and what a man must do is equally clear but quite immediate. He did feel it, then, and he rather liked it.

"Where's the steward? The one keeping the lists?"

"Over by the ale barrels, last I saw. Lord Amval. Here, though — you're not going to enter, are you?"

"I am. No doubt I'll be eliminated in the second or third round, but by every god in the sky, I'm going to try to spoil that piss-proud excuse for a noble lord's fake vistory even if I ride home covered with bruises and shame both."

When he predicted that he'd be eliminated in the second or third round, Sligyn was not being modest but precisely describing his usual level of skill at mock combats with blunt blade and wicker shield. The rules were simple, but artificial enough to hamper a man like him, used to banging and hacking his way through a scrap. The contestants began at either end of the contest ground, approached and circled for position, then fenced and feinted until one or the other had either scored three touches or driven his opponent into the ribands that marked the ground. Although bruises were ignored, hitting hard enough to break his skin gave your opponent the victory. Holding back on anything had never been Sligyn's style.

But Sligyn had no idea of how useful cold fury can be to a man. He won his first round easily, since it was against the clumsy Lord Cinvan, then went on to win the second as well. For the third, in a state of controlled bloodlust he took the field against the formidable Lord Gwion, who had royal trophy daggers won in Dun Deverry itself hanging over his hearth. When Sligyn beat him handily, everyone, including Sligyn, assumed that Gwion had been stupidly overconfident. There was no such excuse in the fourth, when he beat an equally skilled lord who also happened to be a close friend of Gwarryc's. At that point the crowd began to grow uneasy. When the next batch of fourth-round contestants took the field, many spectators made no pretense of watching them; little clots of men formed to mutter among themselves and look Sligyn's way every now and then with troubled eyes.

As for Sligyn, he felt as if his whole body had become a weapon in the hands of his righteous rage. While he waited for his turn at the fifth round, he drank cold water instead of ale and glared at Gwarryc, standing a good fifty yards from him in a press of followers. Yet, in spite of the distance, it seemed that Gwarryc was aware of him, because at intervals he would look up, and his eyes would search out Sligyn the way a tongue searches out a chipped tooth. Sligyn also noticed the pair of silver daggers, one blond, one dark enough to have some Bardek blood in his veins, watching him, but from their hard and indifferent faces it was hard to tell what they might have thought. Peredyr, on the other hand, who was by then acting as Sligyn's second, bringing him damp rags to wipe his face and water by the flagonful, was beside himself with holy joy.

"Keep it up, man! I'll pray to any god you want, just keep it up! Look at that bastard-born traitor's face, wondering what's wrong with his little womanly scheme! Gods, the vanity of the man!"

The words were more inspiring than the praise-song of the finest bard in the kingdom. On their tide Sligyn won the fifth round, and the sixth, until only the seventh lay between him and Gwarryc himself, who had made his expected easy progress through his rounds.

Unfortunately, Sligyn's opponent for this penultimate trial was Lord Retyc of Gaddbrwn, known throughout Eldidd for his finely tuned skill with a sword. When Sligyn marched out to face him, he was consoling himself by thinking that at least he'd given Gwarryc a good scare before his inevitable defeat. Most of Gwarryc's supporters seemed to agree; they had all relaxed and stood smiling on the sidelines while their champion limbered his enormous frame by twirling the blunt blade round and round his head. But then the gods took a hand, or so every man in Eldidd saw it. Nevyn would later say that Sligyn's supernormal rage was affecting the men around him, troubling their auras as well as their minds, but at the time, every onlooker there saw it as an omen, and that's how the story spread.

When the contest began, Retyc strode toward Sligyn in confidence, but not overconfidence—he'd profited from Gwion's painful lesson earlier. For a few moments they sparred, the blunt blades striking the wicker shields with an odd, squishy thwack. Out of sheer fury Sligyn managed to score one touch; then Retyc feinted in from the side, drew back, danced to the front—and scored two touches in quick succession. Yet, as he grinned in triumph, he dropped his guard ever so slightly, and Sligyn got his second touch, too. Even now in the count, they circled, feinting cautiously from one side or the other, drawing back a little, trying to draw their opponent in, then closing again ever so delicately when the other refused to be drawn. Around and around, back and forth they went, and the length of the fight was beginning to tell on Sligyn, who was a good twelve years Retyc's senior. He was puffing a little as he made a sharp stab—and Retyc slipped. His left foot simply shot out from under him, and down he went, flailing and cursing, to strike the ribands to his left and pull them down.

"Disqualified!" yelled the nearest judge, and though they hated to do it—you could see it in their faces—the other two judges also called out, "Disqualified! The winner is Lord Sligyn."

With a whoop of joy Peredyr rushed out to take Sligyn's sword and shield like a page. Sligyn could hear Peredyr's men as well as his own cheering and calling for wagers as he walked off the field, and the two silver daggers had joined them to celebrate, too. It was between him and Gwarryc now. Except for Sligyn's tiny faction, by then the entire mob of onlookers, lord and riders alike, were strangely silent, looking back and forth at Gwarryc and Sligyn and muttering old proverbs, all of which centered around the way the gods take a dim view of presumption on the part of men. At that point the judges announced a long delay, to allow both contestants to rest and the servants to smooth out the contest ground. No one doubted that the delay would also allow Gwarryc and his supporters to regroup and regain their confidence after Retyc's god-touched defeat.

"Let's go well into the trees," Peredyr said to Sligyn. "Rest in the shade, and I'll get you cold water from the stream."

"My thanks. I'll admit to needing a bit of rest. Hah! the bastards! Their own delay's working against them, eh?"

When Sligyn sat down in the relative privacy of the ash grove, he realized that he ached all over, and that his wind was going fast. Well, by the gods, you gave the bastard a turn, anyway, he told himself. Teach him to put on little shows like a blasted gerthddyn, eh? Then he saw the blond silver dagger strolling toward him, and his heart thudded once. Jill! He cursed himself, wondering how he could have been so blind as to not recognize her earlier. With a grin and a bellow of welcome, he started to get up, but she rushed over and knelt beside him.

"Not so loud, my lord! We've got a little surprise planned for our Gwarryc and his friends."

"Oh, do you now?" With great difficulty Sligyn made himself speak softly. "Is *he* here?"

"He is, and I wonder if he could take your place in the final round."

Sligyn stopped himself from howling with glee just in time.

"He may at that, by all the gods! Here, that other lad with you—didn't recognize him, either. It's not—"

"Na, na, na, just a friend. *He*'s with Blaen—and quite a lot of men, actually—hidden in the woods up the road. Gwin's gone to fetch them."

"Peredyr ought to go make some formal excuse to the contest judges, eh? Or do we just let our lord walk out there?"

"Oh, just let him walk out, I'd say. There's no use mincing around. They'll know soon enough that the dragon's flown home. And Nevyn's here, too, or rather, he and a friend of his are close by. They're planning on keeping out of sight till the shouting's over."

"Probably for the best, though I don't know, the old man can be pretty impressive when he wants. What about your father?"

"He's here. He wouldn't miss this if you offered him the High King's throne."

When Peredyr came back with the water, he nearly wept at the sight of Jill. Once he heard what was afoot, he trotted off to round up his men and Sligyn's and bring them back down to the trees on the pretence of fetching more ale and food and the like. Now that he knew he wouldn't be fighting, Sligyn could at last have a good foaming tankard of ale, and as he drank it, he was feeling that the gods were in their heavenly duns and showering justice upon the world.

The contest was further delayed when Blaen and a warband of fifty men and a couple of captains rode round the dun and dismounted, calling out friendly greetings and jests as they led their horses over and joined the tourney. Although Talidd was as happy to see them as a miller finding weevils in his flour, there was nothing the lord could do, since he had no desire to insult a gwerbret by barring him and his from an open tourney. Sligyn was anxiously looking over the crowd around Blaen and trying to see Rhodry when he felt a friendly hand on his shoulder and spun around. Wearing a battered old cloak Rhodry stood there, his head tossed a little back, his face burning with the half-mad berserker's grin that Sligyn remembered so well. Right behind him was Cullyn of Cerrmor.

"Your Grace." Sligyn suddenly found it hard to speak. "Your Grace."

"Don't kneel!" Rhodry grabbed his arm just in time. "Blaen's keeping them distracted, and they haven't seen me yet."

"Right. Of course. Eh!" Sligyn grabbed a damp rag, blew his nose hard, and wiped his eyes on his shirt-sleeve before going on. "This'll show the bastards, eh? What comes of all their cursed plotting and scheming."

Since Blaen's men all descended upon the food and drink at once and distracted everyone, no one did notice Rhodry, who kept well back in the trees among Sligyn and Peredyr's riders. When the judges called for the contestants, Sligyn walked at the head of his pack with Rhodry in their midst. Gwarryc was already there, pacing back and forth at his end of the field. As Sligyn went toward his end, the judges came forward to inspect his sword and shield as the rules required. Sligyn handed them over with a little bow.

"My lords, someone else will be taking my place. I was only fighting as his champion, a thing you all know blasted well, whether your ugly weaseling hearts would admit it or not, and well, by the black ass of the Lord of Hell, here he is."

The judges turned dead-white as Rhodry shoved his way through the pack and stepped up beside Sligyn to take the blunt sword and shield. He'd thrown off the cloak to reveal a shirt encrusted with embroidered dragons and interlace, and brigga in the blue-green-and-silver plaid of Aberwyn. Down at his end of the ground, Gwarryc paced in happy ignorance until Rhodry strode onto the field. There was a moment's silence; then a mutter, a roar, of whispers, then talk, and finally cheers from Rhodry's loyal men and from the prudent among his enemies, just as when a farmer's earthen dam begins to crumble, with the water trickling through, until the flood bursts out at last and comes roaring down the streambed. Sligyn had a brief moment's admiration for Gwarryc. With a proud toss of his head the lord strode to meet his enemy and saluted him with the blunt sword. The talk and the cheers died.

"Your Grace," Gwarryc said. "Do you want to replace these with real steel?"

"I don't, because you've done me no harm—not enough to warrant your death." Rhodry brought his own blade up in salute. "And lest you think I'm only boasting, let's have our contest, shall we?"

Deliberately and insolently Rhodry turned his back on the lord and strode off to his end of the contest ground, leaving Gwarryc with no choice but to do the same or be thought a coward forever. Licking nervous lips, the judges hovered, glancing at one another, until Sligyn could stand it no longer.

"Well, begin, for the sake of the gods! Don't just stand there sniveling, eh? Begin!"

As the two combatants started walking toward the center, the crowd pressed close, sighing a little. Dropped to a fighting crouch, Gwarryc moved cautiously as he circled, but, even though his sword was at the ready, Rhodry merely turned in place to face him. Gwarryc hesitated briefly, then feinted to one side, back again, and in with a smart slap of his blade. Rhodry didn't dodge so much as step away, smoothly, almost languidly. When Gwarryc spun round and charged, Rhodry was gone again, angling a few yards down the field and grinning when Gwarryc ran right past. Although he could easily have scored three touches and ended the match right there, he waited until Gwarryc caught his mistake and turned back. Like a fool Gwarryc went after him and repeated the whole little farce. By then the crowd was snickering.

"Curse you!" Gwarryc snarled. "Stand and fight!"

"Very well. Here I am."

Rhodry lowered the point of his sword till it trailed lazily on the grass, tossed his shield some ten feet away, and smiled at him. Gwarryc looked this way and that with the scowl of a man who realizes he's been set up as the butt of a joke just when there's no escaping it.

"Well, come along," Rhodry said. "You wanted a bit of sport with a helpless opponent, didn't you? So make your strike."

If Gwarryc had had the sense to throw his own shield and face him on even terms, he might have salvaged a bit of honor out of the situation, but instead, he merely charged, swinging hard at Rhodry's unprotected side. Rhodry jumped back with a little leap that brought him round to Gwarryc's flank as the enraged lord tried to stop his forward movement—too late. Rhodry slapped him three times on the buttocks, as if he were spanking a recalcitrant page. When the crowd burst out laughing, Gwarryc threw his sword and shield onto the ground, and strode off the field. In front of him the crowd parted, still laughing, and let him through. Although his own warband followed him, most of his erstwhile friends rushed forward to congratulate the winner.

"So much for their loyalty, eh?" Sligyn said to Peredyr.

"True spoken. Ah, this is a day to tell our grandsons about, sure enough!"

In the confusion men began milling about, shouting and laughing, or slinking away downcast. A lot of the recent recruits were trying to get close to the new gwerbret to speak with him, a few in sincere and obvious regret and humility, most with false bright smiles, as if they'd been hoping for his return all along. Rhodry himself was greeting everyone with great courtesy, smiling and nodding agreement even when it was plain they lied. Sligyn also saw Jill, standing off at the edge of the crowd and watching with a peculiarly melancholy smile. He worked his way through to join her.

"Oh, he'll make a fine lord for Aberwyn," Sligyn said. "Look at him, all diplomacy, eh? Good lad, good lad. And when will the wedding be, by the by?"

"Wedding?" Jill said with a start.

"Just that. Come now, we all know the lad's going to marry you, eh? If Blaen hasn't laid land and title upon you, why, someone else will."

"Oh. That wedding." She looked idly away. "You're right enough about Blaen. I've got land of my own in Cwm Pecl now, a wilderness, he tells me, but it'll serve."

"So, you're Lady Gilyan, eh?" Sligyn gave her a friendly slap on the back. "Good, good. We'll have a splendid feast when the happy day comes, eh?"

Jill smiled, but her melancholy was almost palpable, as if she stood in a darker light. By then the crowd around the gwerbret was breaking up; the truly loyal warbands had gone to fetch their horses, the flatterers were slinking away. Not far from Rhodry stood Cullyn, listening as Blaen, goblet in hand, talked on and on about something, and the silver dagger Jill had called Gwin was standing just behind Rhodry himself. Down at the tables frightened servants were hurriedly clearing away the food and drink under Talidd's supervision. Although there was no sign of Gwarryc or his warband, some of his supporters were hovering around—trying to put a good face on things, Sligyn supposed. Among them was the Bardek man called Alyan, sipping a tankard of ale and smiling in a dazed way, as if he still couldn't believe what had happened to his employer's cause. He finished the last of his drink, then strolled off toward the busy servants, the tankard dangling in one hand, as if he wanted one last refill before the barrels were rolled away. When he reached the gathering around the new gwerbret, he paused as if listening, then dropped the tankard and moved.

Jill suddenly swore and ran toward the clot of men just as someone yelled an alarm. Frozen by surprise, Sligyn saw Rhodry twist around barely in time as steel flashed beside him and the shouting rang out all round. Like dweomer Alyan had produced a dagger, and he was striking down as Rhodry flung up an arm to protect himself.

"Ware!" Gwin leapt in between assassin and lord.

The dagger struck into Gwin's shoulder, and the bright blood ran as Gwin grabbed his enemy's hair with one hand and shoved the other hard under his chin. There was a crack, a sickening crack like a stick breaking under a boot. Alyan slumped dead as Gwin flung him to the ground. Sligyn was never sure when he'd started running; all at once he was pushing his way through the gathering crowd to reach Rhodry's side just as the gwerbret caught Gwin by the arm and steadied him.

"It's not much of a cut, Your Grace," Gwin said.

"Better get a chirurgeon anyway, eh?" Sligyn rumbled. "Where's that blasted Talidd? Curse the man—he's not much of host, eh?"

And Sligyn was honestly surprised when everyone burst out laughing.

It was well into the evening watch by the time that Rhodry and his retinue came back to Lord Edar's dun. Nevyn lingered in the great hall just long enough to hear that the would-be rebels had been properly shamed; then he insisted that Gwin come up to his chamber and have his wound treated. Jill came along, too—she'd done a clumsy but serviceable job of binding the wound earlier—and cut fresh bandages while he washed it out and stitched it up. Painful though the procedure must have been, not a muscle of Gwin's face moved during it. Nevyn sent him back to the great hall with orders to drink a couple of goblets of mead, then helped Jill as she cleaned up.

"You look sad, child. I would have thought you'd be dancing in glee tonight."

"Well, I'm happy enough for Rhodry's sake."

"Not your own? Come now, soon you'll have a splendid wedding, and you'll be the most powerful woman in all Eldidd."

"Everyone keeps talking about my rotten wedding. Do you realize that Rhodry never even asked me to marry him? He just assumed that I was going to, and so does everyone, and you and Blaen are the worst of the bad lot, and I don't want to be the wretched most powerful woman in all anywhere, curse you all!"

For a moment he thought she was about to cry, but instead she merely stood there openmouthed and shocked at her own outburst.

Nevyn himself was so surprised that it took him a moment to find something to say.

"Indeed? Then what do you want?"

"I want to study dweomer and have Rhodry, too."

"No reason you can't."

"Oh, stop treating me like a child or a half-wit!"

"I wasn't aware that I was."

"Then answer me honestly." Her voice was calm again, even cold. "If I marry Rhodry, am I going to be able to master the dweomer? I don't mean study the odd bit of lore or the odd mental trick. I want to be a master like you and serve the kingdom like you do, too. A couple of months ago, I could never have said that—it would have sounded conceited—but I know better now. That's what I want, but if I marry Rhodry and get turned into his chatelaine and castellan and the mother of his heirs and the Goddess herself only knows what else, am I going to be able to have it?"

"You're not, truly." He stopped himself from adding, "not in this life, anyway." She would have to ask before he could reveal that secret. "There just quite simply won't be enough time."

"So I thought. But can I just leave him? He needs me."

For a moment the room spun around him. His face must have gone white, because Jill rushed over and took his arm.

"What's wrong? Is it your heart? Here, sit down. There's a big chest right behind you."

With a sigh Nevyn sat and leaned back against the wall for support.

"My heart's fine, my thanks. You just took me by surprise, and I *am* getting on a bit, you know. Are you honestly thinking of leaving Rhodry?"

"I am. I suppose you think I'm a fool. Most women would. Or a harridan—most men would think that."

"I don't think you're either, frankly. I will say that the decision has to be yours and yours alone."

"Well, I rather knew that." She smiled at him, then turned to pace restlessly back and forth. "I wouldn't mind a bit of advice, though. Do I have the right to leave him and put the dweomer first?"

"I'm the absolutely worst person in the entire kingdom to ask that question. Once, and a good long time ago it was, too, I had to make this same choice. I chose wrong."

"You took dweomer instead of the woman you loved?"

"Not instead of, exactly. I could have had both. I was just so greedy and impatient for power that I saw her as a nuisance—which she wouldn't have been at all—and so like the arrogant dolt I was, I deserted her."

"I see. But I can't have both."

"That's true enough."

"Did she need you badly?"

"She did. Very badly, just because of the ugly circumstances she was born into. Without me, she had no life at all."

"But Rhodry's gwerbret, and he's got more prospects in life than any man but the High King himself. I keep saying he needs me, but he doesn't, really. Ye gods, any lass in the kingdom would throw herself at his feet for the chance to marry him, and there's hundreds better fit to be a ruler's wife than I am. How am I going to devote myself to his wretched rhan, when all the time I'll be wishing I could be studying my craft?"

"That's all true and splendidly logical, but can you bear to leave him?"

She went still, utterly still, except for the tears that welled up in her eyes and ran in two thin trails down her face.

"Nevyn, I keep feeling like I'm drowning. It's not even Rhodry himself. It's his position and his rank and Aberwyn and everything. It's like a river, and it'll just sweep me under if I let it." All at once she tossed her head and laid a hand on her chest. "I really do feel sometimes like I can't breathe. Do you think I'm daft?"

"I don't. I think you see things clearly. But you never answered my question. Can you bear to leave him?"

The tears came again, and she stared at the floor for a long time before she answered.

"I can, and I have to. I'm going to do it tonight." She looked up. "I'm going to do it now, or I never will."

"I'll be here and awake."

She started to speak, then merely nodded a distracted understanding and left the room. For a long time Nevyn stared at the closed door while his hands shook with a hope that he'd never allowed himself before, not once in the long four hundred years since he'd made his rash vow.

Lord Edar's chamberlain had of course given the gwerbret the most luxurious bedchamber in the broch, a big wedge of a room with an enormous bed, hung round with embroidered panels and covered in embroidered blankets. When Jill came in, she found candles burning in the silver sconces and Rhodry sitting cross-legged in the center of the bed and reading from a long piece of parchment. He tossed it aside and gave her a grin that wrung her heart.

"Edar's terms of fealty to Aberwyn. I see no reason to change them, but he wanted me to look them over just to be sure, so I did. Ah, my love, it's so good to have a moment alone with you. I've been feeling like a hound on a leash. Every time I try to walk your way, someone yanks me back again."

When she said nothing, merely stood hesitating at the foot of the bed, his smile disappeared.

"Is somewhat wrong, my love?"

"I can't marry you." It came out in a blurt that made her despise herself. "I've got to leave you."

"I've never heard a jest I liked less."

"It's no jest, Rhoddo. I don't want to go, but I've got to. It's because of the dweomer."

"What? I thought we'd settled all that. Back in Elaeno's ship—remember?"

"I do remember, but I didn't say everything. I'm saying it now. I've got to study, and I can't study if I'm married to you, and I'm leaving. On the morrow."

"Just hold your tongue! You're not doing anything of the sort. If you need time for your studies, well and good, then. Time you shall have. I—we'll—arrange things somehow. I don't know how yet, but we will."

"I know you mean that with the best faith in the world, but it won't ever happen. Be honest. You know it won't. There'll always be one thing or another that needs me to tend it, and if I don't, then all the courtiers will gossip and tell you what a lazy wife you have, and after all a while, you'll resent it, too. Or what if everyone starts muttering that I'm a witch? I've thought all this out, Rhoddo. What if you deny some lord a thing that he thinks he should have, and then he starts saying it's because your woman bewitched you?"

"That's not the point!"

"Then what is it?"

"I don't want you to go. Jill, how could you do this to me? Ye gods, you risk your life chasing after me, and just when we're finally safe and I can shower you with comfort and privilege, you say you want to leave."

"I don't want to leave. I have to leave."

"Just to study a lot of moldy old books with Nevyn? What are you going to do, wander around the kingdom with a mule and lance farmers' boils for them?"

"If I have to, I will. It's not a bad calling, healing people's ills."

"You're daft!"

"You just can't understand what the dweomer means—"

"Of course I can't understand." His voice was rising steadily. "There's naught to understand except you've gotten this daft idea in your head, and now you won't listen to reason."

"Rhodry, it aches my heart to hurt you this way."

He started to speak, then stopped himself. He got off the bed and walked over to catch her by the shoulders. His hands were so warm and comfortable that she wanted to weep.

"Don't go. Jill, please. I need you so much."

"You don't need me. You just want me."

"Well, isn't that enough? I love you more than I love my own life, and that's not enough?"

"I love you, too, but the dweomer—"

"Oh, curse the dweomer! I don't give a pig's fart about dweomer! I want you."

"And I want you, but I can't have you and the dweomer—"

"So, I'm only second-best, am I?"

"That's not what I meant! By the hells, you're as stubborn as a mule and twice as nasty! Why won't you listen to what I'm saying?"

"Why won't you talk sense, then?"

Later it would seem to Jill that they argued for half an eternity. Even at the time she realized she was quarreling only to keep her pain at bay, that she was desperately trying to find some reason to hate or at least despise him, but merely realizing wasn't enough to make her stop. Rhodry, she supposed, was genuinely furious with her; she needed to believe so, anyway. Round and round they went, the same circling arguments, the very same words, even, until she wondered what she wanted from him, why she was dragging out this agony instead of merely leaving. Finally she realized that she wanted him to say, very simply, that he understood, and that this was the one thing he never would say.

"You don't love me at all anymore, do you?" By then his voice was hoarse and cracking. "Tell me the truth. It's some other man, isn't it?"

"Oh, don't be an utter dolt! I've never loved anyone but you in my whole life."

"Then why could you possibly want to leave?"

"Because the dweomer—"

"See! It does mean more than me."

"Not more than you. More than love itself."

"That's ridiculous! No woman feels that way. Who is it? It can't be Nevyn, and Salamander's back in Bardek, and—"

"Rhodry, hold your ugly tongue! There isn't any other man. You're just trying to salve your cursed wounded pride."

"May the gods curse you! Why shouldn't I try to find some shred of pride to cling to? I'm the one who's going to have to announce to the entire rhan of Aberwyn that a silver dagger's daughter didn't find me good enough for her."

All at once she saw the way out. It was a lie, of course, an utter and complete lie, but at that moment she was desperate to break the chains of recrimination and hurt that were binding them round.

"Well, I've got pride of my own, and how do you think I could live shamed, after you cast me off one fine day?"

"Jill! I'd never do such a thing! Haven't you listened to one cursed word I've said?"

"There's somewhat you don't know." She turned away, embarrassed that she'd stoop so low.

"What is it?" His voice had changed to a frantic sort of worry. "What's so wrong?"

"I'm barren, you dolt. Couldn't you put that together on your own?

After all these years, you've never gotten me with child, and there's little Rhodda at home, waiting to call you father. It's not your trouble."

He was silent for so long that she finally forced herself to look at him. For the first time in that miserable evening he was weeping. She felt that she could taste her lies as a fetid thing in her mouth, but she forced herself to go on.

"You've got to think of Aberwyn, Rhodry. What's going to happen to the rhan in twenty years' time when there's still no heir? I can't do that to Aberwyn and her people, not even for the man I love, and I love you with all my heart and soul."

"You could still—" He stopped his rush of words, hesitated, then wiped the tears from his face before he went on. "Forgive me. I was going to say that you could still be my mistress, but you can't. After everything we've gone through, the battles we've fought—you couldn't live like that."

"Thank the Goddess herself that you understand! I refuse to grovel around your wife and hear her gloat every time she has a babe."

"Oh, my love." He could barely speak. "Of course you couldn't do that. Ah, by every god in the sky! I'm sorry I pushed you this far. Forgive me. Oh ye gods, forgive me, too, for cursing the bitter Wyrd you've given me!"

"You do understand why I'm going?"

"I do."

He slipped his arms around her and held her close while they sobbed in one another's arms, but she was weeping because she hated herself for lying to him. It's a silver dagger's ruse, she told herself, and that's all you are at heart, a rotten silver dagger still.

"I'll never love another woman," Rhodry said. "I promise you that."

"Don't bind yourself to that! I wouldn't want you to, ever. But you can promise me this: never love another woman the way you loved me, and I'll promise you I'll never love another man that same way."

"Done, then."

When he bent his head to kiss her, she twisted away.

"Please don't kiss me, my love. It'll only make things worse."

Before he could answer she turned and fled, running from her lie as much as him. She flung open the door and burst out into the corridor only to charge smack into Gwin. She grabbed him by the collar and shoved him back against the wall.

"Were you spying on us?"

"Couldn't understand a word you said. All I heard was the gwerbret yelling, and I'm supposed to be his bodyguard now, you little hellcat!"

When Jill let him go, she realized that it was sheer luck that had kept her from reopening his wounded shoulder. She took a deep breath to calm herself down.

"My apologies, truly. You'd better go in. He needs someone to talk to." She started off down the corridor, then hesitated. "Oh, Gwin? Guard him well, will you? He's going to need you badly in the next few weeks."

Then she hurried on, leaving him staring puzzled after her, and ducked into the safety of Nevyn's chambers. The old man was standing at the open window, and she realized with a profound shock that the first hint of dawn was turning the eastern sky gray.

"Nevyn, I've got to get out of here. Can't we just pack and leave right now?"

"We can. My poor Jill, I—"

"Oh, don't pity me! I can't stand it, and I don't deserve it. I lied to him, Nevyn. I stood there and told him I was barren, and that's why I couldn't marry him."

"And what's so wrong with that? No doubt he had to have some reason, one he could understand and cling to."

"But a lie's a wretched way to start a new life."

"True, but there are lies, and then there are bandages for the soul."

The dawn was full and golden by the time Jill and Nevyn were saddling their riding horses out in the ward, and Cullyn came out of the barracks to join them. He glanced at the laden pack mule, then nodded in understanding.

"You're not marrying Rhodry." It was no question.

"I'm not, Da. I just can't. It's the dweomer."

"Ah."

He looked round the ward, glanced down at the cobbles, then turned to look back at the stables.

"I'll ride with you aways. Let me just fetch my horse."

As he walked off, Jill realized that she'd be leaving him behind irrevocably, too. For the briefest of moments she wavered; then she caught Nevyn watching her.

"You were right," he said. "The sooner we get on the road, the better."

They took the east-running road from Belglaedd, heading south toward the coast road that ran to Deverry proper, just as the sun was turning hot with the promise of summer. When, after about an hour, Cullyn paused his horse in the road and announced he'd best be getting back, Nevyn rode a little ways along to give them a private word with each other. Cullyn led Jill down a side lane into an apple orchard, where the branches, heavy-laden with white blossoms, hung down over a whitewashed stone fence, so that it seemed they sat on horseback in the midst of clouds.

"Well, my sweet, it's a strange road you've chosen to ride."

"It chose me, Da, and a long long time ago."

He nodded his agreement, his eyes distant, as he thought something through. Through the perfumed mist around them the sun came in shafts.

"A better road than mine," he said at last, and he rose in the stirrups to catch a branch and break off a cluster of apple blossoms. "Want some?"

He broke the cluster in half, handed her a sprig, then tucked the other behind one ear with a laugh for the surprise on her face.

"A warrior's like these flowers, Jill. Like them we have our splendor in the spring, and it's over cursed soon. I've been lucky enough to see my summer through, but not a lot of us are. Think about that when you remember me."

"I will, Da. Promise."

He watched while she tucked the sprig behind her ear; then he turned and rode off without another word. Her eyes filled with tears, but she wiped them away, thinking how odd it was that her last sight of him would be with flowers in his hair.

Rhodry rode home to Aberwyn on a day that seemed to have been arranged by the gods as the perfect backdrop for spectacle: brilliantly sunny, yet cool with a soft spring wind that kept the banners snapping and the horses' manes flowing. All along the road the grass and the spring wheat stood tall and green; the trees shimmered in new leaf. Farmer and lord alike rushed out as the procession rode by to cheer and wave to their new overlord. When they reached the city gates, they found them mobbed with well-wishers, and the city walls, too, were lined with a cheering crowd. As they worked their way along the twisting streets to the dun itself, women threw flowers and little children ran after the warbands, turning the trip into a ragged parade.

"Looks like they're glad to see you, Your Grace," Cullyn remarked.

"No doubt." Rhodry grinned at him. "It means there won't be war. They'd welcome the Lord of Hell himself if he had a clear claim to the rhan."

From Cullyn's slight and ironic smile, he knew that his captain agreed.

At the massive gates of Dun Aberwyn Lady Lovyan stood waiting, wearing the plaid of Aberwyn in her role as regent, but her kirtle was woven of the browns and reds of the Clw Coc to remind everyone that she was a lord in her own right as well. She was also wearing the ceremonial sword of the gwerbrets, slung over her shoulder in an antique baldric, because she was too short to carry it gracefully in a sword belt. As Rhodry dismounted, she strode to meet him, and the golden hilt winked and the jewels sent long sparks of sunlight around her face.

"Am I welcome here, regent?" Rhodry said.

"Always, my lord, to what is rightfully yours." With a flourish bespeaking some practice, Lovyan drew the sword and handed it to him hilt-first. "It gladdens my heart to welcome you home."

The crowd shrieked and screamed like banshees as Rhodry hoisted the sword and held it over his head so all could see. Cullyn stepped forward and smoothly drew Rhodry's own sword so he'd have a free scabbard to sheathe the golden one, then fell in behind him as he and Lovyan walked into the dun. Their path was lined with servants and riders, all cheering and waving, and on either side the door the dragon banners fluttered in the wind, as if they too greeted the heir. Just inside stood a handsome dark-haired woman with her hands on the shoulders of a beautiful little girl, all scrubbed and combed and dressed in a cut-down version of adult finery.

"My wife, Your Grace," Cullyn prompted. "And your daughter."

From the way the crowd was watching him, Rhodry knew they expected a grand gesture; a simple acknowledgement of paternity would be far too paltry for the occasion. He knelt down in front of the child, whose enormous violet eyes studied him with all the haughtiness of a great lady. Around her clustered a gaggle of gnomes and sprites, and in the air above hovered a pair of sylphs. She brought such a feeling of wildness with her that seeing her was like stepping into a forest.

"Know who I am?" Rhodry said.

"My da."

"That's right." Ye gods, he was thinking, what have I sired? She's more an elf than I am! "Want to sit at the table of honor with me?"

"I do."

When he held out his arms, she allowed herself to be picked up, and the gnomes danced round his feet as he carried her across the great hall.

Because of the pomp and ceremony, Lovyan had no chance at a private word with Rhodry that day. First all the noble-born servitors had to welcome the Maelwaedd home; then his vassals appeared to swear their oaths of loyalty; finally there was an enormous feast that lasted until well after midnight. Since she went to bed long before the revelers, when she came down the next morning, she was expecting to find the great hall empty, but Rhodry was sitting alone at the head of the honor table, drinking a tankard of ale and staring into the peat fire smoldering at the hearth.

"His Grace is up early," Lovyan said.

"I never did need much sleep." He rose, making her a half-bow. "Come sit down, Mother. I've much to thank you for."

A servant appeared, bringing her usual morning bowl of warm milk and honey and a basket of fresh bread and butter. Rhodry took a chunk of the latter and nibbled it while they talked over the current business of the rhan, the spring taxes and the feuding lords who might or might not need his judgments on their affairs. She was surprised at how seriously he listened, asking her often to explain some detail or to recommend some servitor to tell him more. Finally he grinned at her.

"I can practically hear you thinking: ye gods, how much he's changed!"

"Well, you have. I haven't seen you for three years—or a bit more now, truly."

"Do you remember, Mother, when you told me that I'd never been raised to rule? You were right enough, and now I know it, too. There's much work ahead of me, but I promise you, I'll tend to it."

"I'm pleased to hear it, Your Grace. At least you can read and write. I insisted on that, you know, even though your father thought it a waste of time for a younger son."

"No doubt he did." For a moment Rhodry looked oddly distracted; then he smiled. "There's one thing particularly pressing at the moment. I've got to marry, and soon."

"Just so." She hesitated for a long moment. "I don't mean to cause you grief, but what's happened to Jill?"

"She left me. That should be cursed obvious."

"Very well. I don't have to know why."

"Oh, in a year or two I'll tell you. Once the wound's not running blood."

When he stood up, pacing restlessly to the hearth, she followed, willing to let the subject drop for a while to spare him pain, but he continued it himself.

"I'm going to marry out of the rhan."

"It would be best that way. When I heard you were safe, I started negotiations with the tieryn of Elrydd. His elder daughter is lovely as well as shrewd."

"Too bad, because you'll have to break them off. I've sent Blaen off to be my second and ask for Ygwimyr of the Auddglyn's sister. Aedda, I think her name is. I don't give a pig's fart what she looks like. I want that alliance."

"What? Rhoddo, I've met that child at court, and she's one of the worst choices you could make! She's a pretty little thing, with lovely manners but no brains at all, and she's as timid as a field mouse."

"Too blasted bad."

"Rhodry!"

By then the great hall was coming alive, with sleepy lords and riders alike stumbling in for their breakfasts. In a mutual silent agreement they went up to her reception chamber, a spacious room where the windows stood open to let in the soft spring sun. In a shaft of dust-flecked light they faced each other.

"If His Grace had only sent me a messenger, I'd have naught to say about it," Lovyan said, picking each word carefully. "But as it is, things are most awkward . . ."

"If Her Grace had only waited to consult me, all the awkwardness would have never arisen. I'm sorry, Mother, but you'll have to deal with Elrydd and put them off. Come now, you're good at that sort of thing. You'll doubtless enjoy all the politicking and wrangling."

Lovyan suppressed an impulse to slap him, the way she would have once. All over again she felt that she was dealing with a stranger.

"I cannot believe that Blaen, well-intentioned though he is, is the proper person to arrange an important marriage."

"And I disagree. It's too late, anyway. By now his speeded courier will be at Ygwimyr's with the letter asking for his sister."

"Rhodry, you've never met the lass. I have."

He shrugged and strode to the window to look down.

"Why are you so set on a marriage-bond with the Auddglyn? I simply don't understand."

"My apologies, Mother. There's somewhat you don't know." He turned with one of his unhuman sunny smiles. "On the Auddglyn coast there's a town called Slaith. Ever heard of it? Of course not—neither have most people. It's a pirate haven, and Ygwimyr's known of it for years and done naught about it. Why? Because he doesn't have a fleet. When he marries his sister to me, he'll get the use of mine, because in return I'll get the right to sail into his rhan and burn that stinking filthy hellhole to the ground."

Although he was still smiling, his eyes were terrifying, not with the blind berserker rage she'd seen so many times before, but with an icy hatred, self-aware and murderous. Involuntarily she stepped back a few paces.

"By all accounts Aedda will make a decent-enough wife," Rhodry went on. "Since the one woman I want in all the kingdom is beyond my reach, any other will do well enough—so long as she's related to Gwerbret Ygwimyr."

"I see." Although she wanted to say more, her mind seemed to have failed her, and for the first time in her life, she truly did feel that she was growing old. "Well, there's naught that I can do about it, then, is there?"

"Naught." He smiled again, more normally, and softened his voice. "Ah, Mother, my apologies. We'll soothe Elrydd's feelings with a good chunk of gold, and in a year or two, it'll all be forgotten and done with. If his lass is a great beauty, she'll have better men than me hunting her."

"Well, *that's* certainly true enough."

At the steel in her voice his smile disappeared.

"Since His Grace has matters so well taken care of," she went on, "I'll be returning to Dun Gwerbyn soon, if indeed His Grace intends to leave that rhan in my hands."

"By every god! What do you think I'd do, steal your rightful inheritance over some little thing like this?"

"It's not a little thing, Rhodry. That's what you're refusing to understand. For a man like you the wrong kind of marriage can poison his whole life—and his rule. You need a partner, not a mouse. Why can't you just make some ordinary war pact with Ygwimyr . . ."

"Because he's a jealous, suspicious bastard, and there's not a hope in all three hells of him letting me on his lands unless I'm kin. Mother, I'm not discussing this any more."

"Then listen to one last thing I say. If I've read Aedda aright, she'll grow to hate you, and if she does, you'd best make very sure who fathers her younger sons."

For a long moment he paused, his mouth half-caught in the strangest smile she'd ever seen on a man's face, a stunned amusement, a laughing disbelief. Then he did laugh with a toss of his head, an utterly elven gesture that froze her heart as she realized what that smile must mean.

"Oh no doubt," Rhodry said. "Mother, on that matter I'd trust your word beyond the oaths of a thousand priests, I would indeed."

The time for fencing was long gone.

"You know the truth, then, don't you?" she said, forcing her voice calm.

"I do, at that. I'd never blame you for a thing, mind."

"My thanks." Slowly, and as casually as she could manage, she found a chair and sat down. "You know, I never told you about your father because I was afraid you'd abdicate. You did have such a fine sense of honor, Rhoddo, and I somehow always knew that the rhan would need you one day."

"So I did, and so it did, and you were right enough, weren't you?" All at once he sighed and ran both hands through his hair. "But all that's a long time behind us, Mam. Aberwyn's mine, and cursed and twice-cursed I'd be before I gave her up."

At last she could smile, thinking that after all was said and done, she'd raised him well.

"When do you think Aedda will arrive for the wedding? Would you like me to plan it?"

"A thousand thanks, Mother. I'd like nothing more."

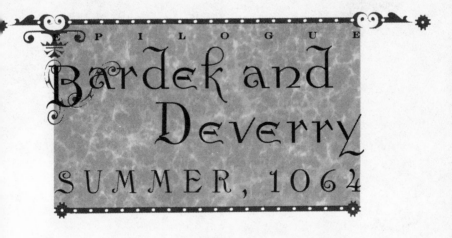

EPILOGUE

Bardek and Deverry

SUMMER, 1064

GWENYN YNG NGOGAWR, GWAN GWAR ADAR;

DYDD DIWLITH;

CASULWYN CEFN BRYN, COCH GWAWR.

BEES IN CLOVER; BIRDS ARE SHRILL;

A DEWLESS DAY. DAWN:

A RED ROSE ON A WHITE-CLAD HILL.

Llywarch the Ancestor

ONE

For some weeks now Alaena had had trouble sleeping. Every morning she would rise before the sun, throw on a linen shift, and go out into her night garden, perfumed with jasmine and honeysuckle, to pace aimlessly back and forth among the statues of her husband's ancestors, until the dark sky turned to gray. At times she would sit on the edge of the marble fountain and run her hand back and forth in the water like a child while she wondered if she would ever hear what had happened to her barbarian boy. Now that his good looks were far away from her, she was nothing but pleased that she'd never gotten pregnant or persuaded him to stay. Marrying a freedman would have been the mistake of my life, she would think, but I do hope he's safe and well. Once the sun came up, she would hurry back inside where it was dim and cool and take out her fortune-telling tiles. Although her readings were always inconclusive, still she pored over them, often for hours at a time, hoping desperately that she would see something—even some bearable misfortune—that would break the tedium of her days. She never found anything more thrilling than the usual love affairs and news from afar.

Yet those common predictions did come true for her in a spectacu-
lar way—or so she saw it. One particularly hot afternoon, she was
lounging on her cushions and desultorily studying a lay-out of tiles
when Porto appeared in the doorway.

"Mistress? There's a Deverry man to see you, Evan the horse
trader by name. He says he has news that might interest you."

"Really? Is he an old friend of my husband's or someone else I
should know?"

"No. I've never seen him before."

"Well, show him in, and have Disna bring some wine."

Her visitor was wearing a pair of gray Deverry trousers and an
embroidered shirt instead of red-and-gold robes, all his rings and
jewels were gone, and his pale hair was soberly cut and neatly
combed, but Alaena recognized him the moment he strolled into the
room.

"Horse trader, indeed! Or have you cast a spell on yourself,
wizard?"

"Do you realize that you're the only person in this town who's
recognized me?" Without waiting to be asked, he stepped up onto the
dais and sat down next to her on a purple cushion. "Everyone else
remembers my finery, not my face, which is, I must admit, all to the
good. For this trip, at least, I prefer to be known as a shrewd
merchant, not a theatrical fool."

"I never thought you were a fool at all."

"Really? Then my disguise was not, alas, impenetrable."

Disna came in with the wine and set the tray down on the low
table. She glanced at this so-called Evan with a perfectly ordinary
curiosity—apparently she too failed to recognize the wizard of last
autumn.

"I'll pour, Disna. You may go."

But Evan picked up the pitcher before Alaena could reach it and
filled both their goblets. When he looked up with a lazy, soft smile,
she felt a flickering of sexual warmth, simply because his mouth
reminded her so much of his brother's.

"Is Rhodry well?"

"Most definitely. Do you realize who he was? The gwerbret of
Aberwyn? He'd been kidnapped by political enemies and sold into
slavery in a vain attempt to keep him from an inheritance."

"No!"

"Yes, oh yes indeed, and so, my paragon of all things beautiful, I wouldn't bother feeling shamed if I were you. He may have been a slave here, but at home I think he'd qualify as your equal."

"In social position? Certainly." She had a sip of her wine. "What a fantastic story! And here I was just thinking that nothing interesting ever happened to me."

"Although normally I'd hate to correct one so lovely as you, in this case I must point out that you were indeed mistaken. Not only did something of great interest happen once, perhaps something even greater may happen in the future."

"Oh, really?" She allowed herself a lazy smile to match his. "Is your brother going to come my way again?"

"I doubt that. He's nicely safe and married off by now, I imagine, to Jill—the woman who was pretending to be my slavegirl."

"Only pretending?"

"Only pretending. She was Rhodry's betrothed the whole time."

"Fascinating! It was kind of you to come tell me—that Rhodry's safe, I mean." She had a sip of wine. "Were you passing this way on business?"

"No. I came specifically to see you."

"Very very kind, then."

"Kind? Perhaps, but to myself. It would be a cruel man indeed who'd deny himself the pleasure of seeing you again after having met you. All winter long I've thought about the lovely Alaena and this room, filled with your presence like some rare perfume."

She smiled again, but delicately, while he sipped his wine and merely watched her. He's the same rank as the brother of an archon, really, she thought to herself—a very important man. And what if he really were a sorcerer? She remembered, then, how frightened she'd been by seeing him perform his marvels, and how exciting that fear had been.

"Will you dine with me tonight, Evan? I've never shared a meal with a wizard before."

"I should be honored. I've never shared anything with a woman as beautiful as you."

When he raised his goblet, she clinked hers against it, and for a moment their fingers touched.

TWO

After he slipped away from the gwerbret and his men in Abernaudd, Perryn rode north, keeping away from the main roads and sticking to country lanes and patches of fallow country. At first traveling was difficult. Although he was used to being out on the road, often for weeks at a time, he had none of his usual gear with him, no woodsman's axe, no kettle, no fishing lines and rabbit snares. His pitifully small cache of coppers dwindled faster and faster as he bought meager provisions at one farm or another. Since he didn't even have a flint and steel to light a fire, he slept cold under hedgerows or covered with leaves in copses. With Nevyn's strictures about stealing fresh in his mind, he resisted all the small temptations that Wyrd put in his way: chickens loose from their pen with no farmer in sight, meat pies left cooling on untended windowsills, axes carelessly left in woodpiles. Finally his newfound piety was rewarded when he reached Elrydd and found a caravan, heading north into Pyrdon, that needed a man who was good with horses. From then on he was decently fed and a good bit warmer.

While they worked their way north, Perryn tried to avoid thinking of his future, but when they left Eldidd behind and headed toward Loc Drw, the question became unavoidable. With a soul-numbing weariness he realized that there really was nowhere to go but back to his Cousin Nedd and Uncle Benoic. At first they would rage at him, but they'd take him in. For months, of course, maybe even for years, he would be the butt of hideous family jokes and humiliating references, trotted out as an example of stupidity and dishonor—but that would be nothing new. He could live with it, as he had before.

At Dun Drwloc the caravan disbanded, and the master paid over Perryn's wages, a generous four silvers' worth of coppers, enough money in that coin-shy area to replace his gear and provision him for the long ride to Cerrgonney. By talking with the local merchant guild, which had a map of sorts, Perryn figured out that if he rode northeast through the province of Arcodd, he had about three hundred and fifty miles to go to reach his uncle's town of Pren Cludan.

The locals, however, suggested that he take a longer route by heading straight east to the Aver Trebyc, which would lead him to the Belaver, which he could then follow straight north to Cerrgonney.

"You could get lost if you just head north, lad," the merchants all said with grave nods of their heads. "The roads aren't too good, and there's long stretches of naught but forest. The Arcodd men call their blasted wilderness a province, but there's only two proper towns in the whole thing, and them far apart at that."

Perryn didn't bother to tell them that Arcodd sounded like paradise to him. When he rode out, he headed north, angling east whenever the roads and deer trails would allow and following his inner lodestone that pointed, grimly and inexorably, to his kin and their version of a welcome. During his first four days of riding, Perryn saw no human beings at all. Soon enough, though, he came to farms and fenced meadows, where white cattle with rusty-red ears grazed under the watchful eyes of young lads with dogs. Everyone he met asked him where he came from, but in a kindly way, and when they found out he came from the south, they treated him as a marvel, that he should travel so far and not get himself lost. Since the spring was blossoming and the threat of winter's famine over, everyone was generous, too, offering him a meal here or oats for his horse there.

Perryn avoided Arcodd's two towns completely. About a hundred miles apart, they lay on a tributary of the Aver Bel that the locals called Aver Clyn, Moon River, but Perryn found a crossing about halfway between them, where the men of a farming village that was growing toward a small town had banded together to build a wooden bridge across a narrows. For a copper in toll they not only let him cross, but stood him a tankard in the local alehouse in return for a bit of news from Pyrdon. As he headed northeast and back toward wilderness, he realized with a sinking heart that he was a good third of the way home. In his mind he could already hear Benoic's accusatory bellow.

That evening he camped in a little dale where a glass-clear stream tumbled over rock and pooled under willow trees. He caught himself a pair of trout, stuffed them with wild mushrooms and wild thyme, then wrapped them in clean leaves to bake in the coals of his fire while he bathed, panting and blowing at the water's cold. Once he was reasonably dry he pulled on shirt and brigga, dug his dinner out of the coals, and built up the fire again. Cursing at singed fingers he pulled open the charred leaves to release a cloud of wonderful steam and the smell of herbs. For the briefest of moments he was happy; then he remembered his uncle, and he groaned out a long sigh of despair.

"What's wrong?"

The voice was soft and female, so close at hand that he yelped in sheer surprise. Not even his horse had heard her coming, it seemed, to nicker a warning. When he looked up he saw her standing among the willows, a lass of about sixteen, barefoot and dressed in a dirty brown smock torn off at the knees, with her waist-length tangle of bright red hair loose and flowing down her back. Although no one would ever have called her beautiful—her mouth was too generous, her nose too flat, and her hands too large and coarse for that—she had lovely green eyes, as wide and wild as a cat's. For a long moment they contemplated each other; then her eyes strayed to the fish.

"Ah, er, oh well," Perryn said at last. "Are you hungry? There's two of them."

Without a word she sat down, a wary distance from him at the fire, and accepted one of the trout on a plate of leaves. She ate neatly, delicately, flaking the tender flesh off the bones with thumb and forefinger and pausing every now and then to lick her fingertips with a pink and healthy tongue. By then the sun was going down, and the night wind had picked up cool, rustling the willow leaves and her long twists of hair, which was shiny clean in spite of the mess it was in. It occurred to him that he couldn't just let her wander off into the cold night all by herself. If nothing else, there were bears in this part of the country, hungry, irritable bears just out of their winter dens.

"Ah well," Perryn said. "Do you live near here?"

"I do. With my Da."

"And is he a farmer, then?"

She shook her head no and began popping baked mushrooms into a greedy mouth.

"Er, when you've finished that, we'd best take you back to him. Going to be cold tonight."

"Cold doesn't bother me."

"Ah. Er, oh, well."

In the end, though, her father found them. They had finished the fish, and a chunk of bread apiece, and were sharing a cup of stream water, when Perryn heard men calling, a long long way away, and the barking of a dog. She went still, crouched like a rabbit in the bracken, then sighed with a melancholy of her own.

"They would have to find me! I was just starting to have fun."

The calls came closer, sharp with worry and fear.

"Caetha! Caetha, answer us! Caetha, where are you?"

She sighed again, then stood up, tossing her arms over her head and stretching her back, shaking her head to tumble her long hair down in the firelight.

"Over here, Da! Here I am!"

In a few minutes three men and a black-and-tan hound came clumping and slipping down the dell. Two of the men, both about twenty, seemed to be a noble lord and one of his riders, because they both wore shirts embroidered with rowan leaves, but one had a pair of much-mended plaid brigga. The third, a slender man with coppery hair going heavily gray about the temples and a silvery red beard to match, was dressed in a long smock like Caetha's, but his was clean, neatly hemmed, and worn over a pair of gray trousers. About his waist was a belt clasped with a buckle in the shape of a golden stag, and from a leather loop hung a small golden sickle. As they came into the firelight Caetha lazed over to him and smiled winsomely while he hugged her and the hound danced round in drooling joy.

"You wretched little creature! You've done it again, and here you promised! Look at this—you've dragged Lord Norryc and poor Badger away from their fire again, and curse it all, Caetha, you promised you'd stop wandering off like this!"

"Did I?" She frowned in concentration. "Oh, well, I suppose I did, truly. I'm sorry, Da. I'm sorry, Lord Norryc. But Badger looks glad of the run to me."

The hound wagged frantically, as if agreeing.

"That's not the point!" the father snarled.

"I know, Da. Er, well, you see, I had to come out. There's someone here I wanted to meet, and you should meet him, too."

Her father gave her a little shake, then let her go, turning and staring at Perryn as if he'd just noticed him standing there.

"Er, ah, she was hungry. So I gave her some dinner. I was going to take her home, but she wouldn't tell me who you were."

"No doubt, good sir. She's a wild thing, truly, and more than a bit simple, as no doubt you've noticed."

"I hadn't at that. Wild, truly, but er, well, she doesn't seem simple to me."

All three men stared, no doubt bestowing the title on him as well.

"Well, my name is Middyr, and as you've doubtless guessed, this is my daughter." He turned to Caetha. "What do you mean, someone I should meet?"

She looked down and began drawing a line in the dirt with one big toe.

"I just knew it," she said at last. "I felt he was here."

Middyr glanced Perryn's way, found him equally bewildered, then shrugged the problem away. Apparently he was used to ignoring much of what his daughter told him.

"You have my thanks, young man, and my blessing, too, for that matter. You see, I'm the priest of Kerun hereabouts."

Perryn made a little yelp of pure joy, like the chirp made by a hungry child when it sees honeycake coming out of an oven. He felt his eyes fill with tears.

"Of Kerun, good sir? Truly, I thought his priesthood dead and gone. Er, no insult, but it's gone where I come from."

"And in most of the kingdom, no doubt. I'm most likely the last of my kind, much as it aches my heart to say so. You seem much moved, good sir."

"I am, truly. I worship him, you see. I mean, he's my god. The other ones aren't. I don't know why."

Middyr cocked his head to one side and considered him for a long moment with a certain strange hope dawning in his eyes. Lord Norryc coughed in a deferential sort of way.

"Uh, Your Holiness? It's getting a bit cold out here to stand around discussing theology."

"Well, so it is, and my apologies. We can all get on home now. You have my profound thanks, your lordship, for bringing your dog out."

"Oh, Badger always finds her quick enough." He gave Perryn a smile. "She may be simple, but she has an amazing touch with animals. Why, I swear they understand what she says to them! Horses, too, not just dogs."

Perryn's heart thudded once. While his lordship, his dog, and his man were all tromping off again, Caetha looked only at Perryn, her eyes as rich and lively a green as spring ferns on the forest floor. When he risked smiling at her, she smiled in return with a witch-warmth that wrapped his soul. His heart began pounding in earnest — could she truly be like him?

"Well, good traveler," Middyr said. "Can we offer you our hospitality? We have a little house not too far from here in the woods, right beside Kerun's shrine. If naught else, no doubt you'd like to pray at the altar of the god."

"I would. My thanks, Your Holiness. Let me just bury this fire and saddle my horse. I'd like naught better than to visit you tonight."

That night's visit stretched to another, and a few more beyond that, then an eightnight or two more, as Perryn began, almost without thinking or asking, to help Middyr with the work of his holdings as well as the shrine. The local noble-born clan had given the priests of Kerun four large farms to support the temple as well as a large tract of wild forest around the shrine itself, but up in that sparse country the rents and dues from the properties wouldn't have been enough to support the widowed priest, his daughter, and their two servants. Perryn helped Middyr tend his horses and pigs or worked with Caetha in the kitchen garden. Planting and tending living things was something she loved, and her knowledge of herbs and garden lore was so profound for a young lass that he rapidly realized that she was no village idiot or ordinary half-wit.

She had her quirks, though. No one could persuade her to wear any sort of footwear, not shoe nor clog, unless the snow was so icy that an ordinary person's feet would have frozen fast to it. As for her hair, she refused to have it cut, yet she also refused to comb it. At times she was given to fits of horrible temper, when she would throw sticks of firewood or iron pans around the kitchen, then rush outside to collapse weeping on the grass. She would let no one near her then, not even her father or the household cats, whom normally she treated like babies, cuddling them and feeding them with her fingers.

At night, with the work done, Middyr would tell Perryn about Kerun's lore, and his was no idle chatter or storytelling. He would discuss some point of the god's tale, then question Perryn about what he'd heard, patiently correcting his more than willing pupil until Perryn had every detail perfectly memorized. At times they would tend the shrine itself, wiping clean the stone altar and oiling and polishing the wooden statue of the god until it gleamed. Although Middyr gave him scraps of temple lore, there he was cryptic, passing on only those details that an uninitiated man could hear.

When the first crop of wheat was turning golden in the fields, Perryn realized that he was never going to want to leave. He was also certain, however, that he was about to wear out his welcome, simply because he always did wear out welcomes, even among his kin. One cool evening he and Middyr were sitting at the round table by the kitchen hearth, discussing how Kerun had been born in the wilderness and suckled by a doe for a foster mother. Nearby Caetha sat sorting dry beans with six cats round her feet—the ginger tom always liked to sleep with his head right on her feet, in fact—and frowning as she worked. Her hair was its usual thorn bush, clean and gleaming in the firelight, but tangled into thick fuzzy clots at the nape of her neck. At a break in the conversation Perryn mustered what was left of his sense of courtesy.

"Er, ah, well," he mumbled. "Somewhat I've been meaning to say, er, oh well. Um, I've been rather rude, imposing on you like this. Time I er, ah, got on the road again."

Caetha looked up with a howl that sent cats scattering.

"Ah well, I can't stay here forever," Perryn said, feeling close to tears. "Eating your father's food and all that."

She threw the bowl of beans across the room and jumped to her feet, howling again as she rushed out the door.

"I get the distinct impression," Middyr said, rubbing the side of his face with one calloused hand. "That she'd like you to stay. I'm afraid I'm the one who's imposing on you, lad. Caetha's my only daughter, you see, and I've never seen her as calm and happy as she's been this last few weeks. As far as I'm concerned, you're welcome to stay as long as you like. Forever, if you want."

"Truly?"

"Truly. Who will be priest when I die? You're the only man I've ever met who cared one way or the other for Kerun's rites."

"Oh." Perryn considered for a moment. "Oh, er, ah, well. Thank you. I'd love to stay. Truly. Er, well, um."

He looked down to find indignant cats glaring at him.

"I'd best see where Caetha went," Perryn said, mumbling again. "Don't want her running off."

Hugging his welcome he ran out the door into a night washed silver with a full moon. Although the farmyard was silent, the barn door flapped open, and he could guess where she was, because like him, she found the company of horses a comfort. In a pile of hay she was sprawled full-length and sobbing in the dark. When he sat down beside her, she looked up and hissed at him.

"Er, I'm not going after all, you know."

The sobbing stopped while she considered.

"Not ever?"

"Not ever."

In the trickle of moonlight spilling in through a nearby window he could see her long tangle of hair, the palest silvery-red in this light, covering her like a matted blanket. He stroked it lightly; then, starting down near her waist, he picked out a particularly tangled bit and began teasing it out with his fingers. At first she went rigid, then slowly relaxed, as a bit at a time he worked his way up to the nape of her neck and got that one long lock of hair smooth and tangle-free. When he started on the one next to it, she moved a little closer to him, then closer still as he fell into the rhythm of the work. All at once he realized that there was a rhythm, that he was performing some sort of ritual, something half-remembered and half-known that seemed to come from the deepest levels of his soul. She stretched luxuriously and rubbed up against him as he worked, as if she too understood. Although his back began to ache, because it took hours to get that mane smooth, he never once considered stopping.

At last he could comb her hair with his fingers without meeting anything nastier than a bit of straw. She sat up, smiling at him, stretching again, then putting her hands on his shoulders and kneading them like a cat. The warmth of that smile was so palpable that he felt as if they sat in noontide sunlight.

"Er, well, we'd best get married, hadn't we? First, I mean. Er, ah, your father *is* a priest and all that."

She jumped up, slapping him across the face, but she was giggling as she ran out the door. As he followed, he was wondering why he'd never noticed before how truly beautiful she was.

Although in the village the folk snickered about how clever Middyr was, to find a husband for his half-wit daughter and a successor all in one lucky stroke, Perryn himself knew that Kerun had at last heard his prayers and brought him home.

THREE

Up in northwestern Cantrae, on the banks of the Aver Can, is a small town called Brin Toraedic, which gets its name from a strange hill rising out of a meadow about two miles to the south. At the rocky crest of the grassy mound is a ravine, a deep cleft running as straight and smooth as if a giant had sliced it open with a sword. If you ride that way, the townsfolk will tell you that an evil demon once built himself a dun on the hill and waged war on the gods until Bel struck him down with a thunderbolt. The demon sank back down to the Third Hell through the cleft, which to this day will lead you down to the Otherlands—if you have the nerve to try the climb. But even with the demon long gone, strange things still happen on the tor, or so they say, blue lights dancing in the moonlight, half-seen shapes skittering around, and wails, creaks, and knockings in the night.

In Jill and Nevyn's time, the town was only a tiny farming village, some five miles from the tor. Since she'd always assumed that Nevyn would live among the common folk, she wasn't surprised when he told her that he had a home there.

"Or near the village, I should say," Nevyn said. "You need privacy for our kind of work. You'll see when we get there. Now, I haven't visited my house in fifteen years, but I've sent the Wildfolk ahead to air it out, like. I wonder what kind of job they did?"

They found out on the hot summer afternoon when they finally reached the tor. Under a glaring, windless sky it stood dusted with clover, looking like some grim old giant turned to stone with the ravine for a battle scar. As they approached, Jill could see Wildfolk clustering in the cleft. So could her horse—it danced and pulled nervously at the bit until Nevyn soothed it with a few soft words.

"We'll have to walk the horses up," he remarked. "It's too steep a ride."

"Oh here! Is this where you live?"

"I did until about fifteen years ago. I'll admit to being pleased to see it again."

The cleft was about six feet wide, and one side was just a natural cliff of packed dirt and weeds. The other, however, was a proper stone wall, made of massive true-cut blocks, and sporting a wooden door with a big iron ring in the middle. The Wildfolk came to meet them, sylphs like a thickening in the air, gnomes with scrawny faces and long arms, dancing and clustering round Nevyn like children welcoming their father home. A blue sprite with a mouthful of pointed teeth materialized on Jill's shoulder, then pulled her hair so hard that it stung. With a yelp, Jill swatted her away.

"Stop that," Nevyn said to the sprite. "Jill's going to live here, too."

The sprite glowered, then vanished with a puff of air.

"I put this door in myself," Nevyn said. "A carpenter would laugh at the job I did, but it opens and shuts well enough."

As if in demonstration he swung the door wide and walked in, the horse and mule following him gingerly. When Jill led her horse after, she found a stable, a big stone room with four mangers along one wall and fresh hay piled up by the other. Somewhere nearby, she heard the sound of running water. On the wall was an iron sconce with a half-burned wooden torch. Although it took Nevyn two snaps of his fingers to light the old, damp wood, finally the smoke rose straight up and disappeared through a hidden vent. The air was remarkably clean and fresh for a cave.

"The Wildfolk have done a good job," Nevyn said. "But I fear me they stole this hay from some farmer. I'll have to find out who and make amends."

They unsaddled the stock and set them at their hay, then carried their gear down a short tunnel into what seemed to be an enormous room, stretching away and echoing in the darkness. Jill heard the dweomerman moving in the dark; then a fire blazed up in a huge hearth of square-cut blocks. Even though it was breathlessly hot outside, the caves were downright cold. The room was about a hundred feet on a side, with walls of smooth stone and a flat ceiling a good twenty feet above them. Huddled near the hearth were a wooden table with a pair of benches, a narrow cot, a large freestanding cupboard and a wooden barrel.

"Stolen ale, as well," the old man remarked with a sigh. "We'll have to get you a cot of your own. There's a carpenter in the village."

"I can sleep on a pile of straw for now. Did you build this place?"

"I didn't indeed." He paused to give her a mysterious grin. "But I did dig it out with a gnome or two to help me. Let's have a bit of this purloined ale, and I'll tell you the story."

Nevyn rummaged through the cupboard, which was crammed full of books, cooking tools, packets of now-stale herbs, bits of cloth, and a few dusty trinkets. Finally he brought out two pewter tankards, dusted them out, and filled them at the barrel. The two of them settled themselves by the fire away from the chill of the vast room. For some minutes the old man gazed around him fondly like a merchant who, after a long year on the road trading, is finally home and at his own hearth.

"Well," he said at last. "This tor isn't a natural hill. As far as I can tell from poking around in here, it was a village long ago—very long ago, before the Dawntime. The folk threw their garbage out onto the street and built new houses on the ruins of old ones, until the village grew higher and higher above the meadow. Then they left for some reason, still long before the people of Bel rode to Deverry. So the wind blew dirt over it, and the grass grew up. Then, around the Dawntime, someone built a dun on the hill to guard themselves from our bloodthirsty ancestors. Didn't do them one bit of good. I found a room with headless skeletons in it round the other side of the hill. I always thought those skeletons were human, but after meeting Perryn, I'm not so sure. Most of the dun was razed, but this corner of it was untouched when I found it. So, then, the people of Bel rode on down to the coast, and the wind and the grass came back, and with time, it all got covered up with dirt again and the hill was higher than ever. All I've done, you see, is to clear myself a space to live in."

"And what about the ravine?"

"Oh, that runs along the old outside wall. Maybe there was a moat once, but whatever the reason, the ground settled away from the stonework. I happened to see it one day, when I was passing by, and climbed up to investigate. That's how I stumbled onto the tor's little secret." He smiled briefly. "I've been digging like a mole, truly. It amuses me in the long winters. I put a tunnel down here and there, and sometimes I find a bit of pottery or jewelry. They're all in that cupboard." He sighed heavily. "One of these days, I have to clean the cursed thing out."

"I'll do it. I'm your apprentice now."

"So you are." Nevyn's voice dropped to a whisper. "Ah, by the gods, so you are."

The gratitude in his voice stirred the constant strange feeling in Jill, that she had known him before, long long ago in some other country. With it came another, that her whole life had led her to this room, half under the earth, half above it. Hastily she got up and fetched food from their saddlebags, to lay out the meal for the master like the apprentice she was. In the hearth, the Wildfolk of Fire cavorted, rubbing their backs on the logs like a cat will do on a doorjamb. Nevyn stared into the fire while Jill cut bread and cheese and laid the slices on a plate.

"Trying to teach you should be interesting," Nevyn said. "First, I suppose, we'll have to unscramble what that chattering elf taught you. I find it hard to believe there was much order or logic in his lessons."

"There wasn't, truly, but it didn't seem to matter. It's odd, but I almost feel as if I'd studied dweomer before."

"Oh, do you now?" He smiled briefly. "Well, well, do you now!"

During their meal, Nevyn said nothing more, merely ate absent-mindedly and stared into the fire. Against her will, against all her efforts to stop herself, Jill started thinking about Rhodry. Ever since their tormented farewell, she had been trying to put him behind her, as if his memory were a place she could ride away from forever. During the day, she could distract herself, but at this time of night the memories came, when they would have been sharing a meal and talking over the day behind them, whether at a table in some lord's hall or by a campfire on the road. She was surprised, because she'd been expecting that she would miss having him in her bed most of all, but it was his company that meant the most to her. I truly did love him, she thought, but I always knew the dweomer demanded its price. She could see him so clearly in her mind that she almost wept, see him standing by a hearth, turning toward her with his beautiful sunny smile, his cornflower-blue eyes snapping with a jest

and yet he was miserable—she could see that, too—the merriment and the jesting were a feverish attempt to hide how unhappy he was. He was wearing a fine linen shirt, embroidered with the dragons of Aberwyn in silver thread that caught firelight. When a page brought him a silver goblet of mead, Rhodry gulped it down much too fast. Suddenly the vision widened. Jill saw that the luxurious chamber was filled with people in the plaids of the noble-born. Sitting in a chair near Rhodry was a young woman, as slender as a reed and just as fragile-looking, but pretty with her long dark hair and wide dark eyes. Her slender hands were tightly clasped as they lay on her dark-blue dress. With a shock, Jill realized that she was wearing the plaid of Aberwyn for her kirtle. Oh by the hells, Jill thought, is that what they found for him to marry? Yet, when the lass turned her head to look at her half-drunk new husband with a very real terror of this man that the gods and her brother had dumped into her bed, Jill found it in her heart to pity the child. All at once, the side of Jill's face stung like fire. She tried to rub the pain away, found that she was utterly paralyzed as the pain came again

and Nevyn was leaning over her, his hand raised for another slap. Drunkenly Jill looked round and saw the walls of the buried chamber.

"My apologies for hitting you," Nevyn said. "It was the fastest way to bring you back. What were you scrying? Rhodry?"

"Just that. He must be in Dun Deverry. I saw wyvern blazons all over the furniture and suchlike."

"Doubtless the King wants to look over this new vassal of his."

"Oh, no doubt. I saw his wife. She's naught but a little mouse sent to amuse the cats."

"Here, listen to you."

Jill shrugged and looked away. She could feel tears rising in her throat. With a sigh, Nevyn sat down next to her on the bench.

"Child, you have my sympathy." His voice was oddly gentle. "I know you love your Rhodry."

Jill nodded miserably in agreement.

"You had to continue your training," Nevyn went on. "Don't you see what's happened? You've been using your dweomer, but all in bits and pieces, so you've got no control, no true understanding of what you're doing. You sit here longing for Rhodry, you picture him in your mind, and all at once, you slip into a trance."

"And truly, I didn't even know it." Jill was frightened as she thought things over. "What would have happened to me if I hadn't come with you?"

"I don't truly know, but there's a good chance you'd have gone mad."

"But you would have let me stay with Rhodry if I wanted."

"I'd have been there to keep an eye on you, but no matter what the cost, you had to choose freely."

The fire was burning low. Jill got up and laid on a couple of logs, watched them catch as the Wildfolk fell upon them in a shower of flame. The ghost of a memory haunted her mind, an abstract thing without image or word, of a time when she had not been allowed to choose, when she had been marked for the dweomer but some other thing had gotten in her way. She couldn't remember what it was, another man, perhaps, that she'd loved as much as she loved Rhodry. All at once she knew that she had to remember, had to see her Wyrd clearly. She sat down in silence while the memory faded, then rose again, a restless spirit from the Otherlands of the soul.

The time when she should have chosen, the time when her Wyrd had been snatched from her. The time when the man sitting beside her should have brought her to her Wyrd.

"Galrion," Jill said. "That was your name then."

"It was." Nevyn spoke very quietly.

Speaking the name brought a memory image with it, of Nevyn as a very young man.

"You've never died," Jill said. "You've never died from that day to this."

"And how could I have died and be here? When a man dies, isn't that an end to him?"

His voice was humorous. When she realized that she understood the jest, she turned so cold that she got up to warm her hands at the fire.

"It was all a very long time ago," Jill said.

"It was."

"And how many lives have I lived since then?"

"So—you know the truth, do you?"

"I do." Jill turned from the fire to face him. "How many lives has it been?"

"In time you'll remember them all. Let's just say that it was too many, and too many years all told."

Nevyn stared into the fire, and she somehow knew that he, too, was remembering that other life. Jill felt as if she were standing on a mountain top after living in a deep valley. At last she could see the world spread out around her and know that it was vaster than she had ever dreamt. The memories crowded into her mind, ghosts pressing around her to tell her their tales. Finally Nevyn looked up.

"Brangwen?" he said at last. "Do you forgive me?"

"I never held one single thing against you."

"Then you loved me too much. It was all false pride and carelessness, but I betrayed you as surely as if I'd drowned you myself."

Jill remembered the night-dark river, the coldness of the water covering her, choking her. With a shudder she moved closer to the fire.

"Well, perhaps you did," she said. "And truly, I did love you too much." She hesitated, groping for words, wondering if she had the wisdom to say such things but knowing somehow that she remembered their truth. "And that's why I had to lose you. That blind, dog's love had no room in it for the dweomer. Ah ye gods, I wanted to bury myself in you, to *drown* myself in you! It was my doing as much as yours."

"True spoken. But if I'd told you honestly what I was up to instead of sneaking around like a bondsman, if I'd only let you know that you were running toward freedom and not a life of exile and naught more, wouldn't you have found some way to escape from your brother's dun?"

"Well, truly I would have. I would have seen the choice as between life or death, not just as Gerraent or you."

"You would have. You were never a dolt, Gwennie—just so young, so very young." Nevyn was silent a long moment. "But do you forgive me?"

"I do. Easily."

"Then my thanks." His voice almost broke on the words.

Jill sat down next to him again. For a long time they sat in silence, watching the Wildfolk sport in the fire and the light dance over the walls, light and shadow, endlessly moving, endlessly changing, one into the other and back again.

GLOSSARY

Aber (Deverrian) A river mouth, an estuary.

Alar (Elvish, plural *alarli*) A group of elves, who may or may not be bloodkin, who choose to travel together for some indefinite period of time.

Alarðan (Elv.) The meeting of several alarli, usually the occasion for a drunken party.

Angwiðð (Dev.) Unexplored, unknown.

Archon (translation of the Bardekian *atzenarlen*) The elected head of a city-state (Bardekian *at*).

Astral The plane of existence directly "above" or "within" the etheric (q.v.) In other systems of magic, often referred to as the Akashic Record or the Treasure House of Images.

Aura The field of electromagnetic energy that permeates and emanates from every living being.

Aver (Dev.) A river.

Banaðar (Elv.) A warleader and a legal judge for a given group of alarli, elected by their members to serve for a hundred-year term. At any time after the election, new alarli may choose to place themselves under his jurisdiction, but withdrawing from the same is a serious matter, requiring the agreement of all the other groups under his rule.

Bara (Elv.) An enclitic that indicates that the preceding adjective in an Elvish agglutinated word is the name of the element following the enclitic, as can + bara + melim = Rough River (rough + name marker + river).

Bel (Dev.) The chief god of the Deverry pantheon.

Bel (Elv.) An enclitic, similar in function to bara, except that it indicates that a preceding verb is the name of the following element in the agglutinated term, as in Darabeldal, Flowing Lake.

Blue Light Another name for the etheric plane (q.v.).

Body of Light An artificial thought-form (q.v.) constructed by a dweomermaster to allow him or her to travel through the inner planes of existence.

Brigga (Dev.) Loose wool trousers worn by men and boys.

Broch (Dev.) A squat tower in which people live. Originally, in the Homeland, these towers had one big fireplace in the center of the ground floor and a number of booths or tiny roomlets up the sides, but by the time of our narrative, this ancient style has given way to regular floors with hearths and chimneys on either side of the structure.

Cadvridoc (Dev.) A warleader. Not a general in the modern sense, the cadvridoc is supposed to take the advice and counsel of the noble-born lords under him, but his is the right of final decision.

Captain (translation of the Dev. *pendaely*) The second in command, after the lord himself, of a noble's warband. An interesting point is that the word *taely* (which is the root or unmutated form of *-daely*) can mean either a warband or a family, depending on context.

Conaber (Elv.) A musical instrument similar to the panpipe but of even more limited range.

Cwm (Dev.) A valley.

Dal (Elv.) A lake.

Dun (Dev.) A fort.

Dweomer (translation of Dev. *dwunddaevad*) In its strict sense, a system of magic aimed at personal enlightenment through harmony with the natural universe in all its planes and manifestations; in the popular sense, magic, sorcery.

Elcyion Lacar (Dev.) The elves; literally, the "bright spirits," or "Bright Fey."

Englyn (Welsh) A verse form consisting of three lines tied together with alliteration by rules too elaborate to go into here. All the epigraphs in this book are englynion.

Ensorcel To produce an effect similar to hypnosis by direct manipulation of a person's aura. (Ordinary hypnosis manipulates the victim's consciousness only and thus is more easily resisted.)

Etheric The plane of existence directly "above" the physical. With its magnetic substance and currents, it holds physical matter in an invisible matrix and is the true source of what we call "life."

Etheric Double The true being of a person, the electromagnetic structure that holds the body together and that is the actual seat of consciousness.

Fola (Elv.) An enclitic that shows the noun preceding it in an agglutinated Elvish word is the name of the element following the enclitic, as in Corafolamelim, Owl River.

Geis A taboo, usually a prohibition against doing something. Breaking geis results in ritual pollution and the disfavor if not active enmity of the gods. In societies that truly believe in geis, a person who breaks it usually dies fairly quickly, either of morbid depression or some unconsciously self-inflicted "accident," unless he or she makes ritual amends.

Gerthǒǒyn (Dev.) Literally, a "music man," a wandering minstrel and entertainer of much lower status than a true bard.

Great Ones Spirits, once human but now disincarnate, who exist on an unknowably high plan of existence and who have dedicated themselves to the eventual enlightenment of all sentient beings. They are also known to the Buddhists, as Bodhisattvas.

Gwerbret (Dev.) The highest rank of nobility below the royal family itself. Gwerbrets (Dev. *gwerbretion*) function as the chief magistrates of their regions, and even kings hesitate to override their decisions because of their many ancient prerogatives.

Hiraeǒǒ (Dev.) A peculiarly Celtic form of depression, marked by a deep, tormented longing for some unobtainable thing; also and in particular, homesickness to the third power.

Javelin (translation of Dev. *picecl*) Since the weapon in question is only about three feet long, another possible translation would be "war dart." The reader should not think of it as a proper spear or as one of those enormous javelins used in the modern Olympic Games.

Lwdd (Dev.) A blood-price; differs from wergild in that the amount of lwdd is negotiable in some circumstances, rather than being irrevocably set by law.

Malover (Dev.) A full, formal court of law with both a priest of Bel and either a gwerbret or a tieryn in attendance.

Melim (Elv.) A river.

Mor (Dev.) A sea, ocean.

Pan (Elv.) An enclitic, similar to -*fola,* defined earlier, except that it indicates that the preceding noun is plural as well as the name of the following word, as in Corapanmelim, River of the Many Owls. Remember that Elvish always indicates pluralization by adding a semi-independent morpheme, and that this semi-independence is reflected in the various syntax-bearing enclitics.

Pecl (Dev.) Far, distant.

Rhan (Dev.) A political unit of land; thus, gwerbretrhyn, tierynrhyn, the area under the control of a given gwerbret or tieryn. The size of the various rhans (Dev. *rhannau*) varies widely, depending on the vagaries of inheritance and the fortunes of war rather than some legal definition.

Scrying The art of seeing distant people and places by magic.

Sigil An abstract magical figure, usually representing either a particular spirit or a particular kind of energy or power. These figures, which look a lot like geometrical scribbles, are derived by various rules from secret magical diagrams.

Spirits Living though incorporeal beings proper to the various non-physical planes of the universe. Only the elemental spirits, such as the Wildfolk (translation of Dev. *elcyion goecl*) can manifest directly in the physical plane. All others need some vehicle, such as a gem, incense smoke, or the magnetism given off by freshly cut plants or spilled blood.

Taer (Dev.) Land, country.

Thought-form An image or three-dimensional form that has been fashioned out of either etheric or astral substance, usually by the action of a trained mind. If enough trained minds work together to build the same thought-form, it will exist independently for a period of time based on the amount of energy put into it. (Putting energy into such a form is known as *ensouling* the thought-form.) Manifestations of gods or saints are usually thought-forms picked up by the highly intuitive, such as children, or those with a touch of second sight. It is also possible for a large number of untrained minds to make fuzzy, ill-defined thought-forms that can be picked up the same way, such as UFOs and sightings of the Devil.

Tieryn (Dev.) An intermediate rank of the noble-born, below a gwerbret but above an ordinary lord (Dev. *arcloedd*)

Wyrd (translation of Dev. *tingedd*) Fate, destiny; the inescapable problems carried over from a sentient being's last incarnation.

Ynis (Dev.) An island.

Book Mark

The text of this book was set in the typeface
Cochin by Jackson Typesetting, Inc., Jackson, Michigan.

It was printed and bound by
RR Donnelley & Sons, Crawfordsville, Indiana.

Designed by Guenet Abraham